BEHOLD ZION
A Star Original

Amos Landau –
pioneer in a harsh new land; his act of indiscretion
nearly destroys his family.

David Landau –
the eldest son; his quiet manner inevitably explodes
into tragedy.

Simon Landau –
the son who fled to America; he discovers an in-
escapable destiny shared by many thousands of sons
in June 1967.

Mara Gabrielli –
the beautiful actress; her glamour and fame turn to
shattering tragedy.

Yaakov Yeshivat –
the dedicated warrior; he has learned to kill without
regret and make love without sentiment.

Hank McClintock –
the American photographer; he breaks with his old
life to carve out a new one in a nation born in blood.

Also in *Star* by Burt Hirschfeld

'FATHER PIG'
MOMENT OF POWER

BEHOLD ZION

Burt Hirschfeld

A STAR BOOK

published by

WYNDHAM PUBLICATIONS

A Star Book
Published in 1976
by Wyndham Publications Ltd.
A division of Howard & Wyndham Ltd.
123 King Street, London W6 9JG

Copyright © 1968 by Burt Hirschfeld

Printed in Great Britain by
Richard Clay (The Chaucer Press), Ltd., Bungay, Suffolk

ISBN 0 352 39860 4

Behold, he that keepeth Israel shall neither slumber nor sleep.

—*Psalms*

"If I am not for myself, who
will be for me?
But if I am only for myself,
what am I?
And if not now, when?

—*Rabbi Hillel*

ONE

He shall feed his flock like a shepherd;
he shall gather the lambs with his arm,
and carry them in his bosom, and shall lead
those that are with young.

—Isaiah

1949

I

Up from Sodom, the awful deep on the lip of the Dead Sea, into the tangled matrix of limestone cliffs. Still climbing, on past striations of marl, angular promontories, a stony lamination of the history of man. A rugged enigma—eloquent. The Judean Mountains. And the air is light and cooler, the flesh less fevered, the breathing easier now.

The truck, a battered American Army two-and-one-half ton, skidded, slowed, the engine groaning in protest. The driver double-shifted down gear and they moved ahead steadily once more. The driver called a mocking word of encouragement to his passengers in the back. One man swore loudly in faulty Hebrew.

There were four of them, uniforms and weapons coated with grayish-yellow dust, faces masked with it, eyes weary and without focus. Men going home but still bearing the burden of war.

"God has forsaken this place, this Negev," the soldier with the sad eyes said. He was an Orthodox Jew and wore a plain black yarmulke on the back of his head, touching it from time to time, taking small comfort in its presence. "For my part, King Abdullah can have all of it." He had spoken in Yiddish and his head bobbed loosely in self-agreement.

The man next to him, fat-faced and sullen, cursed in French, then went on in flawed Hebrew. "Those Arabs, I would give them nothing, only a bullet in the belly."

"We gave them plenty of that!" the youth with his arm in a sling said enthusiastically. His eyes worked from one man to another, ending finally on the quiet officer. "They won't dare bother us anymore, isn't that so, captain?"

Amos Landau held tightly to the slatted seat hoping to reduce the jostling of his injured leg. The gears ground again and he wondered if there was a Jew in all of Israel who could drive well. They left the mountains and the heat returned, the sun pitiless and blinding. The driver should stop, he thought, and put up the canvas cover to

9

shield them. The truck hit a pothole and bounced. A spasm of pain radiated from the thigh wound. Amos kept his face expressionless.

"Stupid bastard German," the Frenchman said, without emotion. "They are too stubborn to avoid the bad places."

"That's right, isn't it, captain?" the youth with the sling said. "Now that we won the war they'll let us live in peace, the Arabs? There won't be any more fighting, will there?"

Amos lifted the corners of his fine, full mouth encouragingly. He spoke in a Hebrew that was too precise to be natural. "Let us hope so, *adoni*. One war in a man's lifetime is enough."

The youth leaned back, reassured. The Frenchman allowed his eyes to close as if to block off the answer Amos had given, contempt etched in the folds of his fleshy face. The man with the sad eyes leaned forward.

"Was it worth fighting for, this desert? What good will it do us now?"

It was an effort to bring the man into focus. Amos craved the privacy of his own thoughts, to consider Joshua, to *worry* about his son. But there was no privacy. Not with these men. Not in this army. Had he been a British officer or in the Wehrmacht there would have been none of this familiarity. A vision of himself in the uniform of a German officer floated to mind and he almost smiled.

"The English farming experts," he said, "their engineers, always insisted that the Negev was good for nothing, that nothing would grow there."

The Frenchman spat out the back of the truck and watched the issue disappear into the trailing cloud of dust. "If the British say it can't be done, we Jews can do it."

"Israelis," the youth corrected, smiling happily. "Now we're Israelis. A *nation*."

The Frenchman glared at him, then turned away.

"The Negev," Amos said mildly, "has always been important to the Jews."

"Yes, yes," the Orthodox soldier said, tugging at his sidecurls. "Ein Gedi, where David found shelter from the rage of King Saul, and Masada——"

"And the valley of Elah," the youth interrupted, "where David killed Goliath."

"God's own miracle," the Orthodox soldier said.

The Frenchman snorted. "There are no miracles! There is no God!"

They began to argue, the three of them, each quoting from the Scriptures to support his position, invoking the knowledge of the Torah to demolish a point of logic, the characters of the Old Testament as real to them as each other.

Amos listened with interest. All of them had absorbed the Bible as other people learned the geography of their own lands. For a Jew, Israeli, he corrected silently, the Bible was a blueprint to both past and future, a system by which to survive as had prior generations. And by which to prevail. Amos felt that he, that all of them, were the end product of the people of the Old .Testament. In a sentiment seldom expressed, he recognized a continuity that transcended nationality or religion or philosophical concepts. The cynical Frenchman and the naive youth off a kibbutz and the Pietist—all children of Abraham. And Amos Landau, he acknowledged silently. Very much so.

The truck hit a rock and the men in back were thrown around. The Frenchman, jarred off the seat, came up snarling, shouting defiant oaths at the driver.

Amos stretched his bad leg and waited for the throbbing to subside. He sat erect and held the cane in his right hand.

"A bad wound, captain?" the youth asked.

"Not bad," Amos said. The doctor said that the pain would linger, not constant but acute when it came, that a nerve had been injured. In time, it would go and so would the limp.

"You were shot?"

Amos would have preferred not to talk about it but he didn't want to hurt the boy's feelings. "Shrapnel," he said.

"Ah, artillery?"

"A mortar."

The Orthodox man shook his head. "A terrible thing. It happened in the desert?"

Amos nodded.

The man fingered his yarmulke. "It is enough simply to be in this wilderness, but to have to fight too!" His head swung from side to side in commiseration. "To walk in the hot sand."

Amos felt impelled to reassure him. "Mostly I rode, my friend. A tank."

"Ah!"

"And now," the young kibbutznik said, "home to your family."

Amos permitted himself a small smile. The boy was trying hard to be friendly. He was about Joshua's age, and Amos could have been his father.

11

"First, Jerusalem," Amos said. "To see my son. He was wounded in the fighting there. Then home." A soft, pleased laugh came out of him. "I have a new son waiting for me at home. Simon, after Bar Kochba."

"Ah, mazel tov," the youth said.

"Mazel."

"Good luck," the Frenchman said.

"Two sons," the man with the earlocks said. "That is doubly blessed."

"Three sons," Amos corrected. "And a daughter."

In the distance, some wild camel foals, awkward and pale, loped across the sand, veering away from the road as the truck roared toward them. Camels alone thrived in this unchanging land, impersonal and cruel through the centuries, the barren, crusted dunes rolling to infinity. Not even the native cactus, the sabra, would grow here; only patches of sun-scorched broom plants broke the glaring monotony. Perhaps, Amos mused, the English experts were right about the Negev. After all, it had lain fallow for thousands of years. Still, it might serve as a defense barrier against the Egyptians to the south.

"There!" the boy cried. "There's Beersheba."

Amos swung around. He had seen Beersheba before, had been part of the attacking force, had been there when the ceasefire took place. It was the same. Dusty. Battered. Ancient.

Long ago it had been an oasis, a base for Abraham. The Patriarchs had wandered this region with their herds and their people. During King David's reign, the northern portions had been well-populated and Simeon had settled to the south. Solomon had established his copper mines at Timna and Eilat was a busy port for ships coming from Africa and the Orient. King Uzziah had put down a network of roads in the desert.

"We're here!" the youth cried. "Will we be able to get a ride north, captain? I'm so anxious to get home, to see my father and my mother."

"Spoken like a good Jewish boy," the Frenchman said.

"What's wrong with that?" the Orthodox soldier said aggressively.

"If we're lucky," Amos said, "we'll find a plane to take us all."

"That would be a miracle," the Frenchman said.

"Ahah!" the Pietist shouted triumphantly. "You believe! You believe!"

II

Yaakov Yeshivat stretched his thick arms, making a small masculine sound of satisfaction in the back of his throat. He sat up quickly and lit a cigaret.

Leah watched him lazily, and appreciated what she saw. A big man, the muscles thick and swelling, the torso bony and lean, heavy with power.

She yearned to embrace him, let him know how very much he pleased her. That she loved him. She said nothing. Yeshivat was for love-making not love-talk. Not love. Once she had told him how she felt. But only once.

He had laughed at her, raucous and mocking, and had slapped her naked behind. "Go and find some *yeshiva yid* to make you a husband. And when you are ready for some good loving, come and find me."

He swung his legs to the floor and stood up. A tall man with a deep, broad chest and a stomach ridged with muscle, his head rode low between great square shoulders. The face had the look of a sculptor's work, shattered and only partially repaired. It was a rocky assemblage of thrusts and angles, the jaw blunt, strong, the cheekbones prominent as if supporting the deepset, pale eyes. His forehead was wide, and a twisting scar plunged into the left brow. His hair was wiry, dun-colored, spotted with gray. And there was his nose, a defiant gnarl of twisted bone and gristle, broken more than once.

"I'm going to shower," he said.

"Must you go so soon?"

"Yes."

She tried to keep her voice light. "Another woman?" Then, quickly, as if to compensate for the lapse. "Some kind of business, Yaakov?"

He measured her, looking up from under the heavy brows. There was that about him, the promise of swift violence close to the surface. It frightened her even as it drew her to him.

His expression softened, an almost imperceptible luminosity in the eyes. "I'm going to see Chaim Lahav. I think he wants me to come back to Histadrut."

"Are you going to?"

"We'll see. I've been thinking about politics, about standing for the Knesset."

She got out of bed, a full-bodied woman, round and smooth, showing no signs of her thirty-eight years. "You would make a terrible politician, my dear." She slid her arms around his waist. "No man is less a diplomat and you'd antagonize everyone and settle all differences with your fists."

He lifted his chin so as not to burn her hair and dragged on the cigaret. "Fists can be first rate convincers."

"The war is over," she said. "You should stop fighting."

He removed her arms and handed the cigaret to her. "To make war is one thing, to make a country something else. That may be the hardest fight of all, to shape it as I would like it."

"Other people may not want what you want."

"Let them fight for what they want then. We'll see who fights best, who will win."

He left her standing there with the smoldering cigaret. She found an ashtray and put it out.

III

"Wallah!" Mejjid al-Hadad said hotly. His strong brown face was mottled and his prow-like nose jabbed the air as if seeking a target to ram and destroy.

"Ridiculous," he said, making sure to keep his voice down. "The Jews know me. I am a Palestinian. My father and his father also. My friends will look out for my interests."

"Yes," Tewfik said. "Of course." But there was skepticism in every line of his narrow face.

Mejjid placed his elbows on the small round marble table and leaned forward. The large eyes were bright and his full mouth was mobile. A sudden gesture almost toppled the small cup of Turkish coffee. He steadied it.

"There is nothing for me to be concerned about. When I go back, my friends will see to my rights." He became aware that he was speaking too loudly. In a street cafe in

Amman, capital city of Transjordan, there were other refugees like himself, many of them hotheads sworn to revenge on the Jews, men who would take pleasure in causing harm to anyone considering a return to Palestine. Mejjid made such men out to be jealous and foolish, unable to adapt to the changing order of the world.

He, Mejjid al-Hadad, was wiser, stronger than they. He would survive no matter the circumstances. He would return and reclaim his possessions and eventually expand them so that his sons might live in a suitable manner. His strong fingers toyed with the knot of his yellow silk tie. "My friends will look out for my interests," he said again.

"El-ham dillah," Tewfik intoned. "Praise be to God."

"What's mine is mine."

"You are an Arab, effendi," Tewfik replied easily. "And an Arab must recognize certain realities. The Jews have just won a war against us. They have carved a country out of Palestine. It has been my observation that conquerors are seldom generous."

"I have friends," Mejjid insisted.

"Jews have been shooting Arabs and may not look upon any of us, even one as illustrious as yourself, effendi, as a friend in these trying days."

Mejjid tried to clarify his thoughts. Across the frontier, in what now was called Israel, there was property, lands that had belonged to his father and his father and his father before him, houses on which Mejjid collected rents, orchards, stores, his own home. Surely the Jews would not steal these from him. They were reasonable people and would know that he had done them no harm. They had wanted a country of their own and now they had it. Very well. Mejjid al-Hadad had done nothing to oppose them in this matter. He would become one of them. A citizen of the new nation. There. It was simple. A smile exposed his fine large white teeth. He leaned back and sipped the thick coffee.

"Tewfik," he said softly. "If a man wanted to cross the border into Israel, could it be done?"

"Oh, my dear," Tewfik said, grinning. "All things are possible to him who knows the way."

"It can be done soon?"

"Arrangements must be made."

"I wish to go back. At once."

Tewfik grew somber. "The frontier is closed, of course. Jewish patrols are active everywhere, as well as those of the Arab Legion. There is danger. Very great danger."

15

"We are friends, Tewfik."

"We are friends. Still—"

"Can it be arranged? For a price."

"For a price—all things are within reach."

"Myself and my family."

"Women and children. That will be extremely difficult."

"I will pay. But it must be soon."

Tewfik stood up and inclined his head. "I will contact you shortly, effendi. *Allah yofathah.* May God preserve you."

Mejjid watched Tewfik stride down the street, robes flowing behind him, another Arab in a city of Arabs. A spreading emptiness settled into his stomach. He didn't trust Tewfik.

IV

A stranger in a familiar landscape. An uneasy dislocation. Amos Landau was unable to shed the feeling.

Jerusalem, Soul of Israel, city of David the King, high in the Judean Hills, its oldest sections still in Arab hands, the Legionaires of Abdullah, the Hashemite king. There was that knowledge but no other evidence of the recent fighting. People—Jews, Gentiles, Arabs—went about their affairs with citified concentration.

It was warm. Amos removed his officer's cap, mopped his damp forehead, and tried to orient himself. He must have taken a wrong turn. The wound in his thigh was throbbing and a faint weakness had settled into his joints. He looked around for help.

Two men were coming in his direction, moving rapidly, talking simultaneously, their bearded jaws bobbing, gesticulating excitedly. They were dressed identically. Despite the heat, each man wore a knee-length black gabardine coat and a wide-brimmed black hat. Amos recognized them as members of the Hasidic sect. Replacing the cap on his head, he sighed and waited for them to come closer. He braced himself for the encounter.

"Excuse me, rabbis," he said in Yiddish, knowing that pious Jews refused to profane Hebrew, the holy language, by giving it everyday usage.

16

They stopped and stared at him, faces pale and intense. Waiting.

"Rabbis," he said. "I seek the military hospital which I was informed was in this section. Now I am lost. Can you direct me?"

The taller of the two men tugged at his earlocks and muttered under his breath: "Another Messiah with a uniform."

"A shame," said the other.

"Rabbis, please. The hospital. My son has been wounded. I am going to visit him." The pain in his leg was worse now, radiating upward into his groin, reaching down to the scrotum. He felt as if he was going to be sick and fought against it. He shifted his weight off the bad leg.

"Heresy," the taller man said, staring at Amos as if able to penetrate to the back of his skull. "Only when the Messiah appears will the true Jewish nation be restored. To force the end is unthinkable."

"That uniform—an obscenity."

"If a man dresses like a Jew, a man acts like a Jew."

Amos turned away.

"Wait!" the tall man cried after him. "Where are you going? Is it polite to act in such a manner?"

"I will ask someone else for help."

"You have no respect, to turn your back."

"He is no Torah-true Jew," the shorter man said.

"I am tired," Amos said. "I must find the hospital, my son—"

The tall man jerked his head. "That way, you go. You know the Talpioth section. There is where the hospital is. You are walking?"

"I have an automobile, a military car."

The tall man repeated his instructions, in greater detail this time. When he was finished, Amos thanked him.

"One more thing, young person," the tall man said. "You Jewish soldiers, you're such good soldiers, why can't you make it possible for Torah-true Jews to get to the Wailing Wall?"

"The Holiest of Holies," the other man said. "The last remnant of the ancient temple—"

"There are political decisions," Amos said.

The tall man snorted in disgust. "When the Messiah comes, He will make all decisions."

"The Prime Minister," Amos said, "the other leaders, they do their best."

17

"It is God's work they should be doing and He will be found only in that place where He is invited to enter."

The two men shuffled off and stopped. The shorter one looked back and shook a finger in Amos' direction.

"Remember, young person, soon it will be sundown. Keep the Sabbath."

"Yes, rabbi."

The two men left, arguing spiritedly again, hands slicing the air, beaver hats pitching and yawing in emphasis. Amos went back to his car.

The hospital was a sprawl of temporary wooden buildings of no particular distinction. They were an inadequate substitute for the Hadassah Medical Center which was to have been opened just prior to the War of Independence. Now, with Mount Scopus in Arab hands, the hospital was out of reach to Israelis.

Joshua Landau had been a member of an assault team that had fought the Arab Legion in Jerusalem. He had been shot while attacking a Jordanian armored car, taking a machinegun bullet in the left side. The slug had glanced off a rib, tipped one lung and exited just short of his spine. Blood had flooded his mouth and he had screamed out his fear and agony.

"Oh, my God! Help me! I'm bleeding to death!"

He almost did—hovering close to death for two weeks—before the doctors were willing to concede him a chance. That had been two months before. Now the pain and most of the terror was gone.

For a long time he had been kept in a private room, the doctors choosing not to inflict his expected death on other men. When it became clear that he was going to survive, he was moved to a ward with nine other soldiers. It was a pleasant room with large, unwashed windows that admitted considerable light. He enjoyed having someone around to talk to.

And there was Mara. Only in the ward would it have been possible to meet her. Only in the ward would he have been daring enough to speak to her, to make small jokes, flirtatious remarks. Desire flickered in his private parts whenever he thought about her and that made him ashamed. A girl like Mara, beautiful, talented, so full of life. To think of her that way was wrong, dirty. But he couldn't keep from wondering what it would be like with her. Wondering, he would close his eyes and imagine her without clothes, her young flesh burnished and vibrant.

"Joshua."

18

His eyes fluttered open and saw her watching him, her expectant half-smile revealing large, slightly protruding teeth. Her sea-green eyes glittered and he imagined she was laughing at him, that she knew what he had been thinking. He blushed and sat up, rearranging the sheet.

"Don't get up," she said. "I will come closer to you." She took his hand and squeezed gently.

"I thought you weren't coming today. It was getting late—"

"I told you I would *try*."

"The audition! Did you get the job?"

Her mouth moved in secret delight, the corners reaching for her dimples then swiftly retreating. "I am to sing at the Café Aïda beginning a week from Tuesday."

"That's marvelous! I'm so happy for you, Mara. You'll be a great success! People will come from all over to hear you." He sobered. "You'll become very famous, very rich. A film star one day."

Her head went back, long black hair falling past her shoulders. She laughed. "Joshua, you are a child, so innocent."

"I'm nineteen."

"And I am twenty-one and I say you are a child. You know nothing. Girls like Mara Gabrielli don't become film stars. They sing a few folk songs in cafes and do shows for soldiers and that's all. In the end they marry and have babies and become fat and wrinkled."

"Is that so bad?"

"You wouldn't like me fat and wrinkled."

"I meant, to get married."

"And you would marry me, I suppose?"

"Yes. At once. Today."

She laughed. "Fool," she said mildly. "You barely know me."

"Three weeks and I——"

She put a finger across his lips. "Be quiet. You are ill and out of your mind and must rest."

"You'll never be fat," he said against her finger. "You'll always be young and beautiful."

She kissed his forehead, her lips lingering. He was able to look down the front of her low-cut blouse and see the fall of her heavy brown breasts. He knew he should look away but couldn't and there was that familiar stirring.

She straightened up and assessed him gravely. "You will come to see me perform?"

"Oh, yes. And bring all my friends. Everyone I know. I

19

will organize the applause and cry bravo and encore and there will be an onslaught of mail to the management demanding that you be kept on at a very large increase in salary."

"You are mad," she said, laughing. "Perhaps the Arabs shot you in the head and the doctors made a mistake." She sobered and measured him.

"Do you know that there is gold in your eyes?" he said.

"Be quiet," she ordered. "I want to talk seriously to you. Soon you will be leaving the hospital, going home to Tel Aviv, to your father's bakery."

"No," he said. "I decided. It's not what I want."

"Will you finish your education, go back to the university?"

"No. I will educate myself, read what interests me." He hesitated. Mara was a practical girl who craved the good things of this world, material rewards. To her such attitudes as self-sacrifice, dedication to a cause, were ideas to be scorned. But he had convinced himself that this was only a temporary condition, a defensive veneer that would dissolve when someone she cared for made her understand that there were purposes in life more meaningful than profit. Joshua meant to be that someone.

"I am going to join a kibbutz," he said.

She took her hand away and stared at him in disbelief. "It is true, you mean it. Oh, you are a fool. You will never be heard of again. You will disappear into the sands of the Negev—"

"Galilee," he corrected.

"All right, Galilee. Your beautiful brown hair will wither up and fall out. Your smooth white skin will be burned by the sun and turned to dried leather. You will get wrinkles in your face and your body will become old and bent before your time, if Arab raiders don't kill you first. I will never see you again."

"It doesn't have to be that way. We are a nation now and conditions will improve. Life can be good on a kibbutz for a man, especially if he has a good wife. You will see," he ended hopefully.

All the lightness went out of her voice. "I have seen enough already to know what life is like. I know what it is to do without, to have to scratch for a bare living. Don't talk to me about your kibbutz, about hard work. There is no nobility to being poor. I have had enough of it for a lifetime. I want to enjoy my life, *this* life, and I intend to. There is nothing else."

20

"There is God," he said softly.

"There is nothing."

"Surely you understand that life can be better than it is, that it should be better. People can make it better."

A derisive sound sputtered across her lips. "Tell me what *is*, not what should be."

He reached for her hand but she avoided him. "Don't be angry with me, Mara."

"Fool," she hissed. "You're young and handsome and you've been to school and could get everything there is to get in this world. You could become *rich*."

"That's not what I want."

"There is nothing else. I said you were a child. This proves it. Perhaps some day you'll grow up."

"When I'm as old as you?"

"Fool," she said again, softer this time, the hard edge fading out of her eyes.

"When I go home," he said, laughing, glad that she was no longer annoyed with him, "will you come to visit? To meet my parents. My father is a very cultured man. He is an amateur archaeologist, an incessant reader, and you are sure to like him." He reached for her hand and she allowed him to take it.

Neither of them saw Amos enter the ward. He limped toward them, stopping at the foot of the bed.

Joshua's head came around and his face broke open in surprise and delight.

"Shalom, Joshua," Amos said hoarsely.

"Papa." Joshua straightened up, arms outstretched. Then the two men were embracing, talking and laughing at the same time, clutching at each other. At last they drew apart and looked at each other, beginning to speak, stopping, starting again. And Joshua laughing.

"For a boy with a bullet in him," Amos said finally, "you look very healthy."

"The bullet came out of its own power, papa. I'm fine now."

"Skinny and pale."

"But getting stronger." His eyes went to the cane. "What about you? Were you badly hurt?"

"Nothing. A nick." Amos glanced over at Mara. "Joshua, your manners. Introduce me to your friend."

Joshua did. Mara offered her hand and Amos took it. She gazed directly into his eyes, almost on a level with her own. How different the father from the son. Joshua was tall, slender and fair; delicately constructed, with pale

21

almost translucent skin. Amos was medium-sized with a blunted jaw and a short strong nose. Only the eyes were the same lambent brown.

It was this crazy land, she told herself, something in the soil or the water or the sun. It altered the genetic structure of the generations, shattered the rules of nature. Had she been a Talmudist like her parents she might have ascribed it to the will of God. But Mara chose not to think about such things.

She smiled at the two men and made her apologies. "I have to go now."

"But you've just come," Joshua protested.

"You and your father have a lot to talk about."

"You'll come back?"

"In a few days. Shalom."

"Shalom," Joshua said.

"Shalom, Miss Gabrielli," Amos said.

He watched her go, arms swinging easily, long legs reaching, the hair bouncing across her shoulders, hips in a natural rise and fall.

"An attractive girl," he said.

"She's beautiful."

"A good friend?"

"I like her a lot," Joshua said. "She's a singer. An entertainer. That's how I met her, here in the hospital. She's going to sing in a café, the Aïda—"

"Sephardic?"

"I suppose," Joshua said. "We never talked about it."

"She's Spanish," Amos said with certainty.

"So was Maimonides," Joshua said defensively.

Amos laughed shortly. "It is no sin to be Spanish and you mustn't pick on your old father who came to visit, to talk to you, about you. After all," he said with exaggerated boastfulness, "your father is a captain."

Grinning, they touched each other, and began to talk.

V

Haifa stepped up the hillside in progressive terraces, looking down on the Mediterranean in the same watchful way that an audience waits for a theatrical performance to

22

begin. At the water, a strand of beach reached around the harbor to Acre in the north. To Yaakov Yeshivat, a mood of hard work had always been attached to Haifa. Here men sweated and raised callouses and developed bad backs. And died, he recalled bitterly. Many of them died.

He turned the memory aside as the taxi left the port area with its distinctive sounds and smells and picked its way along the ascending road to the third of the city's tiers. Here, on Mount Carmel, everything was different. Gentle breezes and wooded ravines, neat white homes studding the slopes. A peaceful, pretty place, almost dainty and too nice.

The taxi stopped and Yaakov got out.

Like the others on Carmel, Chaim Lahav's house was white, the front door and the window frames painted an electric blue. A smooth green lawn rimmed with high hedges fronted the house. Yaakov knew that in the rear was a colorful garden, Lahav's private preserve. Flowers were his only interest outside of Histadrut, the General Federation of Labor of the Workers of the Land of Israel. Yaakov pushed the bell and heard the chimes sound deep in the house. Footsteps approached and the door opened. Lahav stood there, his triangular little face expressionless.

"Shalom, Chaim," Yaakov said.

"You're late," Lahav said. He motioned for Yaakov to enter, then led him into a book-lined room at the rear of the house. One wall was nearly all glass, providing a clear view of the harbor below. A phonograph was playing a symphony. Lahav went behind his desk and sat down.

"You like Beethoven, Yeshivat?"

"It doesn't matter."

"You have no culture."

"You asked me to come here to talk about music?"

Chaim Lahav was a wiry man with a thrusting head, covered with only a few wisps of mousy-colored hair, and eyes that were never still. He always talked a little louder than was necessary and punctuated each sentence with a downward sweep of his right hand. Yaakov could not remember ever seeing him smile.

"A man should have interests outside his work," Lahav said. "Besides women and fighting."

"How is Anna?" Yaakov said deliberately.

"Fine, fine. She made some hummus in case you wanted a drink and a nibble." He peered narrowly at the big man. "You want a drink, some hummus?"

23

"I like Anna's hummus very much." Lahav rose out of his chair and Yaakov went on. "But later. After we talk."

Lahav fell back, scowling. He had no appreciation of jokes.

"Yeshivat, you're forty-four years old. What are you going to do with the rest of your life?"

"I suspect you are going to tell me what I *should* do."

Lahav frowned. He waved his right fist at the desk top. "A man must accomplish something with his years."

"I intend to—to live."

"But how? The fighting is over."

"With Arabs all around us, there will be plenty of fighting. Maybe I'll stay in the army. I've had an offer to join the Headquarters Staff."

"Idiocy! You belong to me, to Histadrut. I know you, Yeshivat. You're a working man, like me, a good Socialist. Histadrut is your home. The way it is for me."

"Maybe I'll go into politics," Yaakov let out casually. "People know me. The last time I spoke to the Old Man he was not against it."

"Ach! Ben Gurion tells that to everyone. He encourages all the younger men to build up the Party. I heard him tell the same thing to Dayan, who is younger than you, and to men like Eshkol and Sharett. You belong with me, I tell you."

Yaakov heaved himself erect, went over to the glass wall and looked down at the sea. It reminded him of San Francisco. How long ago had that been? Two years? Three. He had toured the United States making speeches, collecting money for the Jewish National Fund, money to buy land for new kibbutzim, collective farms. San Francisco had been sweet, the air clean and fresh, the women bright and chic. Accommodating.

He had enjoyed America, enjoyed the temper of the place, its drive and energy, the variety of its people. But it was too far from the land for him, too big, too sophisticated and sleek. He preferred a country where a man could change things because of his work and see those changes take place.

"You could live here in Haifa," Lahav was saying, pulling him back to the present. "Nowhere else do you have such a view. The sunsets are God's artwork."

Yaakov swung back into the room. "You always were chauvinistic about this place."

"Take my offer."

Yaakov returned to his chair. "I'll listen to it."

24

Lahav raised his fist but did not strike. "We need everything in Israel. Machines, food, goods of all kinds, people."

"There'll be plenty of people, Jews from all over."

"But what kind of people will they be? For the most part broken bodies and spirits, those who barely survived the death camps, people used to running and hiding. It will take time before such people can produce. Until then they must be fed and clothed and cared for. Everything must be brought to them, to Israel, from other places. That means ships."

"You want me to go abroad, to buy ships?"

"Listen, I'll talk. The ships will be bought or built. And the facilities to accommodate them will be constructed. Here, at Jaffa, wherever possible. Even now plans are being made to enlarge and modernize the port facilities. What we need is trained personnel to work the port. Crane operators, winchmen, experienced stevedores, gang bosses. Men who know how to work."

"Hitler left us few of those."

"Yes, and thanks to Arab propagandists, most of the Arabs of Haifa chose to leave the city before the fighting began. Many of them worked the docks of Jaffa. Well, they are gone now and we need to create a whole new work force. I want you to get me a cadre of such workers."

"Sure, *adoni*. I whistle into the wind and longshoremen come flocking around. A miracle, right?"

"There are such men and they might be willing to come, if they understood that they were needed."

The pale eyes fixed themselves on Lahav's face. Yaakov sensed the web that was being strung, designed to entrap and hold him. If he was going to avoid it, now was the time. But curiosity moved him to speak.

"Where do such men hide?"

"Not hide. They are working in the open in Dubrovnik, the Dalmation coast of Yugoslavia. You've heard of it?"

"Go on."

"There Jews work the ships. A backward people, uneducated for the most part. It could be a difficult assignment, if you should accept it. Preliminary contact has been made and some interest in coming here has been expressed."

"Then let them come."

"It is not that easy. Right now the Yugoslavian Government takes a dim view of its people leaving. They can be very rough about such things."

"And you want me to bring them out?"

"As many as want to come. It will be dangerous and without official sanction. A private mission, if you should be caught."

"Very nice."

Lahav leaned back in his chair. "It's a mistake. I shouldn't have suggested it. You've had enough fighting. You look tired and it's time you were given easier jobs."

Yaakov shook his head. "I don't understand you, Lahav. You go to such lengths to get me to do something when you know I always say yes. Do you believe you truly trick me or do you simply enjoy the game?"

Lahav spread his hands. "I don't know what you mean. But you will take the job?"

"Afterwards, what then?"

"There will be plenty to do. Life will move swiftly. There will be many changes. You will have a splendid career in Histadrut and who knows, one day you may take over as head of the worker's council for me. After I die, of course."

"You will never die, Lahav. Now how about some of Anna's *hummus?* I am starving."

VI

The small truck bounced through the night and Mejjid al-Hadad was certain his kidneys were about to be torn loose of their moorings. He swore.

"A thousand devils should dance on your mother's grave!"

The driver laughed and drove faster.

Mejjid glared at Tewfik, seated alongside. "Why go to all this trouble just to kill us? The way this one drives, it is insane."

"The road is an obscenity, effendi," the driver protested. "Am I to be blamed for that? And the night is dark, too dark. Did I insist on making this journey tonight?"

"Ah," Tewfik said. "The night is perfect. Such an exquisite darkness. It will be difficult for the Jewish patrols to see anything."

"When do we cross the frontier?" Mejjid asked.

"Soon. And, Allah willing, all shall go as planned."

They rode hard over a bump and one of the women in the back of the truck squealed.

"Make that idiot drive more carefully," Mejjid said. "I do not want my wives killed."

"*Mafeesh*," Tewfik said. "Nothing can be done. We are almost to the place."

Presently they swung off the road into a stand of tall trees. Out of sight, the truck stopped and the men got out. The driver dropped the tailgate and Mejjid helped his wives and children to the ground; three women, faces veiled and averted, and five children, the oldest a fifteen-year-old boy.

"Here it is necessary to be quiet," Tewfik husked. "The border is not far away."

"Take everything that can be carried out of the truck," Mejjid ordered. When it was done, he turned to Tewfik. "We are ready."

"Good. I will lead you across the frontier into Jewish Palestine, *in sha'Allah,* and then you will be safe in the land of your choice."

Mejjid chose to ignore the sarcasm. He had already paid Tewfik, paid him very well, and he had no choice but to trust him now. "Let's begin," he said. "To remain here does no good."

"Everyone must stay close," Tewfik warned. "Each one is to hold to the one in front. Perhaps one of the women should be last in line, to protect the children."

"No," Mejjid said firmly. "Abdul!" he called, and his oldest son came forward.

"Yes, father."

"You will bring up the rear and make certain that no one gets lost. Also, that no one comes upon us from that direction. You can do that, my son?"

"Yes, father."

The boy took his place and Mejjid ordered Tewfik to lead them into Israel. They moved cautiously out of the trees in single file, picking their way carefully across the rising land, trying to make as little noise as possible.

"Ahead of us," Tewfik whispered finally, "the frontier."

Mejjid could make out no distinguishing signs. "Are you sure?"

"That is why I am here, effendi, because I know the

way as you know the inside of your house. A few more strides and we will be there."

Ten minutes later Tewfik signaled them to stop. "This is where I must leave you and your excellent family, effendi."

Mejjid looked around. He could see nothing to mark this as Israel. The terrain was no different than it had been a few moments earlier. "Is this a bad joke, Tewfik? I am in no mood for joking. We are nowhere." He shoved the muzzle of a pistol against the other man's jaw. "Do not play with me, Tewfik, or I will kill you."

"Effendi, we are in Israel. At this very moment. You have only to walk over that hill and you will come upon the road to Jerusalem. A mere hour's walk, effendi."

"I do not like this, Tewfik. If you have tricked me, I will find you and tear out your tongue."

"May Allah take away my vision and that of my oldest son if what I say is not exactly as I say it."

Mejjid put the pistol away. "Follow me," he said to his family. "Stay close to each other. There will be no talking."

He led them over the hill. The road was where Tewfik had said it would be. He turned south, toward the Holy City, the portion under Jewish authority. How fortunate they had been to avoid trouble, to encounter no patrols. Neither Jew nor Arab. He had been unduly suspicious of Tewfik. The man had done his job well.

A disturbing thought came to life back in his brain and he swore softly. Tewfik *had* tricked him. Clearly, there had been no patrols in this area, no danger; he had paid heavily for nothing.

Wallah, Wallah!

Mejjid walked stiffly and rapidly along a crowded street not far from the Old City of Jerusalem, still in Jordanian hands. It was absurd, he told himself, that he, a native of Palestine, a man who had lived most of his years in this city, should be a stranger in his own land. So much had happened so quickly. Less than a year had passed, eight or nine months since the fighting had begun and he had fled across the border. Very little had happened as he had expected it would, as the leaders of the Arab nations had vowed it would. He sighed and turned into the entrance of the Military Headquarters building.

An efficient-looking girl in crisp khakis provided directions, gazing shamelessly into his eyes as she spoke. He thanked her and climbed to the second floor of the old building where he took his place at the end of a long line of Arabs—peasants mostly, the fellahin. It distressed him that a man of his distinction, a man of property, should be treated no differently than such as these. Two hours later he made it up to the desk where a bearded officer looked up at him with bored patience.

"What is your problem?"

"Salaam aleikum, effendi," Mejjid began, smiling obsequiously. When the officer gave no response, he decided he had made a mistake.

"Shalom," he said quickly. "Shalom."

"What is your problem?" the officer repeated tonelessly.

"I am a native of Palestine, effendi," Mejjid said in Hebrew. "I wish to register myself as an Israeli citizen. I, who have always been a native to the Holy Land as was my father and his father and his father before him back to the time——"

The officer thrust an official form toward Mejjid. "Fill out these papers and turn them in at window number six. Next."

It was that simple. When Mejjid left the building he carried a new identity card. Confident that he was suitably armed, he made his way to the office of the custodian of abandoned property, certain that everything would soon be made right again.

Behind the desk, he found a pale, plump little man with wet eyes and a petulant mouth. He was the kind of man Mejjid had always scorned and he could not understand how men such as these had defeated the combined armies of five Arab nations. He inclined his handsome head in a polite bow and smiled graciously. This time he intended to make no mistakes.

"Shalom. I was directed to you, to regain control of my property. My name is Mejjid al-Hadad and my home is located at——"

The plump man held out his hand and Mejjid gave him the papers. He began to read.

A typical bureaucrat, Mejjid decided, officious, pompous, wielding his small amount of power like a dictator. Such men were everywhere in the world. He had known them in Amman, in Beirut, in Cairo. Less Jew or Arab, they were extensions of their oak desks, rubber stamps and filing systems. Despicable.

The little man arranged the papers neatly on the desk

and looked up. "You made sure the shooting had stopped before you came back, I see."

Mejjid felt the blood rush into his face. He fought back an angry response. *How could they have won with such men?* He arranged a supplicatory smile on his mouth.

"Effendi, I was afraid. There was my family, wives, children. My responsibility."

"You ran because Radio Cairo told you to, Radio Damascus. Clear out, they told you, so that the Arab armies could get on with the business of killing Jews unobstructed. It was going to be a small matter and not take too long. Things didn't go quite as expected, did they?"

"I fled for the sake of my family. Nothing more. I am not a political. I am back now, an Israeli citizen, with certain rights."

He saw the plump face pull together and knew that he had committed an error. He tried to correct it.

"Effendi, please, I wish only what is rightfully mine. I am a man of property, of business. The fighting is over and I would go back to my affairs, to make jobs for citizens of your country, *our* country. That is all of it, effendi."

"You have been absent for a long time and conditions change."

"But now I am back. Of my own free will. I insist on having what is mine."

The little mouth twitched and the wet eyes went out of focus. "These are matters that take time. Some of the houses you own, the shops on which you collected rents, have been taken over by people who did not run away, who stayed and displayed courage and loyalty. Such people are established now. What do you expect us to do with them?"

"Put them out!" Mejjid said hotly. "The shops are mine. The houses are mine. I must be paid what is mine, the rents are mine. Everything. And what of my lands, to the south and in the north? There were groves and farms——"

The little man folded his hands on the edge of the desk. "The lands will not be returned! They fall into sensitive areas, areas vital to the defense of the nation. Already kibbutzim have been built in three locations. The land belongs to them."

"I will not tolerate this! I am being robbed. I have rights. I will go to my friends, Jews in high places. They will protect me, see that what is mine remains mine. I do not have to endure such treatment!"

The little man half rose out of his chair, eyes glazed but steady, mouth quivering. "Your house will be returned to you so that you will have a place for your family. As for the rest, you can go to hell! Straight to hell!"

Every fiber in Mejjid's body trembled with hatred for the plump little man. He ached to drive his fist into his face, to destroy him. He turned without a word and left.

VII

From Jerusalem, forty-two reflective miles by Egged bus. Past the village of Abu Ghosh, home of the Ark of the Covenant, down the slope beyond the valley where Judas Maccabeus was victorious, to where Joshua stopped the sun and gained time enough to defeat the Amorites. Past Ramla and the Tower of the Forty, past Lod, that ancient center of learning. To the Hill of Springtime. To Tel Aviv.

Tel Aviv was conceived to be a suburb of Jaffa, that crowded, noisome Arab port town on the Mediterranean. It was to provide a better place to live and raise children. They named the first streets—in honor of men who had done so much to help them to build their lives in Palestine—Rothschild Boulevard and Herzl Street.

Tel Aviv spread out from its limited beginnings to become the commercial center of the land, its industrial heart. The largest Jewish city in the world.

Amos Landau moved without purpose, aware of the weariness in his wounded leg, trying to ignore it. He reminded himself that at home Ruth was waiting, and his father, and Levi, Rena, the new boy, Simon. Months had passed since he had seen them and now a few more minutes mattered little.

He stopped at a construction site. Amos knew that the apartment building going up would be an exact reproduction of those on either side of it. The color of the desert, it would have small windows and balconies from which housewives would drape their laundry and dust their carpets. The drabness of all the buildings was a concession, he supposed, to necessity. With shelter needed for all the new people coming, there was no time for architects to spawn beauty and variety.

Further along, the street was lined with shops. Here, too, there was a depressing sameness—a dingy grocery, a dry-goods merchant, a fruit market, a kiosk, a bakery that might have belonged to his father. All were the same. They were cramped, without appeal, and offering no stimulation to prospective patrons. Yet what choice did people have? There were no better places to buy.

Something should be done, he told himself. But there was no one to do it. He began to look for a taxi. It was time to go home.

"I have decided," Rena announced firmly, "to become a film star."

Amos sipped hot tea from a tall glass and studied his daughter. In the months of his absence, a radical change had taken place. She had stopped being a young girl and had been transformed into a budding beauty. True, she was only sixteen years of age, but there was a thrusting maturity to her; round at bosom and bottom, she moved in a seductive cloud of femininity that could not be ignored.

She was a happy, healthy and ebullient girl, quick to laugh and sensitive to what went on about her, full of feeling and vulnerable. The skin of her cheeks was smooth, softly olive. Her eyes were large, black, luminous.

"I shall go to Hollywood one day," she continued, "and become famous and make simply marvelous films in which everything comes out all right in the end."

"And what," Amos asked lightly, "if your employers decide that things should not come out all right in the end?"

As she considered that briefly, her generous mouth opened in a wide smile. "I shall marry my producer, of course, and he will, naturally, be the sort of man who believes in happy endings. So it will be all right, you see."

"Yes," Amos said. "I see."

They were seated, waiting for the night to descend in the tiny garden in back of the house, Ruth's garden with its variety of flowers.

"Oh, papa," Rena said, "I know you must think I'm a silly girl but it isn't wrong to dream, is it?"

"I don't think so."

Her face grew somber and she leaned forward and

spoke in a confidential voice. "Papa, do you still dream? I mean, when people get older, that's no reason to stop dreaming, is it? I mean, if you don't have dreams then how can a person know what she wants to do with her life?"

He patted her cheek. "I still dream."

She moved to the edge of her chair. "Do you have a dream now?" He considered the question, then nodded. "What is it, papa? Oh, tell me, please!"

"Not yet. At my age you learn to hoard your dreams until they are letter-perfect, or else forget them."

She frowned. "I don't think I like that way. A dream doesn't have to be *perfect,* just attractive."

He laughed and she joined him. "I think that you may be much wiser than your old father."

"I expect so," she said, in a voice that told Amos she had given consideration to that proposition. "Papa," she said crisply, "there is no need for you to flatter me. I want the truth. Do you think I have a good face, in photographic terms, I mean."

He assessed her for a beat and nodded solemnly. "I believe you have a very good face, in photographic terms, of course."

"I do have a good nose," she said, "and my eyes are quite nice, my best feature, I think."

"You may be right."

"And with proper makeup I shall be able to improve my appearance." When Amos began to speak, she raised her hand for silence. "There is no use in your trying to talk me out of this, Papa. Oh, yes, I expect it to be a very difficult life in the beginning. After all, I am realistic. I know that I am not the most beautiful girl in the world. Nevertheless, it is what I want and I shall dedicate my life to my career, become a serious actress like Joan Crawford."

"You consider Miss Crawford to be a serious actress?"

The eyes went round. "Oh, Papa, she's marvelous!"

Amos was about to answer when Levi came out of the house. A year younger than Rena, he resembled her superficially. The same olive skin, the same black eyes. But where hers shone with vitality and zest, his were veiled, wary, never still. His slender body, the shoulders squared unnaturally, was drawn tight as if anxious to attack.

"Grandfather is going to synagogue," he broke in, blinking in disconcerting spurts. "He says you are to go with him, all of us."

33

"Levi," Rena said. "You're doing it with your eyes."

"Oh, shut up!" he said quickly.

"Enough," Amos said. "Tell your grandfather I'm not going tonight. That I'm tired."

"What do you mean—tired!"

Amos looked up to see his father framed in the doorway, face drawn up in disapproval. Baruch Landau approved of less and less with each passing day and least of all did he approve of the way his son lived or of the manner in which he raised his children. He had always owned a temper—the wrath of righteousness, Baruch termed it—and it seemed to Amos it had become more uncontrollable in recent years.

"My leg is bothering me a little," Amos said, thinking to forestall his father's anger.

"Does it bother you too much to thank God for sparing you from the Arabs?" Baruch demanded in Yiddish. "Too much to pray for your son who was almost killed? Too much to pray for the Jews who died?"

Still standing in the doorway, he seemed to fill it. Though not a large man, he managed to impose himself and dominate any gathering. His gestures were broad and dramatic and his resonant voice could not be ignored. He had a great, round head and deep-set hot eyes. The skin of his face was drawn tight, very pale and almost translucent. His gray beard was neatly barbered to a sharp point which he used for emphasis.

"Heretic!" the old man roared. "You are no Jew!"

Amos was aware of Rena and Levi watching him, measuring his reactions, and he resented being placed in this position. To be a proper father and obedient son at the same time seemed almost impossible.

"Papa, please," he said, in a conciliatory manner. "I'm back only a few days. I'll go to services tomorrow. All right?"

"Not all right. Sabbath commences when the sun goes down. It is right that a son should accompany his father to the synagogue." His eyes turned in Levi's direction. "You too, bandit, you also will come."

Levi began to blink. "No," he muttered.

"I'll give you a *no!*" The old man raised his right hand.

"Papa," Amos said. "Stop it. If Levi doesn't want to go, he doesn't have to. He is my son and that's the way I want it." He heaved himself erect. "I'll go with you." He smiled at Levi, trying to reach him, to make him under-

34

stand that certain compromises were necessary in order to exist. Levi turned away.

"Heretics!" Baruch bit off again. "You call yourself Jews! If the father does not even wear a yarmulke how can more be expected of the son. Jews without earlocks." He brought one fist up to his breast in an ancient gesture of guilt. "It is what I deserve for coming here, for leaving the Holy City———"

"Have you forgotten how we lived in Jerusalem? That old house. No money. Here we live decently and the bakery does a good business."

"Business," Baruch intoned, "is not everything." He glared at Amos. "When do you come back to work? It is time———"

"Oh, *zayde*," Rena burst out. "Papa's only been home for a week. He's been fighting a war. He's entitled to a holiday."

"Did I speak to you? You with your long hair and showing your legs like a *courva*." Rena laughed delightedly at the suggestion that she might be a whore and Baruch jerked his head back to Amos. "Enough talk. It is time to go to synagogue. The whole family."

Amos braced himself. "I will go with you. And Ruth, if she wants to. The children are old enough to decide for themselves."

Baruch realized that he had lost and his face grew dark. He spun away, nimble for his seventy-odd years.

"In d'rerd mit dir. Gornischt helfen," he muttered. "To hell with you. Nothing will help."

Amos spent the next few days trying to isolate his thoughts, to understand what it was he truly wanted, and how to get it. There was one idea, half-formed, silly, perhaps, but persistently returning to his frontal lobes. He knew that he had to give it his full attention, the respect it deserved. He spent long hours strolling around the city, along the docks, watching the men at work, picking his way through the commercial district, going in and out of shops, seldom buying but watching the way the merchants conducted their affairs, listening to the bargaining that went on, impressed with the casual and unbusinesslike way business was conducted.

One night he took Ruth and the children to the cinema, one of those colorful Hollywood musicals. Baruch, stubborn and still angry, refused to come along.

After the movie, they had ice cream and coffee in a cafe on Dizengoff Street and watched the passers-by. It was easy to pick out the Americans among them, especially the women, almost always smartly turned out, their dresses chic, hairstyles carefully arranged.

He glanced at Ruth, pretty in a flowered print dress that she might have made herself, but hadn't. Her hair was pulled straight back off her forehead into a bun at the nape of her neck. Her face was warm, motherly, her smile generous.

Two women passed, their husbands a stride behind.

"Hadassah ladies," Rena said softly, smiling.

"And their hero husbands, coming after all the danger is over," Levi said bitterly.

Ruth looked at him kindly. "And how much fighting did you do, my hero?"

"I would have fought, if they let me. I could be as good a soldier as anyone. Anyone."

"I agree," Amos said. "But still I'm glad you didn't have to."

"Next time I will."

"No," Ruth said quickly. "No next time. No more killing. The fighting is over, isn't it, Amos?"

"Yes," he said automatically. "Everything is settled now." He was still watching the two American women.

That night, as they had every night since his return, Amos and Ruth made love. He enjoyed her, her easy acquiescence, the loving gentleness; and if she was always the same, he took comfort in knowing what was expected of him, that he was capable of providing it.

Yet something was different now. He tried to define it, to discover some alteration in her flesh or her touch, in the pliant acceptance of her lips, the moist heat of her insides. But there had been no change in her.

After the love-making, Amos felt vaguely dissatisfied and he lay back and stared at the ceiling in the dark, only dimly aware of Ruth's fingers on the inside of his thigh.

"It's so good for me," she murmured, after a while. "Exciting, the way it was when we first got married." He offered no response and they lay in silence for a long time. "Your father is worried about you," she said, sitting up, looking at him.

He kept his eyes fixed on the ceiling. "He's got to understand that in my own home I must go my own way. I cannot be the way he is, especially about the synagogue."

"He's an old man."

"He's an ox, that man. He'll live to be two hundred. He'll sit *shiva* for all of us."

36

She laughed softly. "Not for you, my darling. A man with a body like yours is not even close to dying. You're so strong and finely constructed. You have the most beautiful physique I've ever seen."

"What do you know of men's bodies? I thought I was the only man you ever knew."

Her laugh was teasing, reminiscent of Rena. "I go to the beach. I've got eyes."

"Maybe you've done more than look while I was busy saving you from the Arabs."

"Dozens of times with dozens of men. Shall I tell you all about it?"

"Some other time. And I will tell you about all the young girls I had in the Negev."

She glanced down at the scar on his hip, still livid and ugly. She bent and brushed it with her lips.

"Does it still hurt?"

"Not now."

She placed her cheek on his thigh. "I love everything about you."

"And I love you," he answered automatically.

"Amos," she said hesitantly. "How did you become a tank commander? I thought you were a liaison officer."

"It was easier than walking."

"Tell me about it."

He supposed she was entitled to know but he took no satisfaction in recalling his battle experiences. "I was just an over age lieutenant attached to brigade headquarters," he said flatly. "They sent me to a forward position to observe the action near Gaza. Our boys had some tanks, three altogether. One of them was from the first world war.

"War can be very confusing and the men fighting sometimes don't know what's going on. I guess that's what happened and the tanks stopped and the commander opened the hatch and climbed out to look around. I came up from behind in my jeep and we spoke to each other and he made a joke about the heat. He was a nice young fellow. That's when the plane came out of the sun and strafed us. I dived for cover under the tank and held my breath.

"When the plane went away I stood up and brushed off the sand. Men were doing the same thing everywhere, crawling out from under trucks or jeeps. My heart was pounding and my throat was dry. But nobody showed they were afraid so I didn't either. The young officer, he was still on top of the tank, sprawled out with seven bullets in his back."

Ruth grimaced and turned away.

"It was all very neat and clean. There was more confusion then. It seemed that there were no other officers and no one knew what was expected. Well, neither did I. But I climbed up on the tank and said let's go and we went charging toward some Arab positions. The next day a colonel showed up and told me to keep doing whatever it was I was doing and said I was in charge of the unit. That's Israeli efficiency," he ended with a small, tight laugh.

"Amos," she said, almost inaudibly. "Were you afraid?"

"Always."

She kissed his thigh and caressed him, but he felt nothing. His mind kept reaching for some blurred idea, a quicksilver fragment tormentingly elusive.

He had been this way since he had come home, turning in on himself, searching all the dark corners in an effort to find answers, answers to questions that he found difficult to formulate. At forty, nearly forty-one, father of four, he was still unable to perceive life clearly. A man of his years should know who and what he was, what he wanted.

Forty. It had happened so quickly, the years passing almost without notice. He had married when he was twenty and Joshua had been born a year later. They had lived in Jerusalem, on the fringe of Mea She'arim. He remembered the synagogue they used to attend, the men in their black kaftans and beaver hats, their beards long, looking old even when they weren't. The droning of their prayers while the women gathered together behind a latticework screen in the balcony in the Orthodox manner.

Not for him. None of it. Not the somber dress nor the incessant praying, existing in a world that no longer was, rejecting the present.

Amos accepted God, believed sincerely, paid Him that which was His. But he was a man and had to make his own way. The war had taught him that. Unlike the Mandatory time with its irregular raids on British police stations or against Arab villages, the war had exposed him to a continuity of violence and death with no sense of how it would end. Or when. Or if you would be alive at the end.

For Amos, the war had been more than a collective triumph for the Jews. It had been an individual victory and he refused to surrender what he had won.

Forty, he reminded himself, was not too old.

"I am finished with the bakery, Ruth," he said, without special emphasis. "I want you to know that. I never enjoyed it, never wanted it. That's my father's life, not mine."

She lifted herself on one elbow and tried to see his face in the darkness. "What will you do?"

"I don't know. I'm not sure. It isn't that I'm terribly ambitious, or that I want to be rich. But I have to do things my own way, to test myself, to find out what I can do. Do you understand?"

"I think so," she said uncertainly, then: "But what about us? The children?"

"Nobody will starve. I'll see to that. But I've got a lot of thinking to do. I thought I would go into Galilee, dig a little, see what I can find. I want to be alone for a while. To make up my mind. I do have an idea—"

"Can't you tell me? I'm your wife, I could help."

"When I'm sure, I will."

He fell asleep shortly and she held herself very still, looking at him, trying to understand this man who had come back to her. He was the same but different and she was afraid of that part of him that was different. Yet, she loved him still, more than ever, and she yearned to please him, to make him happy.

VIII

Dubrovnik was founded in the Seventh Century and served as a maritime and commercial center in medieval times. It was a pretty place and became a resort city in modern times. Traces of its beginnings were evident in its ancient stone buildings, ramparts and monuments. But Yaakov Yeshivat had not come to see the sights of antiquity or to sun himself on Adriatic beaches. His business was serious and there was no time for frivolity.

It had been simple enough to locate Rabbi Ben-Ezra, to gain the old man's support for his mission, to assemble a number of Dubrovnik's Jews under one roof. The difficulty would be to convince them to come to Israel to live and to do so quickly, before word reached the authorities of his intentions.

The meeting took place at night in the large kitchen of a stone farmhouse seven miles north of the city. In addition to Yaakov and the rabbi, there were about twenty men present. The farmer, a non-Jew, withdrew to another part of the house.

Yaakov studied his audience. For the most part, the men were young, in their twenties, which was good, and they looked like workers. Strong shouldered with thick wrists and that open, almost innocent, look in their eyes that so often belongs to men who labor with their hands. There were three or four others, older, faces weathered and wrinkled, the leaders of the Jewish community.

These were Sephardim, descendants of the Jews of Spain who had been forced to flee beginning in 1492. Some of them had drifted to Italy, others to Greece, while the antecedents of these men had found their way to Yugoslavia and the docks of Dubrovnik. They were swarthy, sharp-featured and serious, with a glint of curiosity in fox-like eyes.

"Shalom chaverim," Yaakov began, then switching to his faulted Yiddish. "Peace, gentlemen. By now most of you have heard why I am here. Well, I am not much for fancy talking so I will tell it to you straight. We need you in Israel, to work the docks in Haifa, to teach our young workers how to operate the winches and the cranes, the tugs, how to unload great weights. How to work hard."

A few of the young men laughed at that. It didn't surprise them to learn that the Jews of Israel were soft and indulgent. To win a war was one thing. To work hard day after day was another matter.

Yaakov's eyes worked from face to face. Here he recognized a friendly expression, encouraging, there one suspicious, another simply patient, waiting to listen, and one that was set, rutted with antagonism.

"Our young men do not have a bad life in Dubrovnik," one of the older men said. "There is steady work and enough food to eat and the officials seldom trouble us."

"But there are few prayer books for the synagogue," Yaakov said, "and the Government forbids the printing of any more. And is any one of you free to criticize the regime if you wish to do so?"

"There is nothing to criticize," one of the young men broke in hotly. "In a Socialist country all things are as they should be, all institutions are designed for the welfare of the people."

Yaakov flexed his mouth in what he hoped was a

friendly smile. "Even I do not accept that premise, my friend, and I have been a Socialist all of my life. I have lived a Socialist life on a kibbutz where no man owns anything but no man goes without." He decided to challenge the speaker, aware of his hostility. "If you choose to, will the Government allow you to emigrate to Israel?"

"I do not choose to go. I am content here. It is not bad here and it will get better."

Yaakov ransacked his memory for the man's name. *Mori.* They had not met, but Rabbi Ben-Ezra had pointed him out walking past the great stone customs house. "He is a member of the Communist Party," the rabbi had said.

"And a Jew?"

"He does not come to the synagogue but he is a Jew still in God's eye."

"In Germany," Yaakov said, issuing the words slowly, "it was not so bad and then Hitler came and promised to make it better. Nor was it so bad in Russia in the Pale of Settlement before the pogroms. Nor in Poland. Nor in Spain, until the Inquisition. For Jews, it is never bad until it becomes bad. And then it is too late."

Rabbi Ben-Ezra was a man of impressive proportions with a massive head. He admitted to being eighty-three, but some of his parishioners were convinced that he was at least five years more than that. He took great pride in his appearance, combing his thick beard and hair every day, and had a wife forty years his junior. He had been seated along the far wall. Now he stood and came forward.

"Yeshivat," he said, voice deep and rolling, "is right to remind us that we are Jews and what it can mean to be a Jew. It is known that throughout history they, the goyim, always turn on us. And with reason. For to be a Jew is to be unlike other people."

"This is a Communist nation," Mori cried out, coming to his feet. "Here there is no anti-Semitism. That is a capitalistic disease."

"Where Jews live among Gentiles," the rabbi said, "there is feeling against our people."

"Except where all men are Jewish," Yaakov said.

"It is so," the rabbi said sadly. "Here the Government insists that all must think in one way politically. To do so it is necessary that all people think and feel alike in all matters. To worship God in a different way, to worship at all, may in time be expected to be termed a threat to those in power."

41

One of the middle-aged men raised a hesitant hand. "You believe the young men should leave, rabbi, go to Israel?"

"They must make their own decisions. But if I were a young man I should go."

"But their families——"

"Their families could come later," Yaakov said. "Such things can be arranged."

"The young men should go," the rabbi said, "for the sake of their families. For themselves. For the sake of all the Jews everywhere."

Now, Yaakov ordered himself. Close the deal. Screw the lid on tightly. Make them commit themselves. End the emotional indecision, that deep tear between the familiar and the unknown. Now, while the impact of the rabbi's words still gripped them.

"Some of you may be afraid," he said.

"Fear is no stranger to these men," the rabbi put in. "They will do what they think is right."

Yaakov accepted the criticism, turned back to the men. "Patrol boats along the coast could be a problem for those of you who agree to go. They will shoot—"

One of the young men laughed. "We know all about the patrol boats."

Another man laughed. "True, true. Whenever we wish to leave, we leave, to fish, which is sometimes frowned upon, or to travel down the coast to court the girls of Hercegnovi. The patrols will offer no difficulty."

"No!" Mori cried. "This must not happen!"

Yaakov watched him, the darting eyes, the taut set of his mouth, the fluttering of his workman's hands. There was too much tension, the tension of a man torn and frightened, the tension of desperation.

"To even talk about this is to move against the state, to act in a counter-revolutionary fashion. How do we know that this is not some capitalist plot? It is known that Israel is little more than an American colony. Do not let yourselves be tricked by this man. Jew or Gentile, it is nothing. There is no God and all churches are corrupt and cheat the workers. We must remain together for the good of all and strive for the Socialist ideal."

"If you want Socialism," Yaakov said, "you should come to Israel, live on a communal farm. All receive a fair share of what is produced."

Mori whirled to face him, face blotched, mouth working. "It is true that America supports Israel! You dare not deny it."

"We have friends in America."

"America was the first to recognize the Zionists."

"And the Soviet Union was close behind," Yaakov said. He took a hard look at Mori and made up his mind. He turned away. "Each of you," he said to the others, "has friends. I ask you to ask them to come, to help Israel, to help yourselves. I can take only the young men this time. If you come and find that Israel is not for you, you will be free to leave at any time and funds will be provided for transportation."

"He is a liar!" Mori shouted. "Once you are there, you will be enslaved, exploited, lost——"

"Which of you," Yaakov went on, "will agree to come, to commit your friends?"

Hands were raised. Three of them represented a total of 13 men. One of the older men raised his hand. Three more. Another hand, reluctant yet steady. "I have two sons and a cousin. They will go with you."

Yaakov continued to count hands.

"And I speak for five young men," Rabbi Ben-Ezra said. "None yet is twenty but they are strong and willing and without families here."

Yaakov figured swiftly. Forty-one men, more than he had hoped for. "About boats. We will need two, perhaps three. Fast ones and with good range."

"How far by water?" someone asked.

"To the Greek island of Corfu. There is a cove where we can put ashore. Then onto the mainland. Arrangements have been made to take us the rest of the way."

"The boats are no problem," the rabbi said.

"Then it is settled," Yaakov said. "I congratulate you."

"When do we leave?" a young man asked, excitement in his voice. There was the promise of high adventure here and he was unable to recognize the dangers.

But Mori did. "You fools! This is treason to the state. You could all be shot for this. And if the patrols find you they will shoot. You will all die. I tell you not to listen to this man. Don't go with him."

"There is danger," Yaakov agreed. "Real danger. And life in Israel is not easy. Those of you who would change your minds had better do it now."

No one spoke.

Mori swore. "Traitors. All of you. You will be pun-

43

ished. I have warned you." Then he was out of the farmhouse, slamming the door.

After a moment, one of the young men laughed without humor. "Mori is too serious about politics."

"He is a threat to us all," Yaakov said.

"Mori is political," the same youth said, "but he is a friend, one of us."

"As was Judas to Jesus," Yaakov said.

"No," the young man said. "No, no—"

The rabbi voiced the rest of it. "If Mori is a danger to those who would go, he is also a danger to those who stay behind. He has the power to betray all of us."

There was a long silence, only the sound of breathing to break it. Someone moved and the scraping of a chair on the wooden floor was exaggeratedly loud.

"We could take him somewhere," a man said. "Keep him until it is safe."

"That will not help those who remain," Yaakov said. "Dubrovnik is a small place. Everyone knows everyone else. There will be no hiding places for Jews here."

The rabbi, still standing, closed his eyes, his lips moving. His words carried to them all—the prayer for the dead.

"No," someone said. "We can't do that. We can't."

A middle-aged man rose heavily, his face tired, eyes lidded. "I will arrange for the boats and on the first moonlit night you will leave. I will also obtain the new schedule for the patrols." His head rose up and he looked into Yaakov's eyes. He found no sympathy there. "You cannot ask us to do this thing."

Yaakov let his gaze go from face to face. "Someone must take me to wherever Mori is. It should be taken care of at once."

The rabbi stopped praying. "Rudolph. Take him now. It is necessary."

Rudolph had a round head and a thick neck and his immense hands bulged with heavy veins. "I have a truck outside. Mori has only his bicycle. We will catch up with him soon."

He was right. Halfway to town they spotted him, walking his bicycle up a steep incline. Rudolph pulled ahead and turned onto the shoulder.

"Keep the motor running," Yaakov said. "And turn off your headlights. I will not be long."

"Will you want my help?"

Yaakov recognized the offer as genuine.

"I will do this myself. Wait in the cab for me."

44

Yaakov walked down the hill and waited for Mori to reach him. Mori stopped ten feet away and frowned when he recognized Yaakov in the moonlight.

"What is it?" he said. "You think I shall change my mind? I will not. I am decided against you. I do not go along."

"Where are you going now, Mori?"

"That is no matter to you," he said. Then quickly—too quickly, Yaakov thought—Mori . added, "I am going home, to sleep. Where else? I am a working man and I need my rest."

Yaakov moved two strides to the right so that the bicycle was no longer between them. He measured the other man. Mori was almost as tall as he was with immense shoulders and a thick, powerful torso. To close with him would be a mistake. To allow him time to put those huge longshoreman's hands to work would be a mistake. Surprise and speed. They were paramount.

"You are going to betray us, Mori. Betray your friends."

"You are a liar. I am going home. Get out of my way."

The voice took on a sharp cutting edge and Yaakov anticipated an attack. Good. It was always easier in combat, with the blood hot. His weight shifted imperceptibly onto the balls of his feet and his knees bent, the tendons and muscles taut.

"All of them know you, Mori, a Jew who uses Jews in order to profit."

"There is no profit! I am a citizen, a member of the party! I do what is right for the state, for the people. Those back there, subversives, tools, refusing to conform to what is proper and good. I will not permit you to take away the young men, the workers—"

Now, Yaakov urged silently. Do it now. Drop the bicycle and charge. The anger is there, Mori, along with the fear and the self-hatred. A gathering well of bile, scorching the lining of your throat, bitter, loathsome.

Here, my friend, let me help you.

"Men like you led the Jews of Germany to the death camps, Mori, pushed them into the ovens. But these men laugh at you, know you for a petty spy, a traitor, a coward——"

A soft moan seeped from between Mori's lips and the bicycle went clattering to the macadam road. At the same time, he launched himself at Yaakov, face twisted in anguish, fists swinging with clumsy fury.

45

Yaakov almost felt sorry for him. He shuffled forward, in a balanced crouch, deflecting the looping right hand easily, moving inside where his hands could work most effectively. First, the fingers of his left hand, together and stiffened, propelled with stunning acceleration, sinking deep into the soft place between the ribs, paralyzing the diaphragm.

The rest was routine.

Mori, doubled over in agony and unable to breath, retched and moaned silently. Yaakov wasted no time. One short step, one descending blow with the edge of the right hand to the exposed place behind the right ear. The soft crunch of bone, a small sound lost in the chirping of the crickets, and Mori went to the ground.

Yaakov found a large rock and crushed Mori's skull. Working rapidly now, he went through his pockets and took his money and the cheap watch and gold chain on his vest. It was important that the police be convinced that the murder was the result of a robbery. Finished, he went back to the truck. Rudolph sat hunched over the wheel, staring into the night.

"Let's get out of here," Yaakov said. "It's done."

Rudolph drove carefully, neither too fast nor too slow. Yaakov leaned back and forced himself to breathe regularly. He marked Rudolph down as a valuable acquisition for Israel, a man who would do whatever was required. A good man. One who would please Lahav very much.

IX

And it came to pass, Joshua took
the city of Hatzor,
and he slew the king thereof, with
the edge of his sword.

—Book of Joshua

Hatzor existed before Solomon lived. And 1,900 years before Jesus, the city rebelled against the Pharaohs Thutmose III, Seti and Amenhotep. Five hundred years later, King Abdi-Tarshix of Hatzor was accused of treachery by the kings of Ashtaroth and Tyre. Subsequently, Joshua, seeing Hatzor as the key to the land of Canaan, captured it and set it afire. Then, Solomon charged the people to "... build the house of the Lord ... and the walls of Jerusalem, Hatzor, Megiddo, and Geser." Two centuries later the Assyrians conquered Hatzor, and five centuries after them the Asmonaeans.

Here Amos Landau came to chip away at the *tel*, the high mound that concealed the layers of all this life and death. Like many others in Israel, Amos was steeped in Biblical history and enjoyed scratching at the land in search of bits of pottery or coins or a tool that would confirm or deny the truth of the Old Testament. Archaeology was too immediate, much too important, to be left to the experts.

To the west of the *tel*, there was a narrow stream and beyond it a stand of eucalyptus trees. Here, he pitched his tent. There was a kibbutz a few miles to the north, but he craved only his own company and appreciated the isolation. Early each morning he climbed up the west slope of the *tel* and began digging, using a lightweight pick. On the third day he uncovered a pottery shard and cleaned it off with the dental tools he carried for that purpose. It seemed to be part of a water jug, but was no more than one hundred years old and of little importance. The next day he found an arrowhead, still attached to a portion of its shaft. It was an exciting find and he wondered what the experts at the Hebrew University would make of it.

He dug only in the cool of the mornings, spending the afternoons around the tent, meditating and reading: the plays of Ibsen, his Bible and a Joseph Conrad novel that he had always wanted to re-read, *Nostromo*.

Twice he spotted other men, diggers like himself, but he made no effort to contact them and they avoided him too. On the night he decided it was time to go home, he heard the sound of voices and laughter, of singing and a guitar. His curiosity aroused, he went to investigate.

A quarter of a mile to the south he found a group of people gathered around a large campfire. There were about twenty of them, young men and women, obviously on a hiking and camping holiday. Two of the men strummed guitars and some of the others danced a hora, circling around the fire. Amos watched for a while, enjoying the graceful movements of the dancers. He was about to leave when he heard his name spoken. He turned and saw a tall girl coming toward him, hand outstretched.

"Shalom, Mr. Landau. You don't remember me. Of

course not. Mara Gabrielli. I'm a friend of Joshua. From the hospital in Jerusalem."

She was wearing khaki shorts and a white blouse. Her long black hair had been plaited into braids and piled on top of her head. Olive skin shining with perspiration, she was breathing hard and her eyes glowed in the firelight. Amos thought her the most beautiful woman he had ever seen. He accepted her hand but released it almost at once.

"Shalom, Miss Gabrielli. I remember you. How nice to see you again."

A mood of annoyance settled over him. He felt awkward and stupid, wished suddenly that he were clever and quick and able to make bright, amusing remarks.

"How is Joshua?" she asked. Her blouse had worked its way out of the shorts and she tucked it back, the thin fabric taut over her breasts. He glanced back at the dancers.

"Better," he said. "Well, I suppose I should go. I heard the singing and came to see. I didn't mean to interrupt."

"Why don't you join us?" She looked down at his leg. "You've given up your cane."

He was pleased that she remembered and, being pleased, was annoyed with himself. "The leg is a little better. Soon the limp will be gone." He took a backward step. "I should go back. I'm camped a little way from here. I've been digging."

She nodded. "I've never understood, this preoccupation with the past."

His smile was unsteady and he found the directness of her gaze disconcerting. "Well, you know what they say— those who ignore the mistakes of history are doomed to repeat them." He berated himself silently for being a pompous, clumsy idiot.

"My only interest is the present," she said evenly. "And how it affects my future, whether or not I get the pretty things it offers—you know, clothes, jewels, money. All those common things." Her laugh was a rising peal of pleasure. "I want to dance some more. Will you dance with me?"

"I don't think so."

Even as he spoke he knew that he wanted to stay. And the wanting frightened him.

"Suit yourself," she said. "Tell Joshua hello when you see him."

Then she was gone, breaking into the circle of dancers, lost in the music. She was graceful and lithe; he enjoyed

48

the play of muscle in calf and thigh, the thrust of her tight round bottom.

Later, lying in his tent and smoking, he listened to the sound of the music and allowed himself to visualize her again. At once something was different. He sat up. The singing had stopped, the music. Now, only the usual night sounds: a quick scurrying through the brush, the rustle of leaves, the crickets.

He settled back and arranged the blanket under his chin. A girl like that, so vital and alive, so full of excitement. A girl like that, all fever and damp, so *exciting*. A girl like that, too much for a man his age, too much in need, too demanding. A giver of coronaries, a girl like that, he warned himself wryly.

He supposed she was with someone now, one of the dancers. There had been one man, tall and handsome, with a deep, strong chest. She would not exhaust him, not in one night.

X

The house of Mejjid al-Hadad was on the outskirts of Jerusalem, beyond Romena, not far from the Armistice Demarcation Line that separated Israel from Jordan. The house was stone, more than one hundred years old, the thick walls providing a thermal barrier against the oppressive heat of summer. Inside, large earthenware jars filled with water, kept the air fresh and moist.

Mejjid greeted Amos Landau in the bare reception hall. *"Miyet marhaba,"* he smiled, bowing rapidly. "A hundred welcomes. My poor house is honored at your presence."

"Abu Abdul," Amos murmured. "Father of Abdul," using the indirect manner to display his respect. "To be invited to your splendid home is indeed to be honored."

Mejjid straightened up. "Enough of this nonsense, Amos. Come inside where we can be comfortable."

Amos followed the taller man down three steps into a large room furnished with heavy oak furniture, carved and darkly ornate. Thick Oriental carpets covered the stone floor and lattice-work screens masked off the doorways to the rest of the house. They settled into oversized chairs covered with dusty red velvet.

"Will you drink with me, Amos?"

"My pleasure."

Mejjid filled two glasses with arak and handed one to Amos. *"Naharak unbarak,"* he said, toasting his visitor, then emptying his glass in one swift swallow.

"And may your day also be blessed," Amos replied, sipping cautiously. He was familiar with the sting of the powerful brandy. He watched as Mejjid refilled his glass. The Arab presented a dramatic picture, darkly handsome in a tan gabardine suit, a yellow shirt and a neatly figured tie. He might have been a French trader or an Italian or a Jew. He swallowed half the arak and turned to Amos, smiling.

"A day could be very long and cruel without such beneficial prescriptions."

"For a Muslim, you have grown very fond of arak."

Mejjid finished the remainder of his drink. "Are all Jews kosher? I think not. And not all followers of the Prophet obey the prohibitions concerning alcohol."

"A point well made, Mejjid." He brought the glass up to his mouth but did not drink. "Your letter surprised me, Mejjid. It has been a long time."

"Friends should not be strangers to each other."

"Circumstance sometimes keeps people apart." Amos put the glass down. "How are things with you these days?"

The dark eyes lidded and the full mouth tightened. Seconds later the tension washed away and Mejjid was smiling graciously.

"Matters with me go well, *habibi,* and why not? Israel is a free country and I am a citizen. But it has been too long since last we saw each other and while we have lunch you must tell me all about your adventures, about your fine family." He stood up.

Amos shook his head. "I can't stay for lunch, Mejjid."

"Ah, but you must. My poor wives have surpassed themselves. There is chopped lamb and squash filled with saffron rice, boiled sheep's brains, some of that salty goat's cheese you are so fond of. Watermelon soaked overnight in a splendid French wine and chilled."

Amos kept his face expressionless. Mejjid was a contemporary man yet he was very much an Arab with an Arab's chronic inability to get to the point of the matter. Always this circuitous route, this mantle of sociability to veil the most serious and even venomous of confrontations. And there was the exaggeration, the inclination to dramatize. Their relationship, for example. Amos had known Mejjid for about five years and during that time they had seen each other no more than half-a-dozen times, frequently by accident. Hardly a close friendship.

"I am certain your wives have prepared a splendid feast, but I cannot enjoy it. I have business back in Tel Aviv. I must be there this afternoon."

"Ah, business. The common denominator among all peoples, yes? You Jews, always in such a hurry to get things done. There is much to be learned about life from those of us who are not Western."

Amos laughed. "You're more European than many Israelis."

An elaborate sigh issued from Mejjid. "It is true. I have put aside many of the old ways, too many. But I am wasting your precious time with useless talk. Oh, my dear, I trust that the recent unpleasantness between the Jews and the Arabs has not affected our friendship. After all, it was not of your doing nor of mine."

"Nothing has changed between us, Mejjid."

"Allah is compassionate." He sat down, leaning forward, the smile back on his mouth, but his eyes remained glazed and watchful. "I am a Palestinian, *habibi*, even as you are. Born and raised here."

"I am no sabra, Mejjid. You know that."

"Ah, yes, but you are here and I do not suggest that you are of less value for that."

Score one point for Mejjid, Amos noted silently.

"There is in me no hatred for men," Mejjid continued. "Not for Jew or Christian nor any other. We worship the same God, you and I, obey the same prophets, both of us the sons of the sons of Abraham, isn't it?"

"Go on."

"My sons are circumsized even as yours have been."

"Mejjid," Amos said, making no effort to conceal his impatience. "I am a Jew and also an Israeli. Now will you please get to the point."

"A thousand apologies." He broke off, spread his arms. "This house, it is all I have left." The dark eyes narrowed and the mouth turned down. "You people have taken it all away!" he shouted.

"What are you talking about?"

"My shops, my apartments, all gone, appropriated by the custodian's office. Lands that belonged to my family

51

for generations. They must be returned to me! They must!"

"Have you talked to the proper officials?"

Mejjid spat. "Talk has brought me nothing. Bureaucrats and regulations. One cannot deal with such people. They will not listen to reason."

Amos understood that to mean that Mejjid had offered bribes without success. Bribery was an accepted business practice among Arabs; to refuse one was considered bad form approaching treachery.

"I don't see how I can help you," Amos said. "You did leave Palestine. You listened to Beirut and Cairo. It was a mistake."

"A mistake. I admit it. A foolishness. I was afraid for my family. And for myself. But I am back now and what is mine is mine. I am no refugee. I am here, a citizen, with certain rights. I returned of my own will and someone must make the Government return what belongs to me."

Mejjid's was no isolated instance, Amos knew. A considerable amount of property belonging to former Arab residents of what was now Israel had been appropriated and the question of what was to be done with it already occasioned debate among Jews. There were those who felt it should be returned to the rightful owners; or that adequate compensation, at the very least, should be made. Still others, bitter and vengeful, insisted that all Arab claims be ignored, that the plight of the refugees was no concern. Amos understood the complexities of the issue. He was convinced that unless dealt with swiftly and fairly, the issue would polarize, become insoluable.

"People feel very strongly about the war," he said mildly. "Many still mourn their dead."

"They are victors and can afford to be generous."

"You expect too much of us. We are no better than other people."

"But there is peace now!"

"Only an armistice."

"There will be negotiations, treaties signed. Cairo will recognize Israel, so will Damascus, Amman, the others. You will see. These matters take time."

"I hope you are right."

"Yes, yes, I am."

Mejjid was standing now, animated, his rasping baritone filling the large room. "You will help me, my dear friend.

Surely you must be well connected with friends in high places in the Government, perhaps Ben Gurion himself."

Amos rose. "You give me too much credit. But I do know a man who might be able to help. His name is Yeshivat. I'll get in touch with him. But there are no promises, no certainties."

"You shall be rewarded with long life and riches and your children after you and their children."

"You'll hear from me."

"*In sha' Allah.* It is in Allah's hands."

It was not until a month after his return from Dubrovnik that Yaakov Yeshivat found time to visit the Landaus. As usual, he appeared without warning, upsetting the routine of the family. After an excited and prolonged greeting, Ruth rushed into the kitchen to prepare for the guest. Rena and Levi insisted on plying Yaakov with questions, demanding that he tell them of his adventures. The word amused him.

"Adventures, no," he laughed. "Tortures. Living in the hills, dodging Arab snipers, eating army food. All army food is fit for dogs, and that is by definition."

"Here you'll eat well," Amos put in. "If I know Ruth, she's making something special for you."

Rena broke in. "You're not married yet, are you, Yaakov?"

He grinned in her direction. "Who would marry an old kibbutznik like me?"

"Rena would," Levi said cheerfully.

"Oh, be quiet," she said, blushing but looking directly at the older man.

He let his eyes work over her. He winked deliberately. "That daughter of yours, Amos," he drawled. "You had better keep her locked up. Already she has too many bulges here and there."

Rena was the only one who didn't laugh but she didn't look away.

"You should get married," Amos said. "You're too old to be running loose. You could still have children—"

"At my age?"

"You are not too old for *that,* I'm sure."

"What kind of talk is that?" Baruch erupted. "And in front of the children. A shame."

"It's all right, *Reb* Landau," Yaakov said. "These Israeli kids, they learn fast."

"Too fast."

53

Yaakov swung back to Amos. "How goes the bakery? I hope you brought some of that strudel home today."

"Hah!" Baruch exploded. "A good question! But my son is too good for the bakery. He is going into another business. At his age, such craziness—"

Amos was about to reply when Ruth announced dinner.

Afterwards, Amos took Yaakov out into the garden. The night air was clear and cool and they sipped brandy and smoked.

"That's a fine new son you have," Yaakov said, after a while.

"Simon's a good baby. Always laughing and so beautiful. The best looking baby I ever saw. I suppose we'll spoil him terribly."

"He is already."

Amos laughed shortly. "Is that bad?"

"Ask me again in about twenty years."

Amos sipped some brandy and allowed his mind to range backward and forward in time. It was then that he recalled his meeting with Mejjid. He told Yaakov the story.

"Can you help him, Yaakov? He is not a bad fellow and he is pretty upset."

"They're all the same, these Arabs. When it looked good to them, they ran. Now they're back and want things to be just as they were before."

"I would appreciate anything you can do for him."

"Next time I'm in Jerusalem, I'll get in touch with him. I'll send him to someone I know. We'll see."

"Good, good." His mind turned back to himself, the course he had chosen. "You heard my father, about the bakery. I am through with it."

"You want to talk about it?"

Amos gazed off into the distance. "Have you ever really looked at the women of Israel, Yaakov?"

"Constantly."

"I mean, *really* looked, at how they look, their appearance."

"I told you, I look. And what I see I like."

"They have no chic, no style. You can always pick out the foreigners, especially the American women or the French."

"I prefer the Americans. They are without that fraudulent Gallic sophistication."

Amos exhaled audibly. "Yaakov, I am going to open a dress shop in Tel Aviv."

"You have lost what few brains you ever possessed!" He laughed, an abrasive mirthless eruption. "Is that a business for a tank captain? Stick to baking bread, a good honest trade. If you must change, become a worker."

"You don't understand. I am going to bring the latest styles from Paris, London, New York. The women will buy them. You will see. I will be very successful."

"A capitalist is what you'll become."

"That sounds very nice."

Yaakov snorted. "The collective effort is what this country needs."

"If things go as I plan, there will be jobs for a number of people and the women of Israel will be prettier, happier. And that will be nice for the men."

"Spare me your daydreams. If I didn't enjoy Ruth's cooking I would never come to this madhouse."

"Ruth agrees with you. So does my father, as you heard, and Levi. I think the idea of his father selling dresses makes him ashamed."

"He'll get over that."

"What about you," Amos said. "What are you going to do with yourself?"

Yaakov cracked the knuckles of his right hand. "Work with Nahal, I think."

Amos could not hide his surprise. "They're going to continue it?"

"It worked well during the War and with proper organization it could be the answer to some of our defense problems. Anyway, I intend to try."

Nahal, an acronym for *Noar Halutzi Lohem,* Pioneer Fighting Youth. A volunteer corps within the Israeli Defense Forces, its members took military training and performed agricultural work in border villages, the first outposts of defense.

"A couple of years," Yaakov said. "Then back to Lahav and Histadrut. Labor and soldiering. That's all I ever do. Maybe you're right to become a capitalist, to get rich. In any case, I wish you luck."

Ruth appeared in that quiet way, a vague smile on her pleasant face. "Yaakov," she said without preliminary. "Come next Sunday. We'll have dinner and then there's a Debussy concert. We'll all go. Maybe I'll invite Paula Stock—"

Yaakov stood up. All at once he was gripped by a thick

craving for Leah, to taste her scented flesh, to bury himself in her. "I'll let you know. But you know how it is with me. Don't depend on me."

Ruth smiled. "But we do, you know. All of us."

Amos looked around. The two salesgirls seemed at ease. Well, why not? This was merely a job to them; to Amos it was a radical alteration in his life, a great gamble of energy, time, money. All his savings had gone into this shop, into the purchase of stock. All his money and three thousand pounds advanced grudgingly, but advanced, by his father. Baruch was a difficult man, carping, stubborn, self-righteous, but whenever help was needed he could be depended upon.

Amos studied the decor, neat and colorful, but not gaudy. Perhaps too much effort and cost had gone into it, perhaps it was, as Baruch had insisted, wasteful and unnecessary. Shops in Israel were generally unimpressive, badly lit, fly-specked, places in which to haggle and argue, the service poor, the proprietors often rude. Take it or leave it, was the expressed attitude of most tradesmen and the public, without choice, took it.

This then was the heart of Amos' plan, to provide high fashion at reasonable prices along with good service. He was certain the women of Tel Aviv would appreciate it and spread the word, assure him of a clientele.

Or would they?

Not according to Ruth. She was convinced he was taking them all down the road to financial ruin. Nor was she alone. Everyone he had spoken to insisted there was no market for Paris fashions in Israel. Living, they pointed out, was casual and so were most events, providing little occasion for women to dress up. Even more, most of the new immigrants were coming from Yemen, Iraq, Soviet Asia, from other remote and backward regions of the Orient. Such women would have no interest in Western fashions.

He had listened to all the arguments, explored them, and proceeded anyway, supervising every detail of the shop from the well-lit dressing cubicles to the deep display windows looking out onto Ben Yehuda Street. He had interviewed almost seventy-five applicants before selecting these two salesgirls, offering unusually high salaries plus commissions in order to have the kind of person he wanted. Both of them were fluent in Hebrew and Yiddish. One girl spoke French and some Italian; the other excellent English. With his own German, and knowledge of Arabic, Amos was certain they could handle most situations.

To obtain the stock he wanted, Amos made three trips to Paris and twice went to London, hiring agents in each city to represent him. He had also contacted a buying office in New York and hoped to begin doing business through it shortly.

News of the new shop had been widely circularized in Tel Aviv, emphasizing the latest styles from abroad and the added services. He advertised in newspapers in Jerusalem and Haifa as well.

"They won't buy," Baruch warned him ominously.

"Other shops are cheaper," Ruth pointed out. "You won't be able to compete."

"I think I will," Amos had argued. "Most shopkeepers are Orientals with no experience in sound business practices."

"And you have *genius?*" Baruch put in.

"I learned from you, papa. I'm going to run the shop the same way you ran the bakery. Good business procedures, bookkeeping, accurate records, courtesy. Attractive displays."

"In this uncivilized country," Baruch growled, "people don't care about such things."

Now, as he glanced around the shop, at the brightly paneled walls, the conveniently placed mirrors, the neat arrangement of dresses, the comfortable chairs in which a husband might wait for his wife, Amos was no longer as confident as before. Outside, people hurried past without pausing, disinterested, and no line of anxious women waited to get in to buy. He forced a smile on his full mouth.

"Well, girls, here we go." He opened the door and stepped back. "I guess we're in business."

It was nearly noon before the first customer entered the shop. By now, Amos, the palms of his hands damp, stood behind the accessory counter, trying not to reveal the depth of his concern, making small jokes to the salesgirls. It was then that a middle-aged woman paused in front of the show windows, appraising the displays from a variety of angles.

"She's going to come in," one of the girls said softly.

"Hush," said the other. "Don't look at her. You want to make her feel uncomfortable?"

The woman walked inside, stopped and looked around aggressively.

"Good morning, madam," one of the girls said in Hebrew.

"The red dress in the window. How much?"

"A lovely design," the girl said. "I'm certain we still have it in your size. Would you like to try it on?"

"How much are you asking?"

The girl lifted the dress off the rack and displayed it across her arm. "It's a very good price, five pounds ten."

The woman snorted and gazed off into space, hands folded across her middle. "It looks better in the window than in person. I'll give you two pounds, more than it's worth."

The girl looked over her shoulder at Amos. "I'm sorry, madam. This is a Paris model and only Landau's carries it——"

"Three pounds is the best I'll do and that's final."

Amos stepped forward, smiling. "Excuse me, madam. I'm Mr. Landau. You understand that our gowns are shipped here specially for us. Our buyers in London and Paris——"

"Three pounds," she said stubbornly. "Take it or not."

Amos was tempted to take it. He wanted desperately to conclude his first sale.

"I'm sorry, madam. Landau's doesn't bargain. All our garments are priced as listed."

The woman turned without another word and left the shop. A moment later she was back. "Landau, you'd let me walk out! What kind of businessman are you?"

"I'm sorry," he said helplessly. "Our policy is——"

"You're crazy," she said, with an incredulous expression. "In a month, you'll be out of business. Less, probably."

By the end of the day, Amos wondered if she hadn't been right, if Ruth and his father weren't right. Seven women had come into the store during the day. Three of them had tried on dresses but none had bought. None of them had displayed any great enthusiasm for the styles or had offered any encouragement.

That night Baruch gloated. "I told you. I warned you. But you, so smart, you wouldn't listen. All right, maybe you'll listen now. Get out while you can. Sell the stock and the fixtures. Take your loss. I'll let you come back to the bakery."

Amos was tempted.

"Tomorrow it will get better," Rena said. But even her optimism was dampened.

An hour after he opened the door the next morning, the first shopper of the previous day returned. Her face was set, her manner no less aggressive. She trundled over to Amos, ignoring the salesgirls.

"Landau, I'm going to give you another chance. Four pounds for the red dress. My final offer. Positively."

He moved his head from side-to-side deliberately. "The price is listed."

For a long interval she gave no indication that she had heard. Then the lines of her face seemed to soften and the mouth spread easily. She eyed Amos with obvious curiosity. "The sign in the window that says alterations and deliveries. It means it?"

"It does. We have an excellent seamstress."

"From where?"

"Why, she's an Austrian lady."

"Oh, well, that's all right. The Russians, they don't do such good work, you know." She glanced around, focusing nowhere. "You remember that red dress, maybe I'll look at it again. Maybe try it on."

The first sale, and that afternoon there were three more. By three o'clock Friday, closing time so that the salesgirls could get home before the start of the Sabbath at sundown, Amos had begun to allow a certain amount of hopefulness to color his thinking. The shop might yet succeed. True, he had fallen far short of meeting expenses, but business seemed to be building. Each day there had been a few more sales. Before long, he was sure, word about Landau's would spread, about the styles, the reliability.

After the girls had gone, he closed the shop and moved down Ben Yehuda Street. Around him men wearing yarmulkes, carrying prayer books, blue-and-white-and-gold shawls draped across their shoulders, shuffled toward the Great Synagogue on Allenby Road. He decided to join them. There would be no public transportation afterward and he would have to walk home, but the exercise would be good for his bad leg.

XI

"Dammit! Men must be given a good reason to die!"

Yaakov made no effort to soften his displeasure. The discussion had dragged on for two hours and he was sick of it. Either they grasped this one point, or they would understand nothing of what he hoped to do. He sucked air into his lungs and decided to try one more time.

They were in the board room at Histadrut headquarters in Tel Aviv. Three of them: Yaakov, Chaim Lahav and Shapiro. General Abraham Shapiro, member of the High Command, a career soldier, like Yaakov a sabra and no less stubborn, no less tough or dedicated. No less sure he was right.

"All right, Abie," Yaakov said to the burly officer. "I put it to you one more time. You want to take young people away from their fun, from their own futures, then you must give meaning to their lives."

Shapiro stared across the table steadily. His round face and tiny eyes effectively masked off his thoughts. He ran a hand through his close cropped brindle hair.

"You listen to me, Yeshivat. You are not the only one concerned about the future of Israel. And your way is not necessarily the only way. What we need is a cadre of young people ready and willing to fight on short notice, a ready reserve."

"And I will give you that!" Yaakov burst out. "But not your way."

"Shalom," Chaim Lahav said soothingly. "Peace. All of us want what is best. Let us work for it in a friendly fashion. For fighting, there are always the Arabs."

"My point exactly," Yaakov said. "They are all around us. Millions of them. They hate us now and will hate us more next year, the year after. We are a thorn to them and they mean to pluck us out."

"The Army stands ready," Shapiro said.

"The Army cannot remain ready," Yaakov interrupted. "A small nation cannot afford a substantial standing military. The economy demands people, young and energetic people. Producers."

"It also needs fighters."

"I will give you both. I say we turn Nahal into an extension of the Palmach. When we needed an elite commando group, it was formed. This time something else is called for. Let me train the young people for two tasks—fighting and farming. Give them a stake in the soil and they will take strength from it. They will fight better."

Shapiro refused to be convinced. "Most of our people are not farmers. They come from Europe, city people, soft—"

"We will make them tougher. And the Asians, too. Make them understand what Israel can mean to them, teach them Hebrew, our history here, about each other. Give them to me and I will turn them into true Israelis, fighting men."

"And when they leave Nahal they will leave the soil."

"Perhaps. But they will have a greater respect for it."

"Say again what you have in mind, Yaakov," Lahav said.

"Let every boy go into the Army as planned. But let those who volunteer for halutziut, pioneering, become part of Nahal. They will take fundamental military training in the regular way. Then I will place them on kibbutzim, in new ones, old ones. At the start, they will do basic work, unskilled jobs. They can pick potatoes, load hay, feed cattle, plant saplings. Whatever is required. Eventually, they will be given more specialized work, a true role in the communal villages."

"I see your plan," Shapiro said thinly. "You do not fool me, Yeshivat. It is your scheme to turn them into kibbutzniks instead of soldiers."

"Abie, listen and think, man. They would live separately and remain under strict military discipline. After a year, all of them would proceed to advanced military training."

"It is a wasted year."

"The opposite. They will have been exposed to a certain kind of life, certain values. They will be able to make a choice based on first-hand experience." Yaakov hunched forward, brows drawn together, pale eyes glittering. "Look at a map of Israel, my friend. You know the statistics as well as I—two hundred and eighty miles long, maybe, and only an hour by plane from Jerusalem to Eilat. Our cities are no more than twenty minutes from the Arab capitals. Every frontier is vulnerable. The kibbutzim are our first defense, the most valuable. Perhaps later it will change. But now, strengthen them, fortify them, give our young people a reason for leading that kind of tough life."

Shapiro looked at Lahav. "I still don't like it. Give me those boys for the full thirty months of their service and they'll become better soldiers for every day of the time."

Yaakov leaned back and tugged at his bent nose. "Yours is the deciding vote, Lahav. What do you say?"

"I always have been partial to workers who are also fighters. Let's try Yeshivat's idea. If it doesn't work, we can always change."

Shapiro stood up and gathered his papers, jammed them into his briefcase. "If the Arabs give us the time."

XII

A rut of concern furrowed the space between Mejjid al-Hadad's dark eyes. He sat deep in one of his red velvet chairs, cramped in on himself, head low, staring sightlessly, a glass of arak in one fist. He had been drinking most of the day, most of every day, since his return from Jordan. All his influence, his contacts, his friends, had brought him nothing. The land of his fathers was still denied him and from the shops and houses that had once brought him so much income there came only a trickle of rent money, hardly enough to pay the agonizingly high Israeli taxes.

Through the alcoholic haze that encased him, he was dimly aware of an intrusion. It was a struggle to concentrate, to iris the nearing figure into focus. Abdul, recently turned sixteen, his first son, pride of his loins, issue of his first night with his first wife. He had drenched her insides with a monumental flood of semen, virile and powerful, full of his own wisdom and courage and manliness. His beauty. The result—Abdul, Mejjid's living connection with the future, with immortality, with Allah, the good, the merciful, the compassionate.

"Father," the boy said, veiling his distaste, holding himself straight and speaking formally.

Mejjid almost smiled. But not quite. This boy was tall and well shaped, would grow bigger and stronger. His skin gleamed soft and brown, the deep, dark eyes steady, penetrating, disturbing. Mejjid drank some more arak. It was as if behind those lambent eyes, in some shadowed niche of his brain, there was secreted some special knowledge denied to less fortunate mortals. There was the high, proud tilt to Abdul's chin, the challenging thrust of his red lips, the pitch of his voice. A mood of depression enveloped Mejjid.

"Father, I want to talk to you."

"Bokra!" Mejjid snapped peevishly.

"Today," the boy insisted, a boldness in his face that Mejjid would not have dared to display to his own father. "I am going away, father."

"Going away? What are you saying?"

"I cannot remain in Israel any longer. Each night I hear the *muezzin* chant *Humdillah* and for a short time I convince myself that everything is the same. But it isn't. I am not a Jew, father. I am not an Israeli. I am a Palestinian Arab. I must go away."

Mejjid refilled his glass. "There is no place to go," he bit off thinly, fighting not to comprehend his son's words. "This is your home, and mine. You must have patience. Things will get better. Last week I talked with Rothenberg for fifteen minutes. He is a friend from the old days. He is a member of the Knesset and he promised to help us, to help all the Arabs. He is a good man and will make a speech, a strong speech, he vowed it to me, to demand that justice be done, that the lands confiscated be returned to their rightful owners."

"Speeches will not help."

"You are young. You don't understand. These matters take time."

"There is no time."

"I am older and for me there is time. There must be time. Be patient, my son." His voice went soft and a note of pleading crept into it. "Be patient."

Abdul set his mouth stubbornly. "I am going to go away, father, and make a life for myself somewhere else."

Mejjid stared at the empty glass in his hand. "Very well," he sighed. "Very well. I will do what I can to help. Perhaps I will be able to supply you with a certain amount of money each month. You will not be rich, of course, but you will be able to live in a suitable fashion. You will go to Paris and study at the Sorbonne. Perhaps it is a good thing to do. You will improve your French and meet important people. There is a place for a handsome young Arab in Paris and you will discover that

63

French women are very anxious to please you." He
laughed suddenly. "When I was there, in 1935, there were
parties and never enough time to sleep."

"I am going to Cairo, father."

Mejjid slumped lower, all passion stranded. This son of
his, what thoughts were born inside that lovely head, what
strange ideas? "Wallah!" he said. "To what purpose Cairo?
You will not like it there. Egyptians despise everything
and everyone not English. They consider Palestinians to be
a lesser order. You will get no money from me to spend in
Cairo."

"I am sorry, father, but I have no choice. I will go to
Cairo."

Mejjid exhaled noisily and pinched the boy's cheek. He
could sustain no anger against this son, not now, not ever.
"Could I allow my first son to wither away on food fit
only for the fellahin? Aiee! You will make me old before
my time. Now leave me alone. I have much thinking to
do."

He waited until Abdul was gone before he poured more
arak into his glass.

XIII

Changes came swiftly. The ingathering continued and
from all over the world people made their way to Israel,
invoking the stated aim of the Government to admit any
Jew who wished to come.

There had been national elections and it resulted in a
coalition between Mapai, the moderate Socialist party,
and the religious parties. The Prime Minister was David
Ben Gurion and Dr. Chaim Weizmann, the President. Both
men had been prime movers in the Zionist movement.

In February, Egypt signed an armistice agreement and
on May 11, Israel was admitted to the United Nations.

"Things are getting better for the Jews," Amos laughed,
when he heard the news. He was watching his infant son,
Simon, crawl around the floor of the living room and now
he lifted him playfully. The boy, pink and fuzzily blond,
laughed silently.

"Bite your tongue," Baruch warned.

"Oh, *zayde*," Rena said with mock disapproval. "You're such a pessimist."

"What's that, a pessimist?"

"A person who only sees the dark side of life."

"And who's got a better right than a Jew?"

It was the second day of *Shavuot*, the commemoration of that sacred moment on Mount Sinai when Moses received the Torah and the Ten Commandments. In celebration, the house was decorated with flowers and greenery.

"It's a good time, Papa," Amos said. "We're all here together and well."

· He smiled at Joshua sitting across the room, and at Mara Gabrielli next to him. His eyes ranged over the remainder of his family. He held Simon high above his head and the boy kicked his chubby legs in pleasure and waved his arms.

"Look at this wonderful new son of mine," Amos said.

"Don't talk," the old man said nervously.

"And I have some good news for everybody," Amos went on. "Something I was saving. Business at the store has been very good, better than I anticipated."

"Don't talk," Baruch repeated.

"I made a couple of trips to Jerusalem," Amos said, ignoring his father. "It's become a very international city, people from all over the world. Cosmopolites. Sophisticated people. People used to the best things in life. What I'm saying is that I found an excellent location, not far from the King David Hotel. I signed a lease."

They were all staring at him soundlessly.

A nervous laugh seeped across his lips. "I'm going to open another shop. In Jerusalem."

This time there was a babble of sound, of excited questions, congratulations, doubts, and from Baruch, mild remonstrations.

"Are you sure?" Ruth said at last. "Everything is so quick——"

"That's it precisely," Amos said. "There is no time to waste. The time is *right*. I saw Yaakov during one of my trips——"

"Oh, how is he?" Ruth said.

"Why doesn't he visit me—*us?*" Rena wailed.

"He told me that the Government will surely be officially transferred to Jerusalem before the end of the year."

"Blessed is the name of the Lord, our God," Baruch chanted in Yiddish. "That I should live to see the Jews returned to the City of David."

65

"I was able to sign a long-term lease at a good price. The workmen have already begun renovations. I am reproducing the Tel Aviv shop. The same front, interior, everything. With two outlets, I'll be able to make better arrangements for merchandise."

"People are saying nice things about Landau's," Mara said.

"With a figure like yours," Rena burst out, "Papa should pay you to wear his dresses."

"Rena," her mother said disapprovingly.

"Well, he should," Rena insisted, unabashed.

Amos put Simon back down on the Oriental carpet. "I was thinking that this might be a good time for Joshua to start in the business. You could work with me here until the new shop opens and then go to Jerusalem and manage it for me."

"Terrific!" Rena exulted, leaping up. She clapped her hands and laughed. "That way I will have an excuse to go to Jerusalem and visit. I'll come to your club, Mara, and see you perform. Aren't you excited, Joshua?"

Levi, his dark face pinched, the black eyes cast down, spoke in a tight, low voice. "He's not going to do it."

"Be still, Levi," Joshua said quickly. "Can't we talk about it another time, Papa?"

Amos tried to ignore the icy uncertainty that worked its way along his limbs. "This time is as good as any other, if there's something I should know."

"We have a guest," Joshua said, "and there's no reason to bore her with family affairs."

Mara rose and smiled confidently. "Why don't I go for a walk, or into the garden."

"No, please," Amos said. "Joshua is right. We'll discuss this another time."

"Hah!" Baruch burst out, voice resonant with righteousness. "Right now I know what it is. Everybody knows. Joshua will not manage the shop for you, will not go into your business. The Bible says the iniquities of the father shall be put upon the children unto——"

"Oh, zayde," Rena broke in. "That means those that transgress against God——"

"Be still!" Baruch ordered sternly. His head came up, the hawklike nose proudly poised, eyes flashing. "You turned away from your father and now it comes down on your head. The Lord is just——"

Amos turned to Joshua, vaguely guilty, fighting to present a casual exterior, to smile. "You tell me, Joshua. I

66

want you in the business, obviously. But you tell me what you want to do."

Joshua hesitated. "I do have other plans, papa."

"Well," Amos said, his cheerfulness strained. "Sons are always deciding their lives for themselves. That's why parents try to teach them to think for themselves."

"Oh, dammit!" Levi burst out. "Can't you see, Joshua wants a better life, something more meaningful." All heads swung in his direction and his manner quieted. "Joshua is going to join a kibbutz," he ended with subdued defiance.

Amos felt stifled, cramped, a victim of unseen bonds. He fought for control over his vocal chords. "In this house," he said to Levi, "you will not swear."

Levi flushed and turned away. "I'm sorry," he muttered, then: "But I'm glad about Joshua. He'll have a *real* life that means something, doing some good. Not just making money and buying things."

Ruth's soft face settled into more determined lines. "You will leave the room, Levi. When you learn respect, you may return."

He marched to the door, jerked around, smooth face drawn and intense. "I meant what I said. I *admire* what Joshua's doing—more than anything else that happens around here, and as soon as I can, I'm going to do the same thing."

After he left, there was a long, uneasy silence, broken finally by Amos. "My apologies, Miss Gabrielli. Levi is a good boy with very deep feelings. Once in a while, they get too much for him to handle."

"I understand."

"Is it true?" Amos said to Joshua. "About the kibbutz?"

"Yes, papa. I decided a few weeks ago, but it's been in my mind since the war. I didn't want to say anything until all the arrangements were made."

"It's all settled?"

"I'm leaving next week. It's a new kibbutz, near Kinneret. We're starting from the very beginning, which is what I want, to truly build something."

"Kosher?" Baruch asked.

Joshua smiled warmly in his grandfather's direction. "I am not a religious man, *zayde*. I'm sorry."

"Apikores," the old man muttered, settling back. "Heretic." He wanted to criticize but the passion wouldn't surface. Not against this boy. It had always been like this, no matter what Joshua did. There was something about him, all that quiet warmth, *goodness,* that prevented Baruch from turning loose his anger. Whatever this first grandchild of his had done, Baruch had always accepted it, if not with approval, then with understanding. Joshua was a special person in his eyes and was treated accordingly.

"You're sure about this, Joshua?" Amos said.

"I've never been totally sure about anything, papa. But this—" he nodded vigorously. "I have a driving need to create something vital for Israel, to give myself wholly to it. To work in the open and make things grow, to build things, to work with my hands." An embarrassed smile ghosted across his mouth and was gone. "It's hard for me to verbalize it, papa."

"I hoped you would go to university, Joshua. I was thinking about Oxford."

"I will read a lot, papa."

"There is no book to read but the Torah!" Baruch erupted, struggling erect, hand slicing at the air. "The authority of the Torah must be accepted without conditions and Torah-true Jews will give no respect to secular powers——" He stamped out of the room, muttering angrily.

"My father," Amos said to Mara Gabrielli, spreading his hands helplessly.

"He is mild compared to mine," she said lightly. "My father insists that Ben Gurion is a traitor to God and he wanted our soldiers not to fight on the Sabbath."

Amos laughed self-consciously, anxious to lighten the mood. "Is anyone else going to walk out on me?"

"Yes," Ruth said, rising. "Rena and I are going to prepare supper."

"In that case," Amos said to Joshua and Mara, "I will also leave. I have to repair my relations with my father and my son both. It is clear that I am of the wrong generation."

When they were alone, Joshua bent quickly and kissed Mara. After a brief interlude, she moved her head.

"Your father is very nice," she said.

"He's an interesting man. Sometimes I find it impossible to believe that he was a tank commander during the war. And he fought with the Haganah. He doesn't seem like the type."

"Neither do you."

"But I am young."

It occurred to her that Amos might be too complex for his own family to comprehend. Soldier, businessman, archaeologist, father and husband. He was a cultivated man, scholarly, yet daring enough to change the course of his life in his middle years. That kind of adventurous spirit drew her admiration. She raised her face.

"Would you like to kiss me again? It is all right."

There was this about Mara, the directness, the unexpected, as if all that mattered was what she wanted when she wanted it. His mouth came down on hers and presently he became aware of the skillful manipulation of her lips. There was the same thick stirring that he always felt when he was with her. His hand caressed her back, slid onto the curve of her side, moving lightly, cautiously, until his thumb made contact with the swelling arc of her breast. She pulled away.

"I suppose you were a good soldier, Joshua," she said flatly. "But you are very careful."

"I don't understand."

"If you want to feel my breast, feel it. Put your hand on it. Squeeze it. Stroke it. But *do* it, at least. You sneak around like a frightened schoolboy." A challenging gleam came into the green eyes. "I'm sure your father would act differently."

"My father! He's old enough to be your father, too."

"But he isn't. He is a very attractive man and not too old for anything. I'm certain he makes your mother very happy in bed."

"Stop it, Mara!"

Her laugh was brittle, forced. "Does it shock you, Joshua? To imagine your mother and father making love?" She leaned closer, voice intimate. "When I was very young I used to think about it, what my parents did. I knew all about such things very early in life, you see. And once I heard them, Joshua, *heard*, so I went and peeked. It was very interesting." She straightened up and adjusted her long black hair. "My mother," she said casually, "was an extremely imaginative woman."

He turned away. "That's enough of that kind of talk."

"You're terribly prudish, Joshua." He offered no reply. She shifted nearer, placed her mouth against his ear, let her tongue touch the pale skin. He jerked away and stood up. Her eyes traveled over him and she pointed. "Perhaps you are not so prudish, after all. Perhaps you would enjoy hearing more."

"It was a mistake for me to invite you," he said.

She stood. "I'll leave. Right now."

He pulled her close and kissed her. She allowed her

body to arch against him, then pulled back, freed herself.

"Will you visit me in the Negev?"

"We'll see." She reached for his hand. "Come on, let's see if your mother can use some help."

Amos was alone in the shop, checking the order list against inventory. He decided to increase the Paris order. Since opening the Jerusalem shop, he had been doing most of the buying through New York, but a change was indicated. More and more American tourists were visiting Israel and they were interested in buying foreign-made items. More and more, Amos had been stocking up in domestic jewelry and had even established a souvenir counter in each store. He suspected that an increasing portion of his business was being done with tourists and wondered how to take advantage of this.

Someone knocked at the door and interrupted his thoughts. He tried to ignore the sound. They were closed; the business hours were clearly stated on the dark green shades drawn at the rear of the display windows.

The knocking persisted. He went to the door. There was always a customer who was convinced she deserved preferential treatment. He raised the doorshade and saw Mara Gabrielli, an expectant smile on her full mouth. His hands fumbled with the lock and he opened the door.

"I was just getting ready to leave," he said, feeling awkward and out of place.

"Oh, I didn't come to buy, Mr. Landau," she said easily. "Just to visit." She laughed, a light, cheerful sound, and moved past him into the shop.

He closed the door and trailed after her.

She swung around, legs planted firmly apart, hands on hips, those sea-green eyes disconcertingly bold. "So," she said, as if daring him to speak, to act. She laughed again.

He gestured toward the counter, where he had been at work. "I was making up an order list, for new things."

Her head swiveled deliberately. "This is very nice. Tasteful. And you have many pretty things." She picked a yellow sheath off the rack and held it against herself. "For me?"

"With your coloring, perfect."

"If it fits," she said gaily, "I will buy it. Where may I try it on?"

Her self-confidence, brashness, was refreshing. No foolish hesitation, no self-conscious apologies about keeping him from his work. Simply I will buy it if it fits.

70

"There is a dressing room," he said, leading the way. "I'll turn on the lights. When you are finished, I'll be out front. My orders."

He forced his attention back to the work until she appeared, wearing the yellow sheath. She did a pirouet and posed for him.

"What is your opinion, Mr. Landau?"

The yellow linen clung to every curve of her body and he could see the outline of her breasts, large and round, the nipples thrusting. He forced himself to look away.

"A bit too tight for me," she was saying. "At the hips. Do you think I should try to lose some weight?"

He kept his manner professionally detached. "It would be a simple matter to let out the seam, if you wish."

She glanced at her reflection in one of the full-length mirrors, turning this way and that, all pelvic thrust and dramatic roundness.

"How is Joshua?" she said.

"It's been about six weeks since he wrote. He is not much for letters, like his father."

"I receive a letter each week," she said.

"Oh. Well," he said, with forced lightness. "You are much prettier than I."

"He says that he is well and working hard and that his blisters have become callouses. I suppose that is all right. But calloused hands would be unpleasant to a girl's skin, I think." She reached back for the zipper of the sheath. "It's not for me." She took a step or two toward the dressing room, stopped and glanced over at him. "Would you do this for me? I can't seem to reach it—"

He came up behind her and worked the zipper down, the sheath gaping open. Her back was strong and smooth, flawless. She was not wearing a brassiere. The sight titillated him and he was annoyed with himself.

"Thank you," she said.

He went back to his work. When she returned, he had finished. "I'm going to close up now," he announced.

Outside, she waited for him to lock the door. "I was on my way to tea," she said. "Will you join me?"

He hesitated, shook his head. "I am taking the family to the theatre tonight. Chekhov."

"Another time, perhaps. I am going to Jerusalem tomorrow. To perform. The Café Royale, off Zion Square, Do you know it?"

He shook his head.

"You must come," she said, "if you can."

"If I can. My daughter is very impressed with you. Rena insisted that her mother buy a guitar for her and she sings and plays every day. Not very well, I'm afraid."

She held out her hand and he took it, her grip firm and cool. "Come to the Café Royale, Mr. Landau. It might amuse you to watch me perform. Shalom."

"Shalom."

He watched her stride down the street, moving easily, long legs reaching with a natural grace, smooth round hips swinging in counterpoint. He turned away and tucked the encounter away in some remote corner of his memory.

XIV

In miles, the distance from Tel Aviv to Sde Yaffee was inconsiderable; in life-style, they were light years apart. Tel Aviv, the contemporary city, sophisticated, increasingly superficial, crowded, a marketplace; Sde Yaffee, a kibbutz, unfinished, mud huts and wooden watchtowers, rutted roads and fields still to be plowed and planted, a place of imminent danger.

Put down to the north of Lake Kinneret, the Sea of Galilee, hard by the River Jordan, it was a fine target for Arab snipers, who used it with increasing frequency, if not much accuracy.

Though much of the community was still to be built, the floor of the recreation hall had been constructed and the school was almost finished. The newest structure was a small house, assigned to Esther Margolis and Shmuel Rosen, whose marriage would be the first at Sde Yaffee.

The ceremony took place under the sky at dusk. An arbor had been erected for the occasion and it was here that the rabbi married them. A glass of red wine was offered and the bride sipped first, then the groom.

"As together you now drink from this cup," the rabbi said, "so may you, under God's guidance, in perfect union and devotion to each other, draw contentment, comfort and felicity from the cup of life; thereby may you find life's joys doubly gladdening, its bitterness sweetened, and all things hallowed by true companionship and love."

72

When the marriage was sealed, the glass was broken underfoot for good fortune and the celebration began.

Tables were brought out of the dining hall and a meal was served, the area lit by paper lanterns made by the children of Sde Yaffee. Candles sent changing shapes flickering across the diners.

The meal was not yet over when someone began to play an accordion. A violin was brought out and three guitars. Some of the younger people formed a circle and began to dance, hands on each other's shoulders, moving a few steps in one direction and back again, fluid and graceful.

Joshua Laudau watched with mingled pleasure and loneliness. An image of Mara kept drifting to mind and he wished she were here. She was in Jerusalem, working, and he feared it might be a long time before they saw each other again. There was so much to do here. He squeezed the thought of her away and concentrated on the present, clapping his hands in time to the music.

First felt was the force of the explosion, an invisible pressure, whipping his head backwards. A hot thrust of air, intense, frightening. Then the flash, brilliant, blinding, and the sound, deep and deadly.

Next, the screams of anguish and terror, hoarse cries for help. There were people sprawled about, some lying very still, others struggling, still others writhing in pain. A few people ran, aimlessly, darting here and there without purpose as if on a wild hunt.

Joshua stood still. The explosion was familiar, the burst of a grenade, the whistling danger of metal fragments. But the sudden improbability was stunning. It was an effort to make his mind function, to move. Someone grabbed his arm and Joshua shook himself free, almost angrily.

"What happened?" the man wailed. "What is it?"

"They are going to kill us all!" someone screamed.

Joshua saw a familiar face and reached out. "Nathan, take some men and scout toward the river. Make sure it is not a general attack. Hurry."

"At once, *adoni.*"

"And find Zvi. I want guards out and ready."

There was no attack, no other grenades. Just another harrassing incident from across the river, Syrian-trained terrorists coming through Jordan. Six people had been wounded, only one seriously, a seventeen-year-old boy. His right arm was amputated at the elbow.

And Esther Margolis, the virgin bride, was dead.

Three days later Yaakov Yeshivat arrived at Sde

Yaffee. He met with the leaders of the kibbutz in the dining hall after the evening meal, the kitchen detail still cleaning up as they talked.

"Have you determined where the grenade-thrower came from?" he asked.

"There's an Arab village about a mile beyond the river, in Syria. Our boys picked up tracks."

"What have you done about it?"

The men around the rough wooden dining table looked at each other. The faces, mostly young, were eager and open. Looking at them, Yaakov realized that only one or two were equipped by training or temperament for the life they had chosen. Joshua Landau, for example, in charge of the community defenses and brave enough, but unused to this kind of fighting and ignorant of what had to be done. Yaakov reached back over the years to his own time at Kfar Akiba, not so very far from here, and not so very different, remembering the lessons his father had taught him.

"Israel needs Sde Yaffee," he said, issuing each word separately for emphasis. "You are here in order to establish a communal village that will strengthen the country economically and militarily, not just to satisfy your own singular cravings. Perhaps you thought that it would be easy."

"No, *Adon* Yeshivat," a burly, bearded man said. "Not easy. Not soft. Nor are we afraid of hard work or of the Arabs. But we are not certain what is expected of us."

"Expected first," Yaakov rasped, "is that you will defend this region."

"We need more men," Joshua said.

"And you'll get them. In two weeks you will receive reinforcements, for working and fighting. Twenty members of Nahal. All soldiers and they will fight well. But you cannot afford to wait for them to come. So we come to expectation second—you must avenge the death of Esther Margolis and make the cost of such raids prohibitive. Let the Arabs know that if they continue to attack, you will strike back, twenty times as hard. Now, somebody tell me the details again."

It was Joshua who rose. "With first light, I led six men in a search for the attacker."

"Too late," Yaakov said. "He was gone, back to his base immediately afterwards."

"Yes. But the trail was clear. We picked up footsteps on

74

the East bank of the Jordan. There were two of them, and we followed to the village."

"Did you enter the village, talk to the mukhtar?"

Joshua flushed and ducked his head. "We came back and reported."

The bearded man spoke up. "It was my decision, Yeshivat, that no action be taken. At least not without higher authority."

"I am that authority." He glared at Joshua. "You should have gone into the village at night and killed a dozen men, burned some buildings."

"We couldn't do that!" Joshua protested. "To kill innocent people . . ."

"What was Esther Margolis' crime?" Yaakov bit off. A thick silence settled over them. "Now listen to me. Your only defense is a strong offense. The Arabs must be made to pay a high price for their terror. And not merely an eye for an eye. They killed a girl. But we won't kill a girl in return. Tell me about the village."

Joshua described it. No more than thirty families, farmers mostly, living in mud huts. There were some date trees, some horses, a few cattle and goats.

"The mukhtar," Yaakov said. "What about him?"

His house was grand by village standards, fairly large and set apart on the slope of a hill.

"Is he wealthy?" Yaakov asked.

"Not really. He has some cattle, some goats, in a corral behind the house. Listen, Yaakov," Joshua said abruptly, anxiously, "we can't just go in there and kill people indiscriminately."

Yaakov stared at Joshua, the pale eyes steady and flat. "You're soft, *adoni*, and it's a weakness. Get rid of it or it will hurt you one day." He stood up and spoke directly to the bearded man. "Tonight. At midnight. Twenty men, all armed."

"We have six Sten guns. Rifles for the rest."

"And knives," Yaakov said. "Sharp knives. I will lead them. Joshua will be my lieutenant."

They crossed the Jordan River in rowboats, the oarlocks muffled, then moved on the village, Joshua leading the way. The Arab village was clearly visible on the side of the hill, the flat white buildings reflecting the cold light of the moon.

Yaakov signaled for the men to halt. They crouched down. "It is hard to believe that they do not keep guards out," he husked. "An indication of how they trust the men of Sde Yaffee. After tonight, they will post guards. All right, the corral."

"This way," Joshua said, moving out.

They swung in a great circle to the north, descending the hill behind the mukhtar's house, approaching the corral. Crickets chirped and once a dog barked.

"There," Joshua whispered. "The corral."

The Damascus cow. An unimpressive beast, wild of eye and lean, with great bone thrust at hip and shoulder. To an Arab, significant of real wealth.

"All right," Yaakov said. "Spread out and work fast. No talking. Do your work properly. There will be a minimum of sound. Let's go."

The men armed with Sten guns took up positions at the far sides of the corral, facing the village, guarding against an unexpected intrusion. The others, knives in hand, slipped into the corral.

They went to work with grim efficiency, the thick scent of blood tainting the night air as the men cut the throats of the acquiescent cattle. One of the beasts refused to expire quietly; Yaakov moved quickly to finish the job with a swift, strong stroke. The plaintive lowing faded away.

When at last it was over, they went back across the river with the noisome smell of death clinging to them.

XV

Levi Landau and two friends, Benno and Arne, swaggered down the shadowed alley past the Ali Baba, once a Turkish bath and currently an exotic nightclub. From inside came the slightly off-key nasal chant of a girl singer. They stopped to listen and a husky doorman in an ornate uniform ordered them to keep moving.

"Big shot," Levi tossed back at the man, as he led his friends down the street toward the waterfront. "Look at him in that uniform, another hero."

They slowed down as they came abreast of another club. "In here," Arne revealed knowingly, "they have a girl who takes off all her clothes."

Benno gave a disbelieving laugh. "Why do you lie so?"

"But it's true," Benno protested. "My brother went here one night and he told me. My brother wouldn't lie to me."

"If it is true," Levi said rationally, "she won't be undressing for long. Not when the chief rabbi finds out. A whole platoon of those insane Pietists will march down here and destroy the place."

"If I can get to the stripper for a little while," Benno said, "I'll give them a hand."

"Benno," Arne taunted. "Would you know what to do with a naked girl?"

"I'd know, better than you."

"You wouldn't know where to put it," Arne cackled.

"He'd learn," Levi hooted, hurrying ahead. "Fast, I think."

Laughing, they ran the rest of the way down the hill until they reached the docks, moving along the dark, deserted stretch fronting the harbor. A line of huge cotton bales were stacked against a warehouse wall. They scrambled on top of them, letting their legs dangle. Benno brought out a packet of American cigarets and each of them took one and they lit up. Arne told a joke and then Benno told one and then Levi. They fell silent and smoked and stared out at the ships moored in the harbor. They began to talk about girls.

It was Arne who saw the two men first. They were strolling along the water's edge, coming nearer, engrossed in conversation, hands moving rapidly in emphasis.

Soon the boys could see them more clearly. "Yemenis," Arne said. "I don't like them."

"Why?" Benno said.

"What does it matter? They're dirty and stupid and they smell different. They're practically Arabs."

"They're Jews," Benno said.

"They're black," Levi said. He jumped to the ground. "Come on, we'll have some fun with them."

"What are you going to do?" Benno said nervously.

"If you're so frightened, stay here," Levi said.

"I'm not frightened," Benno replied, following reluctantly.

They intercepted the Yemenis. Dark, birdlike men with clean-lined face, with earlocks and yarmulkes, they were no taller than the three youths.

Seeing the three boys approach, they broke off their conversation, smiled. "Shalom, chaverim," one of them said.

"See," Benno said, "I told you they were Jews."

"They're nothing," Arne said. He addressed himself to the Yemenis. "You're a dirty bunch and you don't wash or like to work and we don't want you here," he said in Hebrew.

The man who had greeted them replied in a language none of them understood.

"What kind of talk is that?" Levi said.

Still smiling, the two dark men started to walk around the three boys in their path. It was Levi who moved to block the way, holding out one hand. He wasn't sure what he intended, perhaps to show off in front of his friends, to taunt the Yemenis, have fun at their expense.

He squinted into the faces of the two men, saw the uncertainty there and that triggered some strange anger in him. He pointed in the direction from which the men had come.

"Go back," he ordered. "Black men can't walk this way."

Annoyance took its place in the face of the man who had spoken. He brushed Levi's hand aside and said something to his companion. They moved ahead.

Arne laughed, a taunting sound.

The laugh did it, unloosed a scarlet, swelling pendulous rage in Levi, a steaming mist that blocked off his vision and clogged his thought processes. "I said go back!" He pushed the man nearest him hard.

The Yemini swore and swept Levi's hands away. A stride or two forward in short, jerky steps, calling for his friend to come along, took him around Levi, and almost past him.

Levi cursed and sent his fist crashing into the exposed side of the man's jaw. The Yemeni staggered and turned as if to fight. Before he could respond, Levi was at him, both hands swinging, choked sounds, moist and unintelligible on his lips. As the Yemeni went down, Levi kicked out. There was the dull crunch of leather against soft flesh and a wheezing moan, the sibilant whoosh of air.

The second man tried to help his friend. Arne thrust out his leg to send the Yemeni sprawling, scrambling to rise. Again Levi kicked out and the toe of his boot thudded against the man's temple. He collapsed on his stomach, bleeding from the nose.

"Oh, my God," Benno cried softly. "They're dead. I think they're dead. Both of them. Why did you do it, Levi? Why?"

Levi stared at the still bodies in spreading terror. But no answer came.

XVI

The enormity of what he intended, its wrongness, its immorality, the very real threat it presented, jarred Amos, made him hesitate, weigh, measure and consider with a rare thoroughness. But in the end his decision was the same, immutable, certain as the fact that he was alive, and therefore necessary.

He phoned her as soon as he arrived in Jerusalem, at the Café Royale. She wasn't there. A man with a flat, disinterested voice didn't know where she could be reached. Amos left his name and the telephone number of the shop.

The hours went slowly. As he worked, he kept checking his watch, and each time the phone rang he felt himself grow tense and anticipatory. Late, less than ten minutes before closing time, she did call.

"I thought it would be nice to say hello," he said, voice elaborately casual. "Perhaps we might even have dinner one night. Tonight, if you're free."

She wasn't. "Come to the club later. About ten o'clock. We can talk when the show is over."

Concealing his disappointment, he said he'd try to make it. He ate alone on the terrace of the hotel and looked at the panoramic view. Afterwards went for a long walk. He arrived at the Café Royale twenty minutes early, took a table against one wall, and ordered a brandy.

Once a private residence, this building with its thick walls and sturdy archways was testimony to the timelessness of Arab builders. Dim blue lighting softened the rough texture of the walls and contrived a romantic atmosphere.

Ten o'clock came and went. The show did not begin until almost half the hour was gone. First, a sleek young man in a blue lounge suit and long sideburns sang in a weak voice in the style of American crooners. He was followed by an Oriental fire-eater, a muscular man with a Tartar mustache and diaphanous pantaloons. Both acts were received with unenthusiastic applause.

When the fire-eater and his accoutrements were no

longer on stage, the lights went out, blackness holding for a long interlude. Then, a single cone of light, splashing over Mara Gabrielli. The applause that greeted her was prolonged and tinged with excitement. Amos realized that Mara was the featured performer here, that the audience had come to hear her sing, and he took pride in that.

She wore a tight white silk dress trimmed with a geometric design in gold. An abbreviated toga, loosely belted, it draped gracefully over her round hips, stopping at her knees; and it was cut low to reveal the shadow of her cleavage.

The drama of her almost Oriental features was heightened under the light. She held her chin high and allowed the sea-green eyes to traverse the room, as if demanding silence and attention.

Abruptly, a low, nasal tone sounded back in her throat, insistent, penetrating, growing louder. And then she was singing an ancient Bedouin chant. From out of the darkness, a pair of guitars strummed a subdued accompaniment. When the song was over she went right to another, this time an African melody. A soft drum joined the guitars. She moved in time to the insistent rhythm, hips swaying, coming closer to the audience. Amos could see her superb breasts bobbing under the white silk. Again she wore no brassiere. That same excitement coiled through his groin.

She sang only folk songs, and in a number of different languages; her voice was sometimes sensuously throaty, sometimes raucous and mocking, sometimes nasal and sly. And as she sang she used her face and figure to best advantage, supporting the voice. More than support, Amos realized uncomfortably, after a while. Every gesture, every move, was calculated to deflect attention from the voice and its defects, to the perfection of the flesh.

She was singing an American work song, the tempo strong, and she made it stronger. At the last notes, the light faded imperceptibly to darkness, as the sound of Mara lingered.

When the blue lights came on, the stage was bare. The energetic applause failed to bring her back. It was, Amos decided, a very effective performance. Yet he felt peculiarly empty, weary almost, used.

"Shalom, Mr. Landau."

She was standing there, still wearing the white toga, the corners of her generous mouth lifted almost questioningly.

80

He rose halfway from his seat, shook hands with her, and asked her to join him.

"Would you like a drink?"

Her gaze was disturbingly direct. "Nothing, thank you."

"I enjoyed your performance, Miss Gabrielli."

Noting the gleam in her green eyes he suspected that he amused her. He felt uncomfortable; he wished he hadn't come.

"For us to be formal is ridiculous," she said. "We both have given names. You are Amos, I am Mara. All right?"

"All right." There was an ageless quality to her, as if in her few years she had experienced many lifetimes, *knew* all there was to know. "You sing very well," he said, sensing his own inadequacy in this situation.

"I don't think so. I have no range but I can do a few tricks with the voice. If I were a plain woman there would be no work for me. It is arranged—the vocal tricks, the songs I sing, the way I look and move about. I put a lot of time in practicing in front of mirrors so that it would do for me what I want it to do." A quick, taunting smile came and went. "Some day I will find a way to make it do even more for me."

"More?"

"Of course. This place offers very little. I would like to become very successful, famous, wealthy. That is not so easy to accomplish, especially in a new country that puts very little premium on my small talents."

"You have a long-range plan?" he said. "Well, that makes good business sense."

"I have no plan, except to keep exposing myself to possibilities."

"I'm not sure I understand."

She touched his hand as if in reassurance, a brief gesture made without thought. "There is very little to understand. I know what I want in this world, what my goals are. What I don't know is how to get where I want to go. I only know I must keep trying." Again the fleeting smile, this time warm, encouragingly girlish. "I visited your shop last week and bought a dress. I will probably go back."

"Tell me what you want and I will arrange for you to buy it at a discount."

"Tell me about the stores. How are things going for you?"

He spoke with increasing enthusiasm about the difficulties of buying sight unseen in foreign markets, of providing the services that distinguished Landau's from other local merchants and keeping his prices competitive, about ideas that he wanted to test in the near future. She listened, asking an occasional question that revealed a genuine interest. Without warning, she stood up.

"I have to do another show," she said.

He took her offered hand. "Afterwards, if you're free, we might go somewhere for a drink or something to eat."

"I have a date," she said, with that unsettling directness.

"Of course," he managed. What a fool to have come. To her, he was nothing but the father of someone she knew, a middle-aged man away from home and lonely. She was kind and generous with her time, but that was all. In a girl as beautiful as she, there would be many men interested—young, handsome men, men like Joshua. "It was nice of you to sit with me," he said. "Shalom, Mara."

"Shalom, Amos."

He tried to squeeze her out of his mind after that but she kept returning. He fought against phoning her or going again to the Café Royale. On the morning of his fourth day in Jerusalem, she called him at the shop.

"This is my free night," she began without preliminary. "If you are also free, I will let you buy me dinner, if you like."

He hesitated, thinking of Ruth, of his family. A vision of Mara in his mind and a flame of desire in his loins occurred simultaneously.

"Would you like to eat anything special?" he said formally. "Are you kosher?"

Her laugh was spontaneous, clean, free. "I am not kosher. And you?"

"I'll eat anything, except pork and sea food," he ended ruefully.

Again that laugh, tinged with mockery. "I know just the place. Mario's. Only a few blocks from the King David. Do you think you can find it?"

"I'll find it."

He arrived at Mario's early. He ordered a drink and looked at his watch. Where was she? Had she changed her mind, received a better offer for the evening, someone younger and better-looking? Someone unmarried? He reminded himself that this was only a dinner date, nothing more. He was making too much of it, building a juvenile fantasy on her kindness.

She appeared ten minutes late wearing a high-necked black linen sheath that he recognized as coming from his

82

shop. "Rena was right," he said. "I should pay you to wear my dresses."

She laughed. "Perhaps we could arrange to place a flashing electric sign on my bosom, advertising Landau's Jerusalem."

He glanced at her bosom and back to her face. Flecks of gold appeared in the green of her eyes.

"You don't think it's a good idea?" she said.

Amos ordered martinis for them both. They were excellent. Feeling better from the chilled bite of the gin, he said, "When you were late, I thought you might have changed your mind, weren't coming."

There was no change of expression. "I said I would come."

It was that simple for her and she was that confident. There had been implicit criticism of her tardiness in his remark yet she had felt no need to respond to it. At her age, he would have been quick to apologize or explain, fearful of offending. The gap that separated them was, he decided unhappily, even greater than the years.

"How is Ruth?" she said.

He searched her face for some subtle barb, a suggestion that she knew what he was about and meant to have none of it. He found nothing. He leaned back and said that Ruth was well, convinced now that for her this meeting was just what it seemed. Innocent and friendly, nothing more. He struggled for something to say.

"You like singing in cafés?"

"Not really. But it is what I do these days."

"And after that?"

"I have no way of knowing exactly. I do not worry about the details of the future. My chance will come, if I do everything I can do, as I intend to."

He was struck by her certainty that whatever happened she would be up to dealing with it. It contrasted sharply with his own lack of confidence as a young man, some of which he still felt.

"You make me feel," he said, smiling to lighten the words, "as if I am twenty-one and you are forty."

She nodded soberly. "In some ways I am very old."

"Looking at you, one would never guess."

"You think I look young?"

"Very young."

"That's good. Important. To look young, to age slowly, that is important for a girl like me."

"You'll be young for a long time, and beautiful."

"I'm glad I please you."

He hesitated. "I suppose you have always pleased men."

For a moment he was afraid he had offended her. Then that gay laugh and characteristic toss of her head. Her long black hair shimmered across her shoulders.

"You are right. Always. Even as a child, I was the favorite and my father's friends always played with me, fondled me, kissed me. They brought me gifts and sweets."

"Do men still bring you gifts and sweet things to eat?"

"You are buying me dinner," she said very quietly.

"But I am only Joshua's father." Even as he spoke, he was annoyed and ashamed of himself. There was a pleading note in his voice, in his words, as if he were begging for reassurance.

"I am not Joshua's sweetheart."

"He is very fond of you."

"But I am not his girl," she bit off, her voice edged now, insistent. "Joshua kissed me a few times but that signifies nothing. At least for me. Do I shock you? That kissing is so casual to me?"

He studied the tips of his fingers. "Shall we order?"

All the lightness had gone out of her. "It is true that I enjoy the company of good-looking young men. Why not? I am a woman who enjoys men, which is as it should be."

"Please," he said. "I'm sorry—"

"I am not obligated to anyone," she persisted. "Not to Joshua and not to you, either. I am free to do as I wish."

"I meant no offense, Mara."

"I know exactly what you meant to do, Amos, to probe, to discover what I am without risk to yourself. It is enough that I am here with you. Remember, I called you, I *had* to call you, for you would never have tried to reach me again. And we both know that is true."

"Please," he said. "Please, please."

Fear was alive in him, dancing along his nerves, bringing an unsteadiness to his fingers. What was he doing with this aggressive girl and her alien ways? He was used to Ruth, quiet, receptive, almost passive, going about her life without fuss, doing whatever needed doing without rippling the waters of life.

"I think it may have been a mistake for us to meet," he said stiffly. "I will take you home."

"No," she said firmly. "I am starving and you will buy me dinner. As a businessman, you should know that a deal is a deal."

84

They ate swiftly and with a minimum of conversation, anxious to down the food and to cut short their time together. At last finished, Amos paid the check and they left.

"I will get a taxi," he said, "and send you home."

She looked up at the sky. "It is a marvelous night, all those stars—the eyes of God I used to think as a child." Her eyes came down to his. "I want to go for a walk."

He yearned to be rid of her and the heavy burden she placed on him. But he didn't dare insist that they part, afraid of what her reaction would be, what she might think.

"All right. I will walk you to your apartment, if you wish."

She said nothing, moving off briskly, and he hurried to keep up with her. They went past Sham'a Street, near the wall of the Old City, picking their way through rusting coils of barbed wire and concrete tank traps, the high gray wall pocked with bullet holes.

"Did you fight here?" she said.

"In the Negev."

"I don't like the desert. I am a woman for cities, where there are people and things happen. We go this way," she said suddenly. "Are you up to climbing?"

The hill that rose ahead was high. "You live around here?" he said dubiously.

Her laugh was short. "This is Mount Zion. We are going to King David's Tomb."

"At this hour!"

She had started up the incline and he hurried after her. Two-thirds of the way up, she paused.

"The view," she said, "is beautiful."

From where they stood, Amos could see the tower of the YMCA, Israel's tallest building, and the King David Hotel, the cluster of stones that marked Herod's Tomb, even the windmill built in the previous century by Sir Moses Montefiore.

"Look," he said. "You can see the minarets over in Jordan. Listen!"

The muted trilling of a *muezzin* rode through the night.

"A beautiful sound," he said.

"Ah, that accounts for it. You are a follower of Allah, an Arab."

"I have nothing against the Arabs. After all, they are not so different than we and this is their land, too."

She tried to read the expression on his face in the

85

darkness. "Look there," she said, pointing to the east. "You see those lights. Campfires of the Arab Legion. If they knew we were here, one of them might take a shot at us."

"Yes, and one of our boys might do the same thing to them. Listen to the *muezzin*. Is his praise of Allah so different than how we praise Jehovah?"

"You have the soul of a poet," she said without rancor.

"Just a dress salesman."

"And a baker," she said quietly. "And a soldier and an archaeologist. What else?"

He took her elbow, suddenly embarrassed. "Come on, if we're going to the top."

At the crest, they paused, catching their breath, letting the soft wind cool their cheeks. To the left was the Dormition Monastery, to the right the black-domed Tomb of King David.

"There," Amos said. "That cave. Up on that ridge. Let's look at it."

"No," she said quickly. "I've had enough."

He insisted and she trailed reluctantly after him. He stopped at the mouth of the cave and squinted into the deeper blackness.

"Let's go inside."

She stepped back. "There are those who believe that King David is really buried in this cave."

"Nonsense. Besides, if there is anyone in there at this hour it will be some futile old beggar." He took her hand and strode into the blackness, feeling her unhappy presence.

"Oh, let us leave this place."

"There is nothing to be afraid of."

"Come out!"

The voice was strange, hollow, echoing ominously. *"Come out!"*

A faint cry of fear trickled out of Mara. "Oh, *imaleh—* mama!" As she clutched at Amos his arms went around her, held her close, aware of the firm thrust of her breasts against him. He led her outside where a bent old man in a black kaftan and yarmulke waited, his bearded face tight with disapproval. A trembling hand extended in reproach.

"Why are you here?" The Yiddish spewed out from between unsteady lips. "To pray where King David sleeps, out of love of that which is holy? Oh, yes, indeed. A dark place is what you seek, to commit what obscenities!" His fingers combed the gray beard. "The night time is our time without tourists. Go away and leave those of us who believe to our praying which is a serious affair."

Amos murmured an apology and backed off. Holding Mara's hand, he hurried back down the road, neither of them speaking until they were at the bottom.

"Please," she said. "Take me home."

She lived in the Bukharan quarter of the city and Amos was unable to conceal his surprise as they picked their way along the narrow streets.

"Why not?" she replied. "This is where I was brought up. My ancestors came from Spain. My people have lived in this country for a very long time."

"Since the Spanish expulsion in 1492?"

"Perhaps not that long, but long enough." In front of a house that showed the signs of wear and long years, even in the darkness, she stopped to face him. "My memories of this place are very sweet, Amos. Though we were poor, always poor, there was a lot of laughter, a lot of singing and dancing. A mixture of the Spanish and Asian Russia. And everybody ate Arab food. And always there was music, goat-skin drums and lyres and flutes."

"And guitars?"

"That is how I learned to play and to sing." She gestured toward the old house. "This is where I live." He followed her inside. She had a small apartment on the second floor, with old furniture. She offered him some brandy and sat next to him on the frayed pettipoint sofa. "So now," she said, grinning, "you know all about me."

"Not all, but it sounds like a fine childhood."

Her mouth drew down. The yellow flecks seemed to dissolve into the green of her eyes. "But so poor. Everyone was, I suppose. My mother had seven children and there was seldom food enough to feed us all. I was the only one who survived."

"I'm glad that you did."

A playful gleam appeared in the green. "Shall I tell you how I came to live? I owe it all to my Great Uncle Israel, who was a female goat."

He laughed hesitantly.

"Reincarnated, of course. You know the Cabala?"

"A little. The mystery literature. Cabalists believe that revelation was a continuous mysterious process, not an original act."

"Supernatural."

"Yes. Years ago I tried to study the Zohar, the Book of Splendor. It traces the entire Cabalist movement. It was too much for me and I gave up after a while."

"Very good. That proves you are healthy and sane. The Zohar is too much for anyone who isn't mad."

"What about your uncle who was a female goat."

"Since my mother had lost her other children, she was determined to save me and so she consulted a cabalistic rabbi."

"And he told her about Uncle Israel?"

"You do understand! Right after I was born, my father sacrificed a pet goat—"

"Uncle Israel?"

"Yes."

"Poor man."

"Uncle Israel was especially robust, you see, in all of his lifetimes, as a man and as a goat, and the idea was to transmit his good health and strength to me. The goat skin was kept under my bed until my existence was assured, my thirteenth birthday."

"I hope Uncle Israel is happy, wherever he is these days."

"I hope so. I know that I am." The laughter washed out of her face and she leaned closer, the sweet heady scent of her in his nostrils, the clean lines of her face framed in a blur of black hair. "My dear, wouldn't you like to have me now——?"

There was a surging sense of his own strength, retreating and coming on again; a gathering storm, swinging heavily, swelling; a hot liquid force. His hands were rough and insistent, pulling her across himself, twisting and maneuvering until he was on top of her, aware of her belly reaching up as if to make it easier. Her mouth was damp and gaping, and her hands groped and grabbed and explored with abrupt need.

Rolling, attacking fastenings, they went to the floor. The flesh was moistly prepared, sweetly accepting, bellies thumping. The soft smothered cries grew louder, more demanding, pleas to be filled with him, to be flooded with his essence, screaming finally into his mouth in spasmodic counterpoint to a vaginal ecstasy that broke with incredible force, subsided and returned, again and again until each of them was drained. And fulfilled.

After that, they saw each other two or three times a week. And more often, after Mara's engagement at the Café Royale ended and she returned to Tel Aviv. They would lunch together almost every day and go to her apartment afterwards. Soon, they put an end to the lunches and he went directly to her place. Sometimes they would eat and then make love, and other times they would make love first. And sometimes they would forget to eat.

Guilt was a living part of him these days, and he sought to expiate it in different ways. To Ruth, always the busy wife and mother, offering no complaint of neglect, he brought gifts, flowers or a recording or a piece of costume jewelry. He listened tolerantly to Rena's babbling about becoming a movie star and offered no objections when she insisted on playing her guitar for him. And he forced himself to make an even greater effort to understand Levi, to break through the defensive barrier the boy had erected around himself. In this he failed, even as he failed to find ways and means of turning away Baruch's constant carping and criticism.

None of this diminished his desire for Mara, his need of her. She dominated his thoughts and the hunger for her flesh was always present, an inexorable lure that could not be withstood.

"I feel like David," he told Mara one afternoon, as they lay side-by-side in her bed.

"David of the Bible?"

"Yes."

"And I am Bathsheba?"

"Something like that."

"But I don't have a husband whom you can order into battle in order to get him killed. So you see, it is quite different, my darling."

He allowed his hand to fall onto her thigh, firm and round, the flesh warm, stroking until he found the feathery confluence of limb and torso. Oozing a sigh, she positioned herself for him.

"I want us to be together always," he said into her mouth. "Not to get out of bed, ever."

"Lecher."

"It is true. In an earlier life I must surely have been one of those Patriarchs of Biblical days."

"Were they lechers too?"

"Insatiable. Don't you remember those begats? What did you think they were doing, those fiery old warriors, those old Hebrews? They killed or raped with equal passion."

"Ah, then you are in good company."

They kissed and his manhood stirred and reached for her. She rose to meet him.

"I always thought it was over for me, this way," he muttered, voice rasping through the thick glob in his throat. "The way my flesh feels, all muscular and manly."

89

"Very manly."

"Sometimes I want to beat my chest and flex my biceps—".

Her breath was hot against his cheek. "How lovely! For me, after, it's always a sort of bursting with what you give me."

He bowed his neck and his mouth found her breast, teeth carefully manipulative. A quick gasp came out of her, and her hand touched the back of his head. He went after her mouth.

"So long, so long. I didn't think it would happen again, me making love more than once. Everything had become routine, twice a week like taking an iron supplement for the blood."

When she laughed, their teeth clicked together. "Persist in this unseemly behavior," he said, "and you will ruin my attempts to be a suave and sophisticated lover. It is not fair to an old man."

She squeezed his thick shoulders and stroked his arms. "So strong. Everything about you. So strong and so young, the youngest man I've ever known."

"You've known many?" Tension slithered along the twist of his gut and he hated himself for putting the question, even in jest.

"Two or three hundred."

"And you enjoyed them all?"

"Don't talk. Love me."

"Is it the same with all men?"

The green eyes were lidded, wary. "Must you know?"

"I love you," he said. "It doesn't matter."

"You're a liar." She spoke without expression. She rolled away and sat up, looked off into space, oblivious of her nakedness, of the fine, almost statuesque lines of her body. "The first time, I was fifteen. I was curious, I wanted to know, I did it. Before that, I had done things to myself, with my hand, with things. It was not very hard to find a willing man. I was almost as developed then as I am now and I was always pretty."

"You found a man?"

"I found one. He was thirty years old and I seduced him." Her eyes flickered close, then opened. "It hurt but I knew that it was right for me, something necessary, that I would find pleasure in." Her head jerked around. "You understand, about some things you know, not with the brain, but you *know*. I knew the pain would not last and I went back to the same man until there was no more pain.

But he was a terrible lover, pompous and arrogant, and he believed that just being with him made it good for me. I had to teach him what I enjoyed."

"How did you know."

She shrugged, and her breasts rose and fell with the movement. "I did know, I did." She lowered herself back down to the pillow and glanced at him. "Now, my dear, I would appreciate it if you would make love to me. You see, I am going away in the morning."

"What are you saying?"

"I am going to travel around the country, singing for the kibbutzniks."

"Don't go. If you need money, I'll give it to you."

"I'm an entertainer," she said coldly. "I must build my reputation, polish my skills."

"How long will you be gone?"

"Three weeks."

"Oh, my God, I can't be without you for three weeks. I'll go too."

"Yes," she bit off tightly. "And bring Ruth along. And Levi and Rena. Perhaps Joshua can join us."

"There's no need to be cruel."

"And you, do you have a need to be cruel to me?"

"What do you mean?"

"I am yours now, my darling, and that is the best I can do. But you have no right to ask about what went before, and you mustn't expect eternal devotion from me. It is not the way I am. I live in my own style, you see."

He started to speak, to apologize, but her hand covered his mouth, cut off the words. She was smiling, the green of her eyes warm and peaceful. "Ah, it's over. Here," she murmured, taking his hand. "Here is where you left off. Do you remember?"

He remembered...

The unsigned note arrived at the Tel Aviv shop on the tenth day. She said that she missed him, wanted him to visit, and listed the remaining stops on the tour. One name struck him—Dov Hadorom, near the *tel* of Hatzor. He made up his mind.

That evening, during dinner, he announced that he was tired, was going to Hatzor for a few days. "I need a change," he said.

"A holiday will do you good," Ruth said. "You haven't been yourself recently."

He searched her face for some hidden meaning, some veiled criticism. There was nothing. Her expression was without guile. He looked at Levi. "Would you like to come along? It might be fun." He felt his heart pounding and hated himself for what he was doing.

"Digging for old pots," Levi said sullenly. "Not for me."

Amos arranged an indulgent smile on his mouth. For once, he was pleased by Levi's parochial interests, limited only to city matters, to the street activities of himself and his friends. It occurred to him that Levi seemed to be turning in on himself more each day. He made a mental note to talk to the boy, after Dov Hadorom, to try and reach him.

"What about you, Ruth? Would you like to come along?"

She shook her head, laughing. "Take the *zayde*. That digging is not for me."

Baruch glared at Amos. "There is no need for me to dig in dirt to find out what has been. Study the Holy Scriptures if you want to learn the truth."

"Papa," Amos said placatingly, "archaeology tends to support the historical accuracy of the Bible."

Baruch sniffed. "A good Jew knows where to find God, my genius son. He is where He is invited."

Two nights later, Amos was with Mara in his small tent no more than a quarter mile from the Jordan River, about fifty feet from where the road bridged a deep gulley. They had made love and dozed; and, waking, talked, and made love again. By now most of the night creatures had ceased their noise and a deep quiet moved across the land. Amos felt sleep settling over him when he heard them.

A baritone voice, gutteral, unmistakably Arabic. He sat up, suddenly awake.

"What is it?" Mara asked lazily.

He placed his hand gently over her mouth. "Arabs," he hissed. "Terrorists."

Sitting up, eyes wide in the dark, she watched him pull on his trousers and walking boots. He took a pistol out of his rucksack.

She clutched at him. "Don't. It's too dangerous. You don't know how many there are."

"Listen to me," he husked out intensely, gripping her face in his hand. A harshness she had never before heard salted his voice with authority. "You circle around, away from the river. Get to Dov Hadorom as quickly as you can. Tell them there are three, maybe four raiders. They're moving along the gulley, past the bridge now. I figure they'll head for the crossroads about a half mile from here. You know it?"

"I think so."

"They must have timed the night patrol. They'll take up a position in those rocks above the road."

"I know that——"

"I'm going to try and get there first."

"You'll be killed."

"I won't do anything unless I have to. Tell them at the kibbutz. Tell them to hurry."

"Let me go with you."

"Don't be stupid. Get help. Hurry."

He left her and picked his way through the rugged terrain, moving quietly, mind ranging ahead, trying to anticipate what would happen. He came from the west, moving cautiously among the rising rocks until he had achieved a clear view of the crossroads. The moon had gone down but there was light enough to see. Three men were placing mines in the road. They worked speedily and Amos made them out to be well-trained. His eyes moved off the road to the outcropping that dominated the crossroads. Two other men were assembling a lightweight machine gun in a protected place. Amos heard the bolt click, then click again. The gun was ready to fire.

Amos forced himself to think. By now Mara would be no more than halfway back to the kibbutz. Help would not arrive for at least fifteen minutes, probably longer. To attack five armed men with only a pistol was foolhardy and could have only one ending, his own death. He hoped the patrol car was not due for a while, that the kibbutzniks would be able to reach him first.

The Arabs on the road joined the men at the machine gun, took up firing positions. Five minutes later, the sound of a heavy car engine could be heard coming closer.

Amos listened to the Arabs chattering among themselves. Their plan was obvious—to disable the car and kill the patrol members, half-a-dozen soldiers who would have no chance.

The car now closer, Amos picked it out of the darkness, advancing slowly, showing only blackout lights. The Arabs were silent, ready.

Amos cocked his pistol and forced himself to breathe regularly. He would not be able to wait for the kibbutzniks. He stood up and leaned his right elbow on the rock shelf in front of him, brought the pistol to bear, steadying it with both hands.

He fired.

The machinegunner screamed and pitched over his weapon. The patrol car stopped and soldiers came tumbling out, taking cover.

Amos fired again, and someone swore in Arabic. One of the raiders shoved the dead gunner aside; tracers sprayed through the night in the direction of the patrol car. The soldiers returned the fire.

Amos shot at the gunner and missed. He aimed again and that's when he noticed that two of the Arabs had vacated their position. They were coming after him. Without hesitation, he moved deeper among the rocks. Moments later he heard a pebble clatter down the slope. He shifted around, pistol ready. A man appeared, rifle in hand. Amos shot him in the belly and he screamed over and over again.

Amos backed out of sight.

The second Arab made a fundamental error. He kept the safety on his Sten gun and now, coming up behind Amos, he unlocked the weapon. Amos heard the ominous click and swung around, shooting in the direction of the sound as he whirled. It took two shots to bring down the Arab whose finger held on to the trigger, unloosing four rounds.

Amos took one high in his chest, just under the right shoulder.

Lying there, he listened to the continuing battle, to Israeli soldiers moving on the machine gun, calling to each other. A dull explosion and another. Grenades. The silence announced the end of the fighting.

Holding the wound, blood warm between his fingers, the pain throbbing and a numbness spreading, he cursed himself for being a fool. There would be no hiding what existed between himself and Mara now, for the story of this raid and his role in it would be known all over Israel by the middle of the next day. He cursed himself for allowing the Arab to come up behind him, for not killing him with the first shot.

He thought of Ruth and the children. Of Joshua at Sde Yaffee. All of them would know that he was an adulterer. His brain seemed to pitch and yaw on its axis and his forehead came to rest on the ground, grateful that at last the need for further deceit was past. His eyes fluttered shut, and he waited for Mara to find him.

TWO

Amos Landau

I

Shlomo Landau knew who he was, what he was. All the details of his existence served to remind him and reinforce that knowledge. Each morning he wore tefillin, those small black boxes containing fragments of parchment inscribed with verses from the Books of Exodus and Deuteronomy, affirming God's providential care, His unity, and one's faith in Israel's deliverance from bondage. According to ritual, he wrapped the straps of one around his left arm and attached the other to his forehead, symbolizing his emotional and intellectual commitment to God's truth.

And each evening, before returning home, he visited the old Orthodox synagogue just beyond Konigstrasser, not far from the River Elbe itself, to pray.

His home was kashruth and he kept the Sabbath in all ways. He studied the Torah, considered its words, debated the fine points it contained with his friends, and often wished he were a wiser man and could have become a rabbi.

Born in Bremen, Shlomo Landau was six when his parents moved to Hamburg, capital of the state, where they opened a small dry goods shop.

Shlomo was not interested in the shop. From childhood on, he was captivated by the sights and smells of his mother's clean and efficiently run kitchen. And it was Shlomo, when he was twenty-three years old, who decided to open a bakery, despite the skepticism of his father. The operation was an immediate success: people soon heard about his delicate pastries, the fine *cholla* and kaiser rolls, and came from surrounding neighborhoods to buy.

Three years later, Shlomo married Paula Katz and eventually they had four children, one of whom, a girl, died at birth. There was Anna, the oldest, Moshe and Baruch.

The years passed and the children survived despite the normal complement of broken bones and childhood crises.

The bakery thrived and if it failed to make them rich, it did allow them to live in comfort. And when Anna married a clothing salesman, there was a proper dowry. A year later they gave Shlomo his first grandchild, but the year after that they emigrated to South Africa, and none of them ever saw Anna again.

In January of 1909, Baruch met Hannah Borkenstein. They were married that spring and the following year Hannah gave birth to a son, quiet and good, with a shy cast to his face from the start. They named him Amos.

Baruch, with a family to support, continued to labor alongside Moshe in the bakery, kneading dough, tending the ovens, and waiting on customers. When war broke out in 1914, Moshe enlisted in Kaiser Wilhelm's Army. A month later, despite the protests of his father and the pleas of his wife, Baruch followed his younger brother into the military.

Moshe was wounded in the Argonne Forest and spent two months in a hospital, but he survived without after effects. Baruch went through the war unhurt. At the end of the fighting, weary and disheartened by Germany's defeat, both men returned to Hamburg and went back to work in the bakery.

Despite the years of upheaval and unrest, Amos' childhood was full and rich with tradition and form, with obligations. He attended cheder where he learned to read and to speak Hebrew. He began to study the Torah and he was, when he came of age, bar mitzvah. He also worked in the bakery, learning from his father, his uncle, and his grandfather. Mostly he learned from Baruch who was often quick to criticize, his tongue barbed. Yet Amos felt no resentment, instinctively aware that to his father the bakery was less a business than a symbol, a private and unspoken measure of his significance.

When he was nineteen, Amos met Ruth Schroeder, whose family had come to Hamburg from Vienna. She was a gentle girl with lambent eyes and a woman's body. Her manner was modest, and though she offered Amos no encouragement, she made no effort to turn aside his attentions. After a few months, Amos went to his father and told him that he wanted to propose marriage to Ruth.

"An Austrian," Baruch snorted, with apparent disdain. "There are no nice German girls?"

"I love her, Papa."

"Find a German girl to love." Baruch rolled his eyes to the sky. "All right, all right. *Love.* Can she cook and does she keep a clean, kosher house? These are the important things. You asked her?"

"Not yet. I wanted to talk to you first."

Baruch layed his strong baker's hand along his son's cheek and slapped him with affectionate roughness. "You'll have to ask the permission of her father and mother."

"I hope they approve of me."

Baruch's eyes blazed. "You are the son of Baruch Landau. Perhaps I will not approve of them!"

The Schroeders approved, and that same evening Amos proposed to Ruth. Her hands clasped in her lap, eyes gleaming with pleasure and excitement, she accepted. That was when Amos kissed her for the first time—a cool, chaste brushing of lips.

A year later, Joshua was born, and three years later a girl, whom they named Rena, and eleven months after that Levi came.

That same year, Shlomo was reminded, by an apple-cheeked young man with bright blue eyes and straw-colored hair, who he really was. What he was.

"Jew bastard!"

It was a Friday night and Shlomo was on his way home from shul, his old head crowded with God's wisdom. He moved slowly, almost unaware that the season's first snow was falling, coating his neat beard.

"Jew bastard!"

The words came from another time in his life, and had he tried, he might not have been able to count the years which had expired since he last heard those words. For an elongated moment, he was a boy again, playing in the streets of Bremen.

"Jew bastard!"

The words owned a strong pull toward the present and his attention came into focus. He saw a young man with a nice face, and his laughing friends, young men like himself, and three pretty girls. He saw the red bands with the black swastika in a white circle on their arms. Recognition set in. These were National Socialists. He had heard about them, about their plans for reclaiming Germany, about their promises of building a great empire, about their hatred of Jews. Well, he was too old and too smart to waste himself on that kind. He shuffled away, a slightly bent old man in a long black coat and a black beaver hat, head bobbing sagely.

One of the young men heaved a snowball after him, but

the snow didn't pack well and it disintegrated without striking its target.

"Men like that," he said, reporting the incident to his sons—"they are not true Germans. Gangsters is what they are. This country will never tolerate such behavior. Soon the authorities will see that they are properly dealt with."

"I hope you're right," Baruch said.

"Of course papa's right," Moshe said. "Germany is too civilized to tolerate the anti-Semites."

It was Amos who expressed stronger concern. Only a week before, a friend had given him a copy of *Der Stürmer,* Julius Streicher's newspaper with its virulent denunciations of Jews and its loathsome caricatures. He tried to convince himself that it was all meaningless, a passing mood. After all, he was the fourth generation of his family to be born in Germany. His father and his uncle had served honorably in behalf of the Fatherland, as had his grandfather in his youth. Yet he could not shake off the memory of the hard young men he had seen, men in uniforms and jackboots, shouting their fury as they thumped through the streets.

"Juden Raus!"

He assured himself that Shlomo was right, that this was Germany, the most civilized nation in all of Europe, a country of science and art and philosophy. A cultured people. And the Landaus were Germans. *Germans.* This unrest had nothing to do with them.

That was the winter of 1933 and in July of the year Adolph Hitler was appointed Chancellor of the disintegrating Weimar Republic.

The weeks, months and years that came after served to make certain that men like Shlomo Landau remembered who they were. In the winter of 1937, Shlomo, old and unsteady, moved slowly along the icy sidewalks, mumbling his prayers, lost in a Talmudic mist, oblivious to his surroundings.

He failed to see the three young men so strong and tall and proud in their exquisitely tailored uniforms, and their girlfriends. But they saw him.

"Look at the old Jew. Come on, let's have some fun."

It was a gay moment, the six young people laughing as they hurled mild insults at the old man, at his clothes, his beard, his watery eyes and trembling hands. His Faith.

"This is not right," Shlomo told them, waggling a gnarled finger. "This is not proper, young people.'"

"Were you in the synagogue, old man?" one of them

cried. "What did you do there—butcher some good German babies for your barbaric rituals?"

Shlomo shook his head. What was this? He didn't understand.

"It is getting late. I must get home. I live with my son. He will be worried about me."

One of the young men shoved him and Shlomo stumbled backwards against the building wall. "You'll go when we tell you, Jew."

"Yes," Shlomo muttered. "I am a Jew——"

The same young man spit in his face. For a moment, the old man failed to realize what had happened. Then, wearily, with a large white handkerchief, he wiped the spittle away.

"That is not right," he said. "I am a German citizen——"

His words angered them. A crowd which had collected to watch the fun, urged them on. Someone snatched Shlomo's hat and scaled it aside. Muttering, he shuffled to where it fell, and bent to retrieve it.

The biggest of his tormentors came up behind him and kicked out with all his strength. Shlomo went sprawling. Most of the onlookers thought that was very funny, so when the old man tried to stand, the Storm Trooper kicked him again. Shlomo moaned softly. One of the watchers turned away, but no one did anything. No one spoke.

"Dirty Jew," the big Storm Trooper snapped, glaring at the still form. "Men like him caused the downfall of Germany. They are criminals." He delivered another kick to Shlomo's side, driving the breath out of the old man. Shlomo fainted. The fun was over and all of them left. Shlomo lay there alone until a city policeman happened along and summoned an ambulance.

The next afternoon Shlomo regained consciousness and peered up at the dim outlines of his two sons standing alongside the hospital bed. His lips moved and they bent forward to hear.

"What did I do wrong?" he said—and he died.

Along with the other members of the family, Amos sat *shiva* for his grandfather, mourning for the proscribed period, saying Kaddish three times each day, affirming the wisdom of God's decrees.

And all this time, Amos tried to understand what Shlomo's crime had been. He was an honest, hard-working man who caused trouble for no one, paid his taxes and obeyed the laws. He had raised his family quietly and without ostentation, had lived according to the best teachings of man and of God—he deserved to die peacefully in bed.

What *was* wrong?

Amos considered the situation from every possible vantage and concluded that the problem was arithmetical, proved out by the violence of his grandfather's death. Since the Nazis had come to power, the number of Jews in Germany had steadily declined. Not one Jew remained in the city of Danzig, for example, and in Poland, the death rate for Jews was five times that of other people. There were stories of sealed trains carrying a thousand Jews at a time to—to where? The answers were vague but no less terrifying. All over Europe, Jews were fleeing.

Like Shlomo, Amos knew who he was. A Jew. And Jews were no longer welcome in Germany. Under the circumstances, Amos could reach only one conclusion. It was time to leave. When he mentioned this to his father and his uncle, they looked at him in disbelief.

"Go!" Moshe said. "Where is there to go?"

"This will all pass," Baruch said. "The people—"

"The people are part of this," Amos said. "The people brought Hitler to power. They want him and his policies. They don't want us."

"You are mistaken."

Amos filled his lungs with air. "I cannot stay here. I will not risk the lives of my wife and my children."

"Where will you go?" Moshe asked. "Where has it ever been better for the Jews?"

"I have given it a lot of thought. I'm going to Palestine, to the Holy Land."

"When did you become a Zionist?" Moshe asked witheringly. "I go nowhere. I am a German. All this insanity will end soon. This Hitler, he is only trying to solidify the country, to get the economy moving once more."

"Palestine," Baruch snapped to his son, "is for the *Ost-Juden*. We belong in Germany."

Ost-Juden. The Jews of East Europe, an inferior category. The German Jew was a different breed, a higher order, cultured, intellectual, an integral part of the state.

Amos was not convinced. Nazi flags were draped from balconies and windows all over the city. Each week there were reports of stores smashed and looted, of people beaten, of men and women molested. When Joseph Goebbels, Hitler's propaganda chief, visited Hamburg, there was a torchlight parade of brown-shirted marchers singing the Horst Wessel song; and afterwards a huge rally took place in one of the city's squares. No Jew dared venture out that night. Listening to the sounds, Amos made his decision and told Ruth.

"What about your father?" she asked, fearful yet believing in her husband, never thinking to oppose him.

Amos spoke to Baruch the next day at the bakery, told him what he intended. "Papa, I want you to come with us."

Baruch shuddered. His wife had died three years ago and if Amos went away he would be left alone. There was Moshe, but he had his own family, his own life.

"It is worse in Palestine," he protested. "In Palestine, Arabs massacre Jews."

"That happened in 1932, Papa. Now things are different."

"Still they kill Jews."

"And here in Germany? It will be worse here. Everything will be done according to system, Papa. The Germans will be very scientific, very efficient."

"We are Germans."

"We are Jews."

"In Palestine, there is malaria—"

"Papa, listen to me. Dr. Weizmann, other Zionists, they work to secure better relations with the Arabs. And the British are there. They are a civilized people. They can be depended upon to pacify the country. It will be a good place to live, to make a new life. The Holy Land is the right place for a Jew, Papa, and we can be happy there."

"How could that be, in a strange land, among strangers, people who don't want us?"

"They don't want us here," Amos said. "Papa, I'm going, and I want you to come along."

They fought over it that night and into the next day and the day after that. Baruch marshaled every argument he could think of and battled with all his energy. In the end he agreed to go, unable to bear the thought of separation from his son and the grandchildren.

Without success, he spent the next three days trying to convince Moshe to accompany them. A month later, he kissed his brother goodbye and led Amos and his family up the gangway of a ship that would take him away from his homeland.

None of them ever saw Moshe again. The letters stopped coming after a year and inquiries drew no information. Years later, when the stories about concentration camps began to filter through—impossible tales of mass murders, of ovens, of a systematic elimination of a whole people—Baruch came to understand what Amos had sensed. He knew what must have happened to Moshe and his family. And he sat *shiva* for them and said Kaddish every day for a year.

"Magnified and sanctified be the name of the Lord. . . ."

Jerusalem.

No other place would do. Baruch insisted that they settle in the City of David. They found a small house in the Zichron Moshe quarter, not far from the Mea She'arim, the ultra-Orthodox sector. This pleased Baruch who felt at home with the Pietists, the Talmudists, the Hasidim; and he spent much of his free time in their company.

Amos located a suitable store, built two ovens in the back, and began baking. Business was not as good as they would have liked but it paid the rent and fed them all.

Shortly after their arrival, Baruch joined Agudat Yisrael, the political party which stood for only the most orthodox interpretation of the Torah and its application to all matters. He took part in demonstrations and attended meetings and inveighed against political Zionism, against all secular education for Jewish youth, against the increasing number of agricultural communities springing up all over Palestine. He was adamant in his opposition to the creation of a Jewish nation.

"But, papa," Amos argued, "even the British recommended separate Arab and Jewish states in the Holy Land. Back in 1937, the Royal Commission under Lord Peel——"

Baruch spat. He held a very low opinion of everything English. "Enough! Only when the Messiah comes will the Jews be a nation again, and that is as it should be."

Early in 1939, with Germany's aggressive intentions becoming clearer, the British Mandate authorities arranged a conference, to be attended by both Jewish and Arab leaders. Partition plans were discussed and the Arabs stated their objections in the strongest terms, leaving no question about their opposition.

With war coming closer, England was anxious to enlist any help it could get, anxious to woo the Arabs away from Germany, to protect her interests in the Middle East. To this end, a White Paper was issued restricting

Jewish immigration over the next five years to only 75,000 people. More than sixty percent of the territory in Palestine was forbidden to Jews and the Jewish Agency was frustrated in its attempts to buy more land.

Amos could understand the position of the country's Arabs who looked upon the Jews as foreign interlopers come to take away their land. But he did not fathom the English attitude. The British knew what was happening in Germany, knew that Hitler intended to wipe out all of Europe's Jews.

He was convinced that if he had been able to talk to some of the British officers in Jerusalem he could make them see the pressing need that existed for Jews to have a place to come to. But few Englishmen made themselves available. They kept to themselves, to their own kind, to their own clubs and bars. Once in a while you saw them in the cafés or on the terrace of the King David, cool, aloof, unapproachable.

Amos grew more uneasy. There were reports of Arab raids on Jewish villages, Jewish counter-attacks, Jewish patrols, kibbutzim growing despite the terrorism. He was at once confused and proud, curious about the kind of Jew who knew how to use a gun, knew how to fight. Gradually he came to believe that he should be taking some kind of an active role in all this, that he was part of this land now, that for him and his children there would be no place else to run to.

It was Abba Nathan who supplied the answer. Abba was a slight man of English descent, fluent in seven languages, who worked as a reporter for the *Jerusalem Post,* the English-language newspaper.

He and Amos had become friends. Once a week they met at a café, speaking in English so that Amos could sharpen his accent. On a day, bright and pleasant in the middle of March, they drank tea and munched pastry and talked about *Ulysses,* the James Joyce novel which both had recently read. Abba, a slight man, wore spectacles and they kept sliding down his thin nose as he spoke.

"I don't think you are very interested in Joyce today, *adoni,*" he said finally.

Amos agreed. "I have something on my mind."

"Yes?"

"What is going to happen? Here, I mean. To us Jews."

Abba looked at the people strolling along the sidewalk. "Who can say for sure? There are all kinds of rumors—"

"I hear about raids and fighting."

"Haganah," Abba said. "And the Irgunists, the Stern Gang."

"Are you active in such things, Abba?"

The newspaperman sipped his tea. He set the glass down and nodded. "Haganah."

"Why Haganah? Why not Irgun?"

"I don't believe in terror for its own sake, my friend. Haganah is well-disciplined, acting out of long-range purpose, not killing and destroying for the joy of it."

Amos gave a short mirthless laugh. "It is hard for me to visualize you with a gun, Abba, killing anyone."

"You do what has to be done," he said self-consciously, then forced himself to laugh. "Let's talk more about Joyce and less about trouble."

Amos frowned. He hunched forward, resting his chin on his clasped hands, his brown eyes serious and searching. "Have you actually fought against the Arabs, Abba?"

"Yes."

"There was shooting?" Abba nodded. "And weren't you frightened?"

"Yes, always," Abba said gravely.

"Have you—killed a man?"

"I'm not sure. Sometimes, when there is a lot of shooting, it is hard to tell. I don't know. But I would if it became necessary."

Amos struggled to clear his mind, to think carefully before speaking. "Abba," he said at last. "Would it be possible for me to join Haganah?"

"What about the bakery, your father?"

"Please, Abba. Tell me what I must do."

"There is a training school in the Zebulon Valley, at Ramat Yochanan. It might be possible for you to go there."

"Can you arrange it for me?"

"I will let you know."

Baruch was surprisingly mild in his reaction when Amos announced he was going away, and why. His protests were automatic but lacked any of his usual rage.

"There is a bakery to run. Who will do the work?"

"I'll help," Ruth said. "I can wait on customers."

Baruch glared at her. "You will stay with your children as a mother should. I will hire someone to work the front of the store. It will not be the same but it will have to do." He turned to Amos. "There are not so many Jews left in the world—do not get yourself killed."

On his first day at Ramat Yochanan, Amos was issued

an Enfield rifle and other essential equipment. He sat on his cot staring at the weapon. It seemed ominously heavy and powerful lying across his knees. Feeling apprehensive, he hesitated to touch it.

Coarse laughter broke into his thoughts. He looked up to see a brawny man on the next cot laughing at him.

"Don't worry, *adoni*," he roared cheerily. "It won't kill you. But maybe the Mufti's men will."

Amos stared in fascination at the other man. They were about the same age, but there the resemblance ended. Amos felt dwarfed and inadequate alongside the other. Even seated, he loomed up like some massive rock formation, all angles and planes, hard bulges and bony thrusts. A great black-thatched head and a sun-browned face, vaguely reminiscent, yet unlike any he had ever seen before. A chunk of bone and gristle, the nose a short twist, the brows plunging, the jaw defiant, the eyes pale, shining, far-seeing. Chilled.

"You never fired a rifle." It was an accusation and Amos nodded in affirmation. "Ah, we need soldiers and they send us ribbon clerks."

"I am a baker."

"Worse luck. You are no sabra?"

"I'm a German."

"A lucky *Yecke*. You got out in time. Soon there won't be a Jew left in Germany. That Hitler bastard will kill them all."

Amos blanched. "Oh, no. Labor camps, only——"

"Don't be dumber than you must be. He means to kill them all and there isn't a pious Christian country anywhere in the damned world that will lift a hand to stop it. Well, *adoni*"—he slammed one big claw of a hand down on Amos' thigh and squeezed; pain shot through to the bone—"*here* Jews don't die so easy." He took his hand away and Amos stretched the leg. "You have a name?"

"Landau. Amos Landau."

"I'm Yeshivat. Yaakov."

The stranger was almost too much for Amos to accept, too powerful in body and in personality, overwhelming, an alien force that imposed itself by sheer force and energy. Amos had never met anyone like him.

"You are an apprentice baker?"

"I work for my father."

"A capitalist!" Yaakov growled disdainfully. "I have no use for the profit motive."

Somehow that made Yaakov seem more acceptable; not

frail, not less formidable, but more visibly human. His tension draining, Amos grinned at the big man.

"It is only a small shop. But I would have no objection to becoming rich."

Yaakov grunted and lay back on his cot, hands clasped behind his head. His naked chest bulged upward, broad, deep, ridged with muscle.

"And you," Amos dared. "What kind of work do you do?"

"Whatever there is. I was a kibbutznik and I built houses and lay brick. I moved rocks and dug ditches and planted trees. I unloaded ships and drove a truck. I am a worker," he ended aggressively.

"I see," Amos said uneasily, then, trying to make amends: "Your father is a farmer?"

"My father is dead."

"I'm sorry."

Yaakov sat up and swung his feet to the floor. His pale eyes gleamed with unnatural brightness. "Some Arabs killed him. They raided our village one night and there was a long fight until we beat them off. When it was over, we found my father. The only one of our people who got hurt that night."

"I'm sorry."

"It took six bullets to kill him and they weren't satisfied because they knew what a tough guy he was. So they cut off his head."

A part of Amos rebelled at the meaning of the words. These were things of which adventure novels were made, stories of Lawrence, or Gordon at Khartoum. But it wasn't true. But Yaakov's stony face, the flat gutteral voice, told him otherwise.

"I went out to the Arab village, which wasn't far away, that same night. There were guards out, eight in all. I circled the village and killed each one of them with my hands. Not one man made a sound. Then I went into the village, to the house of the sheikh, Ibn Amer. A man of Allah. A Hajj. A man who three times had made the pilgrimage to Mecca. I woke him up and told him who I was and then cut off his head and placed it on the gatepost where they would all see it in the morning and understand. Then I went back and dug a grave for my father and buried him. The next day I left the kibbutz."

Amos didn't want to believe any of it, but looking at Yaakov, he knew that it was true. Just as he had told it.

Training began at sunrise the next morning. A quick

108

breakfast: a Jaffa orange, some sardines, raw carrots, cucumbers and black and green olives, yogurt and tea. Finished eating, and loaded down with all their field equipment, they set out on a forced march across the countryside. Halfway back on the return leg, Amos had to fall out, his feet bleeding, his calf-muscles swollen and aching. A truck carried him back to camp.

"You are not strong enough," Yaakov informed him bluntly that night. "You would be better off back in the bakery growing fat and rich."

Amos lay on his cot, eyes closed, feet throbbing. A muscle in his thigh leaped erratically.

"Tomorrow," Yaakov continued, "we go even further, thirty miles. You will not make it."

Amos wet his mouth.

"You will never become a soldier. It takes more heart than you *Yeckes* have."

Amos kept his eyes closed and spoke very softly. "I will be on the march tomorrow and I will finish. I will become a good soldier. Better than you. Now shut up and let me rest or I'll smash your ugly skull with my rifle."

Yaakov fell back on his cot, a cascade of raucous sound pouring out of him. The idea of this pale, weak, city *yid* threatening him was very funny. After a while, he stopped laughing and glanced over at Amos.

"I tell you, Landau," he said earnestly. "A man like you needs someone like me to take care of him. And I shall do it for you. In fact, I think we shall become very good friends."

"Go to hell," Amos said, not looking at him.

Yaakov laughed again, but briefly and quietly. After a hard day, a man was entitled to his rest.

The days that followed were crowded. Each minute was accounted for and it seemed they ran everywhere, whipped into motion by caustic officers and non-coms. And always there were those damned rifles, slung across their shoulders and slamming against their hips as they ran, or hanging like lead weights as they marched, or filled with dirt and mud while they ran a battle course.

Then it was the night before they were to go onto the firing range for the first time and Amos grew tense and irritable. Yaakov taunted him.

"Do not be afraid, my little friend. Just make sure to point the muzzle away from yourself. That way you will not get hurt."

"I would like to point it at you and pull the trigger."

"Excellent!" Yaakov burst out. "You are becoming a killer, as all good soldiers are."

"Oh, go away."

"You would like to punish Yeshivat, eh? I will help you." He pulled a chessboard and a boxed set out of his duffle. "Come on, I will give you a chance to gain a victory over me. But of course you shall lose."

Amos' brain clicked over with a voracious anticipation. Surely this crude lump of muscle would be no match for him. He had learned to play chess when he was six, had been able to defeat most adults by the time he was eleven, had competed in tournaments in Hamburg. "I suppose you consider yourself a very good player?"

"Naturally," Yaakov said. "Would you like to play for money, *adoni*? A pound or two, to make it worthwhile. I can use the money."

Amos drew two pounds from his billfold and placed them on the cot.

Grinning, Yaakov matched them.

They assembled the pieces on the board.

"You are white," Yaakov said. "Begin."

Amos advanced his pawn to king 4. Yaakov duplicated the move.

"You see," he chuckled. "I am not too proud to imitate your moves."

Amos made no reply. He moved his pawn to queen 4. Yaakov took the pawn. Amos moved his pawn to queen's bishop 3. They continued the play, exchanging pawns on the fifth move. Two moves later, Amos placed his knight in king's bishop 3. This drew a throaty exclamation from Yaakov who angled his bishop to knight 5.

"Check," he muttered, not looking up.

Amos wet his lips and moved his king to safety.

The tempo of play slowed. The hard edge had been worn off Amos' confidence. Yaakov played with such daring and strength that Amos was kept on the defensive. By now he should have been able to perceive the road to victory. Instead he felt threatened, fearful, weak. He hunched over the board, and with increased concentration, considered all possibilities before each play.

It did no good. On the tenth move Yaakov lifted his bishop with a pawn. When Amos took the bishop in retaliation the craggy-faced man laughed aloud. He countered with his rook to knight 1 and Amos slid his queen over to bishop 3. Yaakov won Amos' remaining bishop with his rook. Amos swore and quickly took the rook.

Without hesitation, Yaakov penetrated his queen to queen 8. "Check," he said, eyeing his opponent narrowly.

Amos blocked the check, placing his knight in king 1. Yaakov looked up and grinned. "You are finished, you know. Beaten. I have seen it coming for five moves now."

"Play," Amos said grimly, staring at the board.

Yaakov shifted his bishop to rook 3. "Check," he gloated.

Amos' eyes scanned the squares desperately. He tried to anticipate Yaakov's attack, weighing his choices. He had no choice. He withdrew the beleaguered king to the adjoining square.

Laughing happily, Yaakov lifted Amos' knight with his queen. "Checkmate," he said softly.

Amos frantically sought a way out. There was none. He didn't want to believe it had happened. Not this quickly, this easily. How could it be? He had been so sure of himself, so sure that in this at least he could defeat Yaakov. He couldn't recall ever being so humiliated and he plumbed his mind for some explanation.

As if in answer, Yaakov spoke. "When you have considered the game, my friend, you will no doubt recognize that this was the famous Danish Gambit with which Reti defeated Nyholm at Baden in 1914."

"You bastard," Amos bit off.

A full-throated laugh of triumph broke out of Yaakov. "You were doomed from the start. Oh, but you were cocky, little *Yecke*, underestimating your enemy. A terrible error. This will teach you humility, respect for your betters." The laugh was taunting.

Amos lurched forward, a blooded veil drawn over his eyes, lashing out. With a swift motion, Yaakov caught Amos' fist in his left hand, muscled him backwards onto the cot, held him in place, helpless.

"I told you we were going to be friends, Landau, and friends do not strike each other. I will teach you things, how to fight without losing your temper, to *think*, to anticipate and so be able to win. Winning is all that matters, in chess or in war." He stood up and displayed his strong white teeth in a warm smile. "You are okay, *adoni*. I like you."

Amos had trouble on the firing range the next morning, from the first shot. Intimidated by the powerful weapon in his hands, he held it loosely and it bucked with each round, slamming into his upper lip with terrifying and painful force. Even worse, he only occasionally managed to be on target. By night, his mouth was swollen out of shape and he was unable to eat.

Yaakov stole some ice from the kitchen and brought it back to the barracks and, wrapping it in a towel, jammed it against Amos' mouth.

"Keep it in place," he ordered, making no effort to conceal his disgust. "That lip is the ugliest thing I ever saw and you have only yourself to blame. That rifle scares you more than the Arabs. Well," he sighed, with exaggerated indulgence, "better that than the other way round. In any case, we are bound to be defeated if men like me don't teach men like you how to survive."

"To hell with you and your help."

"Shut up and listen. You think we can afford to wait for you to grow smart and tough. We can't. The Arabs won't give us time." He picked up his own rifle. "Look at me," he commanded. "See. The butt goes securely against the shoulder. Tight. Eh, like this, see. And hold the grip firmly. This is a rifle and you must control it or it will leap around like a fish on a hook and fight back. I watched you shoot. You curled your thumb over the top of the stock. Don't. Lay it alongside, pointing forward. See! Now there is no way it can bounce back against your mouth. Be strong. Control the weapon without stiffness. Aim, float the target, stay low on a man, the middle of his belly. That way you're sure to get at least a part of him. Dead or alive, he'll be out of the fight. And squeeze the trigger. Jerk it and you'll never hit anything. You'll catch on after a while."

"Is that all?" Amos said with bitterness.

"Far from all, but enough for now. Get some rest. Tomorrow we have battle drills. The new commander of the school has changed the routine. Live ammunition is used."

"Live ammunition!" Amos sat up. "Someone could get killed!"

"Yes."

Amos found it difficult to form the words. "I heard Haganah was short of ammunition."

"The British have plenty," Yaakov said. "We steal it from them."

Amos sat on his cot and cleaned the weapon. It was a beautiful item, a lightweight machinegun capable of spitting out a couple of hundred .38 caliber bullets each minute, and he had become quite proficient in its use.

112

It was hot in the barracks and he wore only his under-shorts. His body was tanned and hard, his stomach flat, ridged, a determined set to his mouth. He applied a light coat of oil to each of the parts and reassembled the piece. Finished, he put it aside and lay down and reached for the book, "Archaeology and the Old Testament."

He had been reading for no more than twenty minutes when Yaakov appeared, a satisfied glint in his eyes. "Hey, *adoni!* Some good news. After today, you won't be seeing me for a while."

Amos lifted himself onto his elbows. "I couldn't be that lucky. What's happening?" It had been three months since he had come to Ramat Yochanan and the two had grown close. In one week the course would end and Amos would return to the bakery, to his family. "You said you were coming to Jerusalem with me."

"That's all changed now. They want me for Kfar Vitkin, officers training."

"I see." Amos dropped onto his back. "That is right for you, a soldier's life. Some crazy Arab will put a bullet in your thick skull and that will be the end of it."

"With one bullet! I don't think so. Listen, *adoni,* from time to time, I will come to visit. But on condition."

"To hell with your conditions."

"I understand the girls of Jerusalem are the freest in all of Palestine. Find some good ones for me, dark-eyed girls with meat on their bones and life between their legs."

Amos picked up the book. "Get your own girls."

Yaakov leaned over to study the book. "Why do you waste your time with this nonsense? All that digging into the past. It is the present that counts, the future."

"Savage! You are ignorant and will always remain so. Go. Play soldier. Some of us must preserve the culture of the Jews."

Yaakov lowered his voice. "I think it will take a lot of killing just to preserve some of us Jews."

"Fight enough for the both of us."

"Oh, you will do your share. I want to say it. When you came here, you were a good man, clumsy and not smart, but with a lot of guts. Now you are smarter, thanks to me. When the time for fighting comes, you will do very well. Not as good as Yeshivat, of course—"

"Of course not."

"But not bad."

"I thank you."

"Too bad you did not apply for the officers school.

There will be good men there. You know Shimon Avidar, Moshe Dayan, Karmel, some others."

Amos rolled onto his side and opened the book again, his back toward Yaakov. "If you ever come to Jerusalem, visit the bakery and I will feed you some first-class kaiser rolls. They will make you a *mensch*."

Yaakov opened his mouth to laugh but no sound came out. From his cot he stared at the ceiling and wondered if he would ever see Amos again.

THREE

*Every man shall sit under his vine,
and under his fig tree,
and none shall make them afraid.*

—Micah

1951-1952

I

The ranks of Israel swelled in the year since Amos had been shot at Dov Hadorom. Out of Yemen, forty-five thousand people tracked across the desert to Aden where they boarded planes of El Al, the newly formed airline, and flew to Israel. Here was the gift of the Lord, the prophesy fulfilled: to be transported to the Holy Land on the wings of eagles.

The Yemenis were not the only ones; almost 200,000 Jews came. And others were born in the new nation. And others died, Baruch Landau, among them.

Dov Hadorom had transformed Amos into something of a national hero overnight. The news of his exploits in saving the frontier patrol were broadcast and published and Mara's role received equal attention. By the time the doctors released him—the wound proved to be superficial, though the loss of blood had left him weak—his family had been able to explore the facts of the situation, to decide for themselves what the truth was, to select the stance that suited each of them best, to marshal arguments and decide on action, to allow their emotions to become fixed.

As Amos had expected, it was Baruch whose response was most visible, most audible. His high rage erupted on the day Amos came home, and it seemed to intensify hourly.

"A *courva!*" he cried, voice reverberating with a sense of doom. The parchment skin of his face grew blotched, a thick vein throbbed in his temple, and his bearded jaw trembled. "My own son with a whore! Fornicator! Adulterer! Defamer of God's Commandments! Shame, shame, shame...."

It continued for days, aided by the accusation of Joshua's absence, his failure to visit Amos in the hospital, by Levi's sullen accusatory glances, by Rena's loving confusion, by Ruth's wounded silence.

Unable to tolerate it, he left on the third day and went

117

to Mara, to the comfort of her bed. He remained with her for two full days, and when he returned it was to discover that Baruch had suffered a stroke.

He rushed to the hospital. At the old man's bed, he was greeted with a fresh onslaught of angry curses. Though partially paralyzed, Baruch was unrelenting in his Biblical condemnation. He spluttered out threats of punishments yet to come, waving his fist. Abruptly, he fell back, silent. Amos summoned a nurse and she sent for a doctor. It was too late. Baruch Landau was dead.

The day after the funeral, Joshua left Israel without a word to his father, ignoring his mother's pleas.

"It's wrong," Ruth cried. "Our first child, to run away like this."

"How could he stay?" Levi burst out. "He's been betrayed, all of us have. You especially, mama."

Ruth's face, pouched and sagging, seemed to become more clearly defined. Her mouth set and she assessed her son levelly. "What is between your father and me is for us to settle. It has nothing to do with you. Papa is still your father, remember that."

Levi cursed.

Ruth stood up. "In this house, you will not use such language."

"Oh, Levi," Rena said disapprovingly, "you belong back on the desert with the camels and the jackals. At least they aren't hurt by your words."

His eyes went from his sister to his mother. He had been a member of Nahal for almost six months, part of the nucleus of a training group on a kibbutz not far from the Dead Sea. But the military khakis he wore barely concealed the tension in his coiled body, the building resentment behind his black eyes.

"The two of you," he ripped out, "I don't understand. He made a fool of you, mama, of all of us. He's shamed us all! He killed his own father."

"Shut up, Levi!" Rena said.

"You've got to do something," he said to Ruth. "You've got to divorce him."

Ruth stared at him. The anxious thrust of his head, the features tight and diminished, the wary expression. All that frustration, that hate—at last he had discovered a proper target for it.

"When I get married I'll never betray my wife," he went on.

"No woman will have you," Rena said.

"You must leave him," he insisted.

Ruth sat back down. A deep weariness gripped her, a weariness no amount of rest would exorcise. "I love your father very much, Levi. I can't stop him if he wants to leave me. Or go to another woman. But give him up—I will never do that!"

If Levi was confused by Ruth's reactions, so was his father. Amos had anticipated recriminations, punishment in one form or another. Instead there was only the carefully controlled facade, life continuing as before, as if nothing new had occurred. Once in a while he found Ruth looking at him; perceived the pain in her soft eyes. Otherwise, nothing.

His guilt, deepening and spreading, he told himself that if not for him Baruch would still be alive. When he mentioned this to Mara, she mocked him as a man without emotional sophistication.

"Your father was a self-righteous old man, and you know it. Don't flatter yourself. Nothing you could do would kill that old man. He was too tough. It was his own meanness that killed him, his own anger. Think of what you've told me about him: that he resented your bringing him to Palestine; resented leaving Jerusalem; resented your going into business for yourself, rejecting him and the bakery; resented your not being Orthodox. Oh, my dear, he was very angry with you and the best way he could punish you was to die and leave you feeling responsible."

"I never realized you were this hard, Mara."

The sea-green eyes flickered and glazed over. "I prefer *practical*. A practical woman in a practical world. Your father was mad at a world that refused to obey him, and you were a symbol of that world. If you let him, he would have beaten you for the rest of your life."

More than two weeks had passed since Baruch's death. With Joshua gone and Levi back in the Negev, living was easier for all of them. Amos had time now to sort out his thoughts, his emotions. Finally, one night, as he and Ruth were getting ready for bed, he felt compelled to force the issue, bring it out in the open at last.

"This way is not good, Ruth," he began.

She had taken to undressing in the bathroom, not letting him look at her. She slipped into bed, quickly concealing herself beneath the covers.

"What do you mean?"

"We might as well be strangers, so formal and proper, hiding everything."

"I'm hiding nothing."

"What do you want me to do?" he said, with desperation in his voice.

"You'll do whatever you want to do. You always have, you know."

The words brought him up short. It was true! For as long as he could remember he felt inhibited by outside forces, his father, the family, beholden to them. And yet no one, nothing, had ever stopped him. Leaving Germany, moving to Tel Aviv, opening the dress shop, joining Haganah, his frequent archaeological expeditions, Mara—For better or worse, he had always been his own man, a man of purpose. It was a new idea and he wanted to consider it.

"Do you want a divorce?" he said slowly. "I'll move out—"

She turned and looked up at him, a mild expression on her softly sculptured face. "I believe that marriage is forever, Amos."

"I don't understand."

"Neither do your sons. How proper and moral they are, when it concerns their parents. Levi insists I should order you out of the house with a great wailing and gnashing of teeth. I imagine Joshua feels the same. The trouble is you men are all terribly romantic, not at all practical."

He gazed at her almost without comprehension. There was a core of strength in her he had never before suspected. Or did she simply lack pride?

"You expect us to live as if nothing has happened?" he said. "As man and wife?"

"Not now."

"Not *now*. "You're an amazing woman, Ruth. I never imagined I'd hear you say anything like that."

She faced him squarely. "You do whatever you want, Amos. Why would you expect less of me?"

He issued the words very softly. "I am not going to stop seeing Mara."

"I won't discuss her with you. Not now, not ever. You are my husband, the father of my children. I expect you to act like both."

"You still want me—?"

"What has happened," she began, then: "It would destroy me to have you touch me now. In time, maybe that will change, maybe I'll grow used to things— For now I'm your wife, but not your lover."

Months passed, and Amos refused to permit himself to sink into an emotional morass. His life was neatly structured. There was the business, which demanded an increasing amount of his time; there was his home, his family; and Mara.

The single benefit of Dov Hadorom and its notoriety was that it allowed him and Mara a new freedom: they saw each other openly, without fear of discovery.

Strolling through Dizengoff Circle late one afternoon, Amos commented on her costume, a two-piece knit outfit, sky-blue trimmed with navy. It outlined her figure in every provocative detail and a glutting thickness came into his throat.

He took her hand and squeezed but there was no response. "Is that a new dress?" he said.

"Yes," she said, with sudden animation. "I had it made specially. An Ashkenazi lady in Jerusalem. She does marvelous work."

An idea forming in his brain, he asked her for the woman's address. He visited her the next time he was in David's City. She was a small woman with a flat peasant face and a number tattooed on her forearm. She listened to Amos without response, knitting all the while, not looking at him.

"I have friends," she said finally. "If you want knitting done, they are better than I, and quicker. You should talk to them."

He did. And he arranged for five women to knit for him. At first, he ordered only ladies sweaters from them, cardigans with colorful flower designs. As fast as he put them on display, they were sold, mainly to American tourists. Convinced that he had hit upon something special, he returned to Jerusalem and searched out ten more women to knit for the shops, using designs suggested by Mara and by Rena.

Business increased rapidly and he began to consider the possibility of opening new shops, of expanding the operation to include other items made exclusively for Landau's.

II

The two men embraced and kissed on the mouth.

"*El-ham dillah*," Mejjid al-Hadad intoned. "You look to be in excellent health, my dear."

Mamoud Ayyash acknowledged the compliment with lowered eyes. He was a bulky man in a brown business suit and a graceful white kaffieh, bound securely around his massive head with two black camel's-hair cords.

"Allah has been good to you, *habibi*," Mamoud said. "You have your health and your beautiful home, your possessions, the lands of your father."

A choked cry expired on Mejjid's finely formed mouth. "Nothing is as it appears, my dear old friend. Come, let us be comfortable and we shall talk."

He led the way into the large sitting room and they settled into the oversized velvet chairs. A servant brought thick Turkish coffee scented with jasmine for Mamoud, and Mejjid drank arak. When the servant was gone, Mejjid began to recite a litany of difficulties he had with Israeli authorities.

"Surely," Mamoud put in, "some gold in the right hands may accomplish many things."

"Aiyeeh! The Jews do not conduct matters in the old ways. Promises are what I get. But no results."

Mamoud displayed small teeth in a neat smile. "You are not a man to be without friends in strategic places."

"It is true. But it has done no good. There is Rothenberg, a member of the Knesset, and this Yaakov Yeshivat who is important in Histadrut, and others. Still, nothing has come of all my friends."

"Can a true Arab have friends among the Israelis?"

"I am also an Israeli," Mejjid said carefully. "A citizen."

"You are an Arab, my friend. The Jews are the oppressors of our people, your people. They are the enemy."

"Matters will resolve themselves in time. The Jews will be fair to me. You have been away for a long time, Mamoud, and so you do not know that things are done differently now."

Mamoud spat. "I have not been so far away that I do not know who my friends are and who are my enemies. I, who have been to Mecca, a true son of the Prophet, do not forget who I am and what I am. I am an Arab."

"No more than I," Mejjid said aggressively. He emptied his glass and arranged a conciliatory smile on his mouth. "It is said that King Abdullah seeks an accommodation with the Israelis."

Mamoud cursed. "Abdullah shall pay with blood for his perfidy." He leaned forward. "Is it not so, the Jews have taken away most of your property?"

"I have reason to believe that soon they will return everything."

"Never. The Jewish Army has extended a security line from Nazareth through Emek to Transjordan. All the land to the south of that line, 300,000 dunams, belonging to Arabs, has been appropriated. Eventually they will give the land to Jews. Believe it, my friend, as long as Jews rule in Palestine there will never again be Arabs who own great amounts of land. Mejjid al-Hadad, and others like him, will never again manage property that is rightfully theirs."

"No. It will not be that way forever. You don't understand how things are done now."

"I understand many things. I have been in Damascus, in Cairo. Listen to me. Great events are in the wind. All the people of the Arab Nation will soon be as one."

"It is a hashish dream."

"A historical necessity. Consider the facts, the plight of your brothers, *habibi*. Eight hundred thousand Arabs, Muslims all, forced to flee during the war. They live in squalor in camps and pray for arms so that they may drive the Jews into the sea and return to their homes."

"They are fools. Just as I was. To run away was a mistake. I, too, listened to Beirut and Damascus and I believed. The Arab armies would sweep the Jews away, it was said. A matter of a few days, it was said. All of us would then return and life would be better than ever. Lies, all of it."

He refilled his glass and drank.

"It is not over yet."

Mejjid snorted. "More hashish. You think I do not know what goes on in the world? Last year America and England and France declared that they would support the armistice between Israel and the Arabs. They will act against any country that violates the frontiers."

"They will not act. It is all talk. No one is going to send their own people to die for some Jews. No one did so when Hitler was killing them and no one will do so now. I say to you, great days are just ahead."

"Who will make the days great? The fat playboy who perches on the throne of Egypt? He is too busy readying his bed for a sixteen-year-old bride."

"Nothing is forever, Mejjid, not even kings. There are men in Egypt, soldiers, officers, fighting men who are afraid of nothing."

"There is always talk of such men."

"Have you heard of General Mohammed Naguib?"

"Perhaps"

"And Gamal Abdel Nasser? The Tiger of Faluga, he was called, a fighter of considerable bravery and skill. Such men do not rest until honor is restored."

"Will this return my lands to me?"

"Patience, my dear. Steps are being taken to bring the Jews down. The Arab League boycotts countries that deal with them and the Suez Canal is closed to their ships. Along the borders, our brave fighters continue to strike at their settlements. The Jews fear them and with reason. Soon they will have more reason to be afraid as such activities increase. Remember, last year, Egypt seized the islands of Tiran and Sanafir."

"They are uninhabited."

"True. But they command the entrance to the Red Sea, to the Gulf of Aqaba, and if a strong military force should be placed at Sharm el-Sheikh which overlooks the Strait of Tiran, Arab guns will be able to halt Jewish shipping whenever we wish. You see how matters progress?"

"Wallah. Does it bring me what is mine? Does it bring my oldest son back from Cairo?"

"Hear what I say, oh, my dear. I have come to enlist you in the cause of the Arab nation, to fight the Jews."

"What are you asking? I am no Levantine bedouin to go crawling over the desert—"

"There are many tasks for patriots. You have said you have many Jew friends. From them you may learn things, gather information, carry messages, do even greater tasks."

Mejjid heaved himself erect. His face was mottled and his eyes lidded, his speech thick. "You are welcome in my house and I will shelter and feed you. But you must not talk to me of such affairs. I am a citizen of Israel."

Mamoud stood. They were of equal height but Mejjid

124

would not meet his glance. "As an Arab you will be judged a traitor if you do not make this fight. Soon a jihad will be called, a holy war——"

"No more! You have honored my home and I thank you. But we have nothing to say to each other."

At the door, Mamoud turned, bowed, his hands in a prayerful position. "Consider, *Abu* Abdul, the future of your sons. Recognize the truth, the inevitable. You have no choice but to join us. One day I shall return and we will talk again. Salaam aleikum."

Mejjid shivered after Mamoud had left and no amount of arak seemed to be able to force the warmth back into his limbs.

III

Yaakov Yeshivat was impatient to get there, impatient to tell Lahav exactly what he thought of this peremptory summons, and he urged the taxi driver to greater speed.

For the last three months, Yaakov had been working in the coastal citrus belt between Gaza and Binyamina. In this sandy soil most of Israel's oranges, lemons and grapefruit were grown. The sweet scent of the orchards lingered in the cavities of his skull, making him all the more resentful of this interruption. His work had been so close to completion, the pickers and the packers organized, with a sense of union, of their own strength; negotiations with the owners about to begin. Yaakov found real pleasure in negotiating, in matching wits and guts with those tough planters. They were men not too different than himself and he enjoyed pitting himself against them, beating them. Now all the benefit of his struggle would go to someone else. He meant to let Lahav know precisely how he felt about this.

The taxi drew up in front of the house on Mount Carmel. Yaakov marched up to the blue door and, as if Lahav had been waiting, it swung open.

The two men hadn't seen each other since Yaakov's return from Dubrovnik, his assignment to Nahal. But the bony little man hadn't changed much. The eyes a little more intense, perhaps, more searching, and there was more white in the hair. That was all. Still no smile, no wasted breath or motion.

"There's someone I want you to meet," Lahav began. Was his voice a little louder?

Yaakov marched past him into the house. "What is this all about? You know what I was doing down there. Why call me away when it's almost done."

"Anyone can handle the negotiations."

"Dammit, Lahav. I like to finish what I start. You pull strings and I jump. Leave the Army. Work for Histadrut. Organize Nahal, leave Nahal. *Come to Haifa immediately*. I tell you plain, I don't like it."

"Come into the garden. We have company. From America."

"What! You call me back to meet Hadassah ladies! I have had enough——!"

"You heard of Ira Salisbury?"

"No."

"He's a movie producer. From Hollywood."

"Congratulations. The Americans are going to put you in the cinema."

"Listen for a change, will you? The Old Man called me himself. He wants this to go smoothly." He hesitated and a taunting gleam came into his eyes. "The Old Man suggested you for the job himself."

Yaakov scowled and rocked his craggy head from side to side. "I don't like this one bit. What job?"

"Salisbury is going to make a movie in Israel. It is to be called The Return. He and his scriptwriter are out back."

"What has that to do with me?"

"You are going to help them."

"The hell I am! I got important work to do. Get someone else."

"The Old Man told me and I'm telling you. Come and have a drink and listen. It will be a fine change. You'll get yourself an American movie star and sleep with her and be very happy."

Lahav moved off but stopped when Yaakov spoke his name. The sun-browned face was somber, the voice low and serious. "I don't want to do this thing, Chaim."

Lahav sliced air with his right hand. "Try to understand. The picture will be good propaganda for Israel. Also, Salisbury will spend a couple of million dollars of American money during the filming. We can use the income. It will also create sympathy for us in Europe and America and we need all the friends we can get. They

126

need a man like you, someone who knows how things are here. They are still writing the script and you can tell them things, take them around. If you devote yourself to this project——"

"How long?"

"Three months, maybe four."

"No. I won't do it. They can pick my brains for a few days. All right to that. And I will open doors for them. Yes. And get them other people. Yes. But stay with them and waste my time—no!"

Lahav sighed. "Every year you become more stubborn. All right. I agree. But whatever they need, it is up to you to find it for them."

"Chaim, I suspect that you are an agent of the Mufti."

Lahav turned away without smiling and Yaakov followed him into the garden.

Yaakov spent the next week wandering around the countryside with Ira Salisbury and his scriptwriter, Jim Tate. They visited the cities and the villages, sites of the major battles, listening to people tell of their experiences during the war, and since, and before.

"Surely you must have done extensive research before coming here," Yaakov said one day.

Tate laughed. A fat man with small eyes and bland, fleshy features, he spoke with the flat twang of America's Middle-West.

"This is it, man. A lot of reading, sure. Mostly the reports of the fighting in *The New York Times*, that kind of thing. And I did a rough story outline, much of which we already scrapped."

"We're going to make one helluva picture," Ira Salisbury said, his manner sprightly and optimistic. "I been thinking. Have you ever done any acting?"

"A natural!" Tate crowed at once. "Look at that face. Another Bogie. Perfect. He *is* Avram. A little makeup to make him look younger and we'll have a new star."

Yaakov decided that they were both insane and he told them so. "I don't act, not now, not ever."

"Think of the money," Salisbury said. " I will guarantee you——"

"No!"

Tate broke in, laughing artificially. "Forget the acting. I want to hear about your experiences in the war. They say you were quite a character, a kind of Jewish Sergeant York."

"Right!" Salisbury said. "Let's get the real thing. Listen, Yeshivat, I been thinking. Bring around some of your buddies, old soldiers, you know. We'll get their stuff on paper too. And I got a terrific idea. We're gonna write in one of those girl soldiers, very pretty, naturally."

"Fantastic, Ira!" Tate crowed. "She could be isolated with Avram, cut off by the Arabs, you see. In the Galilee, it's more photogenic than the Negev. Greater color and contrast. All right. He's wounded, maybe, and she stands the Arabs off while he keeps loading guns for her. You dig?"

"I dig," Salisbury said excitedly. "Throw a little sex in. Let her get wounded, nothing serious. A shoulder wound so we can rip open her shirt and show some tit."

"Right! And lots of leg while she sprawls around. Good stuff in that."

"Girls didn't fight," Yaakov said, voice deep in his throat, thick and ominously grating.

"It doesn't matter."

"They answer telephones and do clerical work, operate radios. They don't fight."

"But they *could*," Salisbury insisted. "They could."

"The girls don't fight," Yaakov insisted.

"Okay," Tate said quickly. "I'll come up with something else. You just give us the real scoop."

"That's a fact," Salisbury said. "Give us the information and trust Tate to jazz it up. Okay, Yaakov-baby, begin."

Yaakov stared at the producer. He was a big man with huge shoulders, a round head and no neck. His arms were long and his hands immense and he had a reputation for possessing great physical strength, for using it often against those who worked for him. There were rumors of fist fights and it was claimed that he had never lost one. Yaakov was tempted to test him.

"This is my last day with you," Yaakov said, in that almost inaudible way of his.

"What do you mean?" Salisbury roared. "You're our man."

"I will get somebody else for you. A good man. A businessman."

"Crap on that. Try to follow this, Yeshivat, we're making a drama, an action picture. We want fighting men to advise us."

"When the armies of five states attack a people," Yaakow said very slowly, "everybody is a fighting man. This man will be good for you. He came from Europe,

128

built a new life here, fought the English, fought the Arabs. If you are lucky, he will agree to help you. In any case, I am leaving."

"You can't!" Salisbury sputtered. "I'll go to Lahav. I'll go to Ben Gurion—"

"You can go to hell—"

Drinking tea, Yaakov watched the passers-by from a table under the sidewalk café awning. He thought he detected a subtle change in people. They looked soft, indolent, concerned more with their comfort than the welfare of the country. Already one heard complaints about the harshness of life, and demands were made for the niceties. Each day it became more difficult to find young people willing to pay the price of life on a kibbutz.

Yaakov wondered if this generation would not soon lose all that he and their fathers had fought to achieve. The thought amused him. He was getting older, thinking in terms of competing generations.

Mara Gabrielli turned the corner and came into his line of sight. She moved easily, long legs extending, giving a full swing to her splendid hips, her belly a full round thrust. Under the black blouse she wore, her large breasts bobbled enticingly.

Good health and vitality glowed in her beautiful face, its skin taut and smooth; her long black hair was piled haphazardly atop her head, making her look even younger than she was. He speculated—would she look as good naked? And would she be the fiery lover she appeared to be? He suspected the answer to both questions was affirmative and told himself that she was wasted on Amos.

He stood up so she would see him and she came over and sat down without self-consciousness. "Shalom, Yaakov."

Ah, the informality of things. No matter your status, no matter what you did or were doing, no matter the differences of age or position, everyone in Israel called you by your first name. He allowed his eyes to shift down to her breasts. The nipples, though dormant, were outlined. To sample that would be special.

"You grow more beautiful, Mara," he said gruffly.

The sea-green eyes were cool and steady. "You must be wondering why I contacted you."

"You'll tell me."

"To talk about Amos."

"All right. Talk."

A suggestion of a smile lifted the corners of her mouth.

This one, she thought, enjoying the idea, but a little afraid at the same time, was a dangerous man. That battered face, the gnarled nose and lips almost bloodless and tight against his teeth, those distant eyes, like naked eggs, the eyes of a man who never looked back, a man capable of anything. A man without regrets.

"Amos told me about the movie," she said, "that you asked him to work with the producer and the writer."

"To serve as technical adviser."

"So that you won't have to?"

"Exactly. He would be better for them than I. A businessman understands other businessmen. But Landau can be very stubborn. He refuses to cooperate."

She let the words out deliberately. "I could make him do it."

She wanted something, but what had not yet become clear to him.

"Why should you help me?"

"If Amos becomes this—this technical adviser, what about you? What will your part in this be?"

"I will return to my work," he said, keeping his manner mild, giving her room to maneuver.

"You will no longer be involved at all with the movie?"

"I will remain nominally in charge of the Israeli end of things. Me and Lahav." When she fell silent, he spoke. "Now my question for you: What are you after?"

"To be left alone. By you."

He cocked his head. She puzzled him. "You intend to get something out of this. What precisely?" He measured her and felt a grudging admiration. There was none of that usual female softness about her. She was direct, a short straight line between desire and action. Not many women were that way.

"You expect to get Amos for a husband? It won't work. I know him too well. He won't leave Ruth."

"Just stay out of it, that is the price."

"No," he murmured. "Not marriage. That wouldn't require all this." His mouth flexed in what passed for a grin. "I think I understand. It is the cinema you're after, and Amos is the vehicle." He leaned forward, brow knotted, face seamed and hard. "He is my friend and I don't want him hurt."

"What is between Amos and me is not your affair. There are no illusions for either one of us. Now, do you want my help or not?" She stood up and stared coldly down at him.

"Yes," he said.

"Your word, then. That you won't interfere."

"My word. Why not? It isn't worth much. If it suited my purpose, I would lie to my own mother."

"As would I. It is enough that you keep out of my way. Agreed?"

It was little enough if it would get him back to where he belonged, to the citrus groves. He agreed.

The next day Amos called to say that he had changed his mind, was willing to work with Salisbury. "But there is a limit to how much time I can give to this. I'm expanding my business."

"Another shop?"

"Four more. A second one in Tel Aviv and one in Haifa and two more in hotels an American company is building."

"You will become rich yet."

"And you can come and work for me. Each shop will be larger now, new departments. Not just dresses. The knits are a great success and there will be coats and sweaters and underthings. Each store will carry a complete line of women's things—jewelry, sportswear, nightgowns. So you can see that my time is limited. But I will do my best to help you, Yaakov."

"Appreciated," Yaakov said dryly.

"By the way, will it be all right if I bring Mara along once in a while? She's all excited about these movie people, like a little girl. She won't get in the way."

"That I believe. She's smart. She'll find a way to keep busy."

At first Amos felt out of place with the movie-makers. Salisbury was bright but glib and difficult to understand much of the time. He was different than anyone Amos had ever known; he approached his work with a kind of feverish aggressiveness, able to change plans and direction seemingly in mid-sentence. After a while, Amos came to realize that often when Salisbury sounded most positive, most confident, he was merely hunting blindly for an answer to a question he had yet to formulate.

As for Tate, owning none of Salisbury's surface crudities or drive, his intelligence was deeper; he was slower to reach conclusions; and he was less dogmatic. He lacked Salisbury's driving ambition and cruel ability to use people. He was also very careful not to offend Salisbury or to enter into an extended dispute, no matter how right he might be.

In time, Amos became fascinated with the operation and wondered if all films were made so haphazardly, if such large amounts of money were usually committed without either a prepared script or a cast. It was Jim Tate who supplied the answer.

"Don't be fooled by how it *seems*," he warned cheerfully. "Ira Salisbury is no fool and whatever else he might be, he is a man who knows how to make a profit for his backers. All his pictures make money, big money, which is why he can always raise it, why he gets away with the wild things he does. He's tough and mean and not a very talented director. But he knows how to pull all the various elements together and he's a hell of a good promoter and publicist. You'll see, this picture will be panned by the critics but people will love it and it'll be a huge success."

They were in Jerusalem, strolling the streets, with Amos pointing out sites where some of the bitterest fighting had taken place, recalling stories he had heard. They moved off Yafo Street and Amos indicated the green-domed Russian Orthodox Cathedral.

"And that building next to it?"

Amos frowned. "Headquarters for the Mandate Police." A quick grin broke across the generous mouth. "*Former* headquarters."

"You don't like the British?"

"No Israeli likes the British, but I don't hate them. They did what they had to do, from their point of view. It was a difficult job but they made it worse for themselves and in the end they handled it badly and finally quit on the whole thing. They aren't missed."

They headed back to where they had left their car. "I imagine you find a lot of satisfaction in knowing you played a big role in creating a new nation?"

"The baby is born, but will he survive?"

"You think it might not?"

"There are all sorts of troubles."

"Such as?"

"Such as a population that is growing too fast. More than six hundred thousand people have come here since 1948. In July alone, over 100,000 Jews were flown in from Iraq. More will come and that places a great strain on the economy. We have neither houses nor jobs for them."

"What's going to happen?"

"Chaos and conflict. The people we're getting—Orientals, from Yemen, Central Asia, Africa—not only are they from different places, they're from different centuries, different cultures. Our people speak different languages."

"Hebrew is the national language."

"Most people have to learn it, and I suppose they will eventually."

"I heard that when the Yeminis came many of them were sick."

"Yes. They carried long-neglected skin diseases and other afflictions. They were undernourished, their native diets limited. They have another handicap—they are dark-skinned," he ended dryly.

Tate showed his surprise. "Does that matter here?"

Amos laughed without humor. "Do you expect us Jews to be better than the rest of you? We're not, you see, no more generous or wise or kind. We even fight among ourselves."

"You mean the Orthodox people? What are they after?"

"What all orthodoxies want, to run things their way. Like the Catholics or the Communists, they are trapped by ideology. The way of all true believers, they alone know the way to Rome."

"Man, oh, man, that sounds like my hard-shell Baptist daddy." Tate frowned. "How am I going to weave all this into my picture?"

"You're not," Amos said, laughing. "You'll make a pretty movie about cowboys and Indians, using Jews and Arabs instead."

Tate chuckled. "Which are the cowboys and which the Indians?"

Amos smiled, then quickly sobered. "Maybe we're all Indians."

When they got back to the hotel, they found Ira Salisbury waiting for them. With a young assistant director, Hank McClintock, he had been scouting for locations and was anxious to begin actual filming.

"When are you gonna give me a finished script?" he said to Jim Tate.

"I've got a story treatment worked out, scenes sketched in. But no dialogue, and I'd like to polish."

"Forget it. We begin shooting a week from Monday. Stay close, baby, we'll put in dialogue as we go along, on the set or the night before."

Amos could see that Tate wasn't happy about this change in plan, but he made no objection. "What about your cast?" he said.

"That's another thing. I've signed Harlow Longstreet for Avram."

Amos visualized the movie star. He was a handsome man of at least sixty years, though he still played romantic parts. "I thought you said Avram was going to be in Palmach. As the striking arm of Haganah, only young men were——"

Salisbury broke in. "I read you, friend. Jimmy-boy, better upgrade the part. Make Avram older, a leader of men, a guy who's been around, lived hard. You know, a Jewish Gable. Got that?" Tate said that he had it and Salisbury went on. "And I got Maggie Whalen for Devra."

"Oh, Ira, no. The map of Ireland is on that face. No one will accept her as a Jew."

"To hell with that jazz," Salisbury snarled. He drove his big fist into the other hand. "All right. Let's back it up. Change things a little. Make her the daughter of an English Army guy, a colonel. Lend a little class. One of those colonial types. She could've been brought up anti-Semitic. Yeh. I like that. Gives us another element to play with. Sure, then she comes back to visit the old homestead and gets caught up in the spirit of the fighting, the pioneering thing, and the rest of that crap. That'll play. Let's put it in."

Amos stood up. "Well, I suppose you won't be needing me anymore."

"Wait a minute!" Salisbury said. "What do you mean?"

"There's nothing I can do during the filming."

"Oh, sweetheart, not so fast. We want you around. You're our technical adviser. Who else will keep us straight on how things are done around here? Oh, we need you, we want you."

Amos nodded agreeably. "All right. But I do have a business to attend to, at least some of the time."

"That reminds me," Salisbury said. "Let's work something out. You could supply clothes for our actresses, maybe whip up some special things. And I'll give you screen credit. Miss Whalen's wardrobe by Landau of Tel Aviv. How's that grab you?"

Before Amos could answer, Salisbury plunged ahead.

"To show you the kind of guy I am, Landau, because I like you, the way you're giving us a hand, I'm gonna do you a favor. I was talking to that friend of yours, the pretty girl. What's her name?"

"Mara."

"Yeh. She's got a good face, it'll photograph okay. I decided to give her a part, a real part with lines. She'll play a girl soldier who gets into action and saves the life of her boyfriend. How does that grab you?"

"Well—" Amos began.

"Girls don't do any fighting, Ira," Tate reminded his boss in a mild voice.

"Screw that noise. I'm making a picture not a war. Write it in." A deliberate grin spread across his coarse face. "Besides, it's my style to give young talent a break. A lot of young people got their start with me. That's the kind of guy I am. . . ."

IV

The company was in the hills south of Jerusalem, filming, when Yaakov Yeshivat appeared. It was the fourth shooting day and there was a frenetic quality about the proceedings, intensified by Ira Salisbury's loud bullying. His directing technique included threatening his subordinates and insulting them.

"Another Hitler," Yaakov said to Amos.

"He's one of us."

"A Jew? Well, why not? My father would have said that the Jews were cursed with every other affliction, why not this one? Watch him close, *adoni,* or he'll be running the country."

"Thay's why we have you around, Yaakov, to prevent such things."

"Only for today. Tonight I go to Haifa."

"A new job?"

"You heard about the seamen? Eight hundred men who work for the Zim Line. Every one of them a member of the seamen's union and Histadrut. All of a sudden, they walk out."

Amos hesitated. "Some day something will have to be done to lessen the power of Histadrut. The union controls too much, has too much strength."

"I think otherwise."

"What does Histadrut want? There is a Socialist Government and you can insure the election of a Knesset favorable to your views. All those benefits to the workers. You think employers can support such programs indefinitely, paying higher and higher costs?"

"Exactly what I think. Private enterprise in this country must do so or not exist."

"But not only do employers pay for fringe benefits but we are forced to compete with Histadrut-owned companies, banks, cooperatives and workshops of all kinds, factories. How can we win?"

"Only the people are supposed to win. One day these things may change, out of necessity, but not now. Would you prefer that the standard of living in Israel remain low, that we become just another Middle Eastern country, at the same level as the Arab nations? Listen, *adoni*, if we are going to survive it will be because we are smarter and stronger and raise our people up."

"But Histadrut——"

"Histadrut works for the country and you know it."

"There must be a limit," Amos said firmly.

Yaakov's face hardened. *"Adoni,* it might be better if we didn't talk of such matters. You know where I stand."

"Suit yourself," Amos said easily. "What comes after Haifa for you?"

"Some traveling, I think. America, maybe, to make speeches to Hadassah ladies and raise some money."

Amos' eyes grew troubled. "Yaakov, sometimes you must hear things. If you learn anything about Joshua——"

"Do you know where he is?"

"An island off the coast of Spain, last we heard. Who knows now? Ask around. We want him home. If you could see him, talk to him. All the children respect you, Yaakov."

"I'll see what I can do," he said gruffly. "But no promises. Young men," he snorted, voice rumbling in his big chest, "can be so prim and holy. They should all become rabbis until they outgrow it."

"Try to find him, talk to him. His mother misses him. And so do I."

When Yaakov arrived in Haifa that evening, he went directly to the port area. A strange stillness was everywhere, the immobile cranes outlined against the crimson glow in the western sky, the usual work sounds absent, and even the pungent sea-smell seemed different, less acrid.

He went out onto a pier and sat down on a piling,

136

peering past the tall Dagon silo at the harbor entrance. He remembered this place from the mandatory days, remembered the ship *Patria,* how it had exploded in the harbor, killing 250 illegals, on board because the British had refused to admit them.

He remembered other ships similarly captured, anchored and under guard, remembered thin cries for help, pale blobs of anguish turned toward the Promised Land, imploring arms. Cargoes of human debris, unwanted by anyone except the Jews of Palestine.

There had been other ships to remember, ships that had made it through the blockade, able to deposit their people on the beaches up the coast where Haganah trucks spirited them into the cities and the villages. A few more saved.

Approaching footsteps brought him back to the present. He glanced over his shoulder and saw a stocky man in a black sweater, hands deep in his pockets.

"Shalom," the young man said.

"Shalom. Cigaret?"

A pack was offered and Yaakov took a cigaret, waited for a light. He dragged deeply.

"Okay. What's it about, Agron?"

"Wildcat strikes. First this ship and then that one. For almost ten days. We tell them to go back to work, that the union will handle any grievances. They tell us the union does nothing, insist we are manipulated by Mapai. That we are controlled by the Government."

Yaakov stared across the harbor. At the horizon, there was still a narrow streak of pink. Suddenly it was gone. "Tactics?" he said.

"Demonstrations. Meetings. Hunger strikes. Parades."

There was nothing new there. Yaakov had used the same weapons at various times himself. "Who gives the orders?"

"I told you, individual action. The crew of one ship and then another. Like that."

Yaakov stood up and walked back to shore. Agron fell in beside him. "Does one man show up all the time?" Yaakov said presently.

Agron considered the question. "One man makes a lot of speeches—Yoram Effrati. Whenever there is a problem, he is there."

That was the man, Yaakov decided idly. He would be aggressive and energetic, fiery, with a flair for speechmaking. A man with a vision.

"Tell me about this Effrati."

"A hothead. A disrupter at local meetings. Never satisfied. Against, always against but not for anything that I can see."

"A good agitator?"

"Excellent and he has developed a following."

"His politics?"

Agron shugged. "He is of the Left, but so am I."

"And I. But there is Left for Israel and Left for others. Arrange for me to meet Effrati."

Agron grinned in the dark. "Stay right here, *adoni*. In the morning, he will be here. That ship—" He waved toward a ship moored at the end of the pier. "It is due to sail at midday. It won't. Effrati is striking its crew in the morning."

"Perhaps we will visit, then. It should be interesting."

When they returned in the morning, a crowd of men, the dock workers and the crew, had collected at the base of the gangway leading up to the ship. Their attention was directed to a wiry man standing on a packing case, addressing them in a strong, driving voice.

"Effrati," Agron murmured.

Yaakov listened. It was all familiar, the accusations of betrayal by union leaders, of political sell-outs, of corruption, of the need for action.

"We must have improved working conditions," Effrati was saying. There was a suppressed tension in his voice that evoked a sense of anticipatory violence. There was something vaguely reminiscent about him but Yaakov was unable to discover what it was. "Living quarters aboard the ships are unsatisfactory. We are told to be patient, that matters will improve. When, I say? *When?* The fat cats in Jerusalem can live with patience. We cannot. They do not work with their hands and break their backs for a few pounds each month. We do. We are entitled to more benefits and we want them. Now! We will get them. Now! We will take them. Now! Now! Now! *Now!*"

Yaakov's mind reached back. What was it Amos had said to him? *"There must be a limit."* Where was it and who would decide when it had been attained? Effrati demanded more and still more, seeing the outer reaches of the attainable as being remote. But all things could not be accomplished at once. Consideration for the country, for the whole economy, was in order. They did not function in a vacuum.

"To hell with gradualism," Effrati cried. "Mapai says

we should wait. That the things we want will come eventually. When we are old, they will come. When we are dead. Not for me, chaverim. Now is the time to enjoy the fruits of our labor. *Now*. Mapai and Histadrut, one and the same, two hands in the same bowl, controlled by old men. Ashkenazi with their old-fashioned ideas of progress. I say to hell with democratic process if it gets us nothing. To hell with their gentle Socialism. We must go after whatever we want and *take it*. . . !"

It came slowly to Yaakov. Effrati reminded him of himself, twenty years before. The same proud passion, the same willingness to go out and meet the future, to shape it. To fight. Or was it the same?

He shouldered his way through the men until he was within an arm's length of Effrati. Seeing Yaakov, the young agitator recognized him as a stranger and a threat, tried to ignore his presence. It was impossible. There were those hard pale eyes and those rearranged features, the unspoken power and authority. At last Effrati broke off, faced Yaakov directly.

"See what we have here!" he attacked. "One of Histadrut's muscle men. Have you come to beat me up, to silence me? It will not work. Go back and tell your masters that I do not frighten easily. None of us do. We know our rights and we will have what is ours."

"I promise," Yaakov said in a loud, clear voice. "You will get what is coming to you."

There was an uneasy stirring, a shuffling of feet. Yaakov kept his eyes fixed on Effrati's face.

"I know what you are," Effrati shot back. "One of those tired old men from Histadrut come to subvert our movement. We will not be turned aside. You can be sure of that."

The fingers of Yaakov's hand flexed into rocky fists, strong, tight. This was no tired old man, he told himself silently. He showed Effrati his teeth but it was not a smile.

"Mapam, eh?"

There was a momentary response in the face above, quickly gone. "This is not a political movement and you will not label us with the red brush. We are workers fighting for what is ours by right."

"To stop Israeli shipping when every cargo is strategic and vital to our welfare is nobody's right. Such flagrant disregard for the national good cannot be rationalized."

"We have legitimate grievances." A rumble of approval went up from the men.

"There is machinery established to rectify such matters. Worker's councils."

"The worker's councils achieve nothing. They meet with company officials and there is talk and more talk. We want action and we will have it now. Until our demands are met, we will not work."

Yaakov turned away from Effrati and his eyes worked from face to face. They were new to him, unfamiliar, young for the most part, and set against him. He swung back to Effrati.

"You are a very good agitator."

"We want action!"

"Action is what we must have," Yaakov said to Lahav that afternoon, at Histadrut headquarters. "The time for rhetoric is past."

"What are you suggesting?"

"That the strike be broken."

"No!" Lahav burst out, in a rare burst of emotion. "You cannot expect a union to act against its own membership. It would mean the end of Histadrut."

"If you fail to act, the situation will grow worse. More walkouts. No ships moving. How long can the economy tolerate that? Authorize me to put our shipping back in operation."

"How can I justify such an order?"

"Effrati's goal is to paralyze our ships, to undercut the stability of the nation, to topple the Government."

"You go too far."

"You think so. I've been nosing around, with Agron's help. Effrati has been meeting with Bohorov. *He* is running this business. You know his aims, his politics."

Lahav sighed and leaned back in his chair. "For a Jew in Israel to be a Communist is beyond my understanding. To see his own people as an enemy—" He let it hang.

"Listen to me, Lahav. It suited Moscow's purposes to recognize us in 1948. They thought we would lean toward them, give them a hold in this region. They know better now. They will turn elsewhere and that means the Arabs. Sooner or later the Kremlin will begin wooing Cairo and Damascus and they will succeed. When this happens, the Arabs will have a ready-made agent in Bohorov and Effrati and others like them.

"Such men turn us against ourselves, divert us from the real job. I am a Socialist and to me that means a political technique for achieving the good things of life as quickly as possible for our people. But it may not work for all people at all times and when a change in philosophy is in order I will stand for that change. Listen, *adoni*, I am first an Israeli and then a Socialist. You understand? I say this strike must be put down. I will do it, if you say the word."

"I can't say it."

"Someone must."

They were in Jerusalem the next morning early, going directly to the Knesset Building where they were ushered into a paneled meeting room.

"The Prime Minister will be along presently," the secretary told them, and left.

For the first time in Yaakov's memory, Lahav appeared nervous, ill-at-ease. "This is your party," he said curtly. "It is up to you to convince him. If somebody's head has to roll, let it be yours."

"I'll tell him the way it is. Once he understands that this is not only a local problem, he'll realize that he must take action."

"You're that sure?"

"I'm sure," Yaakov said, then tightly. "But not absolutely."

It was almost two hours before the Prime Minister appeared. A short man and stocky, that familiar halo of gray circled his head. The face was sternly seamed, the eyes serious as he waved them back into their chairs.

"Politicians," he muttered in Hebrew. "God save us all from politicians and parties. Too many of each. Too much talking. For every Israeli, we must have a separate party." He lowered himself into a chair at the end of the long polished table and drew his brows together. "I know all about you, Yeshivat. I was at Kfar Akiba once. You were an infant. That was some old man, that father of yours." He hawked his throat clear. "All right, what is this business in Haifa? Those people should be working. This is no time for ships to be idle. You, Yeshivat, tell me what is going on."

Yaakov filled his lungs with air. There was a hard-edged intellectual muscularity to the Prime Minister. An aggressive quality, and jarring at first, it incurred an unaccustomed defensive mood in Yaakov, almost a sense of inadequacy. Almost, but not quite.

Yaakov began to describe conditions on the Haifa waterfront. He omitted nothing, including his confrontation with Effrati, the information he had gained about him and Bohorov, his arguments to Lahav.

The Prime Minister, chin resting on one clenched fist, listened attentively. "If the strikes go on, what will happen, in your opinion?" he said, when Yaakov had finished.

"The ruin of our shipping industry and widespread economic chaos."

"Aren't you going too far?" Lahav said.

"Maybe not far enough," Yaakov growled. He jerked his head back to the Prime Minister, rocked his big fist in the direction of the old man in the blue lounge suit and white sports shirt. "Let me tell you how it is. Effrati intends to undercut the machinery on which the union's strength is based—collective bargaining. He by-passes the worker's councils. He refuses to talk to company executives. In the name of improving conditions, he is systematically destroying them."

The Prime Minister closed his eyes. "Tell me why?"

Yaakov glanced at Lahav for support. Had the Old Man lost interest? Had he already rejected Yaakov's position? He braced himself and began to talk.

"Effrati wants autonomy for his seamen's union. Once he has it, has shown that the men profit from it, he will set about encouraging other groups to break away from Histadrut. It will mean the end of the solidarity of labor. And the finish for Mapai's base of popular support," he emphasized thinly. The Prime Minister, eyes still closed, gave no indication of having heard. "Could you govern without labor support?" Yaakov challenged. "I say no."

"What else?"

"Let this go on unchecked and Effrati, Bohorov, the Communists, will take over the docks, the seamen's union, Zim itself. Let that happen and you can say goodbye to Israel's relations with some of the most important maritime shippers in the West."

In the silence that followed, there was only the sound of hard breathing, Yaakov's breathing. He had been shouting, using words to bludgeon the Prime Minister into agreement.

"What do you suggest should be done, Yeshivat?"

Yaakov said the words evenly. "Break the strike."

"With force?"

"Probably."

"Jew against Jew. I don't like that."

"Jew against Jew," Yaakov said, calculating swiftly. "It won't be the first time for you." The Prime Minister allowed his eyes to roll open and he gazed at Yaakov with

142

interest. "Have you forgotten the *Altalena?* The Jews on that ship didn't stop you."

The *Altalena,* an Irgun vessel with reinforcements for that terrorist group, with arms, ammunition. It was during the second truce in the War of Independence and this was a direct and flagrant violation. Irgun defied Government orders to surrender the ship and its cargo.

"That was aggression," Yaakov continued, his voice edged, insistent. "It was as dangerous to the Government as the Arabs. You never waited. You commanded the Palmach to stop the landing."

"And it was stopped," the Prime Minister murmured reflectively. "It was stopped. The truce was not broken. The authority of the Government was established."

"I say Effrati and Bohorov are attacking the Government in the same way," Yaakov said hurriedly. "Naked aggression and it must be stopped. There will be protests," he went on, his manner softer, "but there is no choice. The risks must be taken."

"I suppose you are right. The strike is a bad thing. Put an end to it. As for the criticism, I'll take care of that. You do whatever must be done but do it quickly and do it well."

"Yes."

The Prime Minister pushed himself erect and went to the door, looked back, a small smile curling the solemn mouth. "Your father, Yeshivat, that was some tough guy."

After he left, a flash of weakness filtered through Yaakov's middle. He sat down.

Lahav looked at him. "Congratulations, Yaakov. You were a big success. All you have to do now is break the strike."

Back in Haifa, Lahav called a press conference, at Yaakov's urging, and announced that the strike had no official sanction and that the Labor Organization was opposed to it. At that point, he turned the meeting over to Yaakov.

"This strike is illegal," he declared. "It is being led by men not interested in the workers or in the country. I say the interests of Effrati lie outside Israel and Histadrut intends to load the ships in the harbor. To that end, I am calling for volunteers to do the work."

In answer to the announcement, men began to appear in increasing numbers during the next few days and eight ships were loaded, mostly with citrus fruit for Western

143

Europe. But before they could get up steam and sail, Effrati made his move.

His striking sailors boarded the loaded ships and staged a sit-down. At the same time, organized marches were held and public protests voiced against the effort to end the strike, calling for the Prime Minister to resign.

"It is getting warm," Lahav said to Yaakov.

"And it will get warmer."

"What now?"

"That fruit will rot if it's allowed to stand in this heat much longer. I'm going to move it."

"What are you going to do?"

"Take those men off the ships."

"Yaakov, if we can avoid trouble—"

Yaakov kept his face expressionless. "We already have trouble. We are trying to end it."

"There will be violence."

"I hope not. But if there is, I would like some men I can trust around me. I sent for those Yugoslavs of mine. They're on their way here from Jaffa. In the morning they'll be here and we'll take those sailors off the ships."

After he left Lahav's house, Yaakov drove down the hill toward the port. His mind ranged ahead, trying to anticipate what the next day would bring. If at all possible, he intended to avoid violence. But that was up to Effrati. Should it come, he intended to be ready. He speculated that no more than thirty of the Yugoslavs would show up. He supposed Lahav could give him some men but he preferred not to use local people, hoping to keep antagonisms to a minimum when all this was finally ended.

He tooled past the Baha'i Shrine, down Carmel Boulevard, until he came to the railroad station. He parked the car and continued across to the docks. It was dark by now and he was deep in his thoughts, moving in and out of the shadows, striving to solve the problems that the next day would bring.

They were waiting for him, anticipating his need to return to the port area this night. Or perhaps someone had spotted him walking alone, and sent for the others. Or perhaps Effrati had put out the word to find him.

It didn't matter. Not when they came out of the alley in front of him, three of them, each with a short club, advancing in a loose phalanx, stepping closer with that stiff caution so natural to men close to violence.

He stood still and knew what they intended. His head

144

swung around; behind, two more of them, striding toward him, six or eight feet apart.

He swore at his own stupidity. He should have figured on this, realized that Effrati would take direct action against him personally, would think that by eliminating him he could turn back Histadrut's opposition.

He swept his mind clean. There was only the immediate to deal with. His eyes raked the waterfront. To his right was a warehouse, running from alley to alley. No escape there. To the left, fifty feet away, was the water's edge, a help to the five he faced.

He concentrated on the men to his front, ears tuned to the pair behind, brain working rapidly, selecting, rejecting, deciding. Those ahead were twenty-five, maybe thirty feet away, slowing; those at the rear, nearer. Twenty feet and still coming. He took a slow step backwards.

"Who sent you?" he shouted. "Effrati will change nothing this way. After me, there will be another and another."

"Shut up!" one of the men said.

"We're going to finish you, you dirty bastard, finish you for good."

There was no doubt, he meant it. Killing was on their minds, to beat the life out of him. To make a fight was futile. Five were too many.

The footsteps at his rear had become a slow shuffle as the two men advanced cautiously. He could visualize their club arms raised, their bodies tense, attention riveted on the back of his head. The target. He estimated that they were no more than ten feet away. Less maybe. And closer to each other now. A couple of yards at most. The shortest way, the quickest. A straight line.

He jerked around and was running full speed at first stride. A cry went up.

"Stop him!"

He dived for the space between the two men. Instinctively they retreated a step before coming at him, clubs swinging. One of them glanced off his left shoulder spinning him. He fought for balance and kept running.

He swung into the alley and up the incline, legs pumping with all the strength he could muster, hoping to get to a street where there were people. Lots of people.

Footsteps were closing fast behind and he cursed his years and the slowness of his legs. He made it into the third block, within sight of the street, able to see the passing parade of automobiles and pedestrians, before they caught up.

Whirling, he drove on the nearest man, hooking an elbow to his jaw. There was a sharp crack and the man screamed and went over backwards. Yaakov hoped his momentum would carry him on past the second man, away from the club hand. It didn't. He took a heavy blow across the shoulder and went down, rolling, trying to regain his footing.

The man with the club was good at his work. He was at Yaakov quickly, driving him to his knees. Then the other three came pounding up and he was struck heavily behind one ear. Again. And again. He went down, vaguely aware of a heavy boot cracking into his ribs. He was struggling to rise when everything turned deep black and still.

V

Ira Salisbury ordered his camera and lights set up in the narrow street which his scene designer and carpenters had disguised to make it resemble the Jewish Quarter of Old Jerusalem, under control of Transjordan's Arab Legion.

Extras, some in the uniform of the Legion, others playing members of Haganah, lounged about, smoking and talking. All were members of the Israel Defense Force, provided at no cost to Salisbury. To get them, the burly producer had gone over the heads of local officials, disregarded Amos Landau's advice, and contacted the Prime Minister directly.

"I tell you," he had boasted afterwards, "you want a thing done you do it yourself, right to the horse's mouth."

Now Salisbury was huddling with Harlow Longstreet and Mara Gabrielli, instructing them in how to play the next scene.

"What I want," Salisbury bellowed, "is intimacy, the intimacy of personal discovery. You two are meeting for the first time, in the middle of a battle. But not even the fury of war can keep you from recognizing what each is *for* the other. Got it, Mara?"

She nodded gravely.

"Now, Harlow, you have to make me feel that you'd

146

like to put the blocks to her on the spot, war or no. Look at that mouth. Think of that on you. Look at those boobs—" He frowned and reached, began to unbutton the top buttons of her military shirt. "Let's show a little skin, baby, let 'em look at those things. It's the name of the game. Okay."

Rena Landau, in crisp Army khaki skirt and blouse, might have been a member of the cast. In fact, she was doing her compulsory two-year service and had managed a three-day leave, expecting to find Amos in Jerusalem. She had been disappointed to learn that he had gone back to Tel Aviv, and from there to Paris on a short buying trip.

Mara had prevailed upon her to stay, to enjoy the filming. At first a mutual embarrassment forced them into awkward stances and they found it difficult to talk until Rena broke down, laughing and crying, and they embraced.

"I've never been sure whether I was supposed to hate you for making my mother miserable," Rena said, "or love you for making my father happy. I can't stay angry with you, Mara."

"I'm glad, Rena. I want us to be friends."

"And I'm so glad for you, this movie, becoming an important cinema star. You'll be famous and rich."

Mara's head went back and she laughed, a rich pleased sound. "Not yet. But if it happened, I would not object."

"Mr. Salisbury seems to like you."

The laughter ended and the soft, tan face sobered, the green eyes defensive. "He is a boor and a pig."

"Still, he could help you, if he wanted to."

"Maybe I should convince him to want to."

That had been yesterday and now she watched Salisbury rehearse Mara and Longstreet with building interest. How exciting it would be actually to be friends with a movie star! A voice broke into her concentration.

"Bet you'd like to be out there in her place."

Without turning, she knew who it was. Hank McClintock, the assistant director. Ever since she'd arrived on the set, he had managed to be close. A slender man not yet thirty years old, he owned a diffident manner and toed the ground when he spoke to her.

Rena enjoyed the uncertainty of his approach, so different from most Israeli men who tended to bluntness. She liked the way he looked, too, the smooth line of his cheek, cropped hair the color of the desert, the warm gray eyes on those occasions when he dared to look at her. He was

147

all angles, lanky, his shoulders high and square, with large, strong hands. She decided that he was a very dependable person. If only he were a little more aggressive.

She smiled at him. "Once I wanted to be a movie star," she said in accented English. "When I was a kid. No more. Not after watching the way they make films. It is too dull."

"I suppose." He scraped at the pavement. "I did some acting when I was at Northwestern but I kinda leaned toward making pictures instead."

"You'd make very excellent films, I think."

He studied the toe of his boot. Looking at her was difficult for him. There was that direct manner, the way those black eyes stared back without blinking, as if able to see inside. It made him uncomfortable, nervous, and the perpetual purse of her lips, the fullness of her breasts beneath the khaki, the sweet airy scent of her. Whenever she was around, he experienced a wave of weakness in his middle, a headiness, and he found himself saying stupid things, or unable to speak at all. She was a very disturbing girl.

"I've been reading the page changes Jim Tate's made in the script," he said. "A lot of the stuff's based on what your daddy told him."

"My daddy," she said, imitating his Mid-western twang, "is a major of tanks now, such as they are in Israel."

"Tanks! I thought he was a businessman, or something."

"He sells ladies clothing, or something."

He knew she was teasing him and he wanted to be angry with her but didn't dare. He wanted desperately to impress her. Searching for something that might engage her interest, he said, "The part Harlow Longstreet is playing, that's supposed to be your father."

She shook her head. "Not papa. Papa's friend, Yaakòv. He was here during the fighting."

He looked down the narrow street. "That must have been kinda rough."

"Most of the Jews of the Quarter were trapped by the Arab Legion. Old men and women and children. Only a few fighting men. The Arabs sent armored cars against them. Our people sent reinforcements a couple of times but it did no good. The Arabs kept control of the Old City."

"I guess it's something special over there, to do all that fighting over it."

She shrugged carelessly. "Not so special. Small, stone houses with roofs that come out over the streets, where Jews have lived since the time of King David. Only the Wailing Wall is special."

"I heard about that. It must be beautiful."

"Not really. Just a collection of old stones. The last remnant of the Second Temple. It has a meaning."

"Well," he said, stirred by the unexpected gravity of her mood, and not knowing what to say, "some day things'll work out so you folks can go back over there and see it."

"Oh, yes," she said, almost inaudibly. "We'll go back."

Neither of them said anything for a few minutes until he spoke her name abruptly. She looked up at him. He braced himself.

"I wish you weren't going away so soon," he said. "Maybe we could do something, have dinner together, or something."

She laughed and he misunderstood.

"I suppose the last thing you need is to be pestered by me."

She sobered quickly. "I must go back. Orders, you see. And soon it will be Sabbath and everything will be closed until tomorrow night."

"Oh, look. I didn't mean any disrespect to your beliefs. I mean, I'm not a Jewish person myself—"

"You're not?" she teased, straight-faced.

"No, ma'am. I was brought up Church of Christ but I guess I'm kind of a backslider. My folks don't exactly approve of me." He brightened and his puckered brow went smooth. "Did you ever know Ellie Scheinmil. She was Jewish. I dated her for a while at Northwestern, nothing very serious, of course."

"We never met," she said gravely.

"Shoot! What I mean is, I'd like to see you again."

"Yes."

"I know how busy you must be, being in the army, and all. And you must have a ton of boyfriends—"

"I said yes, Hank."

He tugged worriedly at his long thin nose. "You figure your daddy's goin' to be sure sore 'cause I ain't Jewish? I wouldn't want to bring trouble down on you, Rena."

"Are all American men like you?"

"Ma'am?"

"*Oui,*" she said. "*Yawohl. Da. Si.* You understand yes, Hank? Yes, yes, yes."

He grinned and she grinned in return. "I'm not too bright, I guess."

"Well," she said, "you can always learn."

"I'm a very fast learner," he replied earnestly. "When can I see you again? You'll be off somewhere and I'm going to be moving around with the company."

"I get days off and you will, too. The camp is only a few hours from here. Israel is not a very big country, you see, and if people want to meet it is not difficult to arrange it."

"All right!" Salisbury shouted, the gravelly voice slicing through the air. "This is a take!"

Hank went into action, calling for quiet. "Places, everybody! We're going to shoot some film."

Watching him, Rena made up her mind. This was the man, the first man. He was gentle and attractive and though there was no resemblance, he reminded her of her father, the same quiet firmness, promise of strength. And that boyish uncertainty was very appealing. A random thought surfaced and an amused gleam appeared in the black eyes. There was a good chance that she would have to lead him, teach him.

VI

"There!"

Mustafa Shihadeh pointed and Abdul followed the gesture. They had situated themselves just behind the crest of the dune, as they had been taught. In that way, they were assured of a maximum of cover and concealment, yet at the same time were provided with a good view of the surrounding terrain.

No more than one hundred yards to the front, beyond the pebbled wadi, in a gentle bowl of sand, the drilling rig was clearly visible, a great mechanical arm against the desert, thrusting its bit deeper into the earth in its insistent probe for water.

"Allah is good," Mustafa whispered. "Things are as the colonel said they would be." He looked over at the son of Mejjid al-Hadad, recognized the frozen features of that darkly handsome face as an expression of fear. "We are in

God's hands, oh, my dear, and what we do here today is sacred and fit. Do not be afraid."

"I am afraid," Abdul said, in a controlled voice. "But I am no coward. I will do what I was sent to do. The Jews must be punished, swept off the land." He turned his attention back to the drilling rig. He counted three men. Two were in deep conversation, huddled over what appeared to be a map. The other was working on the generator. "Will we wait for darkness?"

Mustafa shook his head. "The colonel said there were only three men and so there are. With darkness, they might get away. I think it is better that we kill them now and blow up the drill. Have you ever fired at a living target before, *habibi?*"

"I am an excellent marksman," Abdul replied.

Mustafa made a sound back in his throat. "Make certain your sights are set. I make the distance to be one hundred yards, no more."

Abdul resented being treated like a stupid child. He was a soldier now, trained, prepared for this moment, able to judge distance as well as Mustafa who was hardly older than he.

"It is a good rifle," Mustafa was saying. "The Americans make excellent equipment. Steady your hand and the rifle will do the rest."

"My hand is a rock."

"Of course, *habibi.* We will shoot the two Jews talking first. The one on the left is mine. The other yours. After they are dead, both of us will fire at the third man. Are you ready?"

Abdul was aware of the strange sensation deep in his bowels, an almost liquid oozing and he braced himself against it. More than anything, he must bring no shame upon himself or his father. What he did was just and his father would be proud to learn that he served in the case of the Arab nation, the Arab people. He squinted along the length of the rifle and in counterpoint his sphincter muscle contracted.

"I am ready," he murmured.

"Then we are in the hands of Allah. When I shoot you shoot and neither of us will stop shooting until all of them are dead."

The tension was almost unbearable and when Mustafa's shot cracked the stillness Abdul could not keep from flinching. His shot missed.

Mustafa had not missed and now he fired again. Below,

the two men were running toward their Land Rover, after their weapons, Abdul supposed. He sighted on one of the men and fired again. Again he missed. The Jews took refuge behind the car.

"Fool!" Mustafa cried. "If you had not missed, we would have killed them now. They have their guns now and we can do nothing more. Come. We will go back."

Abdul stayed where he was, staring down at the Land Rover, at the pumping rig. Without water, the Jews would not be able to settle and develop this Negev of theirs. To prevent them from finding that water was the work of men like himself. He rolled onto his back and pointed his rifle at the standing Mustafa.

"Come back," he said commandingly, "or I will kill you."

"Are you mad?"

"We are going to kill those two and destroy the drill."

"But how?"

"I will force them into the open and then we will kill them."

Mustafa sighed and spread out in a firing position, brought his rifle to bear.

"Prepare yourself," Abdul said, sighting on the petrol tank of the Land Rover.

"I am prepared, *habibi.*"

Abdul fired and there was a muffled explosion, a soft, rolling sound, then a sheet of flame.

The Jews went running for the rig, crouching. Mustafa shot and missed. Abdul, leading his target, fired. The Jew pitched forward, legs jerking. Automatically, Abdul searched for the last man, all his parts functioning by rote now. His bullet caught the Jew low in the back and he went sprawling, digging a rut in the hot sand.

Abdul stood up and motioned for Mustafa to follow. They went down to the rig, Mustafa carrying the dynamite. One of the Jews was still alive, moaning softly. "Finish him," Abdul said. "With your dagger. Bullets are precious. I will begin setting the explosives."

Mustafa did as he was told.

VII

"It's a mistake," Jim Tate said, concern etched on his round face.

"I didn't ask your opinion," Salisbury growled.

"Ira, it's Saturday. To go into the most religious section of Jerusalem on the Sabbath, you can't do that."

"The hell I can't! I got a picture to make. Saturday, Sunday, Monday, it makes no difference. We're behind schedule and I'm not about to let a bunch of fanatics tell me how to do things. I know all about that bullshit. When I was a kid, my old man had a Shabbath goy who came in on Friday nights to light the lights, or whatever my nutty father wouldn't do. He was a real bug on that crap. Well, not me, baby."

"But these people believe——"

"I don't care what they believe." He glanced down the line of cars, buses and equipment trucks, then climbed into the first car, Tate beside him. "Let's go," he barked to the driver.

"I still think this is a mistake, Ira," Tate persisted.

Salisbury whirled to face him, face mottled, jabbing a finger at the other man. "You know what's wrong with you, Tate? I'll tell you. Too much thinking. Yeh, you think too damned much. Now shut up and let me think."

The convoy rolled across Jaffa Road, the streets becoming progressively more ancient, then Yesha 'yahu Street, the houses here flimsy, showing their age. The tiny shops were closed, their grimy windows opaque. Boys in yarmulkes and knickers and girls in somber dresses and thigh-high woolen stockings hurled insults in Yiddish as the caravan went past.

"We can still turn back, Ira," Tate offered.

"Shut up!" Salisbury snapped. "Look at them," he said, with contempt in his voice. "Crumbs, all of them. The way they dress their kids, like it was always a funeral. And this lousy neighborhood. They don't want it to be better, different. They want this dirt, to live like slobs. No wonder Hitler wanted to kill them. What's this section called?"

"*Mea-She'arim*," Tate said. "One hundred gates."

153

"I didn't see even one gate. Not one. What a bunch of crumbs!"

They were about a quarter of a mile into Mea-She'arim when they stopped, beyond a narrow synagogue squeezed in between two buildings as if for support. Salisbury was in the street waving his arms and shouting orders even before the rest of the convoy had come to a halt.

Jim Tate climbed out of the limousine and leaned against the fender, smoking, watching Salisbury direct the crew as they set up the camera and sound equipment, placed lights and reflectors. A crowd was beginning to gather, the men, despite the heat of the day, wearing knee-length gabardine coats and broad-brimmed hats. Most of them were bearded and all wore earlocks. Their women, in long dresses and unadorned scarves on their heads, stood behind. There was an ominous quality to them and Tate wished he were somewhere else. Mara Gabrielli appeared out of the makeup trailer and he smiled wanly in her direction.

"A formidable crew," he said, indicating the onlookers.

The green eyes were unsteady. Tate realized that she was genuinely frightened, couldn't even look at the growing crowd. "We shouldn't have come."

"Why don't you tell Salisbury?" he said.

"I did. He doesn't listen."

He studied her with appreciation. She was a natural beauty, lush, exciting, and he didn't blame Salisbury. Not one little bit. At the producer's direction, he had re-written her part, enlarged it, so that now she played an important role in the picture.

He wondered if she really knew what she was doing, wondered if Amos Landau suspected what was happening. It was the same all over, ambitious girls using their beauty to earn their way. He tried to imagine her with Salisbury, with that gross body, that ugly face. His eyes flickered down to her tight round bottom. Lucky bastard.

"You think there may be trouble?" he said.

"These people, you can't imagine what they're like. There's a religious bloc in Israel, a political force far beyond their numbers. There are some moderates among them and there are the Agudists and zealots. Worst of all are the *Neturei Karta*."

"What does that mean?"

"Guardians of the City," she said. "They are dangerous. Fanatics who are disciplined and single-minded. Slaves of God is what some people call them."

154

"Can you tell which are which?"

"Only by what they do. See," she said worriedly. "There."

Tate saw a solid rank of black-clad men and boys, stretching across the width of the street, moving toward them. A tall man, with an imposing beard and a hawklike face, led the way.

"*Neturei Karta*," Mara said. "Look at them. They're worse than the Arabs. They reject Israel."

"They're Jews, aren't they?"

"Unfortunately, yes. They insist that Israel is a catastrophe for Jews, that only the Messiah can reestablish a Jewish Nation, that only He can rebuild the Temple and feed the righteous with the flesh of Leviathan. They actually consider our Independence Day to be a day of mourning. And they still recite the ancient lament of Passover— 'This year we are slaves. Next year we shall be free men.' "

"Will they make trouble?"

"I wish Amos was here. He would know what to do."

"We'd better warn Salisbury."

"It's too late."

The Neturei Karta spread themselves along the length of the convoy as the hawklike man took up a position to their front. He raised his long arms to the sky.

"Obscenities!" he cried in Yiddish. "To defame the holy day is to bear the cross to the altar. Go from this place. Leave us to our prayers."

Salisbury came rushing over to Mara. "Who the hell are these people? What do they want? Tell them to get out of here. Can't they see we're shooting?"

"They want us to leave the quarter, Ira," she said. "He says we are violating the Sabbath."

"Go!" the leader of the Guardians ordered in full throat, his voice an echo of another time. "Go or the vengeance of Jehovah shall descend upon your heads with a terrible fury."

"What!" Salisbury said. "What's he saying?"

"He's threatening us," Mara said. "He means it, Ira. These people are dangerous. We should leave."

"To hell with them! I've got a schedule. You think I'm going to let a bunch of religious nuts get in my way. You, McClintock! Move those clowns out of the way. Get a couple of the crew to give you a hand. And do it now. We got work to do."

The tall man, as if he had understood Salisbury, placed

155

himself between the producer and his camera, arms spread wide, eyes flashing. "You profane this day, heretic, and the Lord our God will curse you for it."

"Get the hell out of my way, old man," Salisbury stormed. He placed one of his oversized hands on the tall man's chest and shoved hard, sent him backwards, tripping, sprawling to the ground.

A deep resentful sound rose from his followers and some of them rushed forward to help their leader. Seconds later, head high, beard trembling, he roared out his fierce anger.

"Destroy them, oh, Lord! Drive them from our streets and our holy places. Give us the strength to do Your bidding, oh, Lord, to remove this filth from Your sight. Destroy them!"

The black line broke into a hundred angry clusters and at once the air was dark with rocks and vengeful cries. The film crew ducked for cover. One man was struck on the temple and went down in a heap. Another took a rock in the mouth. He spit teeth and blood. Jim Tate pulled Mara behind the limousine.

The street was alive with violent movement. Actors and crew scrambled for the safety of the buses and trucks. Drivers started their engines and the growl of grinding gears added to the din.

Suddenly, like shock troops held in reserve, a couple of hundred young boys rushed forward, hurling rocks at the bus windows at point-blank range. Glass shattered and went flying. One of the wardrobe women was cut and she began to scream.

A few of the boys worked their way in close to the equipment trucks and began pounding huge spikes into the tires. In a matter of seconds, eight of the heavy vehicles had settled onto their rims, unable to move.

A squad of boys launched themselves at the camera and it was toppled over with a great crash. When the crew moved in to right it, they were attacked by a swarm of black-clad men.

"Into the buses," Hank McClintock cried. "Come on! We're getting out of here!"

"No!" Salisbury raged, shoving Hank aside. "Stop the bastards! Fight back! Kill them! Kill them all!"

McClintock made up his mind. Moving swiftly, he slid behind the big producer, twisting his right arm behind his back, the wrist bent, applying pressure, forcing him into the nearest bus. "Mr. Salisbury," he grunted, struggling, "you don't understand. We could all get killed. Let's get out of here!" he shouted to the driver.

"No!" Salisbury raged. "The equipment. They'll ruin everything——"

"Hit the road!" McClintock ordered.

The bus began to roll, people hiding under the seats against the rocks of the righteous.

VIII

Summer in the city of Gaza was a yellow whiteness; life proceeded at a deliberate pace. Abdul al-Hadad, straight and tall in the uniform of a lieutenant of the Palestine Liberation Army, was grateful to get out of the sun, even for a brief interlude. He blinked and tried to accustom himself to the dimness of the interior of the house. Ibrahim Hafez, himself, had admitted him. Hafez, who, it was said among the refugees in Gaza, would be one of their leaders when the return to Palestine began.

Ibrahim, a short, round man in flowing black robes and a white kaffiyeh, led Abdul into his study, a modest room with hundreds of books on shelves along the walls. It was also said of Hafez that he had been a professor at the university in Beirut for many years. A man was seated and as they entered he rose, inclining his head.

"This is Mamoud Ayyash," Hafez said.

"Salaam aleikum," Abdul said, bowing.

"Salaam aleikum."

Hafez invited them to sit in the great brown leather chairs that faced each other across a small table which was inlaid with ivory. He rang a bell. A servant brought tiny cups of bitter coffee and a platter of sweet baklava pastry.

"Though we have never met," Mamoud Ayyash said, "I am a friend to your blessed father. He will be honored to discover that you are an officer in the service of the Arab nation."

"You have seen my father?" Abdul said, concealing his anxiety. "He is well?"

"He is well but confused. He is unable to realize that preparations are under way for Palestinians to go back to

157

their homes and claim what is rightfully their own. Unhappily Mejjid al-Hadad fails to understand where his duty lies in all this."

Abdul glanced quickly from one man to the other. What did they wish of him? The company of such men, older and wiser men, authorities, made him nervous. "I will write to my beloved father and encourage him, tell him that our destiny requires his aid." There, he assured himself. That is what they wanted to hear.

Ayyash smiled coldly. "You are aware of what occurs in Egypt, *habibi?*"

The familiarity, intended to put Abdul more at ease, distressed him instead. Flushing, he tried to pick out the desired answer.

"I am aware that Farouk has surrendered his throne and fled, that all Arabs are better off without that fat obscenity." A despairing chill seeped along his spine. Perhaps Farouk had returned, reclaimed his throne, held power once again. Such extreme language would not be forgotten or overlooked. He shuddered. He glanced covertly at Ibrahim Hafez. He sat easily, a pleased crescent on his mouth. Ayyash seemed unconcerned, picking casually at the baklava.

"You know who Mohammed Naguib is," Ayyash said absently, "what has occurred?"

Abdul hesitated.

Hafez shifted uneasily. He had boasted of Abdul's intelligence and reliability. Surely the boy understood that he was being tested, that his response was a reflection upon them both.

"Speak," Hafez muttered.

"Mafeesh," Abdul said, appalled by his own ignorance. ".Nothing, nothing."

Hafez reached for another slice of baklava.

"Naguib," Ayyash said, with patience, "is a general. With the assistance of a group of young, courageous officers, he took command of the country."

"Yes, yes. I remember now," Abdul said quickly, anxious to repair any damage committed. "Soldiers possess an efficiency about such matters."

"There is more," Ayyash said.

Abdul felt as if he had been tricked. He lowered his eyes, determined to speak very carefully.

"Gamal Abdel Nasser was a member of this group, a young officer who distinguished himself in the war against the Jews. Nasser could see that Naguib was too old, too

158

weak, too indecisive to accomplish what was required and so he assumed leadership."

"I understand," Abdul said, not certain that he did.

"Gamal Nasser will reclaim all the glory of the Arabs." There was a rising tone of joy in Ayyash's voice. "He will forge Arabs from one end of the Fertile Crescent to the other into a single and powerful nation. Once again we shall assume our rightful position in the world. A handful of Jews will be as nothing before our wrath and they will be drowned in the flood of Arab nationalism. No longer will we allow ourselves to be used as pawns by the imperialists. We will take whatever we need from the foreigners and when the right moment comes we will push the Jews into the sea."

"El-ham dillah," Hafez intoned. "God is merciful."

Abdul echoed the words.

Ayyash went on. "Gamal Nasser asks every Arab everywhere to enlist in this holy cause."

Guilt rose into Abdul's throat and tasted of poison. "I myself, effendi, fight Jews at every chance. I have destroyed the tractors of their farmers and their water drills. I have mined roads and blown up trucks—"

"And," Hafez put in enthusiastically, "he killed the engineer at an electric power station and he led the ambush of a convoy in which two Jews were killed and others wounded——"

Ayyash broke in. "It is your father I am concerned with, Abdul. He could be valuable to our purpose but he is a stubborn man and will not see matters in their true light. He resists all arguments." He stared at Abdul until the youth averted his face. "It is the wish of Gamal Abdel Nasser that you return to Jerusalem and speak to your father, convince him where his duty lies—"

"Gamal Nasser wants this?" Abdul said.

"I am his faithful agent. The thoughts of my head and the words of my mouth are *his*. As he thinks, I think. As he desires, I desire. As he would act, I act."

Abdul wet his lips. "I will go to my father, effendi, and inform him of the great events in Cairo, the even greater moments that wait just ahead. But I am only the son and it is not often that he hears my words with favor."

"Say that it is God's will that he take his place in the ranks of the true believers in the Prophet. Say that the work he could perform among the Jews may one day save the life of his oldest son, and the Arab sons of other Arab fathers. Say these things and say too that I, Mamoud

Ayyash, will presently visit him again with instructions from the Tiger of Faluga."

"God give me strength to accomplish His purpose," Abdul said.

"It is ordained," Hafez said, reaching for another slice of baklava. *In sha'Allah.*"

IX

Hank McClintock told Rena about the assault of the Guardians of the City. She sputtered, trying not to laugh.

"Didn't anyone warn Salisbury?" she burst out. "Israel practically closes down from Friday sundown to Saturday night."

"I always thought you Israelis weren't particularly religious."

"We're not. But the Orthodox exert a lot of power. They've all collected in the Mizrachi Party and no Government can even hope to govern without their support."

She leaned back on her elbows and gazed across the desert. He had come to the training camp to visit and she had managed to get away for the evening, to borrow a jeep. They had driven deep into the Negev, deposited the jeep in a wadi, and climbed to the apex of this great dune. The moon reflected off the rolling terrain, a yellow streak broken only by an occasional castus outcropping.

"Anyway, we got out of the religious quarter and no one was seriously injured."

"Salisbury must have been furious."

"That hardly says it. He was insane with anger, storming at everyone. He raged at Jim Tate and the production manager. I practically saved his life and he was sore at me anyway."

"He is a fool. You did what was right," she said protectively. "He'd have known better if he was Jewish."

"That's the whole point, he is Jewish. We were all up in his suite at the King David when the damage report came in, more than one hundred thousand dollars worth. Plus the time lost. He went sky high. All of a sudden, he snatched up the telephone and put a call through to the Prime Minister."

"Oh, no," she began to giggle.

"The amazing thing is that he got to him. Oh, it took a little while but the Prime Minister came on the wire. You should have heard that conversation, at least Salisbury's end of it. 'What kind of a crazy country are you running?' he screamed. 'It isn't safe for people to walk the streets. The Arabs should've won.'

"I suppose the Prime Minister tried to calm him down but it didn't do much good. He began to yell again. 'I spend millions of dollars to help your economy and you let this happen.'

"I suppose the Prime Minister tried to explain things but Salisbury kept interrupting. I could almost hear the Prime Minister saying, 'Now, look, Ira, baby, you shouldn't've gone into Mea She'arim on Saturday. You're a Jew and you should know better.'

"Well, Salisbury turned green, actually. He began to sputter and he shouted into the phone—'It's men like you make me ashamed I'm Jewish!' "

"To the Prime Minister!" Rena managed to get out. Her head came up and there was a short exhalation, a giggle, an inflated tide of uncontrollable laughter. She fell back on the sand, clutching her middle, gasping for breath, unable to stop. At last she lay still, spent, looking up at him, giggling again.

He leaned forward and peered into her face. In the soft light he was able to see the still lingering chubbiness in her cheeks. Soon that would disappear and the lean jawline and wide cheekbones would provide a more womanly line. Her deep dark eyes gleamed and a small sigh seeped across her lips.

He said her name and felt her hand come up, touch his shoulder. He sat up and looked away. What an incredible idiot he was! Alone with this lovely girl in the midst of nowhere, his innards knotted with emotion, yearning to tell her how he felt, and unable to speak. He might as well have been a kid on his first date.

She gazed at him, in profile against the moon. He puzzled her, so unlike the Israeli boys she had known. They were different, aggressive, sometimes to the point of arrogance, insisting on the use of her flesh as if a right. She had held them off, all those young men, but not forever, she told herself wryly. Her own desire and curiosity intensified steadily. There was something about men, the hardness of their arms and shoulders, the insistence of

161

their hands. And the rich masculine sound of them found a responsive visceral chord in her.

If only they were not such insensitive bulls, jabbing at her, allowing no time for her to become accustomed to them, for trust to take hold. They tended to dissolve in her memory, one into the other, and she craved a singular man.

This one. This bony American with his pale, open face, and his direct manner, without guile. That shyness appealed to her and she had considered him often since that first weekend, imagined what it would be like with him. A disturbing thought took hold of her. What if he didn't want her at all? She shivered.

"You're cold," he said. "We should go back."

Still, she reminded herself, he had come all the way from Jerusalem for only this evening, had to make the return trip before morning.

"I don't want to go back," she said. She sat up. "Are you afraid of me, Hank?"

"Afraid of *you!* Heck, no. Why should I be? Well, a little, maybe. You're so damned beautiful."

The corners of her mouth turned up happily. "You think so? You really think so? I don't, you see. I mean, it's a pleasant enough face but not beautiful. Mara is beautiful. And that Maggie Whalen. That's what convinced me not to become an actress, seeing how pretty she is." She hesitated. "Are you friendly with Maggie Whalen?"

"Oh, we talk once in a while."

"Oh. Have you ever been alone with her?"

"What do you mean? A couple of times, I guess."

"And?"

"And nothing."

"You never made love to her?"

He stared at her. There was this about Rena, this directness. So many of the young Israelis were that way. He wasn't sure that he liked it, or could ever get used to it.

"You ask the damnedest questions, Rena."

"Well, did you?"

"No," he answered aggressively.

She leaned back on her elbows and appraised him.

Uneasiness crackled along his nerves and he felt compelled to speak, to fill the void. "What other crazy things are you going to ask?"

"Have you had many women?" The words barely came out, smothered behind her teeth.

162

Resentment began to build in him and he grew defensive, as if under attack. "Now, look here, Rena, you have no right to do this—"

"I just want to know."

"What difference does it make?"

"It's important," she murmured, lowering herself onto the slope of the dune, the sand crunching in the stillness, "that one of us knows what to do. You see?"

"What—?"

"I've never been with a man before—"

He was glad it was dark and she was unable to see the flush that colored his cheeks. His brain turned ponderously and time spent itself with excruciating slowness as he turned to her, seeking her mouth, saying her name in gratitude and wonder.

They saw each other as often as possible after that, keeping to themselves, hoarding each available moment. They explored each other, body and mind, probing, experimenting, risking exposure and hurt, afraid only of missing something tender and valuable. They spoke mostly in Hebrew, because he wanted to learn the language, but she despaired of his flat accent ever improving.

"It would be easier if I were Jewish," he said. "I guess I'll never learn."

"You'll learn."

He frowned and looked out at the Mediterranean, at the orange western sky as dark came on. They had driven to the coast, not swimming, simply basking in the warm November sun. Now they huddled together, a blanket draped across their shoulders against the evening chill.

"Does it bother you, Rena, that I'm not Jewish?"

"Does it bother you that I am?"

"What kind of a person do you think I am!" he said quickly.

Her laugh was full. "You Gentiles are so defensive."

Aware that she was teasing, he ducked his head, lifted the back of her hand to his mouth.

"Rena, I love you."

It was the first time he had said it.

"I love you, too."

He kissed her with a gentle concern as if afraid to bruise her. She thrust herself at him and he went over backwards, Rena arranging herself along the length of his body.

"There," she said at last. "You see what you have made

of me, a shameless lady with an extremely passionate nature."

"Marry me, please."

She sat up and turned away, struggling to keep her voice steady, casual. "Of course not, Hank. That would be absurd."

"I'll make you happy, Rena."

"You'll be going away."

"You could come with me."

Her head swung from side to side stubbornly. "I couldn't leave Israel. I don't want to." Her head swiveled around with the abruptness of discovery. "You're leaving soon?"

He nodded. "Salisbury decided it would be cheaper to shoot the rest of the picture at the studio. It's mostly interiors anyway. We're way behind schedule and the money people have been on his back."

"Well," she said, with forced brightness.

"Come with me, Rena. Marry me."

"I meant what I said, about not leaving here. Let's enjoy the time we have left."

An idea surfaced. For some time he had given it considerable thought, approved of it finally as the sensible, practical answer to the problem.

"What," he said cautiously, "if I were a Jew? Would you marry me then?"

"That doesn't matter."

"I'll convert," he said firmly. "It can't be so difficult. I'll find a rabbi who'll give me instruction, a condensed course."

She laughed, but without mirth. "You make it sound like language study at Berlitz."

"I mean it, Rena."

"I know," she said distantly, then: "It isn't that easy. Jews don't proselytize. Most rabbis discourage would-be converts. And you'd have to be circumcised." He grimaced and she laughed and he laughed with her. "You wouldn't want to take chances with your beautiful thing." He reached for her and she avoided his arms. "You better forget all about it. When are you leaving?"

There was an emotional glut in his throat. He wanted to jar her, to make her accept him, to insist that she come with him. But he didn't dare, afraid of making her angry, of losing her.

"Wednesday," he managed to say.

"So soon?"

He cleared his throat and spoke hurriedly. "Salisbury, Longstreet and Whalen, the leading players, are going first. They want a chance to get settled at home before shooting starts up again. I'm going straight through to the studio with Jim Tate and Miss Gabrielli——"

"Mara! She's going too?"

"I thought you knew. Salisbury signed her to a long-term contract. A personal contract. She belongs to him now and he says he's going to make her a big star. That's a personal matter," he ended, chuckling.

"What does that mean?" Rena said, baffled and full of resentment. "You Americans, all alike, thinking anyone can be bought. Mara is my friend——"

"Hey!" he protested, taking her arms.

She twisted away. "I don't like the insinuation. A dirty mind sees dirty things."

"Wait a minute! *She's going with him.* That's no insinuation. That's a *fact.* What's between them, it's been going on almost from the first day of shooting. Everybody in the company knows it. And it was at least as much her doing as it was Salisbury's. She went after him, after this deal, and she got it. Don't blame me."

Rena made no answer. She was thinking about her father. She knew that Amos needed Mara, had been unable to turn away from her even as Ruth had been unable to let him go. Now this. He would suffer pain and she feared he would be somehow altered for the loss, lose some precious human element in himself.

"Please, Rena, let's not fight."

Her head came around. "What?" All the resentment had drained away.

"It will be three or four months before I can come back." He hesitated. "We'll be married then."

Her smile was wistful and brief. "Your home is in America. You'll become a very successful movie producer. But not like Ira Salisbury, please."

"I love you, Rena, and I'm coming back here to live, to marry you. If you want me to I'll wear a long black coat and grow my sideburns."

He meant it now but everything would be different when thousands of miles separated them. Life in America, in Hollywood, would be simpler and easier, safer. Some pretty actress would discover him and he would never escape.

"I love you, Hank," she murmured.

"We'll be married as soon as I get back."

He kissed her and after a moment she allowed her lips to go soft and part and she drew him back down on the sand. She tried desperately not to think; but one idea persisted, leaping crazily along the convolutions of her brain—she was never going to see him again.

X

The soldiers, three of them, were young and charged with excitement, anxious to find a quiet place to be with the girls. The waterfront had been a fine idea, an absence of people, the assurance of dark privacy. Half-running, laughing, the girls hanging back, but not too much, they turned the corner, plunged into the narrow street. Ahead of them, less than thirty feet away, the rise and fall of clubs, the crunch of a boot against flesh, the thick curses.

One of the girls screamed, "They're killing a man!"

The soldiers hesitated only briefly before charging forward, shouting. The men with the clubs turned and ran.

The six young people stood in awe of the still body, at blood glistening in hair.

"Is he dead?" one of the girls said.

One of the soldiers knelt and touched Yaakov. "We better get help."

Yaakov's eyes fluttered open and gradually focused.

The kneeling soldier spoke to one of his friends. "Find a policeman."

"To hell with that," Yaakov muttered angrily. "Get me on my feet and into a taxi."

"But, man," the soldier protested. "You're hurt bad—"

Yaakov forced himself into a sitting position, setting himself against the pain stabbing along his shoulder and into his chest. "You heard me," he husked out. "A taxi. I have a friend. He'll take care of me."

Lahav said nothing when he opened his front door and saw Yaakov teetering there. He brought him into his study. Yaakov stretched out on the floor, insisting the hard surface made the pain easier to bear.

Lahav phoned his personal physician. When he hung up, he looked down at Yaakov. "What happened?"

"Effrati. My own fault. I wasn't thinking. Listen, *adoni*. You have some brandy for me?"

"I don't know——"

"But I know," Yaakov burst out hotly.

"Ah," Lahav said, going after the brandy. "I am reassured. There is still too much meanness in you to die."

The doctor kept shaking his head in disbelief. "You took an awful beating," he repeated. "You're lucky they didn't fracture your skull. As it is, you have a concussion, I'm sure. You must rest. And your collarbone is fractured."

"You can set it." Yaakov spoke between gritted teeth, the pain acute. It took all his remaining strength to keep from fainting. "Does it require a cast?"

"I will set the bone and immobilize it, strap your arm down. But you must rest. A week, at least."

"Set the bone, then," Yaakov said. "I have to get some sleep. In the morning, there's work to do."

"Nonsense," the doctor said. "Your body will be nothing but aches and pains tomorrow. You won't be able to move."

"I'll move," Yaakov said grimly.

The doctor began to manipulate the broken collarbone. The pain was worse than Yaakov anticipated but he made no sound. Beads of sweat appeared suddenly on his upper lip. The bone in place, the doctor began to strap the arm.

"I'll give you something for the pain."

"Nothing," Yaakov said. "I have to be able to think."

"You're stubborn and brave," the doctor said, "and I'm not sure that's a good combination."

"Bull-headed," Lahav put in.

Yaakov made no comment. He wanted to conserve his remaining strength.

He slept intermittently, waking finally just before daylight. The pain in his shoulder was a steady throb. His ribs were raw and dislocated and his skull felt as if it had been softened and depressed. He eased himself out of bed and struggled into his clothes.

When he came downstairs, Lahav was waiting. He fastened the buttons of Yaakov's shirt. "I'll make some breakfast."

"Tea only."

"You need strength."

"Are you my mother?"

Lahav grunted and made the tea. "Your Yugoslavs are here," he said. "At my office. Some of my own boys will go along. Don't argue. You're in no shape for trouble and if there are enough of you maybe——" He let it end there, aware of the futility of even hoping for a peaceful settlement.

Yaakov drained the cup and stood up.

"I'll drive down with you," Lahav said.

"Stay out of this. You're too big in Histadrut. Me, I'm only a small fry."

Lahav headed for the door. "Come on, let's go."

The Yugoslavs stood in small groups outside the low headquarters building. A murmur of greeting went up as he got out of Lahav's car, changing to concern at the sight of his battered face, his immobilized arm.

"What has happened to you, *adoni?*" It was Rudolph, head set low between his great round shoulders, face bunched with concern, who spoke in flawed Hebrew. Rudolph, his driver the night he had killed Mori outside of Dubrovnik.

"Shalom," Yaakov said. "I have been beaten, as you can see. It was meant to kill me but I am not killed so easily."

"We will avenge you, *adoni*," Rudolph said seriously.

"I called you here to help me. I wish to repair the damage already done, not to create more." His eyes raked over the faces of the Yugoslavs, solemn, set and determined. Behind them, he saw Agron, a huddle of union men at his back. "All of you," Yaakov emphasized, "must obey my orders, no matter what they are. We wish to avoid violence, if possible."

"And if it is not possible?" Rudolph said.

Yaakov jerked his good fist up toward his bandaged left shoulder. "Do not let this happen to any of you."

"Are we to have weapons?" one of the Yugoslavs asked.

"Since when do men with strong hands need weapons?" Yaakov shot back. A taunting grin slanted across his scarred mouth. "Have you grown so soft on our easy Israeli living?"

That evoked a round of derisive laughter.

Yaakov swung around to Lahav. "Which ship is Effrati on?"

"The *Ayelet Hashachar.*"

"Then we begin with the *Ayelet Hashachar*. Give us a five minute start, then send the crew along."

"Good luck," Lahav said.

Yaakov made no answer as he strode down the hill toward the waterfront.

The *Ayelet Hashachar* was a freighter of some 8,000 tons. Destination: Marseilles. Cargo: citrus fruit. As Yaakov marched out onto the pier, he could see a line of pickets shuffling in a circle in front of the ship's gangway. There were thirty of them, each man armed with a length of pipe or a club. Seeing Yaakov and his small army, the pickets formed two lines, blocking the way.

Yaakov stopped twenty feet away from the strikers. Above, peering over the rail, he spotted more men, another thirty, perhaps, or more. And Effrati. And higher, on the bridge, the ship's officers, who had remained aboard during all this. Yaakov took a step forward and smiled agreeably.

"Good morning, chaverim. I see you are prepared to welcome my friends and myself. And I am sure it will be a very competent greeting. Some of you have already paid their respects to me. Last night, five of you, with clubs, against me alone. A brave act, the act of men not prepared to put their convictions to an open test." His eyes worked over them, naked and narrow, searching. "Are any of the five here now? One by one, I would be pleased to meet them, one good arm against two and a piece of pipe." No one moved. "Ah," Yaakov bit off. "They are shy. Well, it is to be expected, in daylight.

"I represent Histadrut," he said matter-of-factly. "And the Government. It is my job to get this ship, and all the others, back to sea. It will be done. Should you turn us back, kill us all—and killing will be necessary in order to turn us away—even then it will be done. Tomorrow someone else will be back and the day after that, more of them, and armed, if necessary."

"Don't listen! He is trying to scare you!"

It was Effrati, standing at the top of the gangway, face distorted, shaking his fist.

"We cannot be moved if we will not be moved. All of Israel is behind us. Our cause is just."

"What is *your* cause, Effrati? It is not the cause of these men."

"Stand fast!"

"Effrati's cause," Yaakov ripped out loudly. "I will tell you about his cause. It is the cause of Professor Bohorov, whose cause is the cause of Moscow."

"Liar! All lies!" Effrati screamed. "Throw them back!"

"I say this is no labor dispute. If you have grievances,

169

and I believe you do have, then submit them to the worker's council. It is your council. Why reject collective bargaining? Why reject, as Effrati has done, all the machinery established to get for you what you are entitled to? I will tell you the answers. Because Effrati is not concerned with bettering your conditions, with enriching your lives. He wants only to slice away the power of the union, your union, to destroy it, and ultimately to overthrow the Government. To what end? I put the question to you, Effrati! What are you after?"

"Don't listen to him! He is a representative of the company. All your words change nothing. We are not slaves and we will not be tricked by any Jewish Nazis. Drive them off the docks. Destroy them."

"He means kill us," Yaakov said to the strikers facing him. "And I don't think you want to do that." He glanced up at Effrati. "Effrati is not worthy of you," he said. "You are men and he is a coward, good only in the shadows, concealing the truth about himself. Look at me now, only half a man, but more than he dares to face. I will show you."

He moved forward. He saw the grim, sullen expressions on the faces of the strikers blocking his way. He kept advancing and gradually, reluctantly, they gave ground, allowed him to reach the gangway. He moved up the incline with a confidence he did not feel.

"Get back!" Effrati shouted. "Get back or I'll kill you!" His hand rose holding a two-foot length of pipe.

Yaakov kept coming and Effrati retreated onto the deck shouting threats. "Get him!" he cried to the men along the rail. "Kill him. Throw him over the side."

Yaakov came on. Effrati pulled away, keeping the space between them constant.

At once Effrati planted one leg, hurled the pipe at Yaakov. It went tumbling past his injured shoulder. He never flinched, came on without pause. Effrati tried to get away, backed into a bulkhead. Yaakov stepped forward, right fist cocked. Effrati cowered. A small sound fading on his lips, he made no move to defend himself. Yaakov let his arm fall.

"Get off this ship," he said, "or I will have you thrown off."

Effrati hesitated, then hurried across the deck and down the gangway. "The rest of you," Yaakov said softly. He watched them file away, then moved to the rail. The crew for the *Ayelet Hashachar* were waiting on the far side of the dock. He waved to them. "Come aboard! There's a ship to get under way."

Within the next few hours, seven ships were cleared of strikers and crews brought aboard. The strike was over.

That night Yaakov sipped his second gin and bitters in Lahav's garden. A deep weariness held his flesh in thrall and he knew it would be with him for a long time.

"This was a rotten business, Lahav. It won't be forgotten for a long time."

"It had to be done."

"But why by me? I am sick of this kind of affair. Let some of the younger ones get beaten for a change. Let them crack heads."

"You think there are any Yeshivats among the younger ones?"

"Not likely. They are soft and indulgent, citybred—" He broke off and shook his head sheepishly. "I must be getting old, such talk. Some of the young ones, they're all right. Hard as they have to be and willing to take risks. The kibbutzniks and Nahal. They'll do." He finished the drink. "What about the docks, Lahav? Those men have legitimate complaints."

"Yes. I intend to schedule an election so that the seamen's union can choose a new leader. Tomorrow I shall go before the worker's council. They must act now, do what should have been done long ago, eliminate the conditions that make this kind of thing possible.

"Once we win a good agreement, and we will, the sailors will understand that Effrati and Bohorov were never truly concerned about them. That Histadrut is. I want to force Bohorov out into the open, get him to admit that he is a Communist, let our people see who he really serves."

"Can you do it?"

"I *will* do it. Enough. You did your work and very well. The rest is my problem." His right hand sliced air in short, choppy strokes. "It looks to me as if you're a man who can use a holiday."

"A day or two to rest. That's all."

"A month. I've changed my mind. You're not going to America."

"The Americans will be very impressed with my bad shoulder. I will tell them it was the work of a crazed Arab. That should be good for a million dollars more in pledges."

"No," Lahav said sternly. "You must regain your

171

strength and good health. You must go somewhere pleasant and restful. Ah, I have it. Monaco. A good idea. Plenty of beautiful women and you can play the tables. You like to gamble."

Yaakov cocked his head. "My nose tells me there is something fishy here."

Lahav's expression never changed. "There is a man in Monaco. Seek him out. His name is Bristol, Harvey Bristol. An American, I believe. He knows everyone there and will introduce you around, show you a good time."

"Lahav—?"

"It is rumored that he sells armaments of all sorts. Perhaps he will have some modern tanks for sale, some jet planes, whatever seems necessary. . . ."

FOUR

Yaakov Yeshivat

I

He never knew his mother. There were stories, pleasant recollections, of a black-haired pretty woman, slender and delicate, with great dark eyes in a pale face. A woman who loved him very much but was unable to survive the hard early years in Palestine.

As a child, he hadn't understood death, had seen it as some enigmatic adult exercise to explain an absence. One thing he did know—there was no soft female to hold him and kiss him, no mother to soothe his hurts and fondle him. His resentment of this lack took hold and grew sharper. He hated her for going, and hated her for not taking him along.

His father was always there. A highly visible man, Aaron Yeshivat had the hands and shoulders of a worker, thick, veined, powerful. And he had acquired a variety of skills—carpentry, farming, building. He had the knack of confronting a problem, seeing through it. An intuitive theorist, he was able to transfer what he had learned from one area to another. He had come to Palestine in 1902, when he was forty-five, from the shtetl, one of those small Jewish villages in the Pale of Settlement in Poland, along with his young wife.

For him, the Holy Land had been a place to go to in order to escape the anti-Jewish outbreaks of Europe, a place to live and work in peace. To raise a family. But now new and provocative information came to his attention and set his imagination on fire. Someone gave him a copy of the brochure, *Der Judenstaat*. Written by a Jewish journalist, Theodore Herzl, it called for a Jewish State in Palestine. It was a startling concept and Yeshivat tried to imagine the Jews he had known with a country of their own, self-governing, independent, doing all the things a nationalist people did to survive. Though at first it seemed like an impossible dream, in time he decided that Herzl's scheme was not without merit.

In those early days, Yeshivat lived with his wife in a

tiny hut in Jaffa. He worked long hours for small wages for an Arab merchant, from whom he learned the language.

Two years after Yeshivat's arrival in Palestine, Yaakov was born. Yeshivat's wife lost a lot of blood and suffered considerable pain from the breach birth. Months after the child was born, she was still pale and weak, barely able to take care of the infant.

It didn't matter to Yaakov. He grew larger and steadily stronger, seeming to thrive on the very air he breathed.

One evening, after work, after preparing supper for himself and his wife, after feeding and bathing his young son and putting him to bed, Yeshivat went to the small Orthodox synagogue near the Arab market. He went not to pray, but to listen and hear a man whose reputation had been spreading among the Jewish community during the last few weeks.

Aaron David Gordon generated a special kind of excitement. He owned a mercurial quality that drew men to him and left them deeply affected. A native of Russia, where he had been steward on the estate of Baron Horace Günzburg, Gordon had been irresistibly attracted to Palestine, arriving finally when he was forty-eight years old.

He was a man gripped by a single, compelling idea, taking nourishment from it—to reclaim the Jewish people, to transform them from a downtrodden, enervated race into a vital and creative force. To this end, it was imperative, he declared with a ringing certainty, that men alter the very substance of their beings. No abstraction, no philosophy, no matter how benevolent, would accomplish that; not Zionism, not socialism.

"It is in the flesh and blood of men, in their personal emotions and sensibilities," he lectured, "that the beginnings of nationhood will be born."

Listening carefully, Yeshivat became aware of a new excitement, a new sense of anticipation. He stood up.

"How," he said, speaking in Yiddish, "are we to do this thing? So many of our people exist only in cities, behind walls, laboring in small shops, pale and fearful for their lives."

"Exactly!" Gordon replied. "We Jews have allowed ourselves to become divorced from nature, from the soil, huddling behind walls real and fancied for 2,000 years, learning to accept indignity and insult, as the world saw fit to deliver."

"And how much there has been!" a voice cried.

Laughter rippled through the synagogue, faded quickly.

Yeshivat, his lean, heavy-boned face intense, curled forward as if pleading for guidance.

"What must be done?"

Gordon held a clenched fist aloft. "Work," he snapped off. "Work will heal us. Work will transform us into a natural people. Work is the core of our hope and our ambition."

"I am a silversmith," someone said. "Is that not——?"

Gordon quieted the man with a gesture. "Till the soil. Let your own sweat fertilize the earth, then it will become yours. Only then will you become the people of the land. Only then will we change ourselves, become different than the Jews of the Diaspora. Work will bring us everything we want."

Yeshivat returned to the small house in Jaffa that night, anxious to tell his wife about Gordon, about what he had decided to do. When he arrived he found her in bed, running a fever, barely able to speak. A physician was summoned. He said she had pneumonia. Given her weakened condition, he offered little hope for survival. Two days later she obliged him by dying.

Less than a month later, Yeshivat went to work on a farm owned by an Arab who made his home in Damascus. The lands were under the suspicious eye of his foreman, a German-Jew by the name of Stein. Stein, a powerfully constructed man who ruled by intimidation and fear, soon singled Yeshivat out for special attention.

"Poles are not good for much," Stein would announce, within hearing of the new man. "Beasts of the field with strong backs and few brains. And slackers. Every one of them. But not in my fields. In my fields, everyone does his share or he is out."

Yeshivat did his best to ignore Stein, to close him out of mind, to concentrate on work, to be aware of his muscles reaching and flexing, to appreciate the feel of good clean dirt against his skin. Each day he went into the fields with his hoe and his water jar. He broke up the lumpy soil and pulled weeds. At first, blisters formed on his hands and when they broke there was bleeding, pain reaching into his wrists. He made no complaint, wrapping rags around each hand, continuing to work.

At night he would return to Jaffa, reclaim Yaakov from the Arab woman who tended him during the daylight hours, feed the boy and put him to bed. Often Yeshivat fell asleep without having any dinner, too tired to eat. But each morning he was back in the fields, hoeing, yanking, enduring Stein's sneers and insults.

After a while, Yeshivat realized that whenever there were easier jobs to do, planting or watering, Stein made sure they went to the Arab workers. He asked a fellow worker, a man named Navorsky, about it.

"So you noticed?" Navorsky said bitterly, head down, pulling weeds. "Stein hates us."

"But we are Jews, too."

"Stein," Navorsky muttered dryly, "has noticed *that*. But we are only workers and not worthy of him. To work with your hands, your body, that is demeaning, to us, to all Jews, and so to Stein. He hates us."

Later that afternoon, one of the Jewish workers fainted under the hot sun. Stein waited until the man had been revived, then prodded him roughly with his boot.

"Get back to work, you lazy bastard! There will be no malingering here."

The man, too weak to stand, fell back to the ground. Without hesitation, Stein swung his right leg and delivered a brutal blow to the man's hip. He groaned and tried to roll away.

"Get up, damn you! You're being paid to work."

Swearing, Yeshivat started forward, clutching his hoe threateningly. Navorsky grabbed his arm.

"Stein wants one of us to attack him. He enjoys beating people."

"I am not afraid."

"You must understand, he is a bull. Afraid or not afraid is irrelevant. Have you fought much with your hands?"

"No."

"Ah! Stein sent one man to the hospital for three months. You must be careful."

Yeshivat looked at the man Stein had kicked. He had struggled to his feet and was scratching earnestly at the soil. Stein watched him with the smug look of the triumphant on his face.

Yeshivat struck at the earth with his hoe. "It isn't right, to work for a man like Stein for a few coins a month, to be treated as a beast of burden."

"To Stein, that is what we are." Navorsky glanced up cautiously. "Men like us, we have no choice."

"There must be a choice. I will work harder, earn more money, discover new ways of earning more. I will save my money and buy my own land."

Navorsky nodded knowingly. "Others have said the same thing. It is impossible to make enough money."

Yeshivat straightened up. He had heard of Jewish settlements—Rishon l'Zion, Rosh Pinah, Yessod Ha'Maala, and more. On them, men farmed and profited justly from their labor. How had they accomplished it? He put the question to Navorsky.

"Rothschild."

"He gives men money for such things? What has to be done? Where will I find him?"

Navorsky laughed bitterly. "Rothschild is in London." He saw the disappointment on Yeshivat's face. "There are others, rich Jews who support farming settlements."

Yeshivat reached for Navorsky's arm. "Who?" he said, with compelling force. "The names? Where will I find them?"

Navorsky wrenched his arm away. "Ox!" he burst out. "You hurt me." He rubbed his arm. "There is Gutman, who represents an English company in Jerusalem."

"I'll go to him."

A cunning glint appeared in Navorsky's eyes. "Gutman is one of those Jews who believes the Messiah has already come."

"Then he is not a Jew."

Navorsky shrugged. "He will insist that you believe as he believes."

Yeshivat considered that. "I am not a pious man but I am a Jew."

Neither of them noticed Stein until he was standing alongside, face livid, big fists clenched. "You think this is a debating club!" he roared. "Back to work or I'll throw both of you off the land. Here you get paid only for what you do."

The two men obeyed without complaint. A swelling urgency filled Yeshivat and he could hardly contain himself. He waited until Stein had crossed to the far side of the field before speaking.

"If there is a Rothschild and a Gutman," he said, "surely there must be others who also have money and will help. Have you another name?"

Navorsky was on his knees weeding. "Abarbanel. A Sephardim and very rich."

"Where is he?"

"He won't give you money. He supports only groups, communities. You are alone."

"Where is he?"

179

"Why should he see you? You are nothing to him."

"Where is he?"

"He is a religious man and favors the Orthodox."

"Where?" Yeshivat said patiently.

Navorsky sighed and turned back to his weeding. "Jerusalem. But it will do you no good."

That week, Yeshivat broke the Sabbath and went to Jerusalem, slept overnight in a tool shed in back of a shop, and the next morning he went to see Abarbanel. At first the great man refused to hear him but Yeshivat persisted. Abarbanel listened finally, then turned down his plea. Yeshivat would not give in, would not leave, continuing to marshal arguments to support his request.

In the end he got what he came for. Abarbanel promised to advance a suitable sum of money, if Yeshivat could create a community of no less than a dozen families, including no fewer than twenty men past the age of eighteen. Yeshivat agreed to the terms.

Kfar Akiba, they named it. Four hundred dunams, roughly 100 acres, on the northeastern slopes of Mount Tabor in the lower Galilee. Led by Yeshivat, the settlers set about clearing the dry, rocky land. In those first days, they lived in tents and spent most of their time removing rocks and digging up roots. It was hard work but they were encouraged when Yeshivat informed them that the soil itself was reasonably rich and fertile.

"We will have good crops," he said, "and good lives. But we must earn both."

Once the fields were cleared, they began to plow the land. At the same time, a hauling detail was formed to bring water from the stream about three miles away. For this, six donkeys were used, each with two large water jugs strapped to his back, going back and forth continually. Water was their most precious commodity and they hoarded every drop, using as little as possible for personal needs, saving it for the unquenchable thirst of the land.

"Why don't we divert the stream?" Navorsky asked one day. "We could dig a new bed that would cause the water to flow directly into our fields."

Yeshivat had considered that and rejected it. He told them why. There was an Arab village five miles to the southeast and its inhabitants depended on the same stream for their water. "If we changed its course," Yeshivat explained, "that village would have no water."

"We cannot go on hauling water this way forever."

"I agree," Yeshivat said. "We are going to build a pipeline from the stream. That way we can drain off as much as we need without doing damage to the Arabs."

When Abarbanel's delegate, a dapper man in an English riding habit, visited Kfar Akiba to check on their progress, Yeshivat broached the subject of a pipeline to him.

"You can see, Frede, how such a project will insure our success. Naturally, we shall require additional money to buy the pipe, but that too will be repaid at the same interest rate as the remainder of the loan."

Frede focused on some point in middle-space. "Mr. Abarbanel has helped you to rent this land. As we agreed, it is your responsibility to develop it, make it pay. I cannot recommend any further loans to this community, at least until we see some positive results, some return on our investment."

"But without water we cannot guarantee a good crop."

"You are expected to meet the yearly payments on the due dates. If you fail, you will lose all right to the land, as is stipulated in the agreement." He gazed at them with slightly raised brows. "Perhaps had you not wasted valuable funds buying goats you would be able to purchase your pipe now."

"The goats give milk for the children," a woman protested.

"And six donkeys," Frede said, shaking his head.

"With no donkeys, there would be no water at all," Yeshivat said, fighting to control his mounting anger.

"I can only wish you good luck," Frede said, "until next time I return."

That night all the members of the settlement gathered in front of Yeshivat's tent. A mood of despair gripped them and there were some who were ready to give up, Navorsky among them.

"If we had a hundred donkeys," he complained, "we still would not be able to carry enough water to properly irrigate. We might as well leave now."

"Then leave!" Yeshivat roared, his voice expanding and echoing in the night. "We have only begun our work here."

"But without water," one of the men complained, "we cannot succeed."

"We will succeed."

"If only we had funds to buy pipe—"

"We will succeed without money. We will find a way."

"If only there was water on the land."

181

A mood of depression gripped the settlers and Yeshivat understood that life was oozing out of the people of Kfar Akiba as he watched. They were willing to accept Frede's denial of additional money as final, an end to hope, to their dreams of a better future. Every emotional fiber in him quivered with resentment and fear. He wanted to bellow out his rage, to attack them for surrendering so easily, and at the same time he had to accept the harsh reality that faced them. There was no water on the land.

"What are we going to do, Yeshivat?" Navorsky asked, a plaintive sound in his voice.

Yeshivat looked at him, at the others. All faces were turned to him, the same uncertain, anxious expressions looking to him for a solution. Why not, he asked himself. He had organized Kfar Akiba, arranged for the loan from Abarbanel, brought them here and led them to this point. It was up to him to take them forward.

"What *can* we do?" another man said weakly. "Frede said——"

"To hell with Frede!" Yeshivat said, seeking time. His brain was a mass of electrified activity, remembering, sorting, assembling, rejecting, conceiving.

"We believed, I believed, that Abarbanel was a philanthropist, a man anxious to help, to see us on the land, improving the land. We discover we were wrong. He is nothing but a landlord and Frede is his collector of rents. I do not intend to allow that to defeat me."

"Without water there will be no harvest," Navorsky said, with devastating logic. "And with no harvest, we will have no money with which to meet the payments. We might as well leave now."

"We are going to have water." The excitement of discovery darted along Yeshivat's spine. "We *will!*" The idea fleshed out and took shape; though imperfect, he knew it would work. "We are going to bring water to Kfar Akiba."

"Without pipes?"

"We will make our own pipe."

A man rose and spoke in an apologetic voice. "Forgive me, *adoni,* but we simply cannot do it. To make pipe we would need certain kinds of clay and forms and——"

"Wood," Yeshivat interrupted. "We will use the lumber we have."

"That is for the houses!"

"Water first. We are going to build troughs. Simple

affairs with a flat bottom and straight high sides, running from a high point of the stream down to here."

"It might work—"

"When the line is finished, we will erect additional feeder troughs to the various fields. Irrigation ditches will do the rest."

"Yes," Navorsky said. "Yes, it might work."

Yeshivat glared at him, the hawklike face frozen with determination. "It *will* work! We will see to it. All of us."

Work began the next morning. Yeshivat chose the route, an irregular line from the settlement into the hills where the stream descended swiftly. Behind him, a detail of men and donkeys dragged lengths of lumber into place. They used one-by-twelves, each piece ten feet long, wood intended for roofing.

While carpenters hammered the troughs together, other men dug holes for the supporting stakes. When these were solid in the ground, the troughs were lifted into place and fastened down. Joints were fashioned and the seams calked with mud dug out from under the rocky stream bed. Sluice gates were built to regulate the flow of the water.

At the same time, other men continued to work the fields and when all the rocks were cleared away, plowing began and irrigation ditches were dug. It took almost a week to build the waterline and there was a certain amount of trepidation when the sluice gates were opened. They waited impatiently for the first flow to make its way down, to run into the irrigation ditches. And when it did, a cheer went up from the people of Kfar Akiba.

Once the fields were properly watered, the first planting of corn, barley and wheat was completed.

That Passover was a joyous time for the people of Kfar Akiba. The Seder was held under the open sky and they read from the Haggadah and ate matzohs baked on their own land. That night they talked of the houses they were going to build and the kind of lives they and their children would have. When they finally went to sleep, it was to dream of a rewarding future that seemed within reach.

During the night, the water stopped flowing.

One of the children discovered it in the morning. Yeshivat sent Navorsky and another man to find out what had happened. They returned excited and babbling.

"The line is broken! The trough has been ripped apart!"

"A hundred yards, in pieces, destroyed!"

"The stakes have been torn from the ground!"

"Who would do such a thing?" they asked one another.

"Who?" Navorsky said to Yeshivat.

That was when Yeshivat realized his mistake. They had gone about their affairs with an absolute disregard of the Arabs in the vicinity, proceeding as if they didn't exist. This was the result. A prideful reminder that Kfar Akiba was not the only village in the area.

"I think it is time we paid a visit to Ibn Amer," Yeshivat said.

"You think the Arabs did this? But why? We have given them no cause."

"Let's find out."

The Arab village was a collection of mud huts of no particular distinction, placed in loose order along a single street that was little more than a goat path. The sheikh's house stood apart on the side of a hill behind the village, its vaulted roof and high archways giving it the look of a military fortress.

A servant greeted Yeshivat and Navorsky at the door with elaborate courtesy and asked them to wait. He disappeared into the house and returned minutes later, saying that his master had consented to see them. He ushered them into a lofty room, bright with sunlight streaming through high, narrow apertures in the thick walls.

Ibn Amer, a small man, bearded and myopic, stood across the room waiting. In his steel rimmed glasses and long robes he appeared deformed, all head and very little body. When they came closer, he inclined his head.

"Salaam aleikum," he murmured. "A thousand gracious welcomes. You honor my home and my village by your presence."

"Salaam aleikum," Yeshivat said.

"Please," Ibn Amer said, motioning for the men to take seats. "Be comfortable." He lowered himself into a straight-backed chair and clapped his hands. A servant appeared from behind a latticework screen with a tray bearing thick sweet coffee, some figs and dates.

They sipped the coffee and nibbled at the fruit. From another part of the house, Yeshivat could hear the clucking of women, never visible in an Arab household.

"How kind of you to receive us in such a generous fashion," he said to Ibn Amer.

The sheikh bared his teeth in a thin mirthless smile. Behind the thick glasses his eyes appeared swollen and malevolent. "Oh, my dears, it is you who are generous to honor me with this visit."

"It is time that we paid our respects," Yeshivat said, "and in neglecting to do so before this we have been remiss. We are simple men of the soil who wish only to live in peace and harmony with our neighbors."

"As Allah wills it. Are we not all the sons of a single father, the cherished Abraham, the blood in us all the same. I too am a simple man, a farmer, and your way is my way and that of my humble people. It is I who have failed in my duty. I should have come to you long before this to welcome you to the land, to offer what help was within my power to give."

Yeshivat recognized the criticism implicit in Ibn Amer's words. It had been a mistake not to pay their respects to him sooner, to bolster his pride according to Arab custom. Perhaps the destruction of the waterline had simply been a harsh reminder of their omission.

"We are not very clever people," Yeshivat said, "and make many errors for which we beg understanding."

Ibn Amer's face was an indulgent mask as he presented it first to Navorsky and then to Yeshivat. "But that cannot be. My people tell me that you labor with great industriousness and have cleared the land and very cleverly brought water to it and have already planted. Now you will build houses and your roots will take hold in the land and—"

"It is about the water we wish to talk," Yeshivat put in.

Ibn Amer extended his right hand, palm showing. "Ah, water, the most precious of commodities. Please, continue, dear sir."

"There has been some difficulty," Yeshivat said deliberately. "It is known that all information must come to your ears, effendi, and so we turn to you for assistance."

"If it is within my power, you shall have whatever you desire."

"As you know we have built a trough to carry water to the land. The stream is swollen and will serve your village and mine equally well."

Ibn Amer curled his mouth and blinked slowly. "If Allah wills it. In this land, where my fathers and their fathers have lived for years beyond counting, rivers have died and lakes have disappeared."

Yeshivat sensed the brittle veneer that encased the sheikh. This ritual, the elaborate word game they were playing, all designed to what end? He allowed impatience to creep into his voice.

185

"Without water nothing will grow. Without water Kfar Akiba cannot exist."

That imperceptible shifting of features, the enigmatic turn of mouth, the distorted eyes—a protective design. "The way of Allah is mysterious and not to be questioned."

Yeshivat stiffened in his seat. They were getting nowhere with Ibn Amer. He was toying with them, enjoying their distress. "Someone has broken our waterline," Yeshivat said, biting off the words. "It is destroyed. We hoped that once the great and powerful Ibn Amer knew of this he would take steps to correct the situation."

"To improve on the work of Allah, to bring water from one place to another. What genius! The ability to conceive of something where there had been nothing. To peer into the future. What marvelous power!"

"We desire only peace, to work and let others do the same."

"The fellahin are simple people. What they do not understand they fear. Who knows what such people may think or do."

"If the great sheikh would speak to his people, reassure them, explain that they need have no fear of a mere handful of farmers."

"From a handful of seedlings, great armies can be fed."

"You remind us wisely that we are all the sons of Abraham, that we are brothers—"

"It is always difficult for strangers in a foreign land," Ibn Amer intoned softly.

"True, some of us come from other countries but we are here now to live and to raise our families. Palestine is the home of our spirits even as it is of yours. There is no cause for conflict. We have much to give to each other, much to learn."

"The ways of my people have served them for many years and will for many more. One lives as one must, as Allah would have us live."

Yeshivat stood up. Tension lodged at the base of his spine and his breath came in short spurts. "Then we can expect more trouble?" he said bluntly.

"We are a gentle people," Ibn Amer murmured, lowering his eyes. "Peaceful—"

"We will not be driven off the land, Ibn Amer. I tell that to you and you can tell the fellahin or not. The waterline will be rebuilt and the next time your thugs try to destroy it they will receive a proper reception. You want trouble, we'll give it to you."

"In sha'Allah."

The trough was rebuilt and patrolled, night and day. On the third night, the guards were attacked and beaten badly. One man had to be sent to Jerusalem where he was hospitalized. Another had a broken arm. The waterline was ripped apart in two places.

"Repair it," Yeshivat ordered grimly.

"We can't go on this way," Navorsky complained, and there was agreement from the others. "If the Arabs don't want us here, we will have to leave."

"Then leave," Yeshivat shot back. "I am staying. This is my land, my home. I won't be frightened away."

"What can we do?"

"We can fight."

"There are too many Arabs."

"Then we must be smarter and tougher than they are." Yeshivat addressed one of the guards who had been beaten. "How many of them would you say attacked you?"

"Ten, maybe twelve."

"And they were armed?"

"Yes, Aaron. Some of them had pistols and others rifles. I saw one man with a long knife, a sword. They waved the weapons and threatened us but there was no shooting."

"And they came on horseback?"

"Yes."

Yeshivat assimilated the information and made up his mind. "All right. We are going to rebuild the waterline and then we will teach the Arabs something about fighting."

It took three days to repair the breaks and get the water flowing again. Two more days passed with no sign of Arab interest, but on the third day a single Arab was spotted on a hill above the waterline.

"When he saw me," the guard reported to Yeshivat, "he ran away. He did not come to fight."

"Tonight," Yeshivat said, "we will go to him. And we will go to fight."

An hour after sunset, Yeshivat led a dozen of his men out of Kfar Akiba, circling the hills that separated them from the Arab village. Each man carried an axe handle. At the outskirts of the Arab village, they took up positions in the ditches on either side of the dirt road.

"Perhaps they will not come," Navorsky whispered nervously.

"If not tonight, then tomorrow," Yeshivat said. "Or the night after that. But they will come."

Four hours passed with no sign of activity. "They aren't coming tonight," Navorsky said. "They may not know the trough is repaired."

"They know," Yeshivat said. "We will wait another hour."

The hour was almost up when they heard a horse whinnying. "Remember," Yeshivat husked out, "wait for my signal."

Tension was a living thing in Yeshivat's bowels, a tight swelling thing. Fear and anticipation. A craving to act, to charge forward, to swing his club. He squinted into the darkness.

He counted ten of them, robes flowing, horses prancing but moving at a deliberate pace, talking among themselves, confident, laughing.

Yeshivat tightened his grip on the axe handle and waited until they were abreast of him. He rose up and launched himself at the nearest Arab. "Back to Jerusalem!" he cried, pulling at the man's robes. At the same time, he swung the axe handle in a short, swift arc. An oath broke out of the Arab, cut short by the crunch of the club against his skull.

After that, confusion. Men and horses milling about in the darkness. Clubs swinging, hoarse cries in Arabic and in Hebrew. A rifle butt caught Yeshivat in the middle of the back and sent him sprawling. He rolled and found himself under the nervous hooves of an excited horse. Still rolling, he came up on the other side of the beast, chopping his club at the rider. A shot sounded and suddenly it was over. Three Arabs went galloping back toward their village, leaving their comrades unconscious on the ground.

"The horses," Yeshivat cried. "Take them and the guns, all their weapons. And let's get out of here. Quickly."

The entire population of Kfar Akiba was awake and waiting for them. A jug of sweet wine was broken out and they toasted their victory and boasted of their exploits.

"We beat them!" Navorsky cried jubilantly, proud of the trickle of blood flowing from a cut in his forehead. "Oh, how we beat them!" He embraced Yeshivat and planted a kiss on his cheek. "Oh, my dear friend, I was so frightened, so terribly frightened. But I fought them."

"You did very well," Yeshivat said. "All of you did."

"It was my first fight," Navorsky said, wonder in his voice. "My first fight of any kind. I didn't think I could do it, but I did. I hit two of them. Two! I beat one of them unconscious and the other until he began to cry for mercy and ran away. He ran from *me*. He was more frightened then I." He laughed shortly.

"It was a good fight," Yeshivat said. "A lesson for us all."

"Now they will leave us alone," one of the women said. "We can live in peace."

"They will not dare to come back," her husband said.

The laughter expired and all eyes turned to Yeshivat. He drank the last of his wine and extended his glass for more. One of the women obliged him.

"Aaron, will they come again?" Navorsky asked.

"They'll come again," Yeshivat said, "and next time they'll be smarter. It was a lesson for them, too."

"Is there nothing we can do?" another woman said plaintively.

"The same thing—fight."

"But they are so many and we are so few."

"Which is why we can't afford to be beaten even a single time," Yeshivat said. "For us a defeat will be total. So we will not lose."

"We have weapons now." It was Navorsky who had spoken, his manner tentative, but his voice steady.

"Yes," Yeshivat agreed. "And in the morning we will learn how to use them and we will establish a strategy for our defense."

"Wouldn't it be better to go somewhere else? If we are not wanted here?"

"Where is a Jew ever wanted?" Yeshivat snapped. "Before we came, this land was covered with stones. Nothing grew here. There was no water, no people. Now we are here and soon crops will grow and we will build houses and raise children. My sweat is in this soil and that makes it mine. To take it away, I will have to be killed."

One of the women began to sob. "I hate this place. The Arabs will kill us all. I don't want to stay here."

"Then leave," Yeshivat said, without softness. "Whoever wishes to do so, may leave. But before noon tomorrow. After that, we learn how to become fighters as well as farmers; we must be able to depend on each other."

Seven families left in the morning. Twenty-three people. That left thirteen men and four youths old enough to

189

do a man's job. Yeshivat distributed the arms among them as he saw fit.

"But there aren't enough guns," one man complained.

"We'll get more," Yeshivat promised.

"How?"

"The same way we got these, from the Arabs."

Yeshivat began to explain the workings of a rifle, breaking one down and reassembling it. He taught them how to hold a rifle and aim, how to lead a moving target.

"How do you know so much about guns, Aaron?" Navorsky asked.

"For that you can thank the Czar. The Cossacks took me into the army when I was only seventeen and kept me for six years. I fought in four different battles and I had to kill for those bastards in order to save my own life. From now on, if I kill it will be for myself, for the Jews of Kfar Akiba." A bitter laugh died on his lips. "It is something we can learn from the Gentiles, my friends, to kill as efficiently as possible."

Arab raids continued irregularly. Men, if alone, or in small groups, were attacked and beaten. Goats and donkeys were stolen and less than a week after Kfar Akiba acquired its first cow, the beast was taken. Yeshivat organized a raiding party which stole six cows and a dozen goats from Ibn Amer's herd.

So it went. But the village took root and grew. Houses were built. In time some of those who had left returned and brought others with them.

It was not an easy life. The men rose at three in the morning to milk the cows and feed the other livestock. After that they ate breakfast and went into the fields. And since there was always the danger of attack, guards were posted twenty-four hours a day.

They soon realized that they could not afford the luxury of remaining idle on the Sabbath for neither the animals nor the earth recognized one day as different than the others. In the years that followed, under Yeshivat's leadership, they learned to diversify the crops, planting almonds, olives, grapes and even some tobacco.

Kfar Akiba was the only world Yaakov knew. He spent four hours each morning in the one-room village school learning to read and write in Hebrew, studying the Bible, solving simple arithmetical problems. Afternoons, like the other children of the village, he worked in the fields with the adults or tended the flocks or did chores with the women. In the evenings, after supper, there was always music and dancing to the strains of a violin and an accordion. Sometimes someone would tell a story about what life had been like in the Jewish villages of eastern Europe: strange stories, filled with happy demons and a God who loved them all but never seemed to make life better for them; and with oppressive and frightening policemen, soldiers, Czars and Princes.

When Yaakov was nine years old, the trouble with Abarbanel finally broke into the open. It was just before Succoth, the Feast of the Tabernacles, which celebrated the ancient fruit harvest in the Holy Land; the agent, Frede, was due for his annual visit.

The children of Kfar Akiba, as they did each Succoth, had built an arbor, hanging it with flowers and fruit.

"So that we will remember," Yaakov told his father, "how the ancient Jews lived in such flimsy places while they wandered in the desert and fought the Arabs."

Yeshivat laughed. "It is entirely possible."

"But they felt safe anyway," the boy continued solemnly, "because they knew they were under the protection of the Lord."

Yeshivat grunted and tousled the boy's dark locks. "A man is as safe as he is strong. You understand?"

The pale eyes were puzzled. "But doesn't God protect us all?"

"You must be willing to fight for what is yours, my son. That is the only protection a man has. Never forget that."

"Yes, father."

The following day Frede arrived and Yeshivat turned over the rents and accepted a receipt. Then, as was customary, the women served tea and *hummus,* mashed chickpeas and olive oil, and *pitah.* Yaakov particularly liked *hummus,* but like the other children he was forbidden to bother the adults at this time. He stood off to one side watching, trying to comprehend their conversation.

"I wish to put a question to you, Frede," he heard his father say.

The agent smiled without humor. "Ask, Yeshivat. There is no harm in asking."

"We, the men of Kfar Akiba, have been discussing a certain matter for some time. It is almost seven years since we came here and built our village. We've leased additional lands from Abarbanel since and we've always paid what was due promptly."

"And the Abarbanel Land Development Company appreciates that."

Yeshivat raised his brows. "When did Abarbanel become a development company?"

"During this last year. It has become a big business."

Yeshivat's shoulders lifted and his head thrust forward. "Good. Then you will understand. We wish to talk business. We have consulted among ourselves—"

"So you said."

Yeshivat's eyes came to rest on Yaakov, silent, watching expectantly. Resentment gathered in a thick glob in his chest, and he swung back to Frede. The agent was trying to embarrass him in front of his own people, mocking him before his son.

"Frede," he said coldly. "This land is ours by every human measure. By our labor and by the lives we live here. We want to own it."

Frede's laughter was harsh. "The Abarbanel Company rents. It does not sell. You will never own these fields."

Yeshivat had anticipated this reaction. "Frede," he said, with deceiving gentleness, "now I speak only for myself. I will pay no more rent to you. No more money to Abarbanel. When you are prepared to set a price for the land, I will pay. But no rent. The land is mine and I will own it."

Frede rose, mouth working, cheeks blotched. His eyes raked over them all. "You'll pay, Yeshivat. All of you. Or else I'll put you off the land."

Navorsky stepped forward. There was a quiet confidence in his manner. "Mr. Frede, there are now forty-one families living in Kfar Akiba. Eighty-five men and boys, each one of whom is big enough to carry a gun, each one of whom knows how to carry a gun, each one of whom owns a gun." A slow smile turned his mouth. "After all, Mr. Frede, it is unreasonable for you to believe you can put all of us off the land."

"Are you threatening me?"

"Explaining, dear Mr. Frede," Navorsky said. "We are peaceful men and never threaten."

"But we warn, Frede," Yeshivat broke in. "Heed the warning. Go away and tell Abarbanel of our position. Then come back. We will still be here."

"I'll come back, all right. And bring men with me, men with guns of their own."

"The Arabs have not been able to move us," Navorsky said mildly. "Neither will Abarbanel."

"Come back when you're ready to sell," Yeshivat said. "We ask nothing for nothing. We will pay. A fair price. But we will have the land."

"You will be sorry about this," Frede insisted.

Yeshivat stared at him without blinking. "Frede, there is one word for you to remember, you and Mr. Abarbanel. The word is violence. Bring trouble upon us and there will be violence. We will fight and you do not know how well we have learned to do that. Bring trouble, Frede, and there will be violence—against *you*, Frede, and unless you kill every one of us there will be no way for you to escape."

Frede wet his lips and took a step backward. "You will pay for this, all of you."

"What do you think, Aaron?" Navorsky said, after Frede had left.

"I think Frede will convince Abarbanel to sell us the land. "Oh, they will bluster and send lawyers and threaten. But in the end he will sell."

"He could hire mercenaries to send against us."

"I don't think so," Yeshivat said. "Abarbanel is a business man and that would be bad business. That sort of thing could not be kept quiet. Abarbanel would find no safe place for himself in Palestine and no man who works for him would be safe either. We have only to stand firm and to wait. Now let's get back to work. We've wasted half a day already."

It was a month after Frede's visit. Yeshivat and Navorsky were constructing an enclosure in which to keep the chickens that the community had recently acquired. Their plan was to develop a considerable flock, selling the eggs in order to earn cash. They hoped to save enough money to purchase some modern farming machinery.

By late afternoon, the last of the fence-holes having been dug, they were now placing the four-by-fours, tamping them securely into place before attaching the chicken wire. It was Navorsky who spotted Yaakov.

"Aaron, look!"

Yeshivat glanced up and saw his son running toward them, bleeding from nose and mouth, tears flowing out of his pale eyes. Dropping his tools, Yeshivat hurried to the boy, going to his knees.

"What happened? Who did this to you?"

"Arabs," Yaakov managed to get out. "They beat me."

Yeshivat made the boy lie down and he examined him.

The only damage was to his face. The inside of his upper lip was cut but the flow of blood had already slowed.

Navorsky came hurrying up with a leather water bag and Yeshivat washed the blood from his son's face. The boy's nose was badly broken, the cartilege pushed to one side, and bruises appeared beneath both eyes.

"You are not seriously hurt, Yaakov. Is the pain very bad?"

The boy fought against his tears. "It's hard for me to breath. My nose hurts."

"It's broken," Yeshivat said. "But perhaps that is just as well. You were becoming too beautiful for my taste anyway. Now you will look more manly."

Yaakov, sitting up, avoided his father's eyes.

"The nose should be straightened out a little bit," Yeshivat said softly. "To help your breathing. I suppose you cannot stand a little more pain."

The boy's eyes, now fixed on the older man, went flat. Without warning, his right fist lashed out. Yeshivat warded it off effortlessly. "I did not break your nose," he said mildly. "I did not beat you. Now. Shall I fix the nose?"

Yaakov nodded and closed his eyes.

Yeshivat held the back of his son's head with his left hand while he took the crooked thrust of gristle between thumb and forefinger. "Now, Yaakov?"

The boy sucked air between his teeth. "Now," he said.

A quick crunching jerk, and the nose was reasonably straight again. A soft moan seeped out of the boy and he slumped forward. His eyes fluttered and opened when Navorsky splashed water on his face.

"It hurts," he said after a moment.

"Can you stand?" Yeshivat said.

Yaakov pushed himself erect. He looked up at his father. "I was very brave, I think."

"You were," Navorsky agreed cheerfully, "and now it is over."

"Not yet," Yeshivat said. "Yaakov, tell me how this happened."

The boy looked away. "There were two of them, Arabs. They came into the pasture while I was tending the goats and they called me names and chased the goats. When I tried to stop them, they hit me."

"Arab men?" Navorsky said.

"Yes," the boy said softly.

"They stole the goats?" Yeshivat said.

"I don't think so," Yaakov replied hesitantly.

194

"Ah. And perhaps they were not men, but boys like yourself?" Yeshivat said. "Men would have taken the goats."

"They were big boys, though. Bigger than me. And there were two of them. There were!"

"What did you do?" Yeshivat said.

"There were two of them," Yaakov said, his manner evasive.

"The boy has had enough, Aaron," Navorsky said.

Yeshivat waved him quiet. "What did you do when they hit you?" he persisted.

"I—I was afraid."

"But what did you *do?*"

Yaakov began to cry softly.

"You did nothing? You didn't fight back?"

"I was afraid. I held my hands over my head to protect myself."

Yeshivat took his son's chin in his hand. "Listen to me. Everyone is afraid when he is attacked. Everyone."

Yaakov stared at his father. So big, so fierce. That hawklike face, that lean, hard body that never seemed to grow tired. "You get afraid, too?"

"Yes. All of us. But fear mustn't be permitted to imprison you. A man does what he has to despite his fears. See, Yaakov, you hid behind your hands and you were beaten anyway." He stood up and looked down at the boy. "What about the goats?"

The pale eyes widened. "They are still in the pasture."

"Untended. Free for anyone to steal. They are your responsibility."

Yaakov bit his lip. He wanted to protest, to explain that the Arab boys had threatened to return, to beat him again every time they found him. Words rose up in his throat but before he could say anything, Yeshivat began to talk.

"It would be good if you found some method of protecting yourself in case those boys come back again. I'm sure you can think of something. Go back to the goats now and make sure none of them have strayed. There is too much work around here to waste more time talking."

He watched the boy move off. He walked slowly, reluctantly, but never hesitated or looked back. Yeshivat liked that.

"Aaron," Navorsky said. "Those Arabs may come back. Is it such a good idea for Yaakov to be alone? After all, he is only a child—"

"They will come back," Yeshivat said quietly. "And Yaakov will do what he has to do."

A week passed and the pain in Yaakov's nose subsided but his memory of the beating he took remained vividly acute. On this particular day, in the late afternoon, Yaakov herded the goats onto the eastern slope of a gentle hillock. He made a place for himself on the ground, his back to the sun, the elongated shadow of a single eucalyptus tree ten feet to his rear falling across his back. He uncapped his water bottle and filled his mouth with the tepid liquid, swished it around, and allowed it to seep into his throat, drop by slow drop, watching the goats at the same time.

He had been there for nearly an hour, aware of the lengthening shadow of the tree, when he sensed a presence behind him. Seconds later, an almost inaudible sound, a leaf crunching underfoot. Yaakov was aware of his heart, a thumping that filled his ears, and the dryness in his throat, the ill-making sensation that spread in his belly. He squeezed his eyes shut and forced everything out of his mind, willing his heart to a more temperate rhythm, resolving to do whatever was necessary. He opened his eyes and began to get ready, according to his plan.

With no particular urgency, he put the water bottle to one side and drew a thick woolen stocking out of his pocket. Still unhurried, he felt on the ground for some stones, none larger than a good-sized grape. He dropped them into the stocking. After hefting it, and satisfied, he tied a knot in the stocking so that all the pebbles were firmly locked into place in the toe. Next, he gathered his legs under him, muscles tense, quivering, ready to spring.

And he waited.

They circled the eucalyptus tree, one on either side. The length of their shadows, compared with that of the tree, told Yaakov exactly where they were. They signaled to each other, gestured, and it was clear that the figure on his right was to attack first, was to kick him in the back for a starter. The shadow went into a preparatory crouch and Yaakov gripped the stocking more tightly.

Even as the shadow moved forward, Yaakov came to his feet, whirling quickly, the loaded stocking pendulous and comforting. He took one step toward the charging Arab youth, saw the startled look on the slender brown face. Without hesitation, Yaakov swung the stocking as hard as he could, aiming for the place between the boy's eyes.

The Arab went down as if shot and Yaakov pivoted to meet his second assailant. Taller than the first boy, and slower on his feet, he tried to scramble out of range of the deadly stocking, to run. Yaakov was after him, his first blow catching the Arab at the base of the neck. He went tumbling forward, slipping and sliding, yelling shrill protests. Yaakov caught him flush on the skull as he tried to stand. He flattened out and lay still.

Yaakov located his water bottle and poured some water over each of the Arabs. The bigger of the two stirred and, groaning, sat up. Yaakov waited for the brown eyes to clear. Then he walked up to the boy and slapped him across the face. Twice, and with all the strength he could muster.

"Coward!" he bit off in Arabic, with the same hard edge of authority he had heard so often in his father's voice. "Take this other dog and never come back. If you do, I will slice off your testicles and feed them to you. And remember that I could have killed you both."

Yaakov waited until they were out of sight, before turning his attention to his goats. They had scattered over the side of the hill. It was nearly dark before he was able to round them up and herd them back to Kfar Akiba. His father was annoyed and said so. Yaakov offered no excuse.

During the next four years, Kfar Akiba thrived and grew, almost doubled its population. A year earlier, Abarbanel had given up trying to collect rents from the settlers and agreed to sell the land to them. The papers had been drawn and signed and money had exchanged hands. Further payments would be forthcoming, but the land belonged to them. Though no apparent alterations in their lives took place, all of them felt a more intensified pride.

Despite the growth of the settlement, there were no pietists at Kfar Akiba, and no rabbi. Not even a proper ritualistic butcher. Still, some members of the community kept the holy days as best they could and each Friday night at sundown and on Saturday mornings they gathered to read from the Torah and to pray. The most knowledgeable among them prepared the boys to be bar mitzvah. In that way was Yaakov Yeshivat made ready to be admitted to manhood according to tradition, to be responsible for his own deeds. His father had other ideas and on the night before the ceremony he took the boy aside.

"Listen to me, my son," he said gravely. "You've been taught the Torah and the Bible. I suppose if your mother was still living she'd have insisted that you be sent to a proper cheder. And I would not have fought with her. But I am grateful that we live here the way we do. Tomorrow, Yaakov, is the Sabbath before your thirteenth birthday and you'll join the men to read the Torah and chant the lesson from the *Haftarah*, the lesson from the Prophets. It's a good thing, I suppose. But I want you to remember always who you are, who your father is, what kind of a man I expect you to become."

"I know who I am," Yaakov said.

Yeshivat stared at his son for a moment. "Yes, but I want to warn you about those Orthodox money-grabbers, those tefillin swindlers who come around begging charity when they should be doing hard work. You will never learn to be a man from such as them. Only men can teach you that."

"I already know how to be a man, father."

Yeshivat scrutinized the boy with a clinical eye. He was growing fast, was thick-boned and broad in the chest and shoulders, and the muscles of his arms were clearly defined. He was going to be at least as tall as Yeshivat and heavier undoubtedly. Stronger.

Yeshivat could see suggestions of his own face in Yaakov. The high forehead and the wiry hair. The same wide mouth, though Yaakov had more fullness of lip. The lean, blunt jaw, the prominent cheekbones. The nose, thick and strong, irregularly pitched. Only the eyes were not Yeshivat's. A legacy from Yaakov's mother, pale and unblinking, flat, quick, perceptive.

"Tonight," Yeshivat said, "we shall see how much of a man you are. Tonight you take your place on guard the same as the others. Alone."

The boy wet his lips. "I won't disgrace you."

"You are my son and you can do nothing to disgrace me. You are my son always. I want you to act in such a way as to create pride in yourself and that can only be done by your own will, your own accomplishments. Expect to be afraid, Yaakov. There is no courage without fear. But teach yourself to think and act in spite of it. Consider what must be done and do it."

"Yes, father."

Yeshivat reached under his coat sweater and withdrew a revolver. He handed it to Yaakov. "It is loaded and always dangerous. It is my gift to you on your bar mitzvah, my son."

He embraced Yaakov and kissed the boy on the mouth.

Yaakov stepped back to assess the weapon. Blue steel, solid in his hand, an emanation of power. His eyes flickered to Yeshivat and back to the gun. He flipped open the cylinder. "It is unloaded," he said accusingly.

Yeshivat, grunting, took some bullets out of his pocket and handed them over. "Let's eat supper and then I will take you to your post."

An hour later, they walked side by side without speaking, to the stand of oak trees beyond the southern perimeter. This zone was considered neither Jewish nor Arab.

"Over there," Yeshivat pointed, "is the road. If the Arabs come, you must act as the situation demands."

"Shall I shoot at them?" The pistol felt very heavy and threatening.

"Consider the choices open and do whatever is best for Kfar Akiba. You are here to protect us."

"If the Arabs come, I will stop them."

"Study them. Learn how they think. Try to anticipate their actions. Now I am going to leave you."

After his father was gone, Yaakov moved deeper among the trees, taking up a position behind a clump of bushes. He settled down to wait.

Gradually he became aware of the night sounds: the wild shriek of a jackal; the hoot of an owl; the movement everywhere, quick scurrying and scratching. He reached for the butt of the pistol and gripped it tightly.

How long he remained in the bushes he never knew. Time seemed to pass with excruciating slowness. It was the sound of camel bells that alerted him. He stood up and saw outlined against the moonlit sky, a caravan returning to Nazareth. A shiver passed down his spine.

Breathing with studied regularity, he made a conscious effort to slow the wild beating of his heart. Now each second was marked by a throbbing pulse in his temple. He ticked them off. Ten times he counted up to sixty. Then he stopped counting.

He almost missed it. A dull thump, distant, and not repeated. Recognition came eventually. Drawing the pistol, he peered across the top of the bushes, straining to penetrate the night. He saw them, four mounted Arabs, the feet of their horses bound in rags to muffle the sound, and riding two abreast.

They came closer, then swung off the road and into the woods. If they continued on their present course, Yaakov judged, they would pass within six feet of his hiding place, have a clear path across the eastern wheat fields to the

199

cattle pens at the rear of Kfar Akiba. Unless he stopped them.

But how? His brain was a heaving sump. He considered allowing them to pass, trying to get back to the village in time to alert his father and the other men. It wouldn't work; the Arabs would have reached the pens and done their work before anyone could stop them. A signal shot; that would reveal his position, make him vulnerable.

He forced himself to think clearly. He had to act before they got closer. He filled his lungs with air and stood up, aiming the pistol with both hands.

"Stop!" he cried. "Stand where you are! Or my men and I shall shoot you down!"

The Arabs drew up, chattering among themselves, trying to locate the owner of the voice. One of them spotted Yaakov and muttered to his companions. The horsemen fanned out, moving with great skill in the darkness.

"There is only the one Jewish bastard! He is alone!"

"*Andak!*" another shouted hoarsely, the traditional Arab acceptance of a challenge. They wheeled their horses in Yaakov's direction.

He pulled the trigger. The pistol leaped in his hands and sent him stumbling two steps backwards. He came back on balance, fired again.

The four horsemen pulled up and milled about. Yaakov shot again. The Arabs swung around and galloped away. Minutes later Yeshivat and four other men came running up.

"Are you all right?" Yeshivat asked.

An excited Yaakov told them what had happened.

"Four of them!" Yeshivat said, showing his skepticism.

Yaakov drew back, eyes glittering. "Four," he repeated coldly, "and when I shot at them they ran."

One of the other men laughed. "The boy did well, Yeshivat. He is truly a bar mitzvah now."

Yeshivat nodded soberly. "Come, Yaakov. We will go back to the village."

"No," Yaakov said stubbornly. "I will finish out my guard time. It is my duty."

FIVE

And God spake unto Israel, in the visions
of the night, and said. . . "Fear not to go
down in Egypt, for I will there make of thee
a great nation. I will go down with thee
into Egypt and I will also surely bring thee
up again."

—Genesis

1956

I

Simon was already at the table when Amos came down for breakfast. He kissed the boy on the top of his head and took his place across the table from him. At six, Simon already displayed a strong physical similarity to his brothers. The face might have been Joshua's, slender and pale with a certain delicacy of skin and line. There Joshua ended. The eyes, hollow and dark, searching and already defensive, were Levi's, and there was the same aggressive facial thrust, the sullen mouth.

Ruth came out of the kitchen with a sliced orange and a glass of tea for Amos. She kissed his cheek.

"What do you want for breakfast?"

"Nothing. I've got that meeting with Monroe this morning. Early. That could be important."

"Will he make the deal, Amos?"

He glanced over at Simon and smiled briefly. The boy averted his eyes and Amos went back to his orange slices. "There's a good chance we'll close things today," he said to Ruth. "If Monroe agrees to buy from the Landau Company, well—" He brushed at his thinning hair, guiding it to one side in a futile effort to mask his balding scalp. "If we make the deal, I'll be able to buy the new machines. Hire another three hundred people, maybe more. Landau will be the second most important fabric manufacturer in all of Israel."

"That's very nice. Did you hear, Simon? Your father is going to become a big textile manufacturer. All since you were born, Simon. A shop on Ben Yehuda to a national chain to a textile factory. You should be proud of your father."

Simon looked straight at her, eyes disconcertingly steady, hooded and almost feral. "Why should I be proud?"

"Why! Because your father's done so well—"

"Not now, Ruth," Amos said quietly. "Simon's got lots of time to be concerned about business matters. First he'll finish school, then his Service, then Hebrew University and—"

"No," the boy said.

"No to what?" Amos said.

"I'm not going to go to the University here."

"Oh," Ruth said. "You're six years old and you decided what university you're going to? Most boys wait until they're a little older before deciding such things."

"As soon as I'm old enough," he said challengingly, "I'm going away to see things, to have adventures."

Ruth knew she should ignore the childish prattling, but she couldn't. "You'll go nowhere. With Joshua running all over the world, and Levi in the Army being shot at by Arabs—you'll stay home. You'll go to school here and get married and go into papa's business."

"Oh!" Simon burst out, struggling to respond without success. At once he was out of his chair and out of the room without a backward glance.

"Oh, that boy," Ruth said.

"He'll be all right," Amos said mildly. He reached for *Al Hamishmar*, the morning newspaper, and donned his reading glasses. The lead story reported that Egypt had consummated a multi-million dollar weapons agreement with Czechoslovakia. Amos sighed. "If the boy were older I'd say that's troubling him. Maybe it is. He's a sensitive child. He can sense what's going on in the world."

Ruth sat down. "It doesn't mean anything. Nasser bought some guns. All right. He'll threaten us again. It's nothing new."

"Maybe you're right. I wish this situation with the Arabs was finally settled. The fedayeen raid us and we strike back. They attack a kibbutz and we destroy a police fort. We would all be better off if there was more business with the Arabs and less killing. Think of all those people, millions of them, and with nothing. If they could be taught modern ways, their incomes raised. We have so much to teach them and we could learn from them, too."

"But if the Arabs keep attacking us—"

"They're frustrated and angry. Well, why shouldn't they be? What have they got out of life? Nothing but poverty and sickness and a world that keeps stepping on them. To them, we're just the most recent oppressors, taking away what they believe is rightfully theirs. But if they were well fed, could live constructive lives, if their children were guaranteed a future, it would all change. There would be

204

peace. I think these punitive raids we make are a political mistake."

"The last time Yaakov was here he said———"

"Yaakov is a firebrand. He measures a man by how many callouses there are on his hands and how many Arabs he's killed. Men like him, like Dayan, B-G, some of those others, they have to learn how to bend, to compromise. That's something every good businessman knows. We need more people to build a peace, not fight a war."

The blood drained out of her face. "There isn't going to be another war. Not again."

He smiled reassuringly. "Of course not. With my connections in Government, I'd have heard if anything was in the wind."

That made her feel better and she allowed her mind to return to Simon. "I want you to talk to Simon, Amos. Yesterday he insulted that old Mr. Cohen. Mr. Cohen said something to him about going to synagogue and Simon called him an old fool and said there was no God."

"I'll talk to him."

"What is it," she said unhappily. "First Joshua, then Levi, and now Simon. They're different than other children. It's as if we're strangers to them."

"I suppose it's my fault," he said. "If I had acted differently then they would be different."

"They have no right to judge you," she said quickly. "You're their father. Besides, that's over a long time." When she spoke again, her voice was very small, hesitant. "Amos, do you think about her ever?"

"Of course not," he lied, careful to give no emphasis to the words, remembering the last time he had heard from Mara. Abrupt, unexpected. The words so formal and strange—*Try to understand . . . best for us both . . . had to end . . . don't mean to hurt. . . .* But it had hurt. A deep shredding of a certain softness and in its place a hardening core of protectiveness. A *letter*. She should have come to him, faced him, told him herself.

A wistful acceptance flickered across Ruth's mouth. Whenever one of Mara's films played they made a silent point of not seeing it. She remembered Mara, that dark and spectacular beauty. A man never forgot that kind of a woman. But he was back now and if the passion of their youth no longer existed, it had been replaced by a milder, less demanding affection.

Amos stood up.

"Will you be home early?" she said, avoiding his eyes.

Every day, the same question. He hated that plaintive query, hated what she had become, what he had done to her. There would always be that fear and suspicion, a wound that would never entirely close. He promised to be on time for the evening meal.

II

Yaakov Yeshivat rubbed a thorny hand over the stubble on his dusty cheeks and glared at the head of the driver in the front seat. He was a young man with thick yellow hair that curled down the back of his neck and he drove with an easy, rankling arrogance.

"Where the hell are you taking me?"

The driver looked boldly into the rear-view mirror and grinned. "My orders are to tell you nothing, *adoni*," he said cheerfully. "Be patient."

Yaakov leaned back in the seat. There was no sense arguing with this one. The young ones today had no notion of what was proper, no respect for their betters.

None of it made sense to Yaakov. This sudden summons from his labors. If this was Lahav's doing, he'd blast the hide off the old man. No more being ordered around like some new organizer. There were too many years behind him, too many successful assignments. He visualized the mines at Timna, that purple and scarlet landscape, the smokestacks belching green and white and black fumes, the distant gray desert. Timna. The mines of Solomon, back in production after all the centuries. He had been part of that miracle, organizing, driving, fighting to get things done. Getting them done and in only ninety days. Now this!

He reached into the pocket of his desert-whitened work shirt and read again the message that had been delivered to him only hours earlier:

OFFICIAL——MOST SECRET
Report Tel Aviv immediately.
Transport to destination will be supplied.
Repeat: Immediately.

No signature. No hint of who wanted him or why. Mysteries distressed him, made him uneasy, frustrated. He liked matters clear and understandable.

A jeep had carried him from Timna to Eilat where a plane had been waiting to take him to Tel Aviv. There, this car and this insufferable driver. Yaakov looked at the thick neck.

"Listen, *adoni*," he said. "I have friends near here. Take me there so I can clean myself and shave, get a decent meal. I haven't eaten since this morning."

"Nothing doing. My orders are clear."

"You're a soldier?"

Again those penetrating eyes in the mirror. "We both are, are we not?"

"What rank do you hold?"

The young, almost baby-face, opened up in a delighted laugh, a taunting sound. "Forget it. You're a lieutenant colonel on reserve. I'm a sergeant. Regular. But today I'm the boss."

"Maybe I will arrange for you to become a private once more."

"I was told you might try something like this. It won't work."

Yaakov grunted and folded his arms. "Are you much of a soldier?"

A twist of mouth, a taunting grin. "Very brave, very smart."

"Then why only a chauffeur?"

Laughing, the driver turned the car into a driveway and pulled up in front of a large white house set back off the road. He got out and opened the door. He jerked his head toward the front door. "Inside. They expect you."

Yaakov went up to the door and opened it.

"Hey, colonel," the driver called after him. Yaakov looked back. "I'm a paratrooper. Very tough outfit."

Yaakov measured the man, stocky and muscular, with that innocent, fearless expression. There was the look of a fighter to him. "Very tough," he agreed, and went into the house.

A voice came from a room to the right. "In here, Yeshivat." There was an authoritative ring to the words.

Yaakov strode across the reception hall into a large airy chamber furnished with French antiques. There was a delicacy to the room that made him feel out of place.

Two men in slacks and sports shirts stood to greet him.

One of them, a husky man with thinning brown hair and a black patch over one eye, came forward, hands extended.

"Shalom, Yeshivat. How long has it been? Not since you were with Nahal at that cooperative in the Negev. Two years, isn't it?"

"Four. You wanted my people to plant those tomatoes of yours."

"But you wouldn't let them. You should've, Yeshivat. Those tomatoes were a good idea, a money crop. You'll see, one day."

Yeshivat scowled. "What is this, Moshe? You want to talk about tomatoes, you don't need me. Dammit, man, my work at Timna is important. What we're doing there, copper, manganese, that matters. These are vital products and——"

"Come," the man with the eye patch said, "I want you to meet Uri Davidov."

Davidov was a tall man with thick shoulders and arms that seemed too long. At thirty, he had the face of a scholar, lean, almost delicate of expression, with hair that curled around his ears. His handshake was strong and his eyes made a swift exploratory journey over Yaakov's battered features.

"Shalom," he said quietly.

"Shalom," Yaakov replied, and turned back to the other man.

"Come, let's sit and be comfortable. We'll talk."

Yaakov lowered himself into a gold-trimmed chair, afraid it would collapse under his weight. "Okay, Moshe, let's talk."

That drew a thin smile. "I think it would be better if Uri explained. He's closer to certain things than I am right now."

"My apologies for all those cloak-and-dagger precautions, Yeshivat," Davidov said in elegant Hebrew. "But it was really quite necessary."

"My work in Timna," Yaakov said, the resentment stirring again, "is also necessary."

" 'The stones are iron, and out of whose hills are dug mines of Brass.' Deuteronomy," Davidov quoted.

"A favor," Yeshivat said, making no effort to disguise his irritability, "spare me the scholarship." He felt drawn tight, weary. Why should that be? It was not yet five o'clock and he had been up for less than twelve hours. After all, he told himself, the night before he had gotten

208

his usual five hours' sleep. Perhaps he was getting old. "All right, what's this all about?" he rasped.

"Take it easy," Davidov said, in a patronizing way. "Last week Moshe was on holiday in Europe and the Old Man called *him* back."

Yaakov tugged at his twisted nose and hunched forward. "I thought B-G intended to stay retired this time, to live it out at Sde Boker. All at once he's back as Minister of Defense. I think maybe he will become Prime Minister again." He glanced sidelong at the man with the eye patch. "What do you think, Moshe?"

"When there's trouble, men like Ben Gurion are indispensable. Now listen to Davidov."

Davidov began. He spoke in a controlled voice, without emotion or emphasis, as if lecturing a class on contemporary history. "Tension between Israel and the Arab countries is on the increase."

"I've been in the Negev," Yaakov broke in. "You think I don't know what's going on?"

Davidov's expression held steady. "There are three reasons for this tension. Reason one: Our ships are prevented by blockade from using the Gulf of Aqaba, thus nullifying our hold on Eilat. There is a coast guard unit at Ras Natsrani and Sharm el-Sheikh is fortified and the islands of Tiran and Sanafir. Our ships are unable to sail through the Strait of Tiran for Africa or Asia. With Nasser continuing to deny us the use of the Suez Canal, this of course becomes intolerable."

"If I had my way, I'd know how to put an end to that blockade. A couple of battalions of paratroopers and I could——"

"Reason two," Davidov continued, as if there had been no interruption: "Terrorist activity on the part of the Arabs. The fedayeen, the self-sacrificers, as they call themselves, are being trained by the Intelligence Branch of the Egyptian Army in three camps in the Gaza Strip, near the sea, west of Gaza City. They are paid nine Egyptian pounds each month plus a bonus for every crossing made into Israel and another bonus for every target destroyed and every Jew killed. From December of 1955 through March of this year, there have been more than 180 acts of sabotage—mining of roads, shootings, and so on and so on. They continue. Our reprisals serve only as a temporary deterrent."

Yaakov started to speak but Davidov cut him off with an upraised hand. Yaakov had suspected it from the moment they met and now he was sure; he didn't like Davidov.

"Reason three," the tall man said. "Egypt continues to prepare for a major war against Israel. You know about Nasser's arms pact with Czechoslovakia, I suppose. And his army is being trained by professional soldiers, former Wehrmacht officers, and an increasing number of Russian people. Technicians and the like. He owns modern weapons and fighting planes. That arms transaction has destroyed the balance of power in this entire region. For every one of our tanks, Nasser has four. He has two hundred jet planes. We have fifty. He has MIGs and Ilyushins which are superior to our Ouragans and Meteors. And the Soviet T-34 tank is far superior to our Sherman Mark 3. These statistics do not include the equipment owned by Jordan, Syria, Iraq, and the other Arab countries."

"As you can see," Moshe put in wryly, "Davidov is extremely thorough. He has developed a private intelligence network of his own and his boys are scattered all over the Middle East."

Davidov directed his attention back to Yaakov. "And unlike the Arabs, my boys tell me what is true, not what they believe I might want to listen to."

Yaakov grunted, a soft sound back in his throat. "You have yet to tell me why I was sent for. I am still waiting."

The man with the eye patch crossed his legs and folded his hands in his lap. "What would you say to coming back on active duty, Yeshivat, with a promotion to full colonel? How does that sound to you?"

"I hear a big but in your voice, Moshe."

It was Davidov who spoke. "We need weapons, a variety of weapons. You have purchased guns in the past."

"From Bristol, in Monaco. You want me to see him again?"

"We must have contemporary armor. Tanks and field guns, halftracks that can maneuver in the desert. And new planes. We don't care where they come from, as long as they can do the job."

"Bristol generally deals in second-hand goods," Yaakov said.

"Then find another source. And one more thing, we do not have much money for such toys, the economics of Israel being what they are. You must hoard every piaster."

"And afterwards? When the job is done and I come back? What then?"

Davidov seemed to turn in on himself, growing absent, almost casual. "A sovereign nation has two choices in protecting its vital self-interests—to negotiate and to use force. The Arabs refuse to negotiate with us."

Yaakov glanced at Moshe. "This Davidov talks like a professor of philosophy."

"He is."

Yaakov folded his fingers into a fist. "All right. I'll get the hardware. But after, if there's going to be trouble I want to be part of it. No rear echelon job, no desk work. You know me, Moshe."

"The Old Man ordered me to take steps to protect ourselves, to be ready to act whenever and wherever we decide is best. That couldn't be done without men like you, Yeshivat."

Yaakov grew thoughtful. There was more involved here than simply talking to Harvey Bristol, checking an inventory. He would want to field test much of the equipment, see it in action, investigate performance records. A reliable assistant would be valuable.

"You know Amos Landau?" he said to Moshe. "The textile man."

"I've heard of him but we never met."

"His son, Joshua, is in Paris. I think he could help me."

Davidov answered. "Whoever you want, as long as the job gets done. And quickly. And one more thing. No one should know about this meeting, or that you are on active duty again. Others are being called back, too, officers mainly, to get matters organized. Plans are being made. But there is no need to create alarm. Or to alert our enemies."

III

"It's barbaric!"

It was Levi, still slender and tense, but tanned and handsome in his army khakis, who had spoken. His dark eyes darted from face to face around the dining room table. Except for Joshua and Rena, the entire family was there. Hank had come up from Jerusalem, and he smiled at Levi's outburst.

"Why do you say that?" Hank asked.

"To do that to a baby," Levi said passionately. "How do you know what deep emotional scars it will leave?" He turned to his father. "Millions of Christians have lived without circumcision."

"We're Jews," Ruth reminded him gently.

"Rena doesn't believe in God, any more than I do."

"Now we know where Simon gets all those ideas," Amos said.

"Maybe," Ruth said, "God believes in Rena. And in her new son."

Levi swung around to face Hank McClintock. "How could you let them talk you into it? I know you. You don't believe in all that superstitious nonsense."

"Maybe you don't know me as well as you think you do, Levi. Nobody talked me into it. I want my son to be circumcised."

"But you're not really a Jew, only a convert."

"Levi!" Amos said sternly. "That's enough. Hank is a Jew, as Jewish as any other. Never forget that."

Hank grinned at the youth. "You don't remember the blessing recited to me by the rabbi. 'May he who blessed our ancestor Abraham, the first convert, and said to him: "Go before Me and be righteous," bless and give courage to this proselyte who enters the fold.'" Hank laughed briefly. "Whether or not you like it, Levi, I'm one of you."

"And Jewish law forbids any convert to be reminded of his former status," Amos said. "Or to be dealt with disrespectfully because of it."

"So you see, Levi," Hank said lightly, "you must treat me gently lest I shatter and break."

Levi squirmed in his chair. "I still think it's barbaric. Two days old and you're planning to cut up the kid."

"Don't be vulgar, Levi," Ruth said.

"Circumcision is a symbol," Hank said, "an external symbol binding a Jewish boy to the faith. I'd better start arranging for a quorum," he ended.

"A minyan," Levi corrected, with scorn in his voice.

Hank grinned that crooked grin of his and Ruth could see what made him so attractive to Rena. He was handsome and charming, his manner mild and agreeable. Ruth had objected to the marriage when Hank had returned to Israel from America, even after he informed them that he had converted to Judaism. But now she was pleased to have him as a son-in-law, pleased that he had made Rena happy, pleased that he had given her her first grandchild.

"Do you know why ten men are necessary for a minyan?" Hank said.

"Why?" Levi challenged.

"There were ten Commandments, ten plagues visited on the Pharoah, ten Days of Penitence during the High Holy Days, ten generations beween Adam and Noah are recorded, ten more between Noah and Abraham, and Abraham underwent ten tests of his faith. Ten is a very important number to Jews."

"You should become a numerologist," Levi said.

"What you should do is enter the Bible contest," Amos said. "Wouldn't that be something, to have a McClintock win the Bible contest in Israel. That would give those pietists something to argue about." He paused and grew thoughtful. "Hank, unless you've decided on someone else, I would appreciate it if you would ask Yaakov Yeshivat to be godfather to the boy. We have been friends for a long time and—"

"Of course, Amos. Rena and I would like that. Where can I contact him?"

"I'll find out and let you know."

"That Yaakov," Ruth said, "it's time he settled down, got married. That way, people would at least know where he was some of the time."

Amos moved forward when he saw him come swinging into the hospital lobby. They shook hands and Amos squeezed his friend's upper arm.

"You're getting soft, Yaakov," he laughed. "Once this arm was like a piece of stone. Now the flesh has some give to it."

"I am as strong as ever. But look at you. Losing your hair, and what is that thickness under your belt?"

They laughed together and linked arms, moved toward the elevators. "You are all gray, *adoni*," Amos said, looking into that hard face, noticing the seams from nose to mouth, the pouches under the clear cold eyes, the thin lines circling that thick neck.

"The women love it," Yaakov said, voice rough and low. "Listen, *adoni*, I am pleased about this. I have never been a godfather before."

At the elevator bank, Yaakov punched the signal button. "They sent your message to me in France. I had to

213

pull strings to get back in time but a thing like this is important, for a kid to have the right godfather."

Amos sobered. "Joshua was in Paris last we heard. Did you see him?"

Yaakov shook his head. "I tried to contact him but he was gone."

"Gone where?"

"Something for the Government. I don't know."

"For the Government? Is he back with the UN delegation?"

"I don't know, I said. Leave it at that."

Going up, they were silent inside the elevator. In the corridor, Amos gripped the other man's arm.

"I can't leave it," he said with whispered urgency. "Joshua is my son. What is going on with him?"

Yaakov disengaged himself. "If I knew, I wouldn't tell you."

A frown rutted Amos' brow. "What's he involved in? That boy shouldn't take chances."

"His father took chances once. More than once."

"It was different. There was no choice in those days. Now we're a nation. There's a regular army, people trained to do those things."

"You know better than that. Every man in Israel is a soldier. One defeat and we'll all be wiped out. Men, women, kids, the bunch."

Amos eyed his friend quizzically. "Do you know something, Yaakov?"

"I only know that the Arabs look on terror as a continuing action, part of their war on us. For them it's revenge, and it restores their personal and national pride. Sooner or later it must be stopped."

"But not by striking back. We have to understand them more, make them understand us. The refugees, for example."

"Their problem, brought on themselves."

"Many of those people are Palestinians. We must reach some agreement with them."

"All right. Let's begin with you, Amos. The land your new factory stands on used to belong to an Arab. Someone like that friend of yours, al-Hadad. The Government took it over and it was passed on until you bought it. That Mejjid al-Hadad, he came to see me again a few months ago. But I can't help him. He's become bitter, just another drunken Arab now."

"Is war the only answer? We can't keep fighting forever."

"I agree. Perhaps one day we shall make it too expensive for the Arabs to continue making war. Then we will have peace."

"What is that supposed to mean?"

"Listen, Amos, you know what's going on. Back in July Nasser nationalized the Suez Canal. That made England very unhappy, and the French. I can't say that I mind seeing the British getting a little of their own back. They've always played both ends against the middle. For all their dealing with the Arabs, fighting their fights, they are out cold. And it will get worse for them in this region. They have no friends in the Middle East and their days are numbered."

They moved very slowly along the corridor. A nurse passed them, carrying a medical tray.

"What was the feeling in France about our situation?"

Yaakov's mind reached back easily. Through Harvey Bristol, a meeting had been arranged in a chateau on the outskirts of Paris. They gathered in a huge room with a massive fireplace and a vaulted ceiling, comfortable in deep chairs and sofas and sipping old brandy. In addition to Yaakov and Harvey Bristol, there were two French generals, a representative of the armament company involved, a naval attache and a political advisor. It was General Henri Marin, a slender man with a neatly barbered mustache, who did most of the talking.

"We have studied your requests, Colonel Yeshivat," he began, "and they are not without merit. Trucks, halftracks, tanks, transport aircraft."

"And fighter planes," Yaakov added. "Jets."

General Marin smiled. "Yes. Fighter-bombers. But the request for spare parts, supplies, fuel, and so on, are puzzling."

"Puzzling?"

"They are so limited. I assume you have other sources of supply available. From what we know of Israel's defense position, I deduce that your forces cannot have resources enough to fight for more than four or five weeks."

"Thirty days," Yaakov said grimly. "At the most."

"Thirty days!" the naval officer exclaimed. "And what happens if you must fight for thirty-one?"

"We won't let that happen," Yaakov replied. "The

215

Egyptians alone, if fighting should break out in the desert, will be defeated within two weeks."

General Marin observed the high gloss on his finger nails with interest. "And if Syria enters the conflict? Jordan? Lebanon? Iraq? Such a struggle could extend for far more than two weeks, more than thirty days. What then?"

"Then we will lose. Israel will expire."

The political advisor laughed, a brittle sound. The others looked at him questioningly. "Well, don't you see? If the Arabs should win, then the Americans will have to come and save all the Jews."

"It won't be worth the effort," Yaakov said, after an extended interval. "We will all be dead. Nasser will finish Hitler's work."

"Oh, come now, colonel," the political advisor said. That broken face, those steady almost white eyes made him uneasy, frightened almost. "It will never come to that."

It was General Marin who broke the silence. "I would like to satisfy your requests, Colonel Yeshivat. But try and understand the problem I face. Our commanders in Algeria keep demanding more weapons, always more. And there are other considerations."

Yaakov believed he knew what those other considerations were. Information had reached him that England and France were readying a joint expedition against Egypt and Nasser, determined to topple the Government and return the canal to the Suez Canal Company. If true, such a campaign would serve Israel's interests as well.

"My superiors," Yaakov said, choosing his words with care, "would be interested in knowing what France's position would be should war break out between Israel and Egypt?"

Marin crossed his legs and smoothed his trouser leg. "France is of course neutral but we do not look with disfavor upon the Jews."

"Israelis," Yaakov said.

Marin nodded agreeably. "We have only warm and friendly sentiments toward your Government and wish them well in all endeavors. However, it seems to us that there is nothing to be gained by giving notoriety to any exchanges that take place between our countries, this meeting included."

"A sensible precaution. I have been curious myself as to what steps if any France will take about the canal."

"Ah, Suez. A problem for so many years to so many

216

people. A Frenchman built it, you know. Ferdinand de Lesseps."

"And the English owned it for a long time."

"True. And now the Egyptian holds it and blusters and threatens. Such matters require maximum consideration. One would be foolish to act in haste—or, possibly, to act at all."

"Are the French sympathetic to Israel?" Amos asked, pulling Yaakov back.

He made an effort to focus on his friend. "Who can say about the French?"

They were outside the room the hospital had provided for the *brith*. Amos sighed and opened the door. "I hope matters can be worked out peacefully." He went inside and Yaakov followed.

Only men were present, friends and relatives. And the mohel, a surgeon who fulfilled all the religious requirements. Amos moved around, shaking hands, introducing Yaakov to the others.

"It is good of you to ask me to be the godfather," Yaakov said to Hank.

The slender man smiled warmly. "You're Amos' best friend. My son couldn't have anyone better."

Yaakov grunted and took his place alongside the mohel. Why didn't they bring the boy and get it over with? What if it all were true, he wondered, if there was a God, some fierce old spirit on high, sending down His demanding words, His Commandments? There were millions of people who had lived and died believing that. Yet millions more were without faith and lived and died well anyway. He studied the faces in the small room. What strange cord bound them all? They were all Israelis, true, and all Jews, even those who, like himself, were hardcore atheists. His gaze met Levi's and he deliberately winked. Levi turned away. A strange one, that boy, Yaakov told himself. All of Amos' sons, removed, loners, imprisoned by their own dreams, their own fears. He thought about Joshua and wondered if he was all right. The job he had undertaken was dangerous, could end suddenly and violently.

A nurse entered carrying Hank's new son. Yaakov took the boy and the other guests murmured the traditional welcome, "Blessed be he who cometh."

Yaakov looked at Hank McClintock. There was no blood in his cheeks and he appeared to waver slightly as he began to speak in Hebrew.

217

"I am ready to perform the precept of circumcising my son, as the Creator, blessed be He, has commanded us in the Torah: 'Every male among you throughout your generations shall be circumcised when he is eight days old.'"

The mohel held out his arms for the child and Yaakov handed him over. "This is the throne of Elijah, of blessed memory," the mohel intoned. "O Lord, I hope for Thy salvation. I wait for Thy deliverance, O Lord, and I do Thy bidding. I delight in Thy promise, like one who finds abundant wealth. Abundant peace have they who love Thy Torah, and there is no stumbling for them. Happy is he whom Thou choosest to dwell in Thy courts, close to Thee."

"May we fully enjoy the goodness of Thy house, Thy holy shrine," the guests said in concert.

The mohel made ready to perform the circumcision. "Blessed are Thou, Lord our God, King of the universe, who has sanctified us with Thy Commandments, and commanded us concerning circumcision."

The baby began to cry as the foreskin was swiftly cut away. When the cutting was completed, Hank said a benediction for his son.

"Praised be Thou, O Lord our God, ruling Spirit of the Universe, who in sanctifying us with His Commandments hath bidden us bring our son into the covenant of Abraham, our father."

"Even as he has been introduced into the covenant," the others prayed, "so may he be introduced to the Torah, to the marriage canopy, and to a life of good deeds."

A portion of the blood was drawn off from the child's organ so that it would not congeal and cause permanent damage. Watching the mohel perform the act with a special instrument, Yaakov remembered that this had formerly been done orally, and still was among the very Orthodox.

Wine was brought forward and the mohel placed a drop of the crimson liquid on the child's lips. The mohel prayed.

"Blessed art Thou, Lord our God, King of the universe, who didst sanctify beloved Israel from birth impressing Thy statute in his flesh and marking his descendants with the sign of the Holy Covenant. Because of this, for the sake of the Covenant, Thou didst impress in our flesh O eternal God, our Stronghold, deliver our dearly beloved from destruction. Blessed art Thou, O Lord, Author of the Covenant.

"Our God and God of our fathers, sustain this child for his father and mother. Let him be called in Israel, Baram, son of Henry. May both husband and wife rejoice in their offspring, as it is written: 'Let your parents be happy; let your mother thrill with joy.'

"Give thanks to the Lord, for He is good; His mercy endures forever. May this child, named Baram McClintock, become great. May this boy grow in vigor of mind and body to a love of the Torah, to the marriage canopy, and to a life of good deeds."

The mohel returned the infant to Yaakov who carried him out to the corridor where the nurse was waiting. She took him and left. Yaakov went back inside. The men were shaking hands and talking cheerfully.

Yaakov congratulated Hank, and Amos. "Baram McClintock," he said, with mock seriousness. "That has a fine Jewish ring to it."

"In honor of my father," Amos said, smiling.

"That was some old man," Yaakov said.

"Yes," Amos said, reflecting briefly. "Now let's all go to Rena's room where the ladies are waiting and we can have a proper celebration. After all, a *brith* is a *mitzvah* over all other *mitzvahs*. We're entitled to a little wine."

IV

On that same morning, at about the same time that Baram McClintock was being circumcised, David Ben Gurion resumed the post of Prime Minister of Israel. When the announcement was made, conflict between various political factions became inevitable. Ben Gurion represented a hard line with regard to the Arabs and there were many people who felt that a less rigid stance, a less militaristic response to Arab words and actions was in order. Ben Gurion offered such men little encouragement.

The stocky Zionist took his place on the dais under a photograph of Theodore Herzl, flanked by blue-and-white Israeli flags, presenting his new Cabinet to the Knesset, making clear his intentions.

"The Egyptian representatives at the UN," he said, "have openly declared that a state of war continues be-

219

tween Egypt and Israel. The Government of Egypt has violated basic international law governing the freedom of shipping through Suez, on which there was also a specific resolution of the Security Council. Thus Egypt now seeks to seal the Red Sea route against Israeli vessels, contrary to the international principle of freedom of the seas. This one-sided war will have to stop, for it cannot remain one-sided forever.

"The Government of Israel is ready faithfully to respect the Armistice Agreements in all their terms and details, preserving them in the letter and the spirit. But this duty is also binding on the other party. An agreement which is violated by the other side will also not be binding on us. If the armistice lines are opened by them to saboteurs and murderers, they will not be found closed to our defenders. If our rights are assailed by acts of violence on land or sea, we shall reserve freedom of action to defend those rights in the most effective manner.

"We seek peace—but not suicide."

That afternoon, with the sun high and hot, at a time least expected by Israeli patrols along the border, Abdul al-Hadad, inconspicuous in a worn brown suit and an old kaffiyeh, his shoes scraped and scratched, and smelling of goats, came out of Gaza and picked his way to the road heading north. In the fashion of the fellahin, he squatted at roadside, patiently waiting. A sedan driven by a stout Israeli sped by without slowing and a truck carrying farm utensils rolled southward. Abdul waited.

About thirty minutes passed before he spotted the ancient truck rattling in his direction. It moved without haste on the wrong side of the road, the driver leaning out the window, peering ahead. Seeing Abdul, he pulled back into the cab and a moment later his headlights blinked on and off three times. Abdul stood up. The truck came to a stop and the driver gazed blankly at Abdul.

"Salaam aleikum," Abdul said, approaching the truck. A quick glance told him that it carried some crated olives and dates. Nothing more. "You have some chickens to sell," he said.

"Ah," the driver said, recognition breaking. Then: "I go to Jerusalem, the Holy City. If that is your destination—"

"It is." Abdul came around to the other side and got in. The driver stared at him with curiosity. "All right, man," Abdul bit off curtly. "Start the truck. I don't want to sit here all day."

220

The driver grunted and turned to the road ahead. They began to move. Like Abdul, he wore a kaffiyeh, but there the resemblance ended. No more than forty, he looked half again as old, his face rutted and seamed, his eyes yellow and crimson. He hadn't shaved in days and his thorny hands were turned and swollen with arthritis.

"Effendi," he said after a few minutes. "I am a poor farmer, nothing more. I am not a political."

"So?"

"For me nothing changes. Life is the same as it was for my father and his father and his before him. There was the Turk and the Frenchman and the Englishman and now the Jew. For me it is the same. I do what I do and I know nothing."

"You are an Arab."

"As God wills it, effendi. I make this journey once every month and you were but a man on the road."

"That is why you were chosen. The Jews would suspect nothing."

"I pray to Allah that you are right. These affairs are not to my liking. Who you are. Where you come from. Why you come. These are not matters for my ears, effendi. In Jerusalem, I will market my olives and dates and return to my family before the sun sets. That is my life and I would not have it change. So I plead with you, effendi, tell me nothing and I will ask nothing. It is better to be silent."

"Then shut your mouth, old man," Abdul snapped hotly. "And we shall have some silence."

The driver nodded and inched closer to the wheel, as if trying to embrace it. Respect was not taught to young people anymore, he told himself bitterly, and it was not right. Not right at all.

Mejjid al-Hadad sat stiffly on the oak bench in the reception room of Rothenberg's office. The bench was hard on his bottom and a dull ache had come into the lower portion of his back. His throat and mouth craved some arak and he wished he had brought a bottle with him.

He eyed the girl at the typewriter, working so swiftly. They were shameless, these Jewish women. This one with her painted eyes and mouth, her big breasts. They showed their legs and were seen publicly without their husbands. It was another sign of Jewish decadence and he told himself that he had always resented such blatant disrespect.

The girl glanced up and smiled apologetically. "Mr. Rothenberg should be back soon. The new Prime Minister is addressing the Knesset this morning. But he knows you are here."

Mejjid inclined his head in response. The new Prime Minister. That was Ben Gurion, back in power again. The man was indestructible, a fearsome figure to every Arab, going on eternally. Tough and stubborn, determined. With Ben Gurion back, it would mean only more trouble for the Arabs. He made Mejjid think of one of those wild old Bedouin sheikhs, implacably fierce, single-minded, wily, fearless. A sigh trickled across his lips.

When Rothenberg returned to his office, he made elaborate apologies for the delay. "Politicians, Mejjid. You know how they love to talk. Everybody had some comment to make after B-G's speech." He ushered Mejjid into his private office, motioned him into a chair, and settled behind his desk. Rothenberg was a short, squat man of mild demeanor. He had a ready smile and his steel-rimmed glasses rode low on his thick nose.

Looking at Mejjid, Rothenberg tried not to reveal his dismay and concern. The once handsome and vital Arab had changed for the worse. His dark eyes were discolored, lifeless, and his mahogany cheeks were blotched and rutted. His ravenwing black hair was coarse and streaked and his big brown hands were palsied.

"You look well, dear friend," Rothenberg murmured.

"Time passes too swiftly each day, yet not fast enough."

"Many years lie ahead of you, Mejjid, full and rich years."

Mejjid rocked his head from side to side and his lower lip began to quiver. "There is no use in lying to each other. I cannot continue this way. My life is empty and bitter and the only peace I can find is in an arak bottle. You are my last chance. You must help me."

"I'm doing my best, Mejjid. These things are difficult, complicated."

"All the bureaucrats, all my friends. No one helps and I am a man in desperate need of assistance. I exist on a few pounds each month that come from the last of my rentals. But worse, all that is mine, has been taken from me. They have torn out my vitals and left me barely alive, struggling to breathe. I must be restored or finished off. It cannot go on this way." His voice began to climb, grow shriller, and he half rose out of the chair. "Always you Jews make a point of reminding people of how badly you have been treated. It's true, it's true. But what about me? The way you treat me! It isn't right, it isn't fair. Something must be done to correct it."

Rothenberg hesitated before speaking. From Mejjid's point of view, injustice had been done. But there was another point of view and it continued to prevail.

"Perhaps," he said softly, "it might be wise for you to accept things as they are."

"I will not! The land is mine. It has been in my family for three hundred years. I want what is mine! I will have it!"

Rothenberg settled back. Mejjid was not alone in his attitude. Others were in the same position and arbitrary decisions were made affecting the fate of such people. Rothenberg, and a handful of his colleagues in the Knesset, had made speeches, appealed to the national conscience to repair the damage, correct a cruel situation. It had done no good. Very little had been accomplished.

"You know that you can receive compensation," he said, the words hollow in his own ears. The law specified that a working farmer, not merely the owner of land, could receive equivalent lands outside the security zones or a cash recompense. But Mejjid had never done a hard day's work in his life.

Mejjid allowed his eyes to close. Weakness took hold of his arms and his legs and he was aware that his will to fight was draining away. He longed to find someone or something to hate. A tangible target to strike at, to destroy. Rothenberg. His eyes opened. No, not him. It was a system that was destroying him, a complex of departments and regulations, of interlocking bureaus. It had been the same under the English, the Military Government insisting on licences and passes and official approvals. But at least his property had not been taken away.

"What will they pay me?" Mejjid asked, without real interest.

"You can be compensated at the rate of twenty-five pounds for every dunam you owned. With the extent of your holdings, Mejjid, that will amount to a substantial sum."

Mejjid's head came up, eyes glittering. "Before my very eyes, they rob me! Twenty-five pounds for a dunam was the rate in 1950. This is 1956. Inflation has caused each dunam to be worth at least six times as much. I will not be cheated! You Jews have no right to do this to me."

Rothenberg felt guilty, defensive, and wanted to help the other man. But there was a deep emotional antipathy toward Arabs in Israel that Mejjid refused to recognize.

"Why should I suffer for Jewish inflation?" Mejjid went on. "You Jews brought it on yourselves. Unlimited immigration. What madness! All those foreigners! I am not responsible for that and should not have to suffer for it. Your people made the inflation, not me."

"Many of those immigrants came from Arab countries. They were driven out, persecuted, forced to leave all they owned behind."

"I had no part in such things!" Mejjid shouted, coming out of the chair. "I did not do it!"

The interview ended a few minutes later with nothing resolved. Mejjid left, angry, defeated and afraid. Back at his house, he opened a bottle of arak and began to drink. When one of his wives appeared with some lunch, he sent her away with an oath. How long he sat that way, drinking and staring into space, he never knew. He never heard the door at the rear of the house open and close, took no notice of the excited babble in the women's quarters, was not aware of Abdul's presence in the large sitting room.

"Father."

Recognition came slowly and when it did his head jerked around. *"El-ham dillah!"* he cried emotionally. "Allah is kind and good! Oh, my son, first born of my loins. I feared for you, that you had been killed and I would never be told."

They embraced and kissed and Mejjid held desperately to his son as if afraid he might disappear.

"Come," he said finally, leading the boy to the sofa. "Sit with me. We will talk. All that matters is that you are home. Allah is compassionate. He sent you to assist me in my struggle to win back what is mine. And now I shall triumph. You are young and your mind is strong and clear. You will discover the way to victory for me. The Government treats me badly and I can no longer deal with them. You must rest and in a day or two you and I will attack the problem together and we shall be victorious."

Abdul's slender brown face gathered together, his deep black eyes clouded with concern. Abdul had never seen his father this way before. He remembered him as a man always in control of his life, able to shape events to his own ends. But this man, drunk and blabbing like an old woman, eyes blurred and hands shaking, was almost unrecognizable.

He thought about his mission. In this condition, Mejjid would be useless to the cause, more of a hindrance and a threat. Still, Mamoud had insisted that one more attempt be made to win him over.

"Father, we must talk now."

"Yes. We must talk. I will explain the situation to you, how the Jews have tricked me and cheated me. Then you will devise a scheme to defeat them."

"Father, listen to me."

"Yes, my son, I will listen. There is much work to do. When the properties are back in my hands, you will serve as my manager, my collector of rents. We will restore the family to its rightful position."

"Father, in the morning I am going back to Gaza."

Mejjid looked at him without comprehension. "Back to Gaza?"

"Yes. I am needed there."

"*I need you here!* Don't you understand, I am in trouble. I need your help."

Mejjid gazed off into space, reached reflexively for the arak. Abdul took the bottle out of his hand. "Father, it is I who must have your assistance. Have you lost so much of your manhood that you cannot aid your son?"

Mejjid forced himself to sit erect and made a concentrated effort to marshal all his senses into working order. His dark eyes came into focus.

"It has not been easy for me," he muttered. "But I will try to understand." His voice took on new force. "What do you want of me?"

"Father, I am a member of the fedayeen. I fight to win back Palestine, for the glory of all the Arabs."

"The Jews are too strong. Ben Gurion has returned and leads them again. He will arrange to have you killed."

"We shall do the killing. Ben Gurion is old and tired and Gamal Nasser is youthful and potent, the wave of tomorrow. We who fight for him are infused with his dreams of Arab glory and greatness and, with Allah's help, we will win."

"You will die in the desert; your bones left to bleach; and I shall never be told of your death."

"Hear me, father. What I do, I do with the support of Egypt, of all the other Arabs. I myself am an officer now and I am responsible for the training of other men.

Information comes to me, facts not known to others. I say to you that it is only a question of time before we destroy this abomination the Jews call Israel."

"There is no way——"

"There is no way the anger of the Arabs can be appeased by less. No one can stop us. The United Nations is nothing. The United States is cowardly and uncertain and will not act against us. England, France, they are no longer powerful and decisive. Our fate is at last in our own hands and we shall do as we wish. This is a glorious time to be alive, father, and all Arabs everywhere must enlist in this holy endeavor. Fedayeen are nourished on hatred for our enemies and we are able to penetrate deep into Palestine, to turn the lives of the Jews into living hell. Nothing can stop us, father. Nothing will."

"The Government will not allow——"

"They can do nothing. Help us. Help *me*, oh, my dear father, join with me in this struggle and you will be honored and rewarded when we march across the bodies of the Jews into Jerusalem."

Resentment lodged in Mejjid's throat. Resentment and fear. "You expect me to crawl about in the desert and play war games with children!" he burst out. The passion was quickly spent. "I am too old for fighting," he muttered. "I want only the return of my property."

"And you will have it. I will see to it, for by right of heritage what is yours is also mine."

Mejjid measured his son. Abdul had become a man, a stranger almost, only a faint residue of the boy he had been, remaining.

"What do you expect me to do?" Mejjid said wearily.

"You have friends in high places among the Jews. You will hear certain things which when put together with other things can tell us what the Jews plan."

"That is all?"

"More. A man is needed to gather such information from the others who work for the cause. To gather it and make sure it is speedily transmitted. A man is needed who will be reliable, someone other Arabs in Palestine will respect and obey. An organization must be formed, plans for sabotage made and men recruited to execute them."

"You are asking me to become a spy, a saboteur! I will be found out and shot."

"You will be acclaimed a hero and a patriot and be honored. Gamal Nasser will embrace you. The Mufti of

Jerusalem will bless you. Your sons and their sons will sing your praises."

Abdul held the bottle of arak aloft. "Before Allah, I ask you to choose. The corruption in this bottle or the holy cause of God and your son."

Mejjid stared at his son. "Tell me what I must do," he said, his voice thick but steady.

Abdul did.

V

Yaakov Yeshivat sat in the front seat of the limousine next to the driver and watched the flight from Rome touch down, roll into the deplaning area.

The first passenger to come off the plane was a small man in a badly-fitted suit and a broad-brimmed hat. He wore dark glasses and he stepped briskly down the steps. Behind him, pale and scholarly, eyes searching, came Joshua Landau. Yaakov climbed out of the car.

Joshua spied him but gave no sign. When he reached the ground, he spoke to the small man and together they walked over to the car.

"Shalom, Yaakov."

"Shalom, Joshua." Yaakov opened the back door of the limousine. "Inside, Professor Thomashevsky. We'll talk while we drive." He spoke in Yiddish. The little man did as he was told. Moments later, they were on the road leading to Tel Aviv.

"In the city," Yaakov said, "you'll be transferred to another vehicle. An ambulance."

The little man scowled. "Are such dramatics necessary?"

"Security, Professor," Joshua said mildly. "The Soviets have been known to try and get people back, one way or another." The little man grunted and gazed at the passing landscape. "This is Colonel Yeshivat," Joshua continued. "A personal friend and a good Socialist."

"Soldiers and politicians," Thomashevsky snorted. "I have no interest in either. Just my work. You promised me a laboratory, that I would be allowed to proceed with my experiments free from official interference—"

"And the promise will be fulfilled," Yaakov said. "The plan is to construct two reactors, one at——"

"Don't fill my head with details. My work is concerned with desalinization of sea water. Nothing else. I am convinced it can be done efficiently and economically. The Soviets insisted that I concentrate on weapons development. I wouldn't do it there and I won't do it here. I do not wish to give death to any creature."

"Make some sweet drinkable water for us, Professor," Yaakov said lightly, "and leave the killing to us soldiers."

The little man squinted at him and shook his head. "You take pleasure in killing?"

Yaakov chose his words carefully. "If there must be killing, Professor, I would rather do it than have it done to me."

The Professor made a noncommittal sound back in his throat and the rest of the journey was made in silence. In Tel Aviv, they drove into a parking area behind an apartment building. An ambulance was waiting.

"Good luck, Professor," Joshua said.

"Mr. Landau, for bringing me out, I thank you. It was impossible for me to live in Russia any longer, but without your help they would not have permitted me to leave."

"That is why Israel is here," Yaakov said, his harsh, gravelly voice tempered. "For Jews who have no place else to go. You will be safe here and free to do your work. Shalom."

"Shalom," the little man said. He climbed into the back of the ambulance and seconds later was driven away.

"I'm glad that's over," Joshua said.

"Rough?"

"There were moments. The Russians can get very sticky about scientists who try to defect. Still, we managed it."

"The names I gave you—?"

"All were very good. Once I got him into Moscow proper we were able to drop out of sight. They passed us along very efficiently. Except in Leningrad. That man no longer exists. Simply disappeared one day about four months ago."

"Did you use the emergency name?"

Joshua nodded. "He isn't reliable. You better do something about him. He could be dangerous to the others."

"I'll see to it. Did you go by way of Amsterdam or Berlin?"

"Both. But in Berlin they picked up our trail. A couple of gunmen."

"Trouble?"

"A little. Some shooting. That Thomashevsky, you wouldn't believe it to look at him, but he is very steady, very brave. I decided to take the long way around and we went to Amsterdam. They are very good in Amsterdam."

"They've had lots of practice helping Jews when the Nazis were there. After Amsterdam?"

"London, then Rome, and back."

"I imagine you can use a little rest. Come on, I'll take you home."

They got back in the limousine. "Yaakov," Joshua began, "I'm not sure, about going home. Maybe it was a mistake to come back. Would you believe that the idea of seeing my father again frightens me more than bringing Thomashevsky out did?"

"Naturally. Amos Landau is much more menacing than Khrushchev. Listen, *adoni*, it is all over with Gabrielli, that was a long time ago."

"I can still see her, remember the smell of her and the taste of her mouth."

Yaakov looked at Joshua with renewed interest. "Ah, you restore my faith, Joshua. You and Mara. *That* must have been something special."

Joshua gave an embarrassed laugh. "Not what you think. I never had nerve enough to try. She terrified me, all that beauty."

"Ah, then you are not the man your father is. Obviously beauty does not terrify him. Don't blame him for doing what you would have enjoyed doing. Maybe it is just as well. Mara hurt him but he recovered. You might not have."

"She hurt me too. They both did."

Yaakov made a disparaging sound. "You were a kid playing a game. Puppy love. Amos was a man and that made it different, gave it a higher value. Anyway, it's over. Your mother was able to forgive him and you should too. Besides, none of us will ever see Mara again. She's a big movie star, rich, famous, unreachable."

A wry expression flattened Joshua's mouth. "That last picture of hers, I saw it. You know, *adoni*, she is really quite an awful actress."

"But beautiful."

"Oh, yes. Beautiful. Well, I suppose it is time I went home. It should be interesting."

Yaakov leaned forward and gave the driver the Landau address. The car eased smoothly ahead.

VI

Yaakov found the next few weeks less than satisfactory. Davidov assigned him to a desk with orders to break the logistical jam that promised to leave the Israeli Defense Force with a scarcity of operable equipment. Yaakov felt as if he were being smothered in paperwork, in columns of statistics, in pessimistic reports of aids who kept insisting that nothing could be done to alleviate the situation.

Frustrated and increasingly irritable, Yaakov decided to get a first-hand look at conditions for himself. He spent three days in the assembly areas of the Negev, inspecting motor pools, talking with mechanics and tank drivers, testing equipment and checking spare parts inventories. He returned to his desk convinced that disaster faced the Army unless adequate replacement parts were obtained for the armored brigades.

That same day, he summoned his small staff to a meeting in his office. "No vehicle can make it across the Negev without tracks," he roared. "And Sinai would be worse. To climb dunes, to cross the soft stretches, will be impossible for us without tracked transportation. There are going to be breakdowns, tanks and halftracks disabled by the enemy. We must have spare parts. Find them. Make them. Steal them. I want our purchasing people overseas to get on this at once. Today. Get them on the telephone. If they can't do the job, fire them. Hire people who can get what we need. We must have at least 500 spare tracks for the tanks. More for the halftracks. Put every workship on this. Top priority. Contact the Kaiser-Fraser plant. They must help us." He glared at the other officers. "Have we heard from Paris yet? Where the hell is the stuff they're sending?"

A major answered. "We received notification yesterday. Shipment is under way now. Two hundred halftracks, 300 6x6 trucks, 20 tank transporters and 100 Super Sherman tanks."

The lines around Yaakov's mouth softened. "Well, that's the first good news I've heard in days."

"Yaakov," the major said hesitantly, "there is also some bad news."

230

"Oh." There was no mistaking the menace in that single word.

"An hour ago I received a dispatch from our people in Belgium."

"So! Tell me."

"The rifles the F.N. Works is making for us failed to pass the tests, fell short of specifications. That means——"

"I know what it means, dammit!" Yaakov roared. "Wire them at once. Tell them—no." He jabbed his thick forefinger at the major. "You will go there. At once. Today. We must have those rifles. Work out some kind of a modification, but get those rifles. And while you're there, speed shipment on the truck parts."

"They're due for shipping next week."

"By air freight," Yaakov said.

"But the cost! We haven't got the money."

"To hell with money! I must have those parts. Get them. We'll worry about money later." His manner softened and he almost smiled at the major. "Do whatever must be done, *adoni*. Somehow I will get the money."

"Yes, Yaakov."

"And have a nice trip. Now goodbye."

The major hurried away. When he was gone, Yaakov glanced at the notes he had made to himself in the Negev. He looked up at the remaining members of his staff.

"Some of our new tanks do not have turrets and others do not have guns. How soon will that be corrected?"

A captain rose and spread his hands helplessly. "We don't know when the turrets will arrive. You see, Yaakov ——"

He waved the man quiet and considered the problem. There was no way to be sure how soon those new tanks might be needed. In their present condition they were useless. His eyes lighted on a burly tank captain, temporarily assigned to his staff.

"Jesse, these new Shermans provide us with greater mobility and speed than the old Mark 3s, correct?"

"Correct."

"Suppose we take the Mark 3 turrets—would they fit the Shermans?"

The captain frowned thoughtfully. "I think so. Some minor adjustment might be necessary, but it could be made in the field. Yes, an excellent idea."

"Do it."

He glanced at the reports in his hand, but before he could proceed, Uri Davidov appeared. He nodded affably

231

to the officers. "Don't let me break up your meeting, chaverim," he said, advancing into the room.

"It is broken up," Yaakov said bluntly. "All right, we resume after lunch."

Davidov pulled a chair in front of Yaakov's desk and sat down, heaved his feet up. "My spies tell me you are doing an excellent job, Yeshivat, that you've got things cracking around here."

Yaakov eyed the younger man steadily. "You wanted to talk to me?"

"We have a small problem."

"We? Or you?"

Davidov's scholarly face remained passive. "It was my problem. It is yours now. We seem to have run out of funds with which to build additional storage sheds for ammunition. Also, we're short of harnesses, drop-sacks and pulleys for the paratroopers. Get on it at once."

Yaakov kept himself from laughing aloud. He had anticipated these matters and would deal with them. "In the south, beyond Beersheba," he said, "we can store ammunition in the open. Canvas covers will be sufficient protection. As for the airborne troopers, I'll do what I can but no promises. It won't matter. Not with those boys. They're tough. Give them a weapon and a 'chute and they'll be all right." Settling back in his chair, Yaakov rested his chin on his fist. "Davidov, you think it will really happen? Another war?"

"I don't know. It's a political decision but it must be based on military realities. The fedayeen have increased the tempo of their raids. They mine our roads and kill our people. And now that Nasser's taken over the canal—" a faint smile lifted the corners of his fine mouth—"who knows what will happen."

"You think the English and French will go to war for Suez?"

"They might. I've heard names of certain military and naval commanders mentioned. Oh, yes, they might."

"I don't trust the English. They are a mendacious race concerned only with their own profit."

"Aren't we all?"

"You forget what they were like during the Mandate, how they sided with the Arabs. But I have forgotten nothing. Before King Abdullah was murdered he let a number of people know that he was prepared to reach an understanding with Israel but the British stood against it. The British Minister in Amman told Abdullah that an agreement would injure relations between England and the Arabs and that ended the matter. If England had kept her dirty hand out of it, there might not be this trouble today. Jerusalem would not be divided. It would be open to Jew and Arab alike. I trust no Englishman, and with good reason."

"Trust aside, Yeshivat, if England attacks Suez it would benefit us. It would divert Egypt's attention and should the English occupy the Canal Zone it would mean free passage for our ships. It would also mean an end of the raiding."

"When it happens I will believe it. Israel's security can be established only by Israel." He leaned forward. "One thing troubles me—the Americans. What position will they take if fighting breaks out?"

"Interesting question. That Secretary of State of theirs, a smug and self-righteous man. And he influences their President. But they will not act. The Arabs have the oil but the Jews have the votes. I agree with you about one thing, Yeshivat—we can depend upon ourselves only. And I can assure you the Government will act solely with that in mind."

After Davidov left, Yaakov went back to work immediately. Time had become precious. There might be too little of it left to him. To them all.

A colonel from Planning & Operations had worked out an intricate formula for mobilization. Personnel attached to armored units—D-day minus 8; units designated to attack Sharm el-Sheikh and Nakhl, opening the port of Eilat—D-day minus 7; troops for the Gaza Strip—D-day minus 4.

"What about the Jordanian and Syrian frontiers?" the Chief of Staff said quietly.

The colonel had his answer ready. "Should those countries launch an action against us—and we are assuming that they will fulfill their obligations to Egypt once fighting breaks out—they will require a certain amount of time to mobilize. This allows us to muster men for those fronts on D-day itself and the day after. That schedule would also apply to GHQ reservists." The colonel returned to his seat, a contented expression on his full face.

The Chief of Staff glanced around the long table. His single eye glittered brightly, coming to rest on Yaakov seated at the far end of the table, head sunk low between his bulging shoulders, graying hair flaring wildly, a closed expression on the seamed face, an almost threatening turn to the mouth.

"Yeshivat. You have an opinion?"

Only the pale eyes responded, looking out from under the thick brows, holding steadily. "About what, Moshe?"

The Chief of Staff repressed a smile. If he knew his man, Yeshivat was ready to explode, would put it straight so no one could misunderstand. The Chief of Staff preferred it this way.

"Ah, you're bored and haven't been listening. Planning is of no concern to you. You are a man of action. Still, it is necessary to think about these details, Yeshivat. We are discussing mobilization. Operation Kadesh. Possibly you've heard it mentioned before."

"I heard, Moshe."

"Will you give us the benefit of your thinking?"

"It won't work."

"Say why."

"Because—hell, Moshe, you might as well let the whole world in on it. Send telegrams to Cairo and Damascus. Eight days before D-Day! This country will be in a turmoil."

"Alternatives, please."

"Secrecy. Surprise. No general mobilization. Not a week in advance." He closed the fingers of his right hand into a fist and held it alongside his chin. "Hit them quick and hit them hard. This way. Call your officers a day or two at the most before you need them. Brief them. Get them ready for the troops. Armored units will need some time to reactivate their vehicles, prepare their guns. D-day minus two."

"Minus 3," Davidov corrected mildly. "They will need twenty-four extra hours."

"Okay," Yaakov said. "All other units the following day. Normal notification procedures, as if it was the usual training exercise."

"Davidov?" the Chief of Staff said.

"I agree with Yeshivat."

"So do I and that's how it will be. Exactly that way. All right, Davidov."

The tall general stood up. "Chaverim, we intend to muster 100,000 reservists in forty-eight hours, a monumental task. If we can get seventy-five percent of them reporting in time, I will be satisfied. More than that will be a pleasant surprise. As usual, transportation is our primary problem. We will call up over 13,000 vehicles—

taxis, ice cream trucks, private cars. Most will be in poor condition. There will be breakdowns. It will be up to the men to get to their assignments anyway. Once Operation Kadesh is begun, there will be no turning back."

A headquarters officer raised his hand. "People will want to know why they're being called."

Davidov went on without hesitation. "Iraq is moving some of her troops into Jordan. That is your cover story. This is a defensive call, in case there should be trouble. That should take care of all questions." He looked around and, when no one spoke, sat down.

"That is all for today," the Chief of Staff said. "Thank you for coming. Yeshivat, you will stay behind, please."

Yaakov remained slumped in his chair as the others filed out. Davidov and the Chief of Staff stood until the others had gone. Yaakov contemplated standing, in deference to rank. To hell with it, he told himself. Davidov was a stuffed shirt and Moshe—well, he was still Moshe and always would be.

"Well, Yeshivat, you think it will work?"

"The boys will come to fight. I'm sure of that. More than seventy-five percent, I think."

"About the strategy," the Chief of Staff said. "If the Old Man orders us into action. A quick strike into Sinai, into Gaza, and down to Eilat. What do you think?"

"It's possible. I would like to know about Egyptian armor, troop displacements, and if the British and French intend to go into Suez."

"Forget about them. It's us and Nasser, that's all."

"What about Jordan and Syria?"

"Let's proceed on the assumption that, for one reason or another, neither country fights. There you have the situation. How would you deal with it?"

Yaakov allowed his eyes to close. A vision of his father drifted onto his brainpan. He could almost hear the big, hawklike man holding forth in that loud, joyous voice of his. "Fight the Arab where he doesn't expect you to be. That will confuse him and he'll need time to understand. Punish him, if you can, but don't kill him unless you must. Frighten him. Bring him close to death and allow him room to run. He will." Yaakov opened his eyes.

"Go after territory, Moshe, strategic position. A blood bath will gain nothing for us. We can never kill Arabs enough to secure Israel. There are too many of them. Put them to rout, get behind them."

"Go on."

235

"Paratroop drops deep in enemy territory. Mitla Pass must be taken in the first minutes. Mitla will be the key to Suez, to Eilat. Armored units should advance swiftly, by-passing and isolating Egyptian units. Leave the mopping up for later. As soon as possible, our people must break through to the canal and get across, move on Cairo."

"We stop at the canal," Davidov said firmly.

Yaakov looked at him, then the other man. "It could be finished for all time, Moshe."

"We stop at the East Bank. *Our* side. That must be understood."

"I don't like it."

Davidov spoke in that schoolroom manner. "It isn't necessary that you like it, as long as you obey."

Yaakov glared at the younger man. "It makes no difference whether or not I obey. Not as long as I must waste my time with paperwork and supplies here in Jerusalem."

"That is all changed," Davidov said quietly.

"It may cause some unhappiness," the Chief of Staff said, "but I have decided to replace certain unit commanders. This is going to be a short war, *adoni,* and no chances can be taken. None. The best men must be in charge." Leaning back in his chair, he assessed Yaakov coolly. "Would you be interested in taking over an airborne brigade?"

A reminiscent stirring came alive in Yaakov's gut. He straightened up and his mouth went flat. "I am interested."

"Those paratroopers are hard boys. Can you handle them?"

"Try me."

"I intend to. Your objectives will be Mitla, Sharm el-Sheikh and Eilat. Enough fighting to fill anybody's belly."

"When do I begin?"

"At once."

The camp was in the desert south of Beersheba. A sprawl of canvas and slit trenches and camouflage nets. The sun was only an hour above the horizon when Yaakov arrived the next morning, and already the heat was thick and oppressive. Men stood naked under field showers and let the warm water run over their bodies while others shaved at car mirrors. Yaakov got out of the jeep that had brought him and walked toward the command tent, eyes working over the scene. A captain and a sergeant were in the command tent.

"I'm Yeshivat," Yaakov announced without preliminary. "Brigade commander. I want to meet with all officers in thirty minutes."

When the officers were assembled, Yaakov entered the situation tent. There was a shuffling of feet as they rose. He let them stand.

"This brigade is likely to be fighting a war at any time," he bit off, pale eyes going from face to face, voice edged and cutting. "Yet I see tanks and halftracks, trucks and jeeps, lined up neatly as if for parade. In precisely—" He glanced at his watch. "—In precisely four hours I shall inspect all positions. I want every tank, every track, all supply trucks, pointed south, toward the enemy, able to be under way in five minutes times. There are orchards around here. Hide the tanks in them. Put the tracks in the wadis. Camouflage the trucks. One man will be on duty with each vehicle at all times. The rest of the crews will remain within visual distance.

"Next. I want reconnaissance patrols out every morning and again just before sundown. Two men to each patrol. If there is any Egyptian armor on the move, I want to know about it. Also, they will keep their eyes open for new enemy emplacements."

"And if they're spotted, colonel?"

"Then they had better get back to their units with all possible speed. No fighting unless attacked."

"Colonel," another officer said. "Arab patrol planes fly over this area regularly. They'll spot the footsteps our men make."

Yaakov nodded. "Have the scouts keep to the wadis as much as possible. If crossing the dunes becomes unavoidable, the men are to wear Bedouin sandals on their feet. All right. That's it for now. Let's go to work." They began moving out of the tent. "One more thing, chaverim," he said. "Mazel tov."

They were smiling when they left.

VII

The main office of the Landau Company was located in a two-story building in the business section of Tel Aviv. Amos' private office was on the second floor, a modest-sized room decorated with antique furniture. There was a Chagall on the wall opposite his desk and a small yellow-green cactus in a patch of sunlight near the windows.

Amos was studying the building costs of a proposed new wing to the textile factory. Profits had been high and the market gave every indication of remaining favorable. His suppliers of raw materials were offering good prices and the potential for the company seemed excellent. He decided to approve the expansion plan and authorize work to begin. His secretary knocked and entered. She was a plump sabra who wore a perpetual smile.

"Excuse me, Amos," she said brightly. "A young lady is outside. She insists on seeing you in person."

"What does she want?"

"To see you. Her name is Braun."

"Braun? I don't know anyone by that name. All right, send her in."

There were two things about Braun: wiry hair that matched the color of her freckles, and a kind of precise, studied walk that Amos recognized immediately.

"Amos Landau?" she said briskly.

"I'm Landau." This couldn't have come at a worse time. There was so much work to do, so many decisions to be reached, decisions that only he could make. And with Joshua home. He yearned to spend a lot of time with his son. He held out his hand. "Let me have it."

Braun showed her surprise. "You know why I'm here?"

"You think you're the first?"

She gave him an envelope and watched him rip it open, read the message:

MOST SECRET.
REPORT TO BRIGADE HEADQUARTERS AT ONCE.
HIGHEST SECURITY PROVISIONS.

He looked up. Braun was still standing on the other side of the desk. "Excuse me," she said. "But how could you tell?"

Amos burned the message in his ashtray. "You girls with your training walk," he said, laughing. "You move more like soldiers than the men do." A look of dismay came onto the freckled face. "Wiggle a little, my dear," he said. "Be less soldier and more woman. It will serve you better."

He watched her leave, swinging her ample hips in an exaggerated arc. He called his secretary. "Telephone my wife. Say I won't be home for supper. Say a forty-eight hour business trip. She'll understand."

"Another one?" the secretary said.

"Another one," he agreed dryly. These practice call-ups. They fooled no one in Israel. How could they? In such a small country, everyone was either in the defense forces or had relatives or friends who were. If this had been a general alert, even women would be mustered, and his secretary would have been called. "If you have to go," he cautioned her, "make the usual arrangements with the office manager. Now see if one of our delivery vans can meet me out front. There won't be any taxis available today."

Levi Landau slung the Uzi sub-machinegun and climbed into the back of the 6x6. He found space between two other men on the slatted seat and shoved his bedroll between his legs. He layed the Uzi across his knees and patted it lovingly.

"Nice baby," he murmured.

"You like the Uzi?" the man on his right said.

"I like it and it likes me," Levi replied. "We're going to take care of each other."

The Uzi was light and rapid-firing and he marveled that Israel had actually been able to manufacture such an effective weapon. Levi pulled an orange-and-blue stocking cap out of his pocket and put it on.

"That makes a fine target," the patrol leader said. He was a hard looking youth about Levi's age with small eyes and a high, thin voice.

"Don't worry," Levi assured him, "if there's any shooting, I'll provide a moving target."

That drew a laugh from the other men in the truck.

"Besides," Levi went on, "there's not going to be any shooting. I've been wearing this uniform for more than a year and I've yet to hear a shot fired in anger."

"This time it could be different," the patrol leader said.

"Not a chance," another soldier put in. "The Arabs

don't dare come around where Landau is. They know when they're well off."

There was more laughter and Levi joined in.

"It's true," he said, when they quieted. "I would destroy them all by myself. I am perhaps the most ferocious Jewish soldier since the Maccabees. I assure you, this is just another futile exercise designed to destroy our kidneys. Israel must have the worst roads in all of Asia, especially here in Galilee."

"Where are we bound for this time?" someone asked.

The patrol leader cursed cheerfully. "How would I know? Can I tell what's in Dayan's head?"

"More important," someone shot back, "can he tell what's in yours?"

When the laughter faded away, the patrol leader spoke quietly. "We're heading for the frontier with Syria. That's all I know."

"Hey, Levi!" the man on his right said insinuatingly. "Tonight, let's sneak into Damascus. I've never had a Syrian girl. With my good looks and your meanness we will love the women and scare off the men at the same time."

Levi stretched out his legs and pretended to yawn. Just as he gave his comrade the finger, the truck lurched into motion.

Rena hovered over Baram tickling him lightly. His mouth gaped open in silent pleasure. Hank stood off to one side, aiming a 16mm motion picture camera at his wife and son.

"Move your head to one side," he directed. "I can't see the kid."

"His name is Baram," she corrected.

"That's better. Make him laugh again."

The doorbell sounded. "I'll go," Rena said.

"No. Stay. I'll be right back."

The messenger was a middle-aged man with watery eyes and an inquisitive nose. "Mr. Henry McClintock?"

"That's right."

The messenger handed over an envelope. Hank recognized it for what it was. "Thank you." He started back inside.

"Tell me," the messenger said conversationally. "If you don't mind, you're Jewish?"

"Of course," Hank said, ducking into the house.

The messenger looked at the closed door, shaking his head. McClintock! Was that a name for a Jew to have!

Joshua and Simon were having lunch in the garden. Ruth had prepared a green salad and iced tea, with melon for dessert. Now Simon was pressing his brother for details of his adventures during his time away from home.

"Were you ever in danger?" the boy asked, trying to disguise the excitement and pride he felt in Joshua's exploits. "They might have shot you if you were caught in Russia."

"I don't think so. People don't get shot so much these days."

Simon considered that. "That's good. Shooting is stupid, I think. Wars and all that killing."

"Sometimes it's necessary to protect yourself or your country."

"If nobody would fight there couldn't be any wars," Simon said with simple logic.

Joshua laughed and ruffled his brother's hair. "There's no arguing with that."

Joshua rose as Ruth returned to the garden. It seemed to him that she, and Amos, had aged perceptibly since he had seen them last. Not that they were old, but the years were apparent. New lines around the eyes and mouth, a slight sagging under the chin, a more measured way of speaking. The inroads of time.

And more. There had always been a remote quality about his mother, a bright vagueness of purpose, a fluttering uncertainty. It seemed more prevalent these days, yet more transparent, a thin veneer barely veiling a deepening tension.

As for Amos, he appeared contented and smug, protective of his success; it was apparent in his careful choice of words and the thickening line of his once trim figure. It occurred to Joshua that Mara Gabrielli and his father would never have become lovers now. It would have presented too much of a risk for Amos to take.

His mind returned to that day when the facts of Mara's relationship with Amos had become known. Was it only five years? It seemed to belong almost to another lifetime. How shocked Joshua had been, how indignant! But there had been no hurt, not really. A kind of grudging admiration for his father and some envy. And the sudden revelation that he was presented with a dramatic opportunity to free himself from the strictures of home and family without guilt. *Everybody would understand.* A flush of shame heated his cheeks at the thought of the subterfuge.

How young he had been. How frightened. Unable to go away except with the support of his own self-righteousness. And how naive. To believe that Mara Gabrielli would cause his mother and father to break up their marriage. Ruth and Amos needed and wanted each other, the gears of their lives meshing smoothly, and nothing, no matter how painful, could disrupt that.

He pulled one of the painted wicker chairs away from the table so his mother could sit. She smiled up at him.

"That was your father's secretary on the phone," she explained. "He won't be coming home for dinner."

Joshua's first thought was that Amos had another mistress, another Mara.

"It's one of those practice alerts the military is always having. He'll be gone for two days this time. We have a little code—" Her smile was apologetic. "—It's so I'll know what's going on and won't worry."

Joshua tried not to reveal his concern. Perhaps it was nothing more than that. But he owned enough private information to know the political situation was worsening each day.

"I imagine I should report in to my old unit," he said, keeping his manner casual. "Some training wouldn't hurt. Get me back into physical condition."

"That's stupid," Simon broke in. "What do you want to do that for? All that soldier stuff—I think it's stupid."

Ruth addressed the boy patiently. "Everything is not stupid because you say it is, Simon."

"Well, it is stupid. All that killing and——"

Joshua stood up. "I think I'll check in," he said. "At least let them know I'm back. Besides, it would be nice to see some of my old friends again."

"Couldn't it wait for a few days?" Ruth said.

Joshua kissed her cheek. "I've got nothing to do this afternoon anyway."

She glanced up at him, face lined and worried. "Is there any real danger, Joshua?"

"Don't be silly. You said so yourself, the Army's always having this kind of thing. It gives those generals something to do."

"Boy, Joshua," Simon said, his voice thick with disgust. "You're as bad as papa, just as stupid."

Violence continued. A farmer was beaten to death near

242

Amir, and his tractor blown up. On the road south of Degania, a schoolbus ran over a mine and burned; it was empty at the time and so only the driver died. A railroad line was dynamited in three places and a kibbutz near Gaza came under mortar fire killing two persons and wounding four more. Demands for counter measures grew louder and officials discussed what steps were necessary to protect the land and the people. A decision was arrived at.

VIII

At 15:00 hours on October 29, four propeller-driven Mustangs of the Israeli Air Force took off from their base and headed into the Sinai Peninsula. Each of the World War II planes was armed with a tow-hook. Their mission was to destroy Egyptian military communications in the desert by cutting the exposed telephone wires.

The scheme was simple enough. At designated points, the planes were to fly so low that the tow-hooks would engage the telephone wires and tear them free of their moorings.

As soon as they reached the target area, the flight commander signaled the planes to dive. On the first pass, they missed the wires completely. A second attempt was ordered. The commander led the way, sweeping in over the desert, lower now, determined to bring the trailing hooks under the wires. This time the hooks failed to hold and as the planes climbed back to the assembly point, it became clear to the pilots that the plan wouldn't work.

"What are we supposed to do now?" one man said in Hebrew over the radio.

"If we return to the base," another said, "no one can find fault for what has happened. We did our best."

"Still," the commander offered, "they are not going to kiss us either."

"Agreed. So?"

"So we will cut the wires with our propellors and our wings," the commander said.

There was an apprehensive silence over the crackling radios. The wires were no more than a dozen feet above

243

ground level, an uneven terrain of rolling sand dunes. The slightest miscalculation would result in a crash from which there could be no escape.

"You know," a voice said over the radio, "a man could get killed around here."

"True. But it's a fine idea."

"Let's do it."

They followed the flight leader as he described a great circle, coming in from the west, diving abreast of each other, some fifty feet apart.

They cut the wires.

The sound was pervasive, the roar of the engines filling every cavity of their skulls, eardrums trembling with it, eyes sensitive to it, skin tingling with it. And anticipation. Fear. The paratroopers sat stiffly in the bucket seats of the Dakotas staring sightlessly ahead. No one tried to speak. There was no need to. Each of them knew what the others were thinking, what they were feeling. It was the same for them all.

At the head of the airstrip, Yaakov Yeshivat in full combat jump gear waited for the last of his officers to crowd in around him. He shouted to be heard.

"We fly at 500 feet in order to evade Egyptian radar. Just before we arrive at the jump zone, the planes will go up to 1,500 feet."

"If those Egyptian MIGs spot us in these slow buses we're finished, all of us."

Yaakov nodded vigorously. There were about 400 men in this force and he had no intention of losing them in the air. He had demanded and gotten fighter cover.

"Ten Meteors will escort us to Mitla and a dozen Mystères are patrolling the Suez area. Anything that comes looking for trouble will find it."

"Those MIGs are excellent ships."

"Men do the fighting, not planes. We have all the Israeli pilots and they have the Egyptians. Enough of that. We will be making our drop within a few minutes' flight of the airfield at Kabrit and hundreds of miles from our own bases. That means we have no time to waste. Once we hit the ground we must reach the assembly areas quickly. Are there any questions?" There were none. Yaakov checked his watch. "All right. Everybody into the planes. Mazel tov, chaverim."

At 15:20 hours, the Dakotas were airborne and two hours later the drop was made without incident. Yaakov

244

hit the ground hard, too hard, and was slow getting up. He swore at a young soldier who tried to help him. He managed to shed his parachute before the executive officer, a captain named Menache, came running up, trailed by the radio operator.

"I want reports from all company commanders," Yaakov snapped. His head swiveled and an oath broke out of him. "There's something wrong, dammit! This place doesn't look right to me. Get me a fix right away."

The radio began crackling. The executive officer was back minutes later, wearing a worried frown.

"Thirteen men injured in the drop, Yaakov. None seriously. But there's been a mistake." He hesitated.

"Tell me."

"The pilots dropped us in the wrong place." He eyed Yaakov apprehensively.

"Let's look at the map," Yaakov said softly.

Menache spread it on the ground and the two men got down on their knees.

"Do they know exactly where we are?" Yaakov said.

Menache put his finger on the map. "In here. No more than a mile from the target area."

Yaakov kept his voice down. Menache was a good man but inexperienced. He would learn. They all would. Unfortunately, some of them were going to die before they could learn.

"Look around. Remember our scouting reports. There are landmarks. See that outcropping to the northwest? And the broken terrain, like some kind of a skin rash." He put his hand on the map. "This is where we are, about three miles east of the target. Here is the monument for Colonel Parker. Let's get to it as quickly as possible. We may make it before the equipment drop is made." He stood up and Menache began to fold up the map. "Get them moving, Menache."

"Yes sir."

"And when this is over, I want a full report on how such a thing could happen. Now move out!"

Two shots echoed over the desert.

"Who the hell is shooting!" Yaakov rumbled.

"We've got prowler guards out," Menache said.

"Find out what it's all about."

Minutes later Menache returned. "Our men spotted a couple of Egyptian scout cars. They destroyed one."

"And the other?"

"Got away. In the direction of Nakhl."

"That's bad. Get on the radio and tell headquarters what happened. Say that we're on our way. Let's move out."

Ras en-Nakeb was a crossroads directly west of the port of Eilat. Joshua Landau had orders to take it. He led his reconnaissance company out of Eilat and into Egyptian territory, into Sinai, under cover of darkness.

A scout sent back word of a possible mine field and Joshua ordered the sappers out. The report was confirmed and the sappers set to work clearing a path. The company huddled around the halftracks while they waited, trying to keep warm.

At first light, the sappers removed the last mine and Joshua sent the halftracks ahead, the rest of the patrol following on foot. With the rising sun, the desert began to change, a succession of shifting shapes and hues, a rolling plain reaching out from distant granite cliffs, all texture and hot color, a wild and esoteric kaleidoscope. And ahead, the long shadows of the halftracks advancing on the irregular horizon.

The radio operator came up to Joshua. He was a pudgy youth with a scraggly beard and earlocks. "The point wants to talk, Joshua."

Joshua took the instrument, "What is it?"

"There's a police fort over the next series of dunes. It controls the track."

"Hold the halftracks where they are. Any signs of people?"

"No one."

"Stay where you are. We're moving up."

He issued orders and they resumed the advance. When they reached the halftracks, he ordered the men into a skirmish line behind them, and surveyed the fort through his field glasses. There was no sign of life. Suddenly a shot rang out and some of the Israelis fired back.

"Cease fire!"

Joshua focused the glasses again. A cloud of dust appeared behind the fort and he made out a single camel galloping toward the horizon, its rider whipping furiously at the beast's heaving flanks.

"Let's move forward," Joshua said.

"You want the halftracks to put a few shells into the fort?" the radio operator said conversationally.

"I don't think so. We'll see what develops."

246

When the men on the point broke into the fort they found it deserted. All the Arabs had departed.

One of the scouts laughed. "It isn't much of a war."

"Patience, *adoni*," Joshua told him. "You'll find your Arab soon enough. It's only a matter of time."

The hills extended west above Kusseima like a spiny ridge, commanding the valley. The Egyptians held these heights, had established fortified positions. Trenches connected firing positions and bunkers and tanks were dug in for use as artillery. Amos assessed the situation. Intelligence had told him only that Egyptians held these hills. They neglected to say how many or what their firepower was. He turned to his second-in-command.

"Freeman, let's probe the center. In strength. Armor and an infantry company."

"Yes, major."

The attack was launched and the sounds of battle filled the air. Amos watched through his binoculars. A tank was hit, one tread knocked off, and it ran in a tight little circle like a creature gone mad. It stopped and the hatch flew open, a man climbed out, another. A machine gun began to chatter angrily. Both men went down. No one else came out of the tank.

He swung the glasses to the left. One of his halftracks lay on its side burning and further along another one was still and he could see a dead soldier hanging over the side. He ordered the patrol to withdraw.

The patrol leader reported. "The center is too strong, Amos. They're dug in along the line. They've brought bazookas and tank guns to bear from both sides. Also machine guns."

"We've got to get up there," Amos said. "Clear them out."

"Can't we go around?"

"There isn't time for that. Freeman, I want the armor to lay a barrage along the ridge, on the trenches." He looked at his watch. "In exactly twenty minutes, all armor will attack the right flank. Two infantry companies in support. That should occupy the center, may even get them to shift some people in that direction. I'll go with the third company at the left flank."

Amos led the infantrymen in a deep circle to the south, picking their way through a deep ravine, coming up beyond what he hoped was the furthest point of the Egyptian defense line. They began moving up the incline.

247

Halfway up Amos began to believe they were going to make it unobserved and said so to the company commander. Seconds later a hoarse cry sounded and a machinegun opened up on them. The men dived for cover.

"We're pinned here," the company commander cried. "If we try to pull back, they'll massacre us."

"We're not going back. See how the machinegun's field of fire ends before it gets to our left flank. He's on their right point, toward the center. And his visibility is limited. A few men might be able to make it around the corner and get to the top."

"The riflemen———"

"We'll take that chance," Amos said. He called to a squad leader lying behind a tree nearby. "You! Bring your men and follow me." Then, to the company commander. "Stay here, open up on the trenches for cover. When that machine gun stops, move forward on the double. Let's go!" he yelled to the squad leader.

Running, crawling, snaking his way across open stretches, Amos led the squad toward the crest of the hill. A scream of anguish sounded behind him but he didn't turn around. He was aware of the dry heat that coated his mouth and how difficult it was to breathe, of his heart thumping in his chest. But the fear of fear, that he had earlier felt, was gone now and only the sense of excitement remained. If his body was less responsive than he would have liked, his brain at least seemed to be functioning crisply and without panic.

That pleased him. He had been worried about his reactions, afraid that the years since 1948 had made him soft and too self-protective. The man he had been then, and before, still existed under the balding scalp and the thickening waist. Yaakov was not the only tough guy in Israel.

The squad leader appeared to his left. "That machinegun. Behind that high point dead ahead. In those trees."

"Can we use grenades?"

"Not a chance. It's well protected. We'll have to do it the hard way, go in and take them out."

Amos squinted into the blue haze lingering over the hills. He didn't have to go. It was a job for young men. Battalion commanders were not expected to attack machineguns. He glanced over at the squad leader, patiently waiting, trusting.

"Well, *adoni*," Amos said. "Let's do it."

He ran as hard as he could up the slope. It was steeper than he thought. The muscles in his legs were clumsy from disuse and it took all his strength to keep them pumping. Once he tripped, but kept going, finally making it into the trees.

A thin curse sounded to his left and he swung around. That movement saved his life as a shot whirred past his ear. He tugged down on the Uzi, finger tightening on the trigger. It bounced in his hands and he saw the bullets hit the Egyptian in the chest. He straightened up, mouth open, dead before he could cry out.

Amos ducked behind a tree and fired as another rifleman came into sight. The man fell over, legs jerking, and then he died. Other Israelis moved in behind Amos and he waved them forward. After that, it was all sound and smoke and cries of rage and terror and pain.

The squad leader had moved ahead. Now he picked his way back to Amos. He pointed. "I've located the gun. But there's a slab of rock between us and them. We've got to go around."

"Let's go."

Crouching, they ran forward. Neither of them saw the Arab officer, pistol in hand, appear from out of the mist. He fired once and the squad leader went down on his face and lay still.

Amos fired, stitching the officer across the middle. The Arab screamed and blood gushed up out of his mouth even before he fell. Amos charged past him to the machinegun, spraying the three soldiers in the nest. A signal brought the rest of the company up the hill and fifteen minutes later, the ridge was taken.

Yaakov established brigade headquarters and called for reports from all units. From Kuntilla, on the Israeli border to Thamad to Nakhl through Mitla to the southern tip of the canal. One hundred and ninety miles, all his responsibility. Word began to come in.

"Kuntilla is taken. It was deserted. The Egyptians have pulled back to Thamad."

What did that mean? Nakhl too had fallen with a minimum of difficulty, the defenders fleeing at the first shots. Perhaps the Egyptians were consolidating their forces to make a strong stand elsewhere.

"We'll find them at Thamad," Yaakov said. "Let's get our people in there and hit them with everything we can."

"We're short of transportation," Menache reminded him.

"Ninety trucks were promised to us."

Menache was unimpressed. "Only forty-six have been delivered so far."

"Then use forty-six. Commandeer any and all civilian transport. If there are breakdowns, march the men. Get them on the road. We've got a schedule to meet. And get me an Intelligence report on Thamad. How many men originally? The kind of weapons. The name of their commander and whatever is known about him. Also, I was supposed to be given a breakdown of our own people. Where is it."

"We just finished the count of reservists. We're 376 men over strength."

"That's impossible."

"I double-checked, Yaakov. You should see some of them. Men from hospitals, older men, men who are not even in the reserves. And they're still coming."

"Crazy Jews," Yaakov rasped under his breath. "Are they anxious to die?"

"Just to live, I think," Menache said, grinning.

"Well," Yaakov said thoughtfully. "See that they have guns and know the difference between the Arabs and our own people. Now let's get to Thamad."

Thamad was a craggy salient with a commanding view of the terrain below. Two Egyptian infantry companies manned the outpost, their guns ready.

At 06:00 hours, Yaakov sent his paratroopers into the armored cars and halftracks, ordered the attack to begin. They swept forward in waves but were met with a withering fire from above. The attack ground to a halt.

"Get the tanks in to help them," Yaakov ordered.

"There are only two available and they're in action now."

"Two! We're supposed to have thirteen! Where are they?"

Menache looked away. "Some of them got bogged down in the sand. Those caravan tracks couldn't support all that weight."

"And the others?"

"The rest aren't here yet. One other got through, but it turned over. A repair crew is working on it."

Yaakov swore. "Those troopers are out there on their own. What can we throw in to help them now?"

"Nothing. The only substantial help is thirty minutes from here."

Yaakov's head swiveled around in the darkness. The sound of combat, the arch of tracers, the crump of mortars and cannon, meant that people were getting hit, dying. *His* people.

"How many mechanics have we got?" he said.

"A dozen, fourteen maybe."

"Get them together. Also radio operators, cooks, anybody who can carry a gun. Hurry up, man! Let's get into this thing before it's too late." He strode back to the command post and spoke to the radio operator. "Can you raise the commander of those people out there?"

"I'll try, Yaakov."

The field set began to crackle. The operator held out the receiver. "Here's Hayeem, Yaakov."

"Adoni," he began, "is it very bad for your boys?"

"It's bad, Yaakov. The Egyptians are putting up a very good fight."

"Can you pull back?"

"Not a chance. They've got us pinned down. Once it gets light they'll have us zeroed in."

"I'm coming up with about twenty, thirty men. That's all I've got to help now."

"It won't be much help."

The sound of battle came over the radio, metallic, distant. "Enough talk. I'm coming and since you can't go backwards, we'll go forward."

Hayeem began to laugh, the slow sound of discovery and delight.

"What is it?" Yaakov said. "What are you laughing at?"

"Daylight, Yaakov."

"Have you lost your mind? What are you thinking, man?"

"Yaakov, listen. The sun is coming up. Beautiful. Bright. So bright."

"Dammit! In the middle of a war and you give me weather reports."

"You know the desert sun, Yaakov. It can blind a man. This is a battlefield, the air thick and full of smoke, clouds of dust, sand particles. When the sun begins reflecting off that garbage—well, it won't be easier for the Egyptian gunners. You understand, Yaakov?"

"Yes," Yaakov said. "Yes. And in another three minutes you'll have the sun right behind you, low, in their eyes. Attack, man! Attack! Throw it all at them."

"Yes, *adoni.* I will talk to you presently."

The connection went dead.

The Chief of Staff hunkered down with his back against

251

the front wheel of a truck and ate field rations out of a can. He wore a peaked officer's cap and a brown sweater and carried a .45 caliber automatic in a canvas holster on his hip. Members of his staff were collected nearby, talking softly, studying maps and reports. A courier arrived and Uri Davidov scanned the message quickly, sought out the Chief of Staff.

"Moshe. London and Paris have issued an ultimatum to Israel and Egypt to stop fighting."

"Not unexpected. Anything else?"

"They want all units withdrawn at least ten miles from the canal. Also, that the Egyptians permit a temporary occupation by Anglo-French forces at Suez, Ismailia and Port Said."

The Chief of Staff swallowed the last of his ration and looked up. There was a hard glitter in his good eye. "They did not stop there, I'm sure."

"No. If, after twelve hours, there isn't agreement, they threaten to intervene in order to protect the canal."

The General laughed softly. "So they are coming. And this is the pretext, the defense of Suez. Well, that's all right from our point of view. They cannot hurt us and they may even help a little."

"Does this affect our plans in any way?"

"Why should it? I'm interested only in what we do, our own efforts, our own war. I'm much more concerned, as a matter of fact, with the Syrians and with Jordan. Has Intelligence come up with anything new?"

"Nobody's making any move to help Nasser."

The Chief of Staff heaved himself erect. "Those rations never get any better, do they? Planes are faster, tanks are bigger, guns shoot more bullets, but field rations for a soldier are as tasteless as ever." He smiled at Davidov. "Tell me, Professor of Philosophy, is it possible that Nasser's friends will not act in his behalf? They have a defense agreement."

Davidov ran his fingers through his thick, dusty hair. "If they weren't Arabs, I would be sure they would attack. But who knows the Arab mind? A dozen different strains run through it and not the least of them is a blind pride coupled with a kind of self-destructiveness."

"A concentrated thrust by the Arab Legion across the narrow belly of Israel would put them at the sea in a matter of hours. It is only twelve miles across at that point."

"Syria has only thirty miles to go to reach the Mediterranean. A joint effort could cut us into three parts—if they attack."

"If they do, we'll fight them, too. Meanwhile, there are other problems. Any new Egyptian air action?"

Davidov nodded. "Four MIGs hit Thamad just after Yeshivat's people took it. Two separate attacks. They wounded three of our boys. None killed." A thoughtful frown came onto the aristocratic brow. "I simply do not understand what Nasser is waiting for. He has at least 200 MIG-15s and maybe fifty Ilyushin bombers. Why doesn't he use them? Our Air Force could never stand him off. Most of our planes are propeller-driven. The MIGS could sweep the skies." He pulled a sheaf of reports out of his pocket. "None of these make much sense to me. I'm a logical man and I don't understand what's happening. Or not happening. We took Kusseima with hardly a shot being fired. For the most part, the Arabs ran. They literally ran away. All our objectives for the first day— Mitla, Ras en-Nakeb, Kuntilla, Kusseima—have been taken. Could it be some kind of a trick?"

"I don't think so. Our people come to fight, their's don't." He offered the empty ration can to Davidov, who accepted it. "All orders hold until I get back. Ben Gurion has the flu. I'm going to pay him a visit. A man enjoys some company when he isn't feeling well."

Hank McClintock, sitting on a five-gallon water can, reassembled the hand camera and loaded it with film. Everything was in perfect order, clean, ready to roll.

"That looks like an extremely complicated piece of machinery," the elderly private said admiringly. His name was Mordechai; in civilian life he was a statistician and a part-time musician. Mordechai had appeared at the headquarters of the Brigade uninvited and insisted that he be mobilized. When his request was refused, he staged a sit-down in front of the commander's tent. To get rid of him, he was assigned to McClintock.

"What am I going to do with him?" he had protested.

"You have extra film and equipment. Let him carry some of it. A man has to feel he's making a contribution."

Mordechai smiled benevolently at Hank. "You learned to use a motion picture camera here in Israel?"

"In America."

"Ah. I could tell from your accent you were no sabra. Hollywood, eh?"

"Yes."

253

"Intriguing. I have always been a devotee of the cinema. Such technical virtuosity. I have always been a man who admires a high degree of professionalism in another's work, you see. And in films—there is a certain precision, you see. I am a man attracted to that which is arithmetical, you might say. Numbers are my passion. Statistics, music, and films, as well. Numbers play a large part in each. Wouldn't you agree?"

"I suppose. I never though about it that way."

"Well, statistics are self-evident, no? And music—a quarter-note, half-note, and so on. And film—sixteen frames to the second and—"

"I see what you mean."

"I knew you would." He cocked his head, a quizzical expression on his face. "You're an American?"

"Yes."

"Ah, I see. An Irish American. During the War of Independence and before many Irishers helped Israel. They don't like the British and came to fight them. I'm not sure I approve of such animosity." he ended apologetically.

"I'm descended from Scotsmen."

"Is that unusual, Scotsmen in America?"

"Not so very. But I'm an Israeli now."

"You're Jewish?"

"Yes."

"You must admit, that is unusual. Very unusual."

Mordechai studied Hank as he peered through the viewfinder, and panned from left to right.

"You can take pictures that way, moving the camera?"

"Yes."

"And it doesn't blur?"

"If you pan too fast, it does. You get a feel for it, after a while."

"Professionalism. Of course. A remarkable instrument. Excuse me, but would it be possible for me to look through that hole, to see what you see?"

Hank handed over the camera and Mordechai placed it against his eye. A soft sibilance seeped across his lips. He smiled his appreciation as he returned the camera.

"Tell me, McClintock, you believe we'll go where the fighting is?"

"I intend to. That's why I'm here."

"And you'll take pictures of it? Tell me, for what purpose?"

"I make documentary films frequently for the Defense

Forces. Afterwards, I'll put together all the film and we'll have an excellent record of what occurred."

Mordechai nodded reflectively. "You must admit, to go where people are shooting at each other with only a camera is slightly meshugga. Crazy."

Hank grinned. "What about you? You're old enough to stay where it's safe, but here you are."

"You're a hundred percent correct. But, you see, I'm a Berliner. The Nazis broke the windows of my house, they beat me up, they threw me on a train and sent me to a factory to make shell casings so they could kill other people. After that, they put me in Buchenwald. I never lifted a hand. Not once. But no more. Now when they attack Jews, I fight. Maybe I am crazy."

"Maybe," Hank said. "When we have a chance, I'll give you a chance to use the camera."

"To actually take pictures?"

"Yes."

A wide grin sliced across the pudgy little face. "Nice," he said. "Very nice."

IX

The English-French ultimatum was accepted by Israel with the stipulation that Egypt do likewise. Egypt rejected it.

Twenty-five hours after the expiration of the ultimatum, English and French forces began bombing airfields in the Canal Zone. Diplomatic pressure for an end to the hostilities increased in the United Nations and in the capitals of the world. Resolutions were drafted and submitted; proposals made; statements issued. Cries for peace went up.

The President of the United States and his Secretary of State arrayed themselves squarely against the Anglo-French action, as well as Israel's campaign.

Such political maneuverings and diplomatic outcries were lost on the men in the field. They were concerned with the icy chill of the desert nights and the scorching heat of the days; with the possibility of enemy air attack; with the accuracy of their riflemen.

255

Yaakov sat at a field desk, a map of the sector spread out before him. Menache stood at his side, patiently waiting.

"Well, Yaakov?"

The brigade commander made no reply. His orders had been to seize Mitla Pass but otherwise to take no offensive action. Surely Moshe would not immobilize him this way. It must be Davidov who was to blame for this ridiculous order. Davidov the professor with his theoretical ways, his concern with politics instead of war. Now was the time to strike, to push ahead before Egypt could comprehend Israeli strategy, before they could bring up reinforcements.

"I'm convinced that we should be continuing through the pass," he growled irritably.

Menache measured his superior. That battered face with its eyes like naked eggs made him uncomfortable. It masked a brain and a will he couldn't understand. What Menache couldn't understand he found frightening.

"We ought to be hitting down toward Sharm el-Sheikh, open up the Strait of Tiran."

"The orders," Menache said, a gentle reminder.

"Yes, the orders." Yaakov looked at the map. Up ahead in the pass, was it free of enemy soldiers and secure, or a deep trap? He had to know. Sooner or later he and his men would be allowed to advance and such information would be vital. He wanted to know. Now. *Now*. Damn Davidov.

"I've made up my mind," he said. "We must probe ahead."

"A reconnaissance patrol?"

"Yes," he replied, with decisiveness. "A patrol. In force. An infantry company with halftracks for support. Everyone motorized. Use Friedman's company. He's a good man. Tell him to maintain radio contact. And Menache, I want information, not heroes. Make sure Friedman understands."

"Yes, Yaakov."

It was past noon when Friedman ordered his company into the pass. Scouts rolled ahead in jeeps, one on the point, one at each flank. Friedman attached himself to the first platoon, riding in the lead halftrack, eyes scanning the hills to each side.

"Keep a sharp lookout!" Friedman ordered. "Report any movement at all."

Now, with the column moving deeper into the pass, the

256

hills were higher, more rugged, threatening. A mood of apprehension gripped Friedman and he reacted to it.

"I want the platoons spaced out. At least two hundred yards between each one. And fifteen yards between each vehicle." The radio operator transmitted the command.

Five minutes later a sniper killed Friedman's driver. A surprised exclamation came out of his mouth and his head went back, a small dark hole over the left eye. The halftrack swerved crazily and Friedman grabbed the wheel, hit the brake.

"Get another driver up here! Hurry up! Did anyone see where that shot came from?"

"On the right!" a private shouted. "High up."

Friedman followed the private's gesture in time to see a puff of smoke. A bullet ricocheted off the side of the halftrack.

"Let's get moving! Open fire!"

The new driver bore down on the accelerator and they shot forward. "Straight ahead?"

"Straight ahead. Radio! Tell Brigade we've run into some sniper fire. One man dead. Say we're going through." The message was sent.

Up ahead, the scouts accelerated and sped out of the pass. Friedman swung around to see the rest of the first platoon hurrying to catch up.

"We're almost out," the driver said grimly.

That was when they heard the rolling bark of automatic weapons behind them. A dull roar sounded back in the pass, echoing ominously.

"What the hell was that?"

"They got the fuel truck."

Thirty seconds later the first platoon broke out of the western end of Mitla Pass. Friedman ordered the driver to take up a position facing the entrance and waited for the rest of the patrol. Nothing came.

The distant sounds of combat told them all what was happening. "They're trapped in there!" the driver cried. "They'll all be killed."

"Shut up!" Friedman snapped. "Get me Brigade," he said to the radio operator. "I'll talk to the colonel myself."

There was no mistaking the raw disapproval in Yaakov's voice. "All right, Friedman, let's have it."

"They were waiting for us. Only the first platoon made it through. The rest are pinned down. The Arabs were in there in force."

Yaakov swore softly. The mistake had been his. He had

disobeyed orders and now the men of his command were paying the price. His brain turned over quickly.

"I'm going in," he said. "With two companies and armor. Give me five minutes, then you come back shooting."

When Yaakov reached the entrapped men, he found them under heavy fire from light artillery, as well as small arms. The Arabs were using mortars with telling accuracy. He leaped out of his jeep before it stopped rolling and dashed for cover behind a halftrack. About a hundred yards ahead, he saw Friedman's halftrack trundle into sight. He waved frantically and the company commander acknowledged the signal and came hurdling over the side, scrambling toward Yaakov.

A big man and heavy, Friedman moved with a lumbering gait that looked awkward but covered a lot of ground. He was three-quarters of the way across the open space separating them when he was hit. His big body continued in the direction he was going, but his legs buckled and he went to his knees, still churning, though it was clear to Yaakov that he was already dead.

Yaakov turned away. "Who's next in command?" he said to a soldier.

"Wexler."

"Get him."

The soldier moved off. He brought back a young lieutenant who was obviously very frightened. "You want me, colonel?" His voice was controlled.

"Casualties?"

Wexler looked at the body of the company commander. He took a deep breath. "My platoon has two killed and seventeen wounded."

"What about equipment?"

"One of the halftracks is useless. They're using recoilless rifles and anti-tank guns at point blank range. I suppose the other platoons have had losses too."

They heard the planes before they saw them. Four MIGs, swooping low along the eastern axis of the pass, guns chattering. They dived for cover. The MIGs made two more passes before withdrawing.

"They'll be back," Yaakov said. "But we won't wait. We're going up into those hills, Wexler."

"The Arabs are in caves. Solidly entrenched——"

"Yes. We're going into the caves after them. We'll dig them out. We move in one minute. Give the order." Yaakov ran back to his halftrack, contacted the commander of the two companies he had brought with him. "I want one company to hit them head on."

"Shouldn't we wait for the tanks?"

"Use the bazookas as artillery and the heavy machine-guns. And nobody stops until we clean them out."

"What about the second company?"

"Put them all on the ground. Circle up to the heights and come up behind the caves."

"Yes, sir. When do we start?"

"Right now!"

He hurried back to Wexler and gave the order to advance. Men broke out from behind their vehicles and ran toward the base of the incline. Yaakov pounded forward, breath coming in short gasps. Ahead, a man went tumbling onto his face. Yaakov kneeled and saw that he was dying from an ugly stomach wound. He picked up his Uzi and moved on.

They picked their way up the hill, scurrying from rock to rock, shooting as they went. Just below the first line of caves, by silent common consent, they paused, as if to assemble, to make sure they were not alone. Then they advanced again. Grenades, bazookas, automatic weapons. All served to clean the Arabs out of their nests.

Now matters grew more difficult. The incline steepened and their field of fire was cut down. In some places, men had to help their comrades to the next highest level and it became impossible to provide a covering fire. Finally, just below the second line of caves, the advance stalled, the men frozen into position.

One look told Yaakov that there was no going back. He spotted the radio operator with the field pack crouched nearby. "Get the other company!" The officer came on. "Where the hell are you? We've got men getting killed here!"

"It's rough, Yaakov. We've had to fight every step. I'm not sure we can make it all the way."

"You will make it! You'll make it or I'll break your neck myself. Now, listen to me. Those bastards fight pretty good in position. But move them out and they'll come apart. Get them out of their holes, understand! I give you thirty seconds and then I hit them again. You do the same. Okay?"

"Okay."

Yaakov looked around. Most of the men were out of sight, concealed behind outcroppings of rock. He knew they were watching him, waiting for his command. These

259

boys, these paratroopers, they were something special and wouldn't quit. They would do whatever had to be done. He filled his lungs with air and stood up.

"Come on!" he bellowed, waving his arm. "Follow me! Back to Jerusalem!"

He charged straight ahead.

It was a tiring night. Moving armored equipment through the defile at Dika, with the bridge out, was slow, hard work, and no one got any sleep. As day broke, in that swift way it comes in the desert, only the halftracks and tanks had managed to make it. Trucks and lesser vehicles were bogged down in the sticky going.

Certain that his movements had been under observance by the enemy for some time, and anticipating an attack momentarily, Amos Landau ordered his command to continue to advance.

"Strung out the way we are," Freeman objected. "If they hit us we'll be in trouble."

"And if we stay in one place we'll be in worse trouble. Keep moving, those are our orders. And they're my orders."

The lead tanks came under attack within ten minutes. Their maneuverability limited, they fought back as best they could against flat-trajectory fire from anti-tank guns.

In his command halftrack, Amos moved up behind the advancing armor. One look convinced him that unless something were done to correct the situation, all the tanks might be knocked out.

"There's a wadi a mile to the left flank. Sweep in there. It will carry you past these guns."

The tank commander objected. "I know that wadi. It is all sand and anything bigger than a Land Rover will get stuck."

Amos reconsidered quickly. "All right. Then take up positions alongside the wadi, in whatever cover exists. You'll still have a good field of fire and can operate as artillery."

"Amos, look!"

The battalion sergeant major had spoken, indicating the right flank. Amos swept the countryside through his own glasses. A dozen armored cars were moving up, supported by a full infantry company, seeking to exploit the gap in his defenses.

"If they break through," the sergeant major said, "we'll be squeezed into this end, helpless."

"Get Lurie's platoon up there and give him some extra bazooka men. He's got to hit those people head on and take out that armor. Break up that formation."

The fight was fierce but brief and in the space of ten minutes eight of the armored cars were destroyed. The others fled, the infantrymen, taking heavy casualties, chasing after them. Amos ordered the entire command to move on Abu Ageila. One hour later they occupied it, and immediately came under a heavy bombardment from Egyptian artillery.

"Prepare for a counter-attack," Amos ordered. "And call for an air strike. We've got to get rid of some of that armor."

The Arab attack lasted for about fifteen minutes before it was beaten off. "They'll be back," Amos decided and ordered some of the halftracks into a range of low hills off to his right. "From there, they can command the entire front."

The halftracks were no more than two hundred yards from the defense perimeter when the Israeli planes came roaring into sight. The men stood up and cheered. They were Ouragans, four of them, diving low over Abu Ageila, heading straight for the halftracks.

Amos leaped to his feet. "No!" he cried, voice lost in the roar of the motors and the barking of fifty caliber machineguns. "They're ours! *Ours!*"

One of the halftracks exploded in a sheet of orange flame. Another rolled over onto its side. Men scurried for safety and some of them fell as the Ouragans made a strafing run.

"Bastards!" the sergeant major cried. "Those dirty bastards!"

"Tell Headquarters what's happened," Amos snapped. "I don't want those planes to come back. If they do, say we'll shoot them down. Now let's get those wounded men back in here."

Seeing what had happened, and hoping to take advantage of the Israeli mistake, the Egyptian commander ordered his soldiers to attack. They were beaten back.

"They'll try again," the sergeant major said.

"We aren't waiting," Amos said. "I want everything that can move—every tank, every truck, every man, everything—in action. Let's go. Infantry rides when it can and runs when it can't. Let's finish this thing right now."

For about fifteen minutes, the Egyptians held the Israelis off. Then they broke into full retreat, leaving behind a

261

trail of wrecked and smoking vehicles. Many also left their shoes, thinking to run faster without them. Nearly a hundred prisoners were taken. Amos ordered them freed and directed back toward the Suez Canal.

"If they're lucky, they'll get there before we do and they'll be able to conceal themselves."

Freeman presented himself, having compiled the figures on casualties and lost equipment. Amos listened attentively. "Send the wounded back, and whatever equipment can move I want ready to roll in thirty minutes." He spread a map on the ground and put a finger to it. "Here's where we're going. Bir Hama, Jebel Livni, Ruafa."

"The men are tired," Freeman protested. "They've been fighting for—"

Amos folded the map and stuffed it into his back pocket. He stood up. There were pouches under his eyes and his skin was coated with gray dust. "I know how long we've been fighting, *adoni*," he replied, keeping his voice mild. "Are you telling me that you are too weary to go on?"

Freeman flushed. "Of course not! Still, the men——"

"The men know why they are here. They'll do what they must. Give the orders."

At dusk, with the air blue-gray, with Egyptian guns unloosing a heavy barrage, Amos ordered the attack on Ruafa to begin. An armored detachment rolled forward. A halftrack was knocked out and another disabled. The others maneuvered evasively.

The tanks came into range and opened up with their guns even as they came under attack. Most of them were hit, but none were put out of action. They rumbled over and past the advance positions. Suddenly the darkening sky was illuminated by a wild display of light and color; an Egyptian ammunition dump had gone up.

Reports came in and Amos checked the disposition of the armor. "We've got them now," he gloated. "Keep the pressure on."

The radio crackled. "The tanks are stopping, major," the operator shouted. "They're out of fuel."

"How long to get the fuel trucks up there?" Amos asked.

"Too long," Freeman said. "Twenty minutes, at least, and if they should be hit——"

"We can't wait. I want the tanks to function as field artillery as long as they have shells. Everyone but gunners and loaders on the ground to function as infantry. They've got grenades and hand guns."

"If there's a counterattack," Freeman began.

"We're not going to wait for that. Every man who can move is in this. Every gun. This time we hit them with everything at once. Come on, let's go."

It was sometime after nine that night when the battle ended. Freeman, his left arm in a sling, a bullet in his shoulder, was happily detailing the extent of the battalion's victory. "We're making an inventory of the captured vehicles, Amos, the weapons. And the prisoners. This is a very important triumph for us."

"Never mind, Freeman," Amos said. He sucked on an orange which he had been carrying in his pack for two days, and smoked a cigaret. There was a heavy, oppressive weariness in his limbs that made him conscious of his age. "There's no time for that now. Put the mechanics to work repairing our equipment. See if brigade can send spare parts and replacements. And get the wounded back to the field hospitals. This outfit is moving on at dawn."

"What about the prisoners? We've got a few hundred of them this time."

"Send them back to Nasser. He can tell them more lies about their glorious victories. We're not going to feed them."

"Yes, *adoni*."

"And I would suggest that you try to get some sleep, Freeman. That's what I'm going to do."

The battalion commander was a man ready to fight. The sleeves of his shirt were rolled to the elbow, his forearms thick and corded. Of medium height, he gave the impression of possessing a considerable amount of power in his square body. His goggles were pushed up on his forehead and there were circles around his eyes, giving him the expression of an angry raccoon. His mouth twisted and he jabbed a stubby finger in Yaakov's direction.

"What the hell are you doing to me!"

"Take it easy, Andrei."

"Crap on that! I need soldiers, fighting men," he roared, "and you send me clerks, pencil pushers, city boys."

Yaakov looked around at the other officers, company and battalion commanders, assembled for this final briefing before they pushed on. He was sure they had complaints to make, that *this* was not perfect, that *that* had its defects. Once this sort of thing began, it could be contagious. The pale eyes worked back to Andrei.

"You requested replacements," Yaakov said, the words rumbling around in his chest. "I sent them."

"They are no good to me," Andrei shot back. "I want officers who can lead, not shopkeepers who tell me what they can't do. Instead of leading the men into action, they explain why they can't fight. They are too tired or have not received their supplies or their weapons are full of sand or it is too hot or too cold. I want men who will fight, not give excuses."

Yaakov stared at the other man. "So do I. I need a battalion commander who fights better than he complains. Who will fulfill his assignments, not explain why he cannot." Andrei flushed under the dirt but his glance never wavered. Yaakov went on, voice rasping with cold irony. "Some of the men you have are too old. Some of them are not well trained. Some of them are not strong and others are not brave. Some do not know the Negev and they cannot judge distances or stand the heat. But they are here and they came to fight. They are not first-class troops. We do not have enough first-class troops. So it becomes necessary to win with second-class men. Third-class." He paused. "Perhaps you cannot do that, Andrei."

"You expect me to fulfill the schedules you've issued with such men?"

"Exactly what I expect." His eyes traveled from face to face. "I expect that of each of you. You are officers and it is expected that you will lead. If you cannot, you will be replaced." He swung back to Andrei. "Have you anything more to say?"

"I'll do my best," he said evenly, no sign of defeat in his voice.

"And that will be good enough. All right. Now I'm sure the men must be wondering what is going on in the world."

"And the officers," a company commander put in.

Yaakov grinned. "And the officers. Okay, chaverim. I spoke to Moshe earlier. This is what he told me. Our friend, Gamal Nasser, has blocked the Suez Canal, which surprised nobody in Israel. Outside, the pressure increases, which also is no surprise. The Yugoslavs, the Soviets, India. They all want us to break off the fighting. For us, the United States generates the most pressure. Eisenhower feels he's been betrayed, a sentiment which Dulles is sure to encourage. From Washington we get pious platitudes

264

about justice and peace but nothing has ever been done to make Arabs stop killing Israelis. The Americans have submitted a resolution in the UN calling for an immediate cease-fire and withdrawal."

"That could damage our position," an officer volunteered.

"Talk is one thing," Yaakov said dryly. "To fight another. Our mission is to put an end to the terrorist camps and to open the Strait of Tiran. We'll do it."

"What does Moshe say about the British? Does he think they'll actually go into Suez?"

Yaakov grew impatient with the direction of the conversation. There was a lingering fear of the English, of what they had once been, once done. That was all past. He viewed them as struggling to maintain an empire that no longer existed, a fact they had yet to recognize. Their Imperial glory was over.

"To hell with the British," he muttered. "The Syrians have blown up the oil pipeline at three points. That will be felt in London. The Syrians may not be anxious to fight us but they are safe enough when it comes to blowing up pipes." Yaakov waited for the laughter to subside. "Prime Minister Eden is in a bad spot. The jackals are after him and I think they'll pull him down before he can bring off this Suez thing. Oil is a life and death matter for England."

"And what about us?"

"We," Yaakov said, "are going to Eilat, my friend, to Sharm el-Sheikh, where the sun always shines and the water is calm and clear. A holiday, chaverim, as soon as we can eliminate the Arabs in our way."

The weapons carrier tipped over and ground to a halt. The driver cursed and shifted into reverse. The wheels spun but there was no movement.

"What's wrong?" the young officer said. "Use the four-wheel drive and get us out of here!"

"I'm trying. It won't work. Everybody out. Push."

"Come on," the officer said. "A little muscle. Before some crazy Arab takes a potshot at us."

Hank McClintock climbed out and placed his camera in its leather carrying case off to one side of the road. Mordechai did the same thing with the film carriers. They took their places at the rear of the weapons carrier, began to shove. The wheels spun, kicking up dirt, but failed to gain purchase.

"Damn low center," the officer grumbled. "Come on. One more time."

The driver shifted down gear, bore down on the accelerator. This time there was some forward motion. "All together," the officer cried. "Keep it moving."

The weapons carrier gained traction and abruptly pulled away from them, swinging back onto the road, coming to a stop. The driver looked back at them, grinning cheerfully.

"Very well done, my friends. Won't you join me? I think we've overstayed our visit."

Hank hurried back for his camera, Mordechai after him. Slinging the equipment, they turned back up the road. Hank saw the young officer, walking easily, suddenly hesitate, stumble, as if his boot had hooked a concealed root, fighting for balance. His hands came up and he pitched forward on his face.

"What's the matter with the officer?" Mordechai asked.

Hank was the first to reach the fallen man. He turned him over. Blood stained the front of his khaki shirt. Hank straightened up and looked around. "He's been shot. He's dead."

"Oh, my God!" Mordechai said, and vomited.

"What are we going to do now?" the driver said bitterly.

A machinegun began to bark. Seconds elapsed before the realization broke through to them that they were the intended target. They scrambled for the weapons carrier.

"What are we going to do?" the driver said.

"Get us out of here!" Hank said.

A 57mm anti-tank gun opened up on them. A shell landed some yards to the rear.

"Get going!" Hank shouted.

The weapons carrier spun forward.

"Where are we supposed to go?" the driver asked.

"How do I know?" Hank replied, resentment mingling with fear. "I'm a photographer, that's all."

"Well, I don't know. What are we going to do?"

"If you say those words again," Hank said thinly, "I am going to crack your skull with this camera."

The machinegun opened up again and they all ducked. Suddenly the weapons carrier swerved and the driver fought the pull of the wheel.

"They hit the tires!"

They jerked to a stop.

Hank dived out the back and rolled into the ditch.

Mordechai came right after him, the driver a moment later. The machinegun swept the edge of the road.

"What are we——"

"Shut up!" Hank interrupted. "Are there any weapons in that lousy truck of yours?"

"Yes, sir. A couple of rifles."

"Get them."

The driver looked at him in disbelief. "Not me. I'm not sticking my head up there."

Hank struggled for control. "I'll be right back," he said to Mordechai. He scrambled out of the ditch and into the cab of the weapons carrier. Two rifles lay on the floor behind the seat. He grabbed them and headed back to the others. He gave one to Mordechai.

"Start shooting! Let's get that sonuvabitch before he gets us."

He put the rifle to his shoulder.

"Excuse me, McClintock," Mordechai said.

Hank turned. "What?"

Mordechai extended the rifle helplessly. "It won't shoot. I think it's broken."

Hank looked at the weapon. "The safety," he said, suddenly very calm and confident. "You must unlock it if you want the rifle to work."

"Ah. So simple, for such a complex mechanism." He pointed the rifle and began yanking the trigger as fast as he could.

From his vantage point atop the gentle rise, Levi Landau peered through the binoculars at the heights on the Syrian side of the frontier.

Another soldier lay on his back alongside, hands behind his head, comfortably sunning himself. "Tell me, *adoni*, what do you see over there? Any girls?"

"I see a Syrian soldier looking at me."

"Nice. Peaceful."

"Some war," Levi said, with disgust. "We study them and they study us. Why don't they attack?"

"Please. Don't give them ideas. I prefer this looking to shooting. It's much quieter."

Levi said nothing. He could remember how it had been during the War of Independence, with his father and Joshua both fighting, both wounded, both heroes. For so long he had been dreaming of the time he would get his chance. He wanted to fight, to kill Arabs, to prove himself. He turned away, looking back into Israel. There was

267

movement on the road which twisted toward the village deeper in the country.

"What's that?"

The other soldier sat up. After a moment, he lowered himself back to the ground. Every morning at this time, the old Arab drove his donkey cart to the village to sell his goat's milk, and every afternoon he returned. It was part of the scene.

"That old man is not Nasser."

Levi picked up his companion's rifle. Without a word, he brought it to bear on the old Arab, held him in his sights. His finger tightened on the trigger.

"Hey!" the other soldier said, "what are you doing?"

Levi fired.

The other man grabbed the rifle away from him. "What's the matter with you! Why did you do that?"

Levi laughed, a flat sound without mirth. "Look at him whip that donkey. I really scared that old man."

The other soldier shook his head. "I don't get it. He's not the enemy. What do you want to shoot at him for?"

Levi lay back on the ground and closed his eyes. "Why not? He's an Arab."

X

The armored car on the point stopped and the formation behind came to a halt. "What?" Amos snapped to the radio man. The soldier tried to raise the lead vehicle. Amos, in the well of the command halftrack, waited silently. His eyes were deep and glazed, streaked crimson. His beard, four days old, was layered with dust and globs of dirt and he hadn't brushed his teeth in three days. His mouth tasted awful and there was a dull, insistent throbbing at the base of his skull. "Well," he rasped. "What is it?"

"A minefield."

"Sappers out," Amos snapped. Then, to the driver: "Get us up there. There's no time to waste."

By the time the command car swung up the line to the front, the sappers had begun their work. A team of them, mine detectors swinging before them like great appendages, shuffled apprehensively forward like men expecting the ground to give way under them. Or blow them up.

Amos took up a position alongside the lead car. Freeman, left arm tied down to his chest, came up behind him. "I think I hate mines more than anything else. If they're boobytrapped——"

At that moment there was an explosion and a cry of pain. Men began running forward.

"Stay back!" Amos shouted. "Stay in your vehicles."

The sappers came out of the field. Three of them were carrying the wounded man. Amos grimaced. His legs were badly mangled and he was bleeding profusely. A medical aide appeared. He took one look and waved them toward the rear.

"We've got to get him to the field hospital."

"Radio for a plane," Amos said. He swung back to the chief of the sapper section. "I want to get moving again. We've got those Egyptian tanks on the run and I think we can catch them before night."

"The men are terribly tense, Amos," the section chief said. "And when one of them is hurt this way——"

"The mine detectors——"

"They didn't help that man very much."

"We must get through at once."

Amos glanced around. A young private stood a few feet away. Amos held out his hand. "Give me your bayonet." Amos took the short green-colored blade and strode into the minefield, to the point where the explosion had occurred. He dropped to his knees and began to inch ahead, hand extended, lightly exploring the soil. He stopped, probed gently with the bayonet. There was a muffled metallic click of metal on metal. Very carefully, he withdrew the bayonet and began to clear away the loose dirt with his hands. The mine came into view, a flat device with a turret-like trigger arrangement which, if even slightly depressed, would touch off an explosion powerful enough to disable a large tank. Working cautiously, Amos defused it, then moved ahead until he discovered another mine and repeated the process. In twos and threes, the sappers drifted back into the minefield and went back to work.

An hour later, a twenty-foot swath had been cleared and, with Amos driving, the command halftrack led the way past the mines.

Parked on the road ahead, waiting for the tanks to begin to roll through, Amos sent out a call for a scout plane. A few minutes later, a white Piper Cub with the Israeli blue Star of David on its wings, passed overhead going south. When it returned, Amos was almost ready to move out.

"Were you able to locate the Egyptian tanks?" he asked the pilot over the radio.

"Most of them have already crossed the canal. "You'll never catch up."

Amos swallowed an oath. He wanted those tanks, wanted to revenge himself for the casualties they had inflicted on his battalion, to destroy them before they killed more Israelis.

"How much further to Suez?" he asked.

"Twelve miles, maybe. No more."

Amos thanked the pilot and put a call through to brigade headquarters. He explained the situation to the commanding general. "I can catch those tanks," he said. "Give me the word."

The brigade commander laughed. "You seem to have forgotten the British ultimatum. We agreed to respect the ten-mile limit."

"To hell with that!" Amos responded, with quick, flaring anger. "I can cross that ditch and be in Cairo in a couple of hours. There's nothing to stop me."

"Indeed!" There was no misunderstanding the chill in the metallic voice over the field radio. "I will stop you, major. My order will stop you. Your private vendetta with the Arabs is not all that's at stake, you see. This morning a British fighter plane was shot down, by the Egyptians. The pilot parachuted to safety and some of our people tried to help him. They were strafed by British planes. It seems, that though we both fight Nasser, to London we are still the primary enemy. To make sure there is no misunderstanding, word has reached us through Paris that if we violate the ten-mile limit, the English will fire on our forces. The Prime Minister and the Cabinet are not prepared to make war on Britain."

"Understood," Amos said, suddenly weary. He signed off and ordered the column forward. Two miles further along the tanks stopped. And waited.

Sharm el-Sheikh perched on a cliff close to the southernmost tip of the Sinai Peninsula and dominated the Strait of Tiran. No ship could pass under its guns with impunity. No ship did.

As a prelude to attacking the fortress, Yaakov Yeshivat

270

ordered a detachment of paratroopers to occupy the airfield at Tor, about sixty miles away. He was the first man out of the first Dakota and led the brief action that ensued. With the airstrip taken, he ordered planes in with more men and supplies. At the same time, his armor and motorized infantry moved up.

He was working out the details for an air drop on Sharm el-Sheikh itself, when Uri Davidov unexpectedly presented himself. He was a sharp contrast to Yaakov and his men. Where they were coated with dirt and dust, he was clean-shaven and neatly turned out in new khakis, his brass brightly shined.

Yaakov became aware of his presence when his staff officers stiffened to attention. Davidov, he reflected with a certain amount of satisfaction, did that to men.

"Shalom, Yeshivat," Davidov began, then briskly: "How soon can you be ready to move?"

"Soon enough," Yaakov said gruffly. He could not conceal his dislike for the tall young general, though he recognized his cool competence. "I'm going to hit them with overwhelming strength. My tanks are being rushed up there on tank-carriers and—" he looked at his watch, "—in forty-five minutes my boys will be airborne."

"No," Davidov said, with finality.

"What are you talking about!" Yaakov broke off. He could feel his officers watching, waiting to see how he handled this arbitrary intrusion. Davidov had a right to be here, the authority to reject and replace, to command. But he was such an overbearing, offensive prig.

If Davidov was aware of Yaakov's resentment, he gave no indication, his words arranged in crisp, academic order.

"This is what we're going to do," he declared. "The attack on Sharm el-Sheikh will come from two directions, to insure quick success," he allowed. "From the north, along the Gulf of Aqaba, an infantry brigade. They're on the march at this moment. Your paratroopers, Yeshivat, will advance down the eastern shore of the Gulf of Suez, and move from the south."

Yaakov felt impelled to object. "You think that is such a good idea. A drop will——"

"There is no time for discussion. The decision has been made and you must start your men off at once. The timing on this operation is delicate."

"An hour more or less doesn't matter now," Yaakov said. "We've got them running."

"An hour might matter very much later on," Davidov corrected pointedly. "Diplomatic pressure for us to stop fighting grows heavier and heavier. Eisenhower and Dulles are having fits. They're giving the British a very hard time and there is no reason to think that Eden can stand up to them. Now the Russians have leaped in on the side of Cairo. Khrushchev is rattling his rockets and talking about hitting Paris and London. The Americans let him know that rockets can go both ways."

"That is almost funny," Yaakov said. "I can't see Moscow or Washington taking action. Sound and fury, nothing else."

"Maybe you're right. But remember, the Russians would love to establish themselves in the region, to give the English and Americans a difficult time. This may be their chance. They've been unable to do much with us so now they'll try the Arabs. Moscow sent a sharp letter to Ben Gurion and recalled their ambassador." Davidov's mouth pulled down at the corners. "It is necessary that we attain all our objectives before the pressure becomes too intense to resist."

"When are the English supposed to land in Suez?"

"According to our French friends, on November 6. But their landing forces are still at sea."

Yaakov laughed shortly. "Those British generals won't make a move unless every plane is flying and every button polished."

Davidov almost smiled. "The French call it a hundred-ship armada. Right now, however, that's not our problem."

"What's happening at the UN?" Yaakov asked.

Now Davidov did smile. Briefly. "The UN sits in New York, not Sinai. It offers an excellent forum for Arab rhetoricians. They are marvelously colorful speakers. But talk can't hurt us now. The British, on the other hand, are close by and the Foreign Office is capable of any duplicity."

Yaakov raised his brows. "You know, Davidov," he bit off dryly, "there are times when I recognize you as a very clever fellow, especially when you agree with me."

Davidov gave no sign that he had heard, the proper military mask back in place. "That infantry brigade should be hitting Sharm el-Sheikh shortly," he said. "In case you're needed, it would be nice if you and your men were there."

"We'll be there," Yaakov snapped. "Bet on it."

272

The private made no effort to hide his fear. He wanted to run away and told his young captain so a number of times.

"The Jews are going to kill us," he protested.

Abdul al-Hadad glared at him. "You will stay here with me and do your duty or I will kill you at once. Is that understood?"

"But, effendi," the private said, with pleading logic. "There are so many Jews and only the two of us. They possess armored cars and tanks and artillery. If we were to withdraw, it would be possible to fight against them another time."

"We must protect the mine field. They can be stopped here. Soon reinforcements will arrive and we will destroy these befouled beasts and drive them away."

The private nodded but remained unconvinced. He turned his attention to the front and watched with interest as a team of Israeli sappers worked a bangalore torpedo under the concertina wire in front of the minefield. When it was fused, the sappers retreated a safe distance and waited for the explosion.

So did the Arab private.

It never came and when he realized that it wouldn't, that something had gone wrong, he laughed happily. The Jews were not very good at this kind of work and that made him feel better. Soon the reinforcements would come and, as the captain had promised, they would push the Jews into the sea. Then at last a new era of Arab glory and unity would arrive. The world would recognize what the Arab was made of.

He frowned. What were the Jews up to now? Infantry-men were advancing on the wire. They attacked the rolls of wire with their bayonets, with their hands, twisting and tearing it, throwing themselves upon it bodily so that others could walk across their backs unhindered and in safety. And now their sappers were clearing away the mines. The familiar hollowness seeped into his bowels and he set himself up against the weakness of his flesh.

"They will be coming soon," he muttered. "The wire and the mines did not stop them."

"We will," Abdul said grimly.

"The reinforcements, effendi. They will not reach us in time. It is not Allah's will that we die for no reason. We should retreat or surrender."

Abdul fought against the rising sense of panic. He swung around and pointed his pistol at the private. "Keep

273

still and listen. Here no one surrenders. Not I and not you. We are going to fight. To stop them. Now. Begin to fight or I will kill you myself."

The private offered no argument. He recognized that the captain meant what he said. He leveled his rifle at the advancing Jews and opened fire. He was aware of Abdul beside him, using the pistol. Neither of them saw the soldier with the submachinegun circling to the rear. Both of them died without hearing the gun that killed them.

Twenty-five miles of coastal land only six miles wide, the Gaza Strip was administered by Egypt as a colony, Cairo viewing the territory as a separate entity, anxious to neither absorb nor support the 200,000 Palestinians who lived there. Ten thousand troops defended the Strip but they functioned in small and independent units, chronically unable to cooperate with each other. This, coupled with the fall of El Arish and Rahfa to the advancing Israelis, made the conquest of Gaza inevitable.

At 06:00 hours, the armored infantry company to which Hank McClintock had attached himself, attacked the village of Khan Yunis in the southern portion of Gaza. Riding in a halftrack, with Mordechai at his shoulder, Hank filmed as much of the action as he could. The advance was so swift, as defenses crumbled, that he was never able to join the infantry as it cleaned out strongpoints.

Anxious to capture on film the work of the foot soldiers, he was pleased when the column ground to a halt beyond Khan Yunis.

"Is something wrong?" Mordechai asked the driver anxiously.

"Barbed wire and mines. Don't worry, the boys will clean it out." He lit a cigaret and lifted his face to the sun.

"Come on, Mordechai," Hank said. "Let's see what's going on."

He leaped to the ground and helped Mordechai down. "You think this is such a good idea, to go up to the front?"

Hank grinned. "I want to get some of this."

They moved up to the fenceline and Hank shot film of the sappers working a long metal tube loaded with explosives, under the rolls of barbed wire.

"Back off, everybody!" the sergeant in charge shouted.

They pulled back and ducked down behind the lead vehicles. They waited. Nothing happened.

"What's wrong?" Hank asked one of the sappers.

He shrugged and spit. "Sometimes those things don't work."

"What happens now?"

The commander of the infantry provided the answer. "Clear that bangalore out of there," he ordered, "and my people will get rid of that wire." When the bangalore was dragged away, the soldiers moved forward. They hacked at the wire with their bayonets and some of them twisted it until it broke, turning back the loose ends. Other men draped themselves carefully over the wire, making a bridge for the sappers to cross. They set about locating and removing the mines.

Behind them, Hank recorded their every move on film. There was implicit drama in the unyielding way the men held themselves, the tentative way their hands reached for the mines, the threat of instant destruction immediate. He wanted all of this he could get and inched closer.

Rifle fire broke out ahead and he looked up. Arab snipers had the sappers pinned down. A rifle squad moved up and Hank trailed them.

A slug whistled past and he went to the ground. From a prone position, he swung his camera up, focusing on the action to the front. Suddenly the swift tenor cough of a Uzi. A second burst. The shooting stopped.

"Okay!" someone shouted. "All clear."

"Hey, McClintock," someone else called. "You want some pictures of Nasser's best? Come over here."

Hank moved up to the edge of the shallow trench and gazed down at the two bodies. One man wore the insignia of a captain and the other was a private. The captain was very young and there was an expression of pained innocence on his handsome brown face. Hank exposed a few feet of film. For the record.

The deep black sky was studded with stars and provided little protection for the advancing Israelis. Minefields slowed the attack on Sharm el-Sheikh and heavy machine-gun fire drove them back. Twice Joshua led his company forward and each time they were beaten back, the night a kaleidoscope of exploding mortar shells, bright flares and colored tracers.

Orders were issued to prepare for another attack. The

dead and the wounded were collected and loaded aboard trucks and sent to the rear.

"This time you'll have mortar support," Battalion assured Joshua. "Big stuff. You jump off at 05:00. Okay?"

"Okay. But I don't like it. It's very rough out there."

"It has to be done, *adoni*. And now."

For the final assault, Joshua loaded his men into a convoy of jeeps, the plan to get the infantrymen into position quickly. They waited for the signal to advance.

The attack began with a halftrack company, supported by infantry. With first light, it became evident that the Arabs were putting up a stiff defense and the advance was faltering. The fighting continued steadily for almost an hour, when Joshua was ordered to join the battle.

The jeeps sped ahead, moving beyond the halftracks, bouncing toward the Egyptian gun emplacements. The lead jeep skidded to a halt. Joshua hit the ground, Uzi leaping in his hands. He could hear his men shooting, calling to each other, shouting hoarsely.

A shot came from Joshua's left and he whirled, firing. An Arab leaped erect, clawing at his face. He fell back dead. There was shooting on all sides now and he lost track of time and place—running, falling, shooting, reloading without thought, reacting instinctively. All at once he found himself in a deep trench and two men with fixed bayonets were coming at him. He killed them both with a single burst.

Joshua went forward, stepping over bodies, past unattended machine guns. From a dugout he heard a sound, a muffled cough. He pulled the pin on a grenade, ticked off three slow beats, and rolled it inside. The explosion sent a rolling cloud through the narrow entrance. Joshua waited for it to settle, then ducked inside ready to shoot. An officer lay on his back, eyes open and staring sightlessly.

Outside, Joshua saw some of his men moving along the trench. He gestured. "Follow me! Keep them running!"

He heaved himself out of the trench. Two short strides toward Sharm el-Sheikh and Joshua was dead. His legs went slack, all tension drained out of the connecting muscles and tendons, and he staggered without direction, tumbling to the scorching sand in ungraceful surrender. A precise, glistening hole above his right eye drew the pale face into an expression of mild regret.

Three hours later, the garrison of Sharm el-Sheikh surrendered. All objectives had been achieved. The war was over. Quiet settled over the desert.

SIX

Amos Landau

It was the summer of 1939 and Amos Landau had reason to be pleased with the course of his life. Coming to Palestine had been the right thing to do. In Europe, Hitler and the Germans were increasingly arrogant, with political ambitions that seemed to make a large war inevitable. Word reached Jerusalem that life under the Nazis was worsening each day.

In Palestine, at least, a man could live in comparative comfort and peace with his family, raise his children with relative security, work without fear. The bakery was doing better these days and though it would never make them rich, they lacked nothing.

Nevertheless, Amos was worried. He was convinced that England and Germany would soon be at war, that there would be fighting throughout the Near East. How, he fretted, would all this affect the Jews of Palestine.

A partial answer was provided late one night. He was in the back room of the bakery, mixing dough for a batch of German rye bread. It was hot in the low-ceilinged room and the back door had been left open to admit the least stirring of cool air.

Amos was stripped to the waist, a handkerchief around his throat and strips of gauze around his wrists, serving as sweat-catchers. He worked swiftly, his strong hands kneading the dough, fingers reaching deep. Satisfied with its consistency, he began to shape it into loaves, arranging them in neat rows on heavy metal trays for the ovens.

A slow sense of being observed came over him and he stiffened with sudden apprehension. He snatched up a long rolling pin and whirled in one swift motion.

"Shalom, my friend."

It was Yaakov Yeshivat, broad and tough in baggy brown slacks and a white sports shirt, lounging against the doorway, a mocking grin angling across that scarred mouth. He straightened up.

"Do you intend to crack me one with that little tool?" he said, stepping into the room. A second man followed closely.

Amos lowered the rolling pin. "That is a good way to get your thick skull split open, sneaking up on a man. Shalom, Yaakov."

Yaakov looked around, gesturing casually to the other man. "This is Joseph, Amos. He helps me in my work." He brought his pale eyes back to Amos. "Look at you, *adoni*. White with powder like a woman. It isn't fit for the second-best rifle shot at Ramat Yochanan to look this way."

"Some of us must earn our living with work," Amos said, turning back to the dough. "I would prefer to wear clean clothes and wander around at night."

"You see, Joseph. The way he addresses me. Without respect, without fear. That is some tough guy, that Landau. Shut the door, Joseph."

Amos swung around, a vague resentment filtering through him. It had been a long time since Ramat Yochanan, a long time since he had seen Yaakov. Now here he was, uninvited, unannounced, casual and sarcastic. Amos had no need of such friends.

"Leave the door alone," he bit off.

Joseph looked questioningly at Yaakov.

"We have some business to discuss," Yaakov said softly. "Privately." He studied a tray of pastries and selected one with great care, chewing enthusiastically. "Ah, excellent. Did you bake these yourself, Landau? Congratulations. I need a favor."

Amos turned away. "I did you a favor when I did not crack your skull. Go away. I am busy."

Yaakov heaved himself up onto a clean work table and folded his big hands in his lap, assessing the baker solemnly. "Outside, Landau, there is a load of goods. It must be tucked away somewhere safe for a while. I am sure you can think of such a place, a staid and proper fellow like you."

"What are you talking about?"

"Guns, Amos."

Amos looked up. "What guns?"

"Rifles. Fine new models. Perhaps you read about them in the papers. Some daring guys took them from the British armory outside the city yesterday."

"You did that!"

Yaakov shrugged. "We've been on the move with them ever since. The British have patrols covering every road. We figured to throw them off the track by coming into the city, but now we can't get out, can't get the goods to the

280

hiding places we had picked. Joseph here was all for abandoning the load. But I couldn't do that and that's when I thought of you. My old comrade Amos, I told him, will fix us up."

"Go to hell." He went back to the dough. "Even if I could, I can see no reason to help you."

"Because you're a Jew," Yaakov said, the gravelly voice sober and flat. "Because we have to prepare to defend ourselves against the Arabs and their British friends."

"The English will have their hands full with Hitler soon enough."

"Agreed. But that will be our fight too, my friend."

"What do you mean?"

"The British will need us against the Germans. They will be happy to take us Jews into their Army and train us, give us experience fighting in their war. But that war will end one day and things here will be exactly as they are now. We must be ready for that day. That is the job of us who are in Haganah, you and me, *adoni*."

"To fight the Nazis will be a privilege," Amos said.

"Bravo! And later to fight for yourself will be an even greater privilege, to make a country for yourself."

"Since when did you become a Zionist?"

"I am a Palestinian. It is enough. Now about the rifles—!"

"You're mad. What am I expected to do with a load of rifles, put them in the ovens?"

Yaakov glanced at the ovens. There were three of them, massive, black cast iron, lined up against the far wall. "You use them all?" he said mildly.

"You *are* insane. Yes. All of them."

"Too bad. Well, you will just have to think of something else then. These are Haganah rifles, Amos, and you cannot ask us to give them back. Think, man, you have some intelligence. Use it. Isn't there some other place? In this shop, perhaps?"

Amos struggled to sort out his emotions. Resentment of Yaakov's cavalier attitude, his casual treatment of their friendship. The desire to help, to be a part of such a thing. And a very real fear of what might happen.

"This is my father's bakery," he said, concentrating on his work. "You cannot expect me to jeopardize the business—"

None of them heard the front door of the bakery open and close. None of them noticed when Baruch Landau, stern and straight, stepped into the back room.

281

"So!" Baruch broke in, after a moment. "If you are so concerned about your father's business, why do you entertain your friends when you should be working?"

Joseph's hand slid under his coat to reappear with a pistol short and ugly. He pointed it at Baruch's belly.

The old man glared at him. "Who is this gangster?" he demanded.

"Put that away," Amos snapped. "This is my father."

"How did you get in here, old man?" Joseph said.

Baruch scowled. "In my place, I don't answer questions from bums with guns." He jerked around to face Amos. "For this you made me leave Hamburg? You think Jewish storm troopers are better than the German kind?"

Yaakov made a motion with his hand and Joseph returned the pistol to its nesting place.

"Papa, this is Yaakov Yeshivat, a friend of mine. I told you about him. The gun was a mistake, papa. You see, they're with Haganah and there's a problem."

"Big shots. Jewish heroes. Did any of you ever fight in a real war? I was four years in the trenches against the French and the English. That was a war, there should never be another."

"We have been fighting the English, too, Mr. Landau," Yaakov said evenly. "Some day we'll have to fight them again. I have a truckload of rifles outside that we took from them. They must be hidden and——"

"I heard," Baruch said. He waved a hand in Amos' direction. "My smart son is not so smart. Why not the ovens? That one, on the end. Inside, there is a fire-pit, deep. The ashes could be emptied. How many rifles are there?"

"Three dozen."

"The pit is deep enough but the rifles may be too long."

"We could break them down," Yaakov said hurriedly. "Separate the barrel from the stock."

Baruch turned to Amos. "Don't stand there, clean out the pit. You," he said to Joseph, "the gangster. Bring the rifles in here. And be quick. I don't want the British to come along and arrest me."

"Papa, it means we can't use the oven."

"We'll use the oven," Baruch insisted.

"The fire will ruin the rifles," Yaakov said.

"There are bricks outside, against the wall. I will need them, about fifty. We'll build a wall to conceal the guns and to protect them from the fire. In the basement, I have sheets of asbestos, to protect the walls from the heat. We'll use them, too."

"How thick is the asbestos?" Yaakov said.

"Three-quarters of an inch."

"That may do it. We can lay some of it over the guns and the rest just behind the bricks. Keep a fire going and the British will never think to look in the oven, if they come around."

"One thing," Baruch said. "To get the guns back, you must give me twelve hours warning, to put out the fire and cool the oven. Understood?"

"Understood."

Baruch grunted. "So bring in the bricks."

When Amos was alone with his father, he said, "I thought you were against Jews doing anything to make a country of their own. I thought——"

Baruch cut him short. "To make a country is one thing. For Jews to protect themselves, especially against the English, that can't be so bad, I think."

Amos was asleep, dreamless. Abruptly he was smothering, frozen in place, muscles weak and useless, a great weight pressing down on his chest, an invisible force closing off the scream of terror that glutted his throat, immobilizing his head. He couldn't be sure whether he was asleep or awake and the blackness was impenetrable. From a distance, his name was spoken. Or was it close at hand and said in a whisper? Again, this time nightmarishly familiar, grating, cautious. He stopped struggling.

"Ah, better. Listen, *adoni*, there is no need to wake your wife."

It swam into dark focus. The voice. The powerful hand over his mouth, another on his chest. Yaakov. Yaakov in the bedroom, with Ruth and himself.

"A woman with a family," Yaakov husked sibilantly, "needs her rest. I will release you now and we will go back downstairs and talk."

Amos felt the hands withdraw and he sat up, aware of the powerful thumping in his chest, of the strength flowing back along his muscles, of the black rage that gripped him. He went downstairs and into the living room. He switched on a lamp and turned as Yaakov entered the room. Without a word, he swung his right fist at Yaakov's face.

The big man caught Amos' hand in his own, held him

283

tightly. "There is no time for such nonsense," he whispered.

"I am going to kill you. There is no other way——"

"There is no time, I said. Now listen to me, or must I hold your mouth again?"

Amos wrenched his hand free and stepped back. Even in the soft light, Yaakov looked weary. There were pouches under his eyes and his face was lined, turned down.

"What are you up to?" Amos said. "It is the middle of the night. You have no right to break into my house, into my bedroom. By God, Yaakov, if you had frightened my children—"

"I must have the rifles," Yaakov said. "Right now."

Amos shook his head. "At this hour! Why couldn't it wait until morning?"

"Because in the morning the rifles will be used. Something's happened. You'll hear about it tomorrow."

"What is it?"

"Some of our people, members of the Night Squads, have been taken by the British. The Army's holding them."

"At Yavniel," Amos said. "I know about that. Forty-three people, including that friend of yours, Moshe."

"No. Dayan and those others are in the prison at Acre. We can do nothing about them. They will have to take their chances, stand trial. But last night, twenty-one others were arrested. They were on a night course for Haganah south of here. A bunch of young guys on their first night operation. An English patrol took them and they're being held in the Army camp near Beit Shemesh."

"What do you want of me?"

"Only the rifles. Joseph is outside. We, and some others, will do what is required."

Amos stared at Yaakov who stared back. "I'll get dressed," Amos said. In the doorway, he turned back. "You're lucky. We haven't used that oven in two days. It'll be cool."

At the bakery, Joseph steered his old Ford around back. Once inside, Amos drew all the blinds before turning on the lights. At the oven, he began breaking down the protective wall, passing bricks out to Joseph.

"Can't something be done legally?" he said, after a few minutes. "Surely the English can be made to understand that we must protect ourselves from the Arabs."

"The English understand only what they believe is in

their own interests," Yaakov said. "When Moshe and those others were imprisoned, Ben Gurion went up on their behalf. He vouched for the forty-three, pointed out that they were patriots, not criminals. He reminded the English of the role Jewish volunteers had played on their side during the World War, explained that the Jewish Agency was cooperating in the maintenance of law and order in Palestine, despite the British White Paper limiting immigration. He advanced logic and facts."

"And?"

Yaakov made an exclamation of disgust. "Here was the man who represented Palestine's four hundred thousand Jews and he might as well have been a beggar off the streets. It did no good. The men are in jail and will undoubtedly receive long prison terms."

"They might be acquitted," Amos said.

"By British standards, they are guilty. But not by ours. Let the British do what they must. We will too. Now let's get those guns where they will do the most good."

It took twenty minutes to remove the bricks and the asbestos shields. Amos passed out the first rifle.

"Only a dozen," Yaakov said.

Amos swung around, amazement etched on his face. "You intend to attack an English Army camp with only a dozen men?"

"Come with us," Joseph said calmly, "and we will have thirteen."

Amos looked at the thin man, then at Yaakov. A glob of icy fear lodged behind his navel and he shivered. To be a member of Haganah was one thing, to go on forced marches, to learn to shoot, to throw grenades, even to patrol against Arab raiders. There was a kind of respectability to it all, almost a national purpose.

But to attack a Royal Army encampment! The British *were* constituted authority in Palestine, an authority armed and ready. Dangerous in their imperial power. He struggled to conceal the trembling of his fingers as he handed over another rifle.

"You haven't answered Joseph," Yaakov said conversationally. "I assume you are not coming with us."

"Assume any damn thing you please!"

"That makes the dozen," Joseph said, accepting another rifle.

Amos straightened up. "I'm going back to bed."

"After we replace the bricks and the asbestos," Yaakov said. "We don't want the rest of the goods ruined."

285

When the wall was rebuilt, they carried the rifles out to the Ford and secreted them under the rear seat.

"Get in," Yaakov said. "We will take you home."

They were halfway there when Amos finally spoke, voice charged with uncertainty and frustration. "You should join Irgun so you could blow up places and kill more people."

Yaakov lit a cigaret. In the glow of the ash, his face was without the softness of flesh, suggesting a rocky cliff, all thrust and sharp ruts. "They do what they have to do and so do we. This is no whim, *adoni*. It is official Haganah action. We are under orders. We can't afford to let the British put more of our best young men in jail. It would be self-indulgent. We need those guys. Right now they're just a bunch of anonymous Jewboys. But they're all trained, the leaders of a Jewish Army tomorrow."

"You'll never break them out."

"We have a scheme."

Joseph's laughter was thin and shrill. Amos realized that the thin man was anxious to go into action, to kill. "We know something," Joseph muttered.

"It's true," Yaakov said. "We have friends everywhere, even among the British."

"Spies?"

"Patriots. In any case, we are going after the boys, and there is no need for you to worry yourself further. Soon we will have you back to your house and your warm bed. To safety."

"I don't think he would look so good in costume," Joseph put in, emitting that thin laugh again.

"Costumes?"

"It is sort of a party," Joseph said. "A costume party. The British are the guests of honor and they don't even know they're invited. We should have fun."

Amos looked out into the passing night. They were almost to the top of the hill and the Zichron Moshe quarter. Soon daylight would come and the streets would be crowded with the men in their black coats and beaver hats, beards and sidecurls; and those who were not Orthodox, other men in sports shirts; and women and children. All unafraid because they were Jews among Jews, not to be insulted or attacked.

He visualized Ruth in their bed. Soon she would awake and if she found him gone she would be frightened.

"I must get word to my wife," Amos murmured.

286

"There is no time," Yaakov said. "We must join the others and get into costume, get to where we are going."

Amos looked at his friend and nodded once. Joseph laughed mirthlessly and swung the Ford into the next side street, heading toward Beit Shemesh.

The Army camp was set in a sprawl of hills, wooden barracks and tents in military formations, all enclosed by wire fencing. A narrow dirt strand twisted its way through the hills to the main road, snaking back on itself in places and so steeply banked that the big military trucks were forced to grind along in second gear.

"There are frequently accidents along here," Yaakov explained.

He and Amos sat in the cab of the 6x6 as Joseph wheeled it around curves and into the short straightaways with alarming speed.

"And we're liable to have one," Amos said, "the way Joseph drives."

Joseph laughed his pleasure, that compressed rising sound. "That's the idea."

"Around the next bend," Yaakov said.

Joseph grunted. Fifty feet further along, he slammed on the brakes. "Let's go," Yaakov said, getting out. He went around to the back of the truck and dropped the tailgate. "Everybody out."

There were ten of them, all wearing regulation uniforms of privates in the British Army. When all the men were out of the truck, gears clashed and the big wheels slipped and slid on the loose dirt as Joseph backed the big truck into the ditch, maneuvering so that the front end effectively blocked the road. His thin head came out of the window, looking to Yaakov for further instructions.

"That should do it, Joseph. Cut your engine and break out the emergency lights and put them out." Yaakov called to another man. "Selig, take your men and get into position. There will be a Land Rover and three trucks. If it gets to that, you know what you have to do."

"Kill each of the drivers."

"Exactly. Now move." He glanced up at the eastern sky. "A few more minutes and it'll be light. Gerstel and Lupino, get on that truck. Dirty yourselves up, hands and faces, smear some grease on your uniforms. Make it look as if you're really mechanics."

"Yes, Yaakov."

Yaakov studied Amos with professional detachment.

"What irony, my friend, that you of all of us should be the only one the uniform fits properly. You make a very fine officer. Very dapper. Very, very English. No one would ever guess that you're a Jew." The other men, lounging along the high bank that lined one side of the road, laughed raucously. "It is clear," Yaakov went on, playing to his audience, "that clothes do indeed make the man."

"Get on with it," Amos said, with no good humor. A mounting anticipation pulled his nerves up tight.

"You look the part. Aristocratic almost. It must be the German in you."

A warning light came into Amos' eyes. "The convoy'll be along," he said, without expression. "Are we going to play games or do what we came for?"

"Ah!" Yaakov exclaimed cheerfully. "See the way you take command! It is the uniform that does it." He sobered quickly and turned to the others. "Space yourselves out. Be relaxed. You're simply waiting for the truck to be fixed, a common enough occurrence. Be suitably bored, smoke, talk to each other. But keep those rifles ready. You know what the plan is and you will take your direction from whatever happens. Once it begins, it's up to every one of you, *us*—" he directed his words toward Amos, "—up to us to improvise on the spot." Facing Amos, he executed a brisk military salute. "The detail is ready, lieutenant. It's up to you now."

Amos returned the salute with a casualness he didn't feel and placed himself in the center of the road, facing the two men who were supposed to be repairing the truck. He lit a cigaret, puffed anxiously. Displeased with the growing tension he felt, with his reflexive fear, he forced himself to wait for a full thirty seconds before bringing the cigaret to his mouth again. Time passed with exaggerated slowness and he became aware of the changing attitude of the other men. All levity was gone now, replaced by a thickening mood.

Yaakov came up behind Amos. "Listen, *adoni*. They're coming."

Amos strained. There it was, the weary groaning of military engines as they ground around those curves, up the steep inclines. Amos moved to throw down his cigaret, changed his mind, kept his back toward the oncoming convoy. The Land Rover would be leading the way, and then three small personnel carriers with their canvas tops. Inside, the prisoners and a couple of armed guards.

"Here they are," Yaakov said, arranging a smile on his

mouth. "They're on the straight road now and they've spotted us, are slowing down."

"I wish it were dark," Amos said.

"Better this way. At night, they would be more cautious, have a large escort." He pointed at the oncoming vehicles. "Now, *adoni*. Now."

Amos turned and gazed at the Land Rover. He took a last drag on his cigaret and tossed it aside. The convoy had stopped and an officer was leaning out of the Land Rover, a captain.

"Hullo, there. You're blocking our path, lieutenant. You'll have to get that truck off to the side somehow."

Amos moved forward. He marveled at his self-control. He smiled apologetically as he came closer.

"We've a bit of a problem, sir," he called. "Something about the steering mechanism, you see."

The captain frowned. "Bad luck. But we must get on through. Top priority mission. Have to put some people on a plane for the north."

Amos spread his hands helplessly. "The men are working on the difficulty, sir. Perhaps you could give us a pull—"

The captain looked over at the soldiers at roadside. "You've enough men of your own, lieutenant. Put them to work and swing the front end in toward the ditch. We must get through at once." He leaned forward and spoke confidentially. "Valuable cargo. Jew terrorists, you see. Can't take chances with a lot like that. So if you'll put your men to work—"

Amos gave a slow salute, brain working rapidly. "Of course, sir. I understand." The driver of the Land Rover had both hands on the wheel. But a stocky private with a Sten gun across his lap sat in the back seat. He owned one of those British pudding faces that look very formidable.

Amos called to Yaakov, who moved up on the other side of the Land Rover. "Sergeant, the captain here must get through at once. He wants us to manhandle the truck over to one side. Do whatever is necessary."

"Yes, sir," Yaakov said, his pale eyes narrowing.

Amos, smiling pleasantly, reached for the canvas holster on his gun belt. The Army pistol was heavy, stubborn, clinging to its nest. Then it was in his hand. He shoved it under the captain's chin.

On the other side of the Land Rover, Yaakov pointed the Enfield at the chest of the soldier in the back seat.

"What is this, lieutenant?" the captain managed to say. "If this is your idea of a joke—"

"No joke, captain," Amos said, keeping his voice down. "One move and you die and that goes for your men too. Yaakov, the Sten gun." He waited until Yaakov had relieved the private of the weapon. "Listen and understand me, captain. I have more men concealed on the high ground above the road. They are zeroed in on the drivers of your trucks. One signal, one bit of trouble, and they will shoot. We want no killing, if it can be prevented—"

"But if forced to we will kill," Yaakov said.

"All right, captain. Out on the road. And you will order your drivers and the guards out of the lorrys."

The captain didn't move. His face was pale but set, the mouth firm. "I think not," he said. "One shot and they'll hear it back at the camp. Two hundred men will be here in less than ten minutes."

"By which time you and your men will all be dead. Ten minutes and we'll be gone."

The captain smiled confidently. "I think not. This looks like a standoff, old boy. Let's strike a bargain, shall we? I'll give you your ten minutes. You have my warrant that neither I nor my men will make a move while you get away. Without the prisoners, of course."

Amos sucked air into his lungs. He whipped the pistol barrel across the captain's cheek. There was the soft crunch of metal against bone and a streak of blood appeared. After a moment, the captain forced his head up and fear was reflected in his blue eyes.

"The choice is yours, captain," Amos said coldly. "Live or die. Now!"

The captain took out his handkerchief and held it to his cheek. "Yes," he said, his voice very weak. He climbed out onto the road and waved at the drivers of the trucks behind. "Out onto the road, men. Down here and we'll give these chaps a hand. Quickly now." He looked back at Amos. "Personally, we English have nothing against you Jew chaps, y'know. Just trying to keep the Arabs from massacring all of you. I mean, we don't have any of that Nazi thing in England. Disraeli and all of that."

"Captain," Amos bit off, "shut up, please."

There were nine guards and three drivers and they sauntered toward Amos and the captain in that way that soldiers have, slow, indolent, challenge to authority implicit in their movements.

Amos made a quick gesture toward his men and the

rifles leaped into their hands, were leveled on the Tommies. "Drop your weapons!" Amos called, displaying his pistol against the captain's chin. "Drop them!"

The soldiers obeyed.

"Get them off the road," Amos ordered. "Bind them. We want as much time as possible before an alarm is sounded."

Joseph hurried back to his truck, worked it onto the road. Moments later the convoy was under way with Yaakov driving the Land Rover and Amos seated beside him.

"You did very well," Yaakov said presently. "How naturally you gave orders. There is the sound of a commander in your voice. I believe you may come to enjoy this game."

Amos made no reply.

SEVEN

*I call heaven and earth to witness
that whether it be Gentile or Israelite,
man or woman, slave or handmaid, according
to the deeds which he does, so will the
Holy Spirit rest on him.*

—The Talmud

1960-1962

I

At dawn on May 22, a blue-and-white turbo-jet airliner landed at Lydda Airport outside Tel Aviv. A slender, nervous man was hurried into a waiting car and taken to a heavily-guarded old Arab house outside of Jaffa.

Later that morning, he was brought into a room where the chief justice for the district of Tel Aviv was waiting. A police inspector, speaking in German, informed the prisoner that he was facing a judge. This brought the slender man to attention, the sharp face expressionless, eyes focused on some point in space.

"What is your name?" he was asked.

"Ich bin Adolf Eichmann!"

The police inspector stepped forward. "You are accused," he said, "of causing the death of millions of Jews of Germany and occupied countries between the years 1938 and 1945, with the intention of exterminating European Jewry while you commanded SS units in Germany, and while you were in charge of the deportation of Jews in Germany and German-occupied territories. . . ."

The two brothers embraced.

"Shalom, Levi."

"Shalom, Simon."

They stood apart, staring at each other, grinning. Levi ruffled Simon's thick curly black hair and the boy tossed his head and laughed.

"You have grown, Simon. Soon you will be a man."

"Hah!" Yaakov Yeshivat snorted mildly. "When I was twelve I was fighting Arabs."

Simon looked up at Yaakov. His thin face was closed, its dark eyes hooded and its finely sculpted mouth angled downward toward the corners. "Fighting is stupid," he said. "Killing is stupid."

"Perhaps you are right," Yaakov said soberly. He squinted up at the sky and wiped his damp brow. "But I will surely be killed here if we don't get out of this sun. This heat is hellish."

Levi led them inside his tent and offered them each a

295

bottle of orange drink. Yaakov sucked on the bottle, then spewed the liquid onto the dirt floor. "Camel piss," he growled. "The juiciest oranges in the Near East grow in Israel but we can't make a decent orange drink."

"What brings you to Eilat?" Levi asked. "And with my baby brother?"

"Papa didn't want me to come," Simon said. He laughed mirthlessly. "I told him I'd run away, if he didn't let me."

"And now you're here," Yaakov said. "And it's as Amos said, nothing. An empty place. A few buildings and some tents and a lot of sand."

"But it will be much more one day," Levi said. "We are doing great things here."

"Nonsense. It is too hot, too removed from the rest of Israel, too damned close to the Egyptians."

"Can we see them?" Simon said. "The Egyptians."

"Why not?" Yaakov said.

Levi led them outside to a Land Rover. They bumped down to the water's edge. "The Gulf of Aqaba," Levi said to his brother.

"I think this place is good for you, Levi," Yaakov said. "You look tan and strong and that is an impressive mustache."

Levi tugged self-consciously at the growth curling down around the corners of his mouth in Oriental style. "I am younger than most of my workers, you see. The mustache makes me look older, I think."

"At least twenty-five."

"I am twenty-eight."

"An old man."

Simon pointed. "What is that?"

Yaakov looked out to the cliffs down the coast. "Sharm el-Sheikh."

"Are there Egyptians there?"

"Not since 1956."

"That is where Joshua was killed?" Simon said.

"Yes."

"Can I go there. I would like to see where Joshua was killed."

"No, it's not safe."

"Not since the politicians decided to give it back to Nasser," Yaakov growled.

"But Israel won the war."

Yaakov ran his fingers through his patch of almost white hair and stared at the fortress. "Our boys died for

296

that and we give it back. Gaza, Sinai, all of it. We still can't use the Suez Canal and anytime Nasser wants to he can cut us off from the Red Sea." He spat. "Those imbeciles at the UN, the Russians, the Americans."

"I hear you're thinking of putting yourself up for the Knesset," Levi said, trying to change the subject.

"Ever since I took over for Lahav after he died, I've been thinking about it. To make sure that our strength doesn't get diluted by some of the soft-headed ones."

"He means papa," Simon said.

"Your papa," Yaakov said, "is too busy getting rich to do anything else." He grinned at Levi. "Listen, I didn't come to talk politics. You applied to Histadrut for help. What's it all about?"

"So that's why you came. Yes. We're after private capital to build but the risks are too great for the bankers."

"And you expect Histadrut to put up money? For what? This is a wasteland. What good is such a place?"

Levi recognized Yaakov's technique for what it was and kept his face solemn, his voice controlled. "The highway to Beersheba has been opened for two years. And men like me are here to work and build because Eilat can be many things to Israel. Important things. A port, for example, our entry to Africa and Asia."

"And where will the ships unload? There are no docks, no barges, no facilities."

"We have plans."

"Ah, plans. Then you have other fantasies as well?"

"The weather, Yaakov. No more than four or five days are without sunshine during the year. This could be a vacation resort—hotels, swimming, boating, fishing."

Yaakov laughed derisively. "A miracle maker! You are going to make this desert bloom."

"Levi can do it!" Simon burst out excitedly.

"That's right," Levi said. "I can. Ever since I studied at Technion I've been thinking about Eilat. I've made projections. Cost estimates. I have plans, blueprints."

"What about water?"

"A problem, but not insurmountable. Rainwater can be stored in cisterns and we are digging for underground desert water. We estimate that will fulfill 70 percent of our needs. Desalinization——"

"Still not practicable. Costs are too high."

"On a limited basis—"

"What do you want from Histadrut?"

297

Levi raised his eyes to Yaakov's. "Build a hotel, a shopping plaza, a hospital, a cinema."

"Wait! Why not ask for an entire city?"

"A hotel with one hundred rooms," Levi said. "With a pool, perhaps, and air conditioning, of course. A study was made and the potential profit is considerable——"

"Now *you* sound like papa," Simon interrupted, "talking about profits."

Image upon image of Amos flashed into view on the screen of Levi's mind, a lifetime of impressions and reflections. No, he told himself firmly, he was not like his father. Not like him in any way.

"You can't possibly understand," he said to Simon, cutting him short. He turned back to Yaakov, the high shoulders coming forward. "This could be important, to all of us."

"Histadrut is interested in providing work for its people, for improving the country. Show me facts and figures. But not out here in this terrible sun. Let's go back. We'll talk more after supper. It'll be much cooler then."

Levi had an extra cot moved into his tent for Simon. Levi lit a cigaret and sat down, facing his younger brother.

"How are mama and papa?"

Simon's face closed up. Levi saw so much of himself in the boy, the same tension and frustration. Unlike Simon, he had been ready to stand openly against his parents, against authority, to strike out. He remembered the Yemenis he had beaten and wished he hadn't done it. Yet, though it was something he would never do again, he still felt an antipathy toward them, toward all foreigners, all people who were different and spoke strange languages.

"Tell me about mama," he said.

"She is funny."

"How funny?"

"Different. It's like she's someone else sometimes, as if she's thinking about something no one else can understand."

Levi sucked his cigaret. "She took Joshua's death very hard. It changed her."

"Sometimes she talks to herself, says Joshua's name."

"She misses him a lot."

"So do I. Sometimes I think about him before I go to sleep and it almost makes me cry. To get killed in a war is about the dumbest thing anybody can do, I guess."

298

"Sometimes it's necessary to fight."

"I'm never going to fight in a war," Simon said firmly. "I'm not going to get killed and make mama talk to herself. I miss Joshua. I miss you, too, Levi. Everybody goes away. Rena lives in Jerusalem and she and Hank never come to see me."

"Never?"

"For the holy days is all."

"People have to make their own lives. When you grow up, you will too. Just like papa."

"He's always working, always busy. What's he so busy about?"

"The business is very big. It has problems, I suppose."

"I don't care about that. I wish he was home more, and you, Levi."

After Levi left, Simon lay in the dark thinking. Nothing stayed the same, he decided, ever. Even people changed. He remembered days when everything was perfect, his mother warm and loving, his father full of laughter with time to play, his brothers coming and going but friendly, willing to explain things to him, and Rena, always happy, a second mother. All of that was gone now and he resented it, resented being forced to do things he didn't want to do. Like being bar mitzvah. All that studying, the memorizing. He decided that he didn't like any kind of school. One day he would be old enough and big enough to do only what he wanted to do. He could hardly wait for that day to come.

They sat around the plain plank table and listened to the radio. Michael, the unofficial mayor of Eilat, in his early twenties, slender with red hair and a sparse orange beard, a measured way of talking. Nadiv, short and muscular, with small eyes and an aura of explosive power. Leon, quiet, gentle, with the big, calloused hands of a laborer and the vocabulary of a poet.

Yaakov approved of them, as he approved of Levi. Somehow they were different than so many people he had known in Israel. A fine difference. It was in the eyes, he concluded. There was no expression of Jewish sadness in them. No haunting sense of imminent danger. No defensiveness. These were men who looked outside themselves, *Israelis*, used to living and working in their own land, a country twice victorious in battle, a country growing and becoming stronger.

Levi came into the dining hall and took his place at the

table. Michael turned off the radio. "Kol Israel just announced that we've arrested Adolf Eichmann."

"Here? In Israel? Who did it?"

"Shin Beit. The Security Services, I suppose."

"They should've killed him," Yaakov said. "There is no point in bringing him back here."

Michael looked up, his glance steady. "There is a question of justice. As much as any of them, he was responsible for the holocaust."

"All right," Yaakov said. "We'll try him and then kill him."

"Why?" Nadiv said, his voice light, almost feminine. "For revenge? I cannot see any reason to bring it all up again, to raise old ghosts. We Israelis don't care about the past, only the future."

"To hell with that!" Yaakov answered hotly. "Let the world know that we Jews are not without claws, that we strike back at our enemies, that we no longer stand around waiting to be made into ashes. An eye for an eye."

"Have you become a Christian?" Michael said lightly.

Yaakov smiled reluctantly. "When the Arabs raid we hit them back, and harder. The punishment fits the crime. It works."

"Not really," Nadiv said. "The Arabs keep raiding. Nasser still calls for the liquidation of Israel."

"Talk is cheap. We have Eichmann. Good, I say. Hang him, I say."

"There never has been an execution in Israel," Levi put in.

"The time is right for the first one."

Michael shook his head. "Here is our chance to establish the rule of international law, in the tradition of the Nuremberg Trials. Justice must rule here."

"Would you turn him free?" Yaakov said.

"If a case cannot be made, yes."

"Tell that to those whose relatives were cooked by the Nazis. On Eichmann's orders."

"It is something to think about," Leon offered quietly.

"That's the trouble with you boys," Yaakov retorted. "Too much thinking. I say finish him off and that would be that. What if they try to get him out?"

"Out of Israel? That would be impossible."

"Was it impossible to get Mussolini away from the Allies when he was captured? The Germans pulled that one off. You boys have a lot to learn about what can and can't be done by certain kinds of men."

300

"Enough," Michael said calmly. "We don't decide such affairs here. Nadiv, let's show Yaakov the plans for the hotel, the cost estimates, the building schedule. Here we deal in the future, *adoni,* and I'm sure Histadrut will want to be part of that future."

Nadiv slid the blueprints over to Yaakov and he stared at them. These young ones, he thought with some bitterness. They understood nothing, as if everything that had preceded them was unimportant, that life, the world, had begun with them and would continue due only to them. They would learn better when trouble came along and they were forced to turn to men like himself for help. Comforted by the thought, he turned his attention to the plans. They were, he admitted grudgingly to himself, quite sensible.

II

Mejjid al-Hadad appraised the two men with clear eyes. They were very young and they held themselves in that awkward, slightly self-conscious way of new military recruits. He glanced at their papers again. All was in order. But papers, he knew, could be forged. He looked at them again. A matched pair, brown-skinned with glowing black eyes, with sad, expectant faces. And they spoke perfectly accented Arabic. The same, he reminded himself, could be said of many Israelis. He sighed and made an inviting gesture toward the big velvet chairs. They sat.

The taller of the young men arranged a tentative smile on his sensual mouth. "You are kind to receive us, effendi," he said, with a suitable amount of obsequiousness in his voice. "We were assured that in the house of al-Hadad there would be a welcome for such as we."

"How do I know you are who you say you are?"

"The papers——"

"Nothing. You still must convince me."

The young men exchanged glances. "The night before last we crossed the frontier from Syria."

"Your commanding officer?"

"Major Aziz Bigbashin."

"And where did you train?"

"At the village of the Mukhtar Abu Fuad edagini."

"Describe him."

"Ah. The mukhtar is a man of immense proportions, tall with exceedingly broad shoulders and a magnificent beard."

"What else?"

"What else?" the tall one said uncertainly. "There is nothing—ah, yes. The eye. The mukhtar has only one eye and that is a terrible orb that glitters and grows larger and smaller according to his sentiments."

"The mukhtar seldom displays much pleasure these days," the other man said.

"You know how he lost the eye?" Mejjid asked.

"In combat with a Jew more than twenty years ago. The Jew gouged out the eye and even as it occurred the mukhtar throttled the pig."

Mejjid clapped his hands and his second son, a boy of fourteen, appeared with coffee in small cups and baklava. He waited until the boy had left before speaking again.

These first interviews were always difficult. The young men were always dedicated, fanatical sometimes, anxious to strike against the Jews and this caused them to be careless and often led to their deaths. But not Mejjid. He was cautious and protective and so lived on to do the great work he had promised Abdul he would do.

"You came into Israel two nights ago," he said. "What have you been doing since then?"

"Last night we destroyed a bridge north of this city and an armored car was wrecked. Six Jews were killed."

Mejjid glared at them. "Do not lie to me! I am not part of the Liberation Army in order to waste my time on fools. Yes, you destroyed a bridge. Yes, an armored car was wrecked. A wheel was broken and it took perhaps twenty minutes for an Israeli mechanic to repair it and the bridge was back in use this morning. As for the soldiers, one man was wounded, no more than a scratch, and no one was killed. No one."

"But effendi from the look of the accident——"

"I was informed," Mejjid went on coldly, "that the soldiers climbed out of their wrecked car, those dead soldiers, and went into the hills after those who had caused them trouble. But those heroes of the Arab cause ran away."

"There were too many to stand against——"

"Ah, so they were not all killed. Allah protect us from those who tell us only what they think we would listen to.

302

Do you know why the Jews twice defeated us in combat?"

"Yes, effendi," the tall man said cheerfully. "Because the Americans and the British and the French helped them. Alone they would not have been able to stand against us."

Mejjid growled his despair. "You remember the story about the *Jeanne D'Arc?*"

"Yes, effendi. A single Egyptian frogman sank the warship during the fighting in 1956. Such skill! Such courage!"

"Idiots! Do you believe everything Abdel Nasser's radio tells you? The *Jeanne D'Arc* still sails the Mediterranean today, and regularly visits Arab ports. It was never sunk. Never even damaged. There was no frogman such as you envision."

"But effendi——"

"Be still and listen. If you are to join my organization, you must obey me in all things and follow my instructions. And most important, you will always tell me the truth, reporting events and situations exactly as they are, not as you believe I might wish them to be. Is that possible for you, to tell the truth? If you blow up a truck, you are not to tell me it was a battalion of tanks."

"We will never lie to you, effendi."

Mejjid sipped some coffee. It was cold and bitter. Of late he had developed a taste for blander pleasures. "You will remain here for the next two days," he said, "while travel permits are prepared for you."

"And what will our assignments be?"

"Water lines." A look of disappointment appeared on the faces of his visitors. "To the Jews, my dears, water is more important than anything else, more precious than gold or oil. Without water, the kibbutzim cannot survive and they are the first outposts of their defense. You will go south, south of Beersheba, into the Negev, and you will blow up wells and pipelines. You will attack water trucks. But have no fear, in time there will be other tasks more to your liking, all for the greater glory of the Arab Nation."

"El-ham dillah."

"When will the final battle against the Jews take place? At the mukhtar's village we were told that it would be soon, that we would destroy Israel. We heard the great Ahmed Shukhairy speak and he said that the Chinese and the Russians have promised us arms."

"Ah, Shukhairy," Mejjid said softly. "That inciter to violence and death who never presents himself where the

303

results of his rhetoric occur. 'We will wipe Israel off the face of the map and no Jew will remain alive.' "

"His exact words, effendi," the tall youth marveled.

"Listen and understand. In 1956, if Ben Gurion had ordered it, the Jewish Army could have marched into Cairo itself as if on a pleasure stroll. Nasser boasts of Sinai as a victory. It was a defeat. He talks of Egypt as a major power. It is a small and unimportant country. He brags of a single Arab nation with a single language, a single faith. All a fraud. The Arabs of the Sudan are black and many Syrians have blue eyes and fair skin. An Algerian cannot even understand a Yemeni and we Muslims have two major divisions in our religion and a dozen lesser ones. And many Arab states are political creations in the same way that Israel is."

"Does that mean we cannot defeat the Jews, effendi?"

To win with such men as these, Mejjid reflected bitterly, would be difficult indeed. But not impossible. Nothing was impossible for a determined man and he was determined. He visualized his son, Abdul, dying as a hero for what he believed. Surely Abdul had been different than these two, clever, imaginative, daring and realistic. His death was a major loss to the Cause but Mejjid had worked very hard in the years since to compensate for that. Abdul would be avenged. Over and over again until the ultimate victory took place.

III

The new Landau factory was set on a gently terraced landscape south of Tel Aviv. A low glass-walled structure in the shape of the letter H, it seemed to have grown out of the smooth green lawns and the carefully tended flower beds. The flowers had been Ruth's idea and Amos had agreed to it. It pleased his aesthetic sense and the workers seemed to like them too.

In his private office, a spacious chamber flooded with daylight, Amos Landau sat behind his contemporary rosewood and stainless steel desk, his attention riveted on the three men seated across from him. There was Moses Chesin, local chief of the textile workers union; and his lieutenants, Goldenberger and Newman, quiet, observant men.

Chesin, a birdlike man with fluttery hands, was speaking, the words tumbling out of him as if in a race with each other. ". . . Everything is more expensive, Amos. Food, clothes, luxuries, services. Everything. The workers must have more money."

"Always more, Moses," Amos said. "Where does it stop?"

Chesin's hands darted and swooped, came to rest, took off again. This was the fourth time he had headed the negotiating team and he was used to Landau's approach, seeking to postpone what was inevitable, trying to save a percentile wherever possible. He was a shrewd bargainer, but had never been inflexible; a realistic man who avoided collisions and was willing to compromise. Chesin appreciated that.

"The standard of living keeps improving, Moses. But it is too much to expect private industry to pay all the costs."

"Agreed. Actually the Government absorbs most of that. Still, businesses such as the Landau Company must contribute fairly."

"And what of Histadrut? What is its fair share?"

"Histadrut is more than just a union, Amos. You know that. It owns companies of its own, housing complexes, shops. It invests in diversified projects. Histadrut is concerned with almost everything that happens in Israel. The point here, *adoni*, is that prices keep rising. In the last two years, the cost-of-living index has risen almost——"

"Five percent," Amos put in.

Chesin looked apologetic. "Our figures show ten percent. That is what we think our workers are entitled to. Ten percent."

"That's unrealistic. Look at the overall situation. This country still falls far short of full employment." He grew thoughtful. "Perhaps I can find justification for two percent, three at most."

Goldenberger shifted in his chair and his round face darkened. "Amos, you are not talking straight to us. Three percent is nonsense and you know it isn't a fair offer."

Amos frowned. He had made the offer in good faith and resented being doubted. That was the trouble with these Histadrut people, they had begun to believe they were always right, with a private, vested interest in the country.

"I suggest," he said coldly, "that we end this meeting, that both sides take time to consider the other's offer."

Goldenberger shoved himself erect. He was a wide man with a belly that hung over his belt and a ridged brow. "What offer, Amos?" he growled. "Three percent is an insult."

"It is the best offer you're going to get." Amos looked at Chesin. "Put it to your members, Moses. Tell them the truth of economic conditions and let them judge. Then we can talk again."

"Oh, we will tell them. But they won't like it."

Amos considered the situation after the three men had left. They seemed to believe that his past reasonableness was an indication of weakness, of softness, that he was an irresolute man who could be threatened and bullied. It was time they discovered that the Landau Company was solely *his* business, that he ran it and all decisions were his. They would be surprised at how tough a negotiator he could be when the situation demanded it.

It was late when Amos got home that evening and Simon and Ruth had already finished supper. He had no appetite but made no objection when Ruth began to serve him, insisting that Simon sit at the table while his father ate.

"It's important that a family take meals together," she explained. "With Levi in Eilat and Rena in Jerusalem—" She hesitated. "It's important," she ended abruptly, almost angrily.

Amos picked at the food without interest.

"I got a letter from Rena today," Ruth said brightly.

"How is she? The children?"

"Hank is going to take movies of the Eichmann trial," Simon put in hurriedly, "for cinema and television all over the world. Papa, why don't we have television in Israel?"

"It's better to read books and listen to music. That reminds me, there's an all-Brahms concert on Thursday. We'll all go."

"I don't like Brahms," Simon said.

"You're not eating," Ruth said.

"I'm not hungry and I'd like to lose some weight. This belly—"

"You look just fine," Ruth said.

"I'm never going to let myself get fat," Simon said.

"Your father's not fat," Ruth corrected.

Amos layed down his fork. "What's this about Hank and Eichmann?"

"I told you," Simon said brusquely. "He's going to make movies of it."

"Isn't that nice?" Ruth said.

"He should have nothing to do with it. That's a mistake. All that is behind us. We should let it lay, forget it, not expose old wounds."

"Yaakov said they should've killed Eichmann," Simon said.

"That's Yaakov's answer to everything these days. To kill. The man is becoming impossible. And now he's standing for the Knesset."

Ruth smiled, a physical alteration in the set of her mouth, but her eyes remained lifeless. "That will be nice."

"Are you going to vote for Yaakov?" Simon said.

"We'll see," Amos said. Yaakov would be on the Mapai list. As the strongest of all the political parties, Mapai would undoubtedly gain more than half the votes cast and so be able to win at least sixty seats in the Knesset, half the membership of that body. "It's time, I think, that Ben Gurion let more moderate men control the country. He should quit."

"But he did resign," Ruth said.

"A device to show his strength, to choose his own successors eventually. He wants to run things even after he's out of power, after he's dead, I suppose."

"I don't understand," Ruth said, with no particular interest.

"You remember Pinhas Lavon," Amos began. "He used to be defense minister." He wanted to stop, to turn his mind to something less trying. But he recognized the expectant expression on his son's face and he went on.

In 1954, an Israeli espionage ring had been exposed in Egypt and the blame for this debacle was placed at the door of Pinhas Lavon's office. He denied responsibility and questioned the role of the Army in the plot. Documents were then produced that implicated Lavon, soiled his reputation.

Lavon refused to permit the matter to expire. Six years later, he forced the case to be reopened and it was revealed that two Army officers had forged the documents, had lied to a commission investigating the case. The scandal rocked the country and a Cabinet Committee was formed which cleared Lavon. But Ben Gurion continued to be openly critical of the decision, claiming that oral evidence against Lavon had not been heard.

"If Lavon was innocent," Simon asked, "why didn't they let him alone?"

"I believe his guilt or innocence was never the point," Amos said. "Central to the issue was his political ambitions. He wanted to succeed to the Premiership after B-G. The Old Man has other ideas."

"Then it's only politics," Ruth said, dismissing it.

"Yes," Amos said. "That's why Ben Gurion resigned. He resigns whenever he doesn't get things his own way. He forces a Cabinet crisis and this time a special election had to be called. If Mapai wins, then Ben Gurion will have his own way once more."

"Will Mapai win?" Ruth asked.

"I think so."

"Good. Then Yaakov will be in the Knesset. How nice for him."

"Papa," Simon said thoughtfully. "It's not right, is it?"

Amos smiled indulgently. "I suppose not."

"Then why don't you do something about it?"

"What can I do?"

"You're an important businessman. You could do something. A lot of people work for you and do business with you. If you told them what was going on they would listen to you, vote the way you tell them to vote."

"It's not that simple, Simon. You don't understand."

"If it's wrong, people should do something."

"A businessman can't afford to antagonize people, Simon. Especially politicians. Besides, I'm only one man and I don't get involved in such matters."

Simon stared at his father for a long silent interlude. "I don't want to be like that, knowing what's right and what's wrong and doing nothing to help."

"Simon!" Ruth remonstrated.

"I mean it," the boy said, voice climbing excitedly. His eyes darted around. "If you don't do what's right, then what is living all about? I mean, is it just to make money and buy things? If it is, I don't want it."

"What do you think life is all about?" Amos said quietly.

Simon was standing now, the pale face mottled, his lip trembling. "Unless you care, do something, then nothing matters. You're rich and you own things but what about when you have everything you want? What happens then? What do you think about? What reason is there for living?"

'Simon," Amos said, trying to placate the boy. "There's

308

so much time for you to worry about such things. You sound so—desperate."

"I want to be desperate when I'm young. It'll be too late when I'm old and ready to die." He spun away and ran out of the room.

An unreasoning resentment slithered through Amos. "That boy is going to have to learn some manners," he muttered. "He's going to have to understand what life is all about." A troubling thought came alive in his brain; perhaps Simon did understand. Everything.

IV

On the day Adolf Eichmann went on trial in Jerusalem, Yaakov's secretary phoned Amos' secretary and made an appointment to see him. It was the first time in the years of their friendship that Amos had known Yaakov to announce his coming.

Two days later, in mid-morning, Yaakov appeared. He marched across the office to the rosewood desk with all his youthful vigor. But time had marked him. Deep ruts angled from the battered nose to his wide mouth and his brow was seamed. The hair was all white now and in need of a barber's attention. At once Amos remembered that Yaakov was fifty-seven. The brawny, vital young man he had met at Ramat Yochanan was growing old.

He considered himself, only four years younger. Unlike Yaakov, he was running to fat, soft from the sedentary life he led. He vowed to counter it. Perhaps he would build a gymnasium in the factory. And sponsor a soccer team. The workers would appreciate both, he was sure. He extended his hand and Yaakov took it, his grip as firm as ever.

"You look well, Yaakov."

Yaakov grunted and sat down, folded his thick arms. Like Amos, he wore a shirt open at the throat. There the similarity ended. Amos' shirt was French silk; Yaakov's worn khaki, faded and threadbare from too many launderings.

"Some tea?" Amos said.

"I came to talk, *adoni*. Off the record."

Amos sat down. Clever, he told himself. Yaakov was entering the negotiations, but unofficially, bringing his influence as head of the Tel Aviv worker's council to bear. And their friendship. Amos almost smiled for this meant that Yaakov had changed, become more civilized, more willing to compromise, to make a deal. Amos leaned back and peered across the desk.

"You came to talk," he said, without emphasis. "I'll listen."

"This business with my workers," Yaakov said. "I want it settled right away, with the least possible fuss."

"Tell that to Moses Chesin and that negotiating committee of his. Unreasonable demands can't be met."

"To match the cost of living increase is not unreasonable."

"Ten percent is out of the question. Over one thousand people work at this plant. One thousand, plus those at the knitting mill and those in the shops. My payroll runs in excess of——"

"Are we accountants, *adoni?*" Yaakov broke in. "We both know the figures. So many pounds for this and so many pounds for that. We are discussing the needs of the people."

Amos was puzzled. Had matters reached an impasse he might have expected Yaakov to enter the scene. But there was still much room for maneuvering. Why was he here?

"Chesin says ten percent. I say five. He wants the full ten, I've offered two."

"You offered three and that is unacceptable."

Amos smiled grimly. "Louis Goldenberger gave me that impression."

Yaakov leaned forward, hands on the edge of the desk. His eyes were penetrating. "Let me explain something, *adoni.* You know what is happening, the special election."

"You would be better off out of politics."

"You would be better off *in* politics. It is your country too."

Amos straightened up. "I don't need you to remind me of that."

Yaakov nodded once after a brief interlude and Amos recognized it as an apology, the most Yaakov had ever offered to anyone.

"All my life," he said, and the familiar edge had left his voice, "working and fighting. That's all I know. I own a small apartment, Amos, and an extra pair of boots. Nothing else for all the years." He swore and the battered face grew hard. A mirthless laugh broke out of him, tinted with self-mockery. "How do you like that! Yeshivat feeling sorry for himself. Well, there is no need for that. I have lived the life I wanted to live and still do. Now I want Mapai to win the election. I want to be in the Knesset, Amos. I want it very much."

"Mapai will probably win and you will get what you want."

"I want these negotiations settled right away," he said, with the old curtness. "I don't want trouble with the Landau Company. My people are talking strike. You don't want that, Amos, to fight with me." A challenging light came into his eyes. "I would win easily."

Amos met his gaze. "Don't be too sure, *adoni*. Anyway, the workers would never strike. The Landau Company has been good to them."

"Paternalism is no answer to a man's dignity."

"That's an odd thing for an old Socialist like you to say. It seems to me that Histadrut is more paternal than any employer could be."

"Enough talk. Let's settle this quickly. Make a good offer, Amos, a substantial one, and my people will make concessions. I guarantee that. There will be no strike."

"Just another easy victory for Yeshivat. And Mapai will win another campaign point. The Old Man will come back as Prime Minister and you will be in the Knesset. Who is it going to be when B-G finally quits, Yaakov? You?"

"You're too smart to believe that."

"Then who? Dayan? Shimon Peres?"

"That is no concern of ours today."

Amos made a small sound of assent. The Landau Company was *his* concern, his alone. Everyone else pursued different goals, sought different rewards. Yaakov was involved with the benefits to his workers, to his own career.

"We do a large export business these days," Amos said. "That means we bring a great deal of foreign currency into the country."

"That is nothing to me."

Amos tried again. "Let me tell you how I see things, the factors that influence me—"

"Spare me the philosophy. I am here to talk money for my people."

"All right. Money. Soon the German reparations will come to an end. More than eight hundred million dollars have come into the country—"

"That is a good thing!" Yaakov flushed and his fists

311

were tight and hard. "I have never approved of any dealing with Germany."

"The Government is negotiating with Bonn right now for a loan and—" Amos grinned thinly, "—and we are selling them thousands of our Uzi submachine guns. Doesn't that amuse you, *adoni*, Jewish guns for Germans?"

When Yaakov did speak, his voice was a cutting rasp. "I am for the killing of Germans whether they are behind the Rhine or building rockets for Nasser or sitting in the dock in Jerusalem."

Amos leaned back and held his hands aloft in a gesture of pacification. "But I am not. The business we do with the Germans is good for Israel. So were the reparations. As for Eichmann, it would better be forgotten, left to history."

Yaakov held himself very still. The old familiar anger seethed through his middle and a misted crimson veil swirled before his eyes. He made an effort to place a tight rein on his emotions.

"Let us get back to the issue. The Landau workers must have a substantial economic increase. Ten percent is——"

"Impossible."

Yaakov plunged ahead without pause. "I represent all unionists in this city and the vicinity. I can bring them into action against you, if I decide."

"You're threatening me, Yaakov."

"Yes, dammit, I'm threatening you!" He came to his feet, his pale eyes deep and unfocused, a fist raised. "My workers want their rights and I will get it for them."

"I am not easily intimidated," Amos said, in an almost inaudible voice. "You should know that." He reached into his brain for information, facts and figures, projections of future possibilities. Ten percent was an exorbitant rate and Yaakov had to realize it. A lesser figure would be acceptable. "I will make you another offer," he said. "Realistic. Five percent."

"No," Yaakov said. "Split the difference and we have a deal. Seven-and-a-half percent. The men will accept that."

Amos made a series of swift estimates. "On condition," he said. "An increase of that size means I will be forced to raise my prices. That means we shall no longer remain competitive in certain markets and there will be a loss of business here and abroad."

"That is your problem."

"Yes," Amos said shortly. "Therefore I will have to cut

the size of my labor force. Seven-and-a-half percent, according to efficiency ratings. Men with the lowest ratings to go first."

"You think that's funny?"

"I'm not joking."

"You go too far!" Yaakov husked thickly. "Such dismissals have always been the result of joint labor-management consultations. That can't be changed. Not now. Not ever. I won't permit it."

Amos shrugged. "Then I can't afford to give the increase you want."

Yaakov's face flushed and he slammed one big fist down on the desk. "You can't get away with this! You sit in this fine office and play God. But not at the expense of my men! Not at my expense!"

"That's what you're worried about, yourself."

"You want trouble, Amos, you'll get it. Trouble such as you've never known. I'll close down the Landau Company, close it down tight. We'll see who quits first in a fight, Landau or Yeshivat."

A moment later he was gone.

Two days later, the workers of the Landau Company went on strike. Amos was furious, convinced that the union, and Yaakov, were being irresponsible and destructive. He vowed to fight it out, estimating that he was financially able to withstand six months of factory inactivity. He placed full-page newspaper advertisements giving his position, outlining the union's demands and his offer, pointing out that he had no quarrel with Histadrut. In plain language, he insisted that the strike was unnecessary, brought about by the personal ambitions of the chief of the local worker's council. Though he mentioned no names, there was no doubt who he meant.

Three meetings took place during the next ten days between the company's personnel manager and the union negotiating team. Neither Amos nor Yaakov were present, but no progress was made, both sides holding to previous positions.

During the fourth week of the strike, three factory executives were attacked as they left their offices one night, and badly beaten. One man had to be hospitalized. The assailants were never found.

Infuriated by the violence, Amos called in the press and accused Yaakov of direct responsibility, insisting that nothing would have happened if he did not give tacit agreement.

"Further," he went on hotly, "there would be no strike if Yeshivat had not injected himself into this affair. Up to now, I have held my tongue. No more. Yeshivat is ambitious and seeks to further that ambition at the expense of the Landau Company and its workers. He tried to blackmail me into giving him a compromise that would be so beneficial to his people that they would reward him and his political party with their votes. That is not my function nor the function of my company.

"I will not be blackmailed. I will not be intimidated economically or physically. To this end, I am hiring armed guards to protect my property and the lives of my executives. The cowards who assaulted them are welcome to try it again. If they do, they will be shot."

A reporter read Amos' statement over the phone to Yaakov. It drew a typical response. "If Landau wants a war he will have it and he will lose by it. Histadrut stands one hundred percent behind its workers. All this talk of violence and blackmail is so much smokescreen to conceal the avaricious nature of the company."

"Landau said that if he had to he would close the Company down permanently," the reporter said. "He pointed out that he was beholden to no stockholders and no partners."

Yaakov made himself laugh to appear unconcerned. "Talk," he told the newspaperman. "Empty talk. Businessmen never let go of the golden egg. Landau has no choice but to settle." But when he hung up a disquieting uncertainty gripped him.

There was nothing to do but wait and Amos was unused to the inactivity. He remained away from the factory entirely, staying home, going for long walks, growing increasingly bored and irritable.

"Why don't you go away," she suggested, "a holiday. You could go to Galilee. I read where they've made some new discoveries, some Roman ruins. You haven't done any digging in years."

"Why don't we go away together," he responded. "A trip. To Paris or even New York, if you like. It would be nice for us both."

She smiled indulgently. "How can I go away, my dear? Simon's bar mitzvah is coming closer every day. I have a

314

thousand things to do and no time. But you could go. By yourself."

He shook his head. "Maybe I'll go to Jerusalem for a few days."

"Good. That'll give you a chance to see Rena and Hank and the children."

He left that morning, intending to spend the evening at his son-in-law's. But when he arrived in the city of David a sense of dislocation took hold of him. He moved through the streets without purpose, turning here, climbing a long incline there, paying no attention to the people he passed, encased in a thick fog that muffled all sound, inhibited all thought, deadened all feeling.

Abruptly the protective mist lifted and he stopped. He stood opposite the recently constructed Beth Ha'am, the House of the People. Here, he thought. Here is where the years of anguish and terror are being brought back to life, the images of that terrible time of the Nazis recreated, here the bloody memories were dredged up once more. Here Adolf Eichmann was on trial.

High fences had been erected around the House of the People and people filed into the front yard, to the temporary wooden barracks where they waited with silent patience to be searched for weapons. The authorities were taking no chances that some bitter Jew would seek a swift and personal justice. Guards were everywhere and Amos knew that the accused man was protected inside the courtroom by a bullet-proof glass booth.

Amos wondered why he had come. Was it the memory of his father's brother and his family, lost to the ovens? He hadn't thought of them in years, felt nothing thinking of them now. Yet here he was. A shiver twisted along his spine. Whatever blood-lure had brought him, he was not going inside, was not going to submit himself to that sordid recounting of murder elevated to a national policy. He turned away quickly, unaware of the man standing close behind him. Their shoulders met and Amos recoiled as if soiled.

"I'm sorry," he said.

The man had been staring at the House of the People and the collision seemed to have little effect on him. Reluctantly, he turned to Amos, not merely his eyes or his face, but the entire body, the feet first, then the hips, the torso, the joints locking into place until he had shifted around totally in a remote and mechanical maneuver.

"You are going to go inside?" he said with polite interest.

Amos looked at the man. There was a strange physical unattractiveness about him, a body almost top-heavy with chest, though the shoulders were narrow and bony. The head was long with only a few strands of colorless hair, the brow ridged and narrow, as if squeezed by giant hands. The face jutted forward, elongated features unnaturally arranged, a perpetual smile on the small mouth. His eyes appeared too small for their sockets and swiveled wildly on hidden axes.

Amos took a backward step and the long head bobbed up and down as if in recognition of the repellent qualities of his own appearance. "No," Amos answered. "There is nothing for me in there."

"Agreed," the other man said. He spoke poor Hebrew in a shriek of a voice. "I do not wish to enter either. What can they tell me, those lawyers and judges?" He held out his left arm, a long, bony limb; and displayed the smooth white underside. The number had been tattooed in clean block digits. "Typically German, no?" The man giggled but the expression on his face never changed. "See how easy they are to read. It facilitated the filing systems."

"Where—?" Amos was compelled to ask.

"Natzweiler. Ah, you never heard of Natzweiler. Why should you? Few people did. It was designed for the private use of Strasbourg University. The men who labored there, men of intelligence and sensitivity. Creative. Imaginative. Scientists looking into the future. Very special types. Experimenters. Ah, yes. Experimentation for the advancement of science and the betterment of the human condition. That one in the House of the People sent many of us to Natzweiler. *His* personal authorization. At Natzweiler, the scholars studied the activities and the achievements of the Indo-Germanic race. Very impressive, no? But what does it mean? Even now I don't know. You think the one in there knew? Not that it matters now. He signed the papers and ordered so many men and women and children into the freight cars for shipment. The logistics of the job must have been very complicated." A glint of remembered triumph came into the bulging eyes. "I was at Buchenwald and it was only a matter of time until I became fuel for the ovens. But I was fortunate." He tapped his pigeon chest. "To look this way is at times beneficial. An anthropologist came to the

316

camp to make a selection for Natzweiler and decided that I was an interesting specimen."

"But you survived."

"Isn't that the first duty? I survived. The others in my group were disgusted, revolted, sickened, and did not eat. I ate."

"The food was very bad?"

"It was quite tasty. The liver and the lungs especially. Slightly salty, but good." He leaned and the glint returned to the eyes. "It was an experiment in cannibalism. Each day they took some out of the group and slaughtered them and fed us their meat. They studied us, our physical health, our psychological reactions. The scholars were very concerned about that."

For a long moment, Amos was afraid he was going to be sick. The weakness passed. "Why?" he murmured. "Why didn't they leave? Or fight?"

A moist sound dribbled out of the smiling mouth. "There was no reason in the beginning to do either. Who among us believed the truth? Would you accept the story of the ovens if told to you? Persecution, yes. Appropriation of property, yes. Deportation, slavery, punishment. Yes to everything. These are traditional forms of civilized behavior. But not yes to the ovens. The ovens were brand new, a creation of Germanic efficiency. They were beyond belief, beyond acceptance."

"Yet you escaped."

"Because I have always believed the unbelievable. The goodness of man. The sacred words of God. When I arrived at Buchenwald an old man showed me a smoking chimney. 'That is where we all end up,' he told me. 'In thin air.' He was insane, of course, but I believed him. And so later, when my chance came at Natzweiler, I ran away."

"Have you testified?" Amos said, straining to control his voice. "Are you a witness?"

The man cackled. "Yes, yes. A witness. All of us. We all knew. We all made it happen. We all encouraged it to happen. All are guilty. All are witnesses. All."

Amos pulled away and the man began to laugh again, a narrow, penetrating wail, a sound that echoed in the cavities of his skull.

Yaakov masked his surprise when Uri Davidov appeared at his office at Histadrut headquarters in Tel Aviv. They had not seen each other since the end of the fighting

317

in Sinai and Yaakov could see no physical change in the tall officer. Time had been very kind to him. His face was still lean and studious, his hair too thick, too curly behind the ears, his eyes still bright and far-seeing.

It was only a few days since Amos Landau's remarks concerning the strike had been published in the newspapers and the reaction had not been what Yaakov would have liked. Editorials had been printed demanding a quick end to the walkout and letters had come in to Yaakov's office from all over the country criticizing the action of the union. All this had hardened his resolve to hold out until all demands had been met; had soured his disposition. And now Davidov.

"I was not expecting you," he said, by way of greeting.

'It is good to see you, Yeshivat," Davidov said gravely. "You are looking very well."

"And you, Davidov. But not in uniform. That suit, is it English-tailored?"

"I bought it in New York. But I am still in the Army."

"I know," Yaakov said dryly.

They were seated in straight-backed chairs on the balcony outside Yaakov's office and drinking tea brought by his secretary. He gazed down the hillside at the harbor, at the ships moored there, waiting to be unloaded.

"I can remember when the port didn't get half this amount of traffic," he said.

"Everything changes. Since 1948, we have taken in more than one million people. That forces us to change. Unfortunately, there are too few jobs for all those people."

"Sometimes competition is a good thing."

"Not in this case. It simply aggravates the differences between people, the Orientals and Europeans, the people of color and the whites, the unskilled, the uneducated—"

"This will all be resolved in time."

"Has Israel ever had enough time?"

"Still the philosopher, I see."

"Philosophy is not as empty a pursuit as you appear to believe, Yeshivat."

Yaakov broke in abruptly. "Let's get to the point. Why are you here, Davidov? We are not exactly friends."

A slow smile tugged at the corners of Davidov's mouth. "You will not accept it, of course, but I have always felt kindly toward you."

Yaakov made a disgruntled sound in the back of his throat.

"Moshe sends his best," Davidov said.

"Minister of Agriculture," Yaakov said, with obvious distaste. "Is that a job for a soldier?"

"Moshe is also an archaeologist, a man of many parts, very much like your friend, Landau."

"Is that why you came, to talk about Landau?"

"Moshe met with B-G recently and they discussed this affair with Landau and Histadrut. Moshe asked me to talk to you."

"He could've come himself, or the Old Man. I would have gone to see either of them." Yaakov braced himself. He understood the authority that was being raised and anticipated what must inevitably come next. "All right, Davidov. What's on your mind?"

"The Old Man is unhappy about this strike of yours."

"Not mine. Landau's. He asked for it and he got it."

"It is not good for Histadrut or for Mapai."

"It is necessary, and when I bring Landau to his knees it will win votes for Mapai. You will see."

"B-G doesn't want to bring Landau to his knees. Nor any other industrialist. They are precious to the country. We must face things realistically. Even if Mapai wins the election, and we expect to, there are very real, very dangerous problems. Economically the country is not in very sound condition. Jobs are in short supply and so is money. Private capital must be found that is willing to invest here. To do that, a proper financial climate must be established."

"We are Socialists. Why this talk of private capital?"

"Conditions change, Yeshivat. Israel must change with them. If private investment is in order to advance the quality of life here, then it will be found. If capitalism, in one form or another, is necessary, then we shall have it. We will not be bound and imprisoned by any single ideology."

"That is Ben Gurion's message to me?"

"His and Dayan's. Though the choice of words is my own."

"And if I reject it?"

Davidov pushed the tea aside and stood up. "Should you be so foolish, you will lose all support of Histadrut nationally. You will be left alone."

The anger came quickly, running deep, giving birth to a hot craving to strike out, to smash his enemies and take whatever he wanted. He forced himself to listen to Davidov.

"A long strike will endanger our chances of getting foreign investment capital. It could disrupt the economy badly. B-G wants it to end. Very soon."

Yaakov struggled to clear away the roiling mist that enclosed his brain. He had to understand what was happening, what it meant to him professionally and personally. The forces arrayed against him were too powerful to be opposed successfully, that much was certain.

"I could continue the strike without Histadrut," he said brusquely. "Without the Old Man."

Davidov looked off into space. When he turned back, his long intelligent face had settled into an impenetrable mask. "Let me disabuse you of such notions. Without national support, you cannot win." He took a deep breath. "I am authorized to say that your name has been placed number eighty on the Mapai list."

If there had been any doubt in Yaakov's mind about the strength lined up against him, it was washed away. Number eighty! Mapai would never collect a comparable percentage of the vote and that meant there was no chance of his being elected to the Knesset. This was Landau's doing. Somehow he would pay him back in kind.

"Further," Davidov was saying, "unless the strike does end promptly, you will be attacked publicly by national leaders of the party and the union. I'm sorry it has to be this way, Yeshivat, but you are a stubborn man and difficult to convince."

A faint weakness seeped into Yaakov's knees and he fought against it. He faced Davidov squarely. "Am I expected to go to Landau, to beg—?"

"Nothing like that. Nobody wants to embarrass you. The entire matter will simply revert to the negotiating committee. The executive secretary of Histadrut will join the negotiations himself, on your personal invitation. He will settle the matter swiftly and all credit will be yours. This will be better for all concerned. Agreed?"

"I don't have a choice. You do your job very well, Davidov. You are tough, tougher than I thought. Now, if you will excuse me, I have work to do."

Negotiations resumed the next afternoon and continued for seventy-two hours, at the end of which time an agreement was announced. A five percent pay increase and a sliding cost-of-living raise for the three-year duration of the contract. Efficiency ratings and discharges remained the province of joint labor-management consultation.

On the following Sunday, the workers returned to their jobs.

That same morning, Yaakov went to a kibbutz near the Dead Sea where he labored at the most menial tasks he could find, with a religious fervor. During the weeks he remained there, he spoke to no one, taking his meals in silence, buried in his own thoughts, seeking answers to questions he had never before raised.

Finally, reinforced and replenished, he returned to his job, convinced that he had to fight harder than ever to prevent another such setback, determined to rely only upon himself, as in the past, to defeat all signs of weakness and softness in himself, to beat life into submission.

And when he learned that Adolf Eichmann, judged guilty and denied clemency, had been hanged and his ashes scattered over the Mediterranean, Yaakov told himself that justice had been done.

But he wasn't sure.

Not of anything any more.

EIGHT

Yaakov Yeshivat

For Yaakov Yeshivat, there had been a great deal of satisfaction to be gained from heading a Workers' Company. It was a position of trust and respect. It showed clearly what his superiors thought of him. Even more, it was the kind of work he enjoyed most.

Publicly the Workers' Companies had been organized to promote sporting activities among the young men of Histadrut. In fact, their purpose was to select and train fighters for the labor organization in order to protect agricultural workers who were often harried and frequently beaten.

As a group, the planters preferred to employ Arabs in their orchards and fields, since they were willing to work for lower wages. But after prolonged negotiations, Histadrut convinced the planters that employment should be opened to all comers. Fearful that this would cost them jobs, the Arabs struck back. Violence broke out with increasing frequency and Jewish workers were attacked. It was the job of the Workers' Companies to put a stop to this. Wherever there was trouble, teams of tough and aggressive Jews went into the fields to meet the Arabs directly.

Whenever fighting broke out, the Mandatory Police intervened on behalf of the Arabs. In a carefully choreographed charade, the Jews would withdraw and the police did likewise. The Jews would promptly return to the attack. It was a slow and painful procedure and eventually it began to show results.

Then came September, 1939, and everything was changed. England went to war against Nazi Germany and the Jews of Palestine were unable to remain aloof from this fight. Almost to a man, they were committed to the defeat of the Nazis. The common enemy took precedence over their distrust of the English.

Thousands of young Palestinians enlisted in the British Army and were formed into all-Jewish companies. Yaakov Yeshivat was not among them. For the first time in his life, he was immobilized, torn between his hatred for the

Germans and his deep antipathy toward the English. He remained at his job but somehow it had paled, become less important, less immediate. A rising irascibility took hold of him.

Shortly after the beginning of the new year, Yaakov received a message from Reuven Bello, an executive of the Jewish Agency, asking Yaakov to visit him the next time he came to Jerusalem. The tone of the message was casual yet it evoked a sense of urgency in Yaakov and he hitchhiked up to Jerusalem the next day.

Bello, a round pink man in his middle years, greeted Yaakov affably, offered him tea and little Arab cakes and asked him how he liked working for Histadrut and what did he hope to do with his future.

"It's not the way I think," Yaakov said curtly. He hunched forward. "Listen, Bello. We have only met once before. We are not friends. And I do not think you asked me here to talk of my health or my future. What is this all about?"

Bello assessed the man in front of him and liked what he saw. Yaakov was a man of impressive physical proportions and that was important. And that face, exuding strength and aggressiveness, the twist of nose, the scarred mouth and brows, the bright, intelligent eyes. Fear would never stop this man from acting.

"I have heard," Bello said, smiling to let his visitor know it was only a joke, "that you are the best fighter in all of Palestine, and the best lover."

"I've done both," Yaakov said, flexing his mouth in what passed for a smile. "I enjoy both. A man can prove himself in both."

Bello made a small sound that Yaakov took for assent. Forming a steeple with his fingers, he said, "I would like to talk to you about another kind of fighting. I hear you don't like Germans very much."

"I don't."

"Nor the British."

"Nor the British." Yaakov scowled and pulled at his nose. "Get to it, Bello. Enough of this dancing around."

The pink man kept his face bland. Yeshivat was no man to be toyed with and that too was good. He was rough and blunt and seemingly without culture. But he appeared to have the kind of quick braininess required. Bello could almost see his mind functioning, the parts meshing effectively, studying present evidence against accumulated knowledge, measuring, deciding.

"All right, Yeshivat. To the point. You come to me well recommended."

"Lahav?"

"Among others. You have impressed many people in your time. You are the kind of man we want."

"We?"

"The Jewish Agency."

"I'm no Zionist. I was born here. The Jewish Agency is nothing to me."

"You're a Jew. You've been bar mitzvah."

Yaakov revealed nothing, as an image of his hawk-faced father, full of animation and life, drifted to mind. He still owned the pistol that had been a bar mitzvah gift, protectively cleaned and oiled once every month and stored in a soft leather pouch. That old man, he thought. That tough old man. He shoved the memory aside and stood up.

"I am wasting my time here."

Bello smiled. "Sit down and listen. I want you to join the British Army."

"Go to hell," Yaakov said, with no special emphasis.

Bello's mouth firmed up. "This is important. The English must be made to understand that the Jewish Agency represents *all* the Jews of Palestine, that we are of a single mind about the land and our futures here. Peace or war, that doesn't change. We want men like you to *be* the Jewish Agency in the British Army, to stand between them and our boys."

"I was never cut out to be a symbol."

"No symbol. An active extension of Jewish national-ism."

"I said I was no Zionist."

"You've fought the Arabs and the English both. You are an officer of Haganah."

"A question of survival."

"Some of us believe that the only chance of survival Jews have is in a nation of their own here in Palestine."

Yaakov shrugged. "I have my work for Histadrut." He went to the door, hesitated, and swung back. "A question."

"Yes."

"Will the British let Jews fight the Germans?"

Bello leaned back in his chair and spoke soberly. "I'm sure of it."

They set the camp down in the gray-yellow sand of the

327

desert, a collection of pyramidal tents and boardwalks that soaked up the scorching sun all day and offered no protection against the cold desert nights. Water and supplies had to be trucked in from the north and there were not enough rifles for the men training there.

The colonel in charge of the camp was a heavy-set man with a thick mustache, the color of the desert, and watery eyes. He spent his days behind his desk trying to think of some way of getting transferred to Jerusalem. It was lovely in Jerusalem this time of year, and there was nothing quite so pleasant as a gin-and-bitters on the terrace of the King David with that very pleasant Dolly Warrens, whose captain husband was off somewhere in Egypt. The idea so captivated him that he made up his mind to take the weekend off.

The sergeant-major interrupted his ruminations. "Sir!" he broke in, with a fine military salute. "A new shipment of Jews has arrived, sir. Two hundred of them. The man in charge is outside."

"Well. Two hundred. There are a bloody lot of them, aren't there? Tell me, sergeant, your professional opinion. Y'think we'll ever teach these Jewboys to be proper soldiers?"

The sergeant had learned to supply the answers his colonel expected. "They'll never be Englishmen, sir."

"Ha! Right about that. Indeed. Well, must see the fellow, I suppose. Show him in, sergeant."

The colonel shoved himself out of his chair and tugged his issue shorts down to his knees, straightened his jacket and arranged himself in front of the Union Jack in the corner, planting his thick legs solidly.

Yaakov Yeshivat walked into the room and glanced around. He didn't like what he saw. This was no combat officer, this fat man with rheumy eyes and cheeks pink with broken veins. He was a pensioner serving out his time. If the British depended on many like him, he decided, the Nazis would soon be in Jerusalem.

"Colonel White," he said easily, "I'm Lieutenant Yeshivat of the Haganah. My orders from the Jewish Agency are to present myself and my men for disposition."

The colonel's mustache quivered with distaste as he surveyed the husky man in the private's uniform. A lieutenant indeed! What a pushy lot these Jews were. They would soon learn who commanded here. Still, his orders were to deal with these Jewish Agency types, to placate them, to prepare them for battle.

328

"You won't mind," he said, issuing the words singly, "if I address you as private, for that is your rank in our Army."

"Suit yourself, colonel."

"Yes, well, the sergeant-major will see to you and your people. Obey orders, Yeshivat, apply yourself, and there will be a fine career for you in the Service. Show yourself to be obstinate and rebellious and you'll learn that we deal with that sort of thing with dispatch. Remember, in the English Army, we take care of our own."

Yaakov managed not to laugh until after he had left.

Six months later, Yaakov, now wearing the stripes of a sergeant on his sleeve, and his fellow Palestinians, were attached to General Wavell's command, going into battle against the Italians in Libya. In a swift campaign, the Italian Army was virtually destroyed.

Soon after, many of Wavell's troops, including most of the Palestinian companies, were sent to Greece. Yaakov and his company remained and made ready to meet the counterattack being prepared by the German General Erwin Rommel.

Rommel launched a concentrated and powerful thrust across the top of North Africa. He captured Benghazi, El Gazala, Tobruk, and his troops rolled forward, seemingly unstoppable. When a stand was ordered, the result was an overwhelming defeat, the British losing 230 tanks to German armor in one terrible battle. All along the line, the British Army was in retreat, falling back into Egypt, where it was hoped to throw up a defense that would hold. To buy time, counter-attacks were called for in an effort to slow the German drive on Cairo and the Suez Canal.

Yaakov's company, under the command of a British infantry captain, was directed to provide support for six light tanks in a quick delaying tactic just east of Halfaya Pass. They advanced across the badlands before daylight. Fifteen minutes after the sun rose, the temperature climbed over one hundred degrees. And thirty minutes after that, they marched into a German trap.

Moving across the rolling desert along a caravan track, the tanks arranged themselves in a convenient file. Alarmed, Yaakov sought out the infantry captain. He was a slender man with a delicate face, long blond hair and a stunning smile.

"Yes, sergeant," the captain said agreeably. "What can I do for you?"

"Those tanks are vulnerable where they are. They should be on the high ground, on the dunes."

The captain flashed his smile. "You don't understand, Sergeant Yeshivat. The tanks have their limitations. I doubt if they can make the climb over those dunes. Too high, y'see."

"Then order them onto the slopes. Where they are, they're helpless. If we run into German armor——"

"That's the whole idea, isn't it? To run into the Germans, I mean. And if we do, we'll give them what for! Right, sergeant?"

"Our tanks won't have a chance. Their guns won't elevate——"

"They are quite quick, y'know, and once the battle is joined, so to speak, they'll make their runs. Leave it to me, sergeant. I appreciate your concern, but this is a matter of tactics and they do quite well by us at Sandhurst in this sort of problem. Now I do think you should return to your post."

The Germans were waiting for them. The track swung south for about half a mile, then veered north again. Here the dunes were higher, closer together, forming a defile. The German gunners waited until they were all in the sandy gorge before opening up. Their tanks appeared without warning on the skyline, guns zeroed in and firing. Two British tanks were destroyed in that first volley.

Yaakov never hesitated, barking out orders in Hebrew. "Up the hills! To the high ground! Stay low and open fire!"

It was a futile effort. He was halfway up the slope when the green line of German infantry appeared on the crest. Machineguns were set in place and riflemen flattened out into comfortable firing positions.

Yaakov looked over his shoulder. Only one of the British tanks remained in action, scurrying about like a mouse hunting a safe hole. It veered suddenly, running up the dune, cannon firing. It's shells fell far short of the target. A German tank lurched around, fired and missed, and fired again. The British tank shuddered and stopped, began to smoke. No one got out.

"Make every shot count!" Yaakov yelled, shooting.

The captain flung himself down alongside. "Tell them to stop," he cried. "Order them to stop shooting! We haven't got a chance."

The captain, recognizing the cold expression in

330

Yaakov's eyes, swung his service revolver around and jammed it against the sergeant's back.

"Make them stop fighting or I'll kill you. I won't allow my entire command to be destroyed. There's no point in it." The pistol wavered and fell away. "There's no sense in it," he said pleadingly. "No sense at all. We must give up."

Every instinct told Yaakov to fight on. His eyes swept the hillside. The men were watching him and he knew they would do whatever he told them to do. And if they fought, all of them would certainly die and for what? They were too important for that. Such men were needed for another fight at another time. He dropped his rifle.

"If you're going to surrender, captain," he said matter-of-factly, "you better get on with it. The Germans may decide to kill us all while we're waiting."

They were marched through the desert to a barbed wire compound and kept there for nearly three weeks, sleeping in the open with only a single blanket for protection. They received too little water and a kind of potato stew, which was fed to them twice a day.

At the end of that time, they were loaded onto trucks and transported to the coast where they were put aboard a ship. Fifteen days later they debarked in Genoa and transferred to a train for the journey through France and into Germany, not far from the Swiss border.

Stalag Neustrelitz. The old castle in the northwest corner was the first thing new prisoners noticed. The walls were black and crenelated, giving birth to images of armored knights and flying colors, of lances and emblazoned battleshields. There was even a moat, but it had been dry for many years. The prison camp itself stretched out almost a mile to the south and half a mile at its widest point. A double wire fence marked its perimeter and watchtowers had been placed down every hundred yards manned by armed guards. At night, searchlights illuminated the compound.

The prisoners were unloaded at the railhead in the tiny village in the valley below. There were about two thousand of them, Englishmen all, with the exception of Yaakov's Palestinians. They were a ragged bunch, emaciated and dirty, their uniforms torn and stained.

German guards, crisp and militarily correct, each of them carrying a submachinegun, lined up along the length of the station platform, eyeing the prisoners warily. A major in polished jackboots, and trailed by a lieutenant and two soldiers, came marching up. He checked the serial number of the freight car against the list in his hand.

"This bunch," he snapped. "All Jews. Keep them apart from the others."

This was something Yaakov had been expecting, to be isolated, regarded by the Germans as another shipment of Jews to be handled in some sub-human manner. He tried to force his brain to function in some orderly way. A pervading weariness circulated in his limbs and there was a vague weakness in his knees. He had not been able to keep food down for nearly a week and he needed rest and medical care. He wanted very much to sleep, but fought against the desire, struggled to think.

The lieutenant stepped forward. He was a very handsome young man, strong and standing very straight. "Attention, Jews! You will form a column of twos and follow me. Anyone falling out of line will be shot on the spot."

The guttering flame of anger flared up in Yaakov and he gathered all his resources, concentrating all his attention on the young lieutenant. He sucked air into his lungs and took three precise strides forward, coming to a heel-clicking stop, swinging his right arm in a wide military salute.

"Sir!" he roared.

The lieutenant turned back, unable to disguise the surprise he felt.

"Sir!" Yaakov shouted again. "Under the rules of the Geneva Convention, as prisoners of war, we do not have to countenance talk of shooting. And—we—will—not! One more such word and I shall order my men to attack you and your guards."

The lieutenant paled and drew himself erect. "What is your name?" Yaakov recited his name, rank and serial number. "Very well, sergeant. I shall remember you. Now march your men up the hill, if you don't mind."

"Under the Geneva Convention, we are obliged to accept legitimate orders." He did a very British about-face, arms stiff at his side. "Company—'tention!" he commanded loudly, in Hebrew. "Fall in! Even it off. Very good. Let's look like soldiers. *Soldiers*. Not sheep." He pivoted back to the lieutenant. "My men are ready."

"Very impressive," the officer said. "But it will do you no good. Here we will teach you what Jews are good for." He waved a hand and the guards moved closer. "Take them up the hill."

A German non-commissioned officer stepped forward

and barked out commands in German. Yaakov's men made no move. He turned back to them and spoke in Hebrew. "Right turn, chaverim. Forward march." They managed to keep Yaakov's cadence for about twenty yards. But the military step was too demanding and they began to shuffle dispiritedly. Yaakov searched desperately for some way to reach them, to inject new life in them.

He began to sing *Hatikvah,* the Zionist national anthem. A few seconds passed and another man joined in. Another. Soon all of them were singing, a swelling masculine chorus, picking up the step. They swung past the ranks of Englishmen and Yaakov could see the smiles of pleasure on those pudding faces, heard the shouts of encouragement from the Tommies, and some of them began to sing along. It occurred to Yaakov that his war was far from ended.

Once inside the prison compound, they were directed into a long wooden barrack. Here triple-decker bunks with straw mattresses lined each wall.

"In the back," one guard told them, "you will find a toilet and some water."

The men remained at attention as long as the guard was present. But as soon as he left, all life seemed to drain out of them. A few slumped to the floor. Others managed to climb into the nearest bunk. Some men began to pray and here and there muffled sobs could be heard.

"Cowards!" Yaakov bellowed, mustering all of his remaining strength. "On your feet! All of you! Nobody dismissed you. Up, out of those bunks. Up on your feet. You're still in the Army, still soldiers, and by everything holy you'll act that way."

It took time for them to assimilate the meaning of his words, the fury that he hurled at them. Gradually it seeped through and they obeyed, coming back into line. All but one man. He lay huddled on the floor, sobbing, murmuring unintelligibly. Yaakov strode over to him, yanked him erect. Reaching into some pit of energy, he struck the man across the face with his open hand, sent him slamming into the wall. He stared up at Yaakov with naked terror in his eyes.

"Here," Yaakov bit off, "you will act like a man or I shall kill you myself. Now get into line." Yaakov waited until he stumbled into place, then moved slowly between the two facing ranks. "Listen to me," he said at last. "Those Nazis would like nothing better than to butcher a few hundred Jews. All they need is an excuse. Well, we're not going to give it to them. Either we deal with this like men or we'll go under and that's not for Yaakov Yeshivat. I am going to live through this mess and you are going to help me. Every one of you. Let one man fall short and he will deal with me. I am going to live and so are you, and if it becomes impossible to live then I am going to fight and take some of those bastards with me. And so are you."

A lance corporal, who had been suffering from dysentery for almost ten days, spoke up. "It is impossible, Yaakov. We have no weapons. We are sick and weak."

Yaakov knew the man had conducted himself very well in combat. But this was no time for gentleness. "You will become well and strong, Shmuel. And like the rest of us, you will survive and go home one day. Listen to me, all of you. We are our own best weapons. Our brains and our guts. We will show these Germans what Jews are made of. I don't want to hear that you are tired or sick. I will listen to no excuses. Every man will shave and bathe himself. And you will do something to make those uniforms look better. They are filthy. The guard said there is water outside. You will clean up by squads. The first squad, first platoon will begin. *Now*."

After an extended silent beat, the squad leader led his men outside.

Only after all the men had cleaned up, did Yaakov see to his own needs. There was no hot water and he made a mental note to complain to the Germans about that oversight, though he anticipated nothing being done about it. Finished, he went back inside and ordered his men to fall out in ranks. He called them to attention.

"Very well. Platoon commanders will take charge of their men for twenty minutes of close order drill. After that, I want this area thoroughly policed. Perhaps the German Army is accustomed to living in dirt. We are not."

He planted himself in the middle of the compound, watching first one platoon and then another. On the watchtowers, the guards eyed the unusual activity with interest and up on the terrace of the castle a handful of officers observed through field glasses. A few of the English soldiers appeared outside their barracks to watch.

Seeing all of them, faces solemn and curious, wary and careful, an idea sprung from some dark corner of Yaakov's brain and broke out into the light where he was able to study it critically and make modifications. And in that moment he knew what he had been reaching for, had *found*, knew what had to be done and how to do it.

That night Yaakov gathered his men around him and told them what was expected. "Each man must adhere to strict military discipline at all times. Jewish discipline. *My* discipline. And it will be a tougher discipline, making more demands on you, than you've ever known before. It must be that way. We will be soldiers in a way that no German has ever seen.

"As for the Nazis, we fulfill their orders to the letter, but only when they act properly toward prisoners. Those orders will come to you only through me and your own non-coms. Is that clear?"

"But if a Nazi orders us to do something—?"

"You will refer him to me, saying that you are *under orders*. Stress that. They must learn that I command here, not they.

"Now as to questions. You will respond only to the point of giving your name, rank, serial number, that you are from Palestine, volunteers in the English Army. Nothing more. You will not discuss unit identification or anything else of a military nature. Almost every man here speaks two or three languages. But from now on only Hebrew will be spoken. I am the only one who will talk to the Germans in German. To enforce these regulations among ourselves, we will elect a board of discipline with authority to punish, up to and including the death penalty. I hope we never get to that, but if we should I will enforce it without hesitation.

"Also, we begin immediately making escape plans. For this, every man is responsible. To this end, we must learn the habits of every guard, every officer, in the camp. I want to know everything that goes on, every vehicle that comes in and goes out, why, and at what time of day. Do they always have the same drivers? Where do they come from and where do they go? Nothing is too trivial to report.

"We must study the guards on the watchtowers and along the fenceline. How long are their shifts and at what times are they replaced? Which ones are careless, which alert? Who can be distracted and how? I want to learn the duty time for the officers at headquarters.

"Also, which of the Germans is susceptible to bribery? Which are homosexuals? Which are braggarts and which are stupid?

"We will discover what the angles of depression are for

the searchlights in the towers. What is the extent of their beams? Do they traverse and if so over what area, and do the beams overlap? Do they sweep on schedule or haphazardly?

"All of you will consider these questions and any others you can think of during the next few days. Then we'll meet again and assign specific responsibilities. Each man is part of this and is obligated to act in the common good.

"One more thing. This company will perform twenty minutes of calisthenics before breakfast each morning, then police the area. And all privates will salute all non-commissioned officers at all times."

"Is it necessary to be so strict?" a soldier asked plaintively. "After all, Yaakov, we are in a prison camp."

"Exactly. That is why we are going to maintain a rigid and carefully structured life here. And as we go along, you may expect an increase in discipline.

"That's all for now. Get to sleep. We must regain our strength quickly. There's a war to be won."

Yaakov's eyes rolled up and he was instantly awake, skin tingling with an awareness that something was wrong. He sat up and swung his feet to the board floors, stood up. A quick dizziness gripped him and he steadied himself, waited for it to pass.

He glanced around. Most of the men were still asleep, but three or four of them were huddled around a bunk at the far end of the barracks. Yaakov joined them.

"What is it? What's the matter?"

One of the squad leaders straightened up. He hesitated, then saluted. Yaakov remembered to return it.

"Something has happened." He gestured toward the bunk. A man lay on his back, mouth gaping. "It's Shmuel. He is dead. It happened during the night. He didn't bother anyone, just died."

At that moment the front door of the barracks flew open. Two German soldiers stood there. "All right, Jews. Everybody up. You have three minutes to get outside. Let's go! There is work to be done, if you expect to get fed."

The men looked at Yaakov. He moved down the aisle between the bunks to the door. "One of my men is dead," he said in German. "He died during the night. We will bury him this morning. Now."

One of the soldiers laughed. "A dead Jew! That's a good thing. It'll save us the trouble of killing him later.

All right, drag the body outside and we'll show you where the oven is. That's where you'll all end up anyway."

Yaakov took two quick strides forward and the guards pulled back, brought their bayoneted rifles to bear. "Stand back," the second guard warned, face tense, eyes wide. "Don't come any closer."

Yaakov jabbed his forefinger at the two guards. "Okay, you sonsofbitches, now this is the way it is. I am going to give you a chance. I am not going to take those rifles and jam them down your throats." He made a commanding gesture with his right hand and there was the sound of shuffling feet as his men crowded in behind him. The guards retreated another step. "You are two lucky Nazis, that I am a peaceful man. But come around here once more talking about ovens and all that will change. Now leave us alone to tend to our dead."

He did an about-face and the men opened a path for him. In that split second before they closed around him, fear crawled under his skin in anticipation of the shock of a bullet or the hard thrust of a bayonet. Then the door slammed and the men began to talk excitedly. They were clustering close to him, offering congratulations.

His face remained set and distant and he showed nothing of what he felt. "It isn't over yet," he warned. "They'll test us more."

"What about Shmuel?" someone asked.

"Remember what I told you. We are our own weapons, dead or alive. We're going to bury Shmuel."

"We have no box for him."

"Use a mattress cover. Take the supporting boards out of one of the bunks and lay him on that. It'll make it easier for the pallbearers."

"We don't have a rabbi."

"Yes," Yaakov said thoughtfully. "Does anyone have a Bible?"

A dark-skinned man with earlocks and haunted eyes presented himself. "I am no rabbi, Yaakov, but I can speak the prayer for the dead."

Yaakov squeezed the man's shoulder appreciatively. "You will do very well, *adoni*. From now on, you will serve as our rabbi. Did you bring your prayer shawl with you?"

"Of course, Yaakov."

"Good. Wear it. And your yarmulke. All of you who have prayer shawls will wear them. And everyone will keep his head covered. No military hats. If you don't have

337

yarmulkes then knot handkerchiefs at each corner and use them. I want the symbols of our Jewishness highly visible. Now, I want some men to go outside and find some tools. Shovels, picks, anything we can use to dig a grave."

Two men started out. They opened the door and closed it immediately. "There are guards lined up outside," one of them said excitedly. "And an officer is coming with more men."

"Quickly. Get Shmuel into the mattress cover. Six of you will serve as pallbearers. Rabbi, I want you up front and don't be afraid. I will be right with you. We are going to have our funeral right now."

One of the men looked out the window. He pulled back. "There's no time, Yaakov. The officer, he is here."

Yaakov strode to the door. "I'll get us the time. Prepare Shmuel and yourselves." He yanked open the door and stepped out, closing it behind him. The low morning sun shone into his eyes. He forced himself to see through the glare. He heard the safety of a rifle click off.

"Halt!" a guard cried in thick German. "Go back or I will shoot!"

Yaakov picked out the officer coming up behind the guards. He wore the uniform of a major, a tight-bodied man with prominent cheekbones and a prim mouth. Yaakov waited for him to move out in front of the guards, then saluted. The major returned it without much interest.

"What is this business about a funeral, sergeant?" he said in a voice thin and disapproving.

"One of my men died during the night, major. We are going to give him a proper funeral."

The major stared blankly at Yaakov for a slow moment. *"We* will dispose of the corpse in the usual manner."

"No, sir. We bury our own dead. In our own manner."

The major reached for the polished black leather holster which held his Walthar pistol. "We know how to deal with trouble, sergeant. With *your* kind."

Yaakov almost smiled at the continued use of his military title. There was no reference to his being a Jew, no talk of ovens. Just an officious German dealing with a rambunctious prisoner. He took one quick step forward and the major stiffened, the Walthar half out of the holster.

"You have never known our kind," Yaakov said deliberately. "Nor the kind of trouble we can make. We are going to bury the man who died. Right now. The only way for you to stop us is to kill us all and I don't think you're prepared to do that. I demand tools so we may dig a grave."

There was a brief hesitation and in that microsecond of time Yaakov understood that he had won another battle.

"Do as you like with the corpse," the major said. "But you will get no help from us. There," he said, pointing to the southern fence. "Bury him along the line. But do not touch the wire. It is electrified."

Yaakov turned back. "Rabbi, are you ready to begin the ceremony?"

The hollow-eyed soldier stepped into the sunlight blinking and nodding. He wore a yarmulke made of white satin and embroidered with blue-and-gold thread and a prayer shawl edged with gold braid, its fringed ends reaching to the ground. He gave Yaakov a plain black yarmulke and he put it on.

The soldier never looked at the guards lined up across the front of the barracks. He opened his Bible and, shuffling forward, began to read in Hebrew in a loud, steady voice.

"In the sweat of thy face shalt thou eat bread, till thou return unto the ground; for out of it wast thou taken: for dust thou art, and unto dust shalt thou return. . . ."

Behind, echoing his words, filed the rest of the Jewish company, six men carrying the corpse in the striped mattress ticking. Some carried Bibles and a few wore prayer shawls. Led by Yaakov and their newly appointed rabbi, they advanced—the guards giving way—moving with slow-paced dignity toward the distant fence.

By now, men from the other barracks were in the compound yard. They maintained a polite distance and watched the strange procession with silent interest.

Ten feet from the fence, Yaakov stopped. He scratched a rectangle in the dirt with the edge of his boot.

"Here is where we bury Shmuel."

"We have no tools!"

"Use the buckles of your belts, spoons, your hands. We will dig in shifts, teams of six. I want Shmuel placed so that he is always within sight of the rest of the camp, and you will arrange yourselves so that the digging is visible to the German officers up on the hill. Those of you who are not digging, will line up along the fence in close formation. You men, begin the digging. The rest of you—keep praying. Loud."

The ground was reasonably soft and they went down almost two feet in the first hour. It was then that a detail of soldiers came marching across the compound, six men and a sergeant. They were bringing picks and shovels.

The sergeant addressed Yaakov. "We will complete the digging. Order your men out of the hole and we shall begin."

Yaakov hesitated. His men were tired and any exertion was a strain on them. He drew himself to attention. "We make our own graves, sergeant. We bury our own dead."

The German's eyes darted about nervously. "But I have orders."

"Your orders don't hold with us. This is a Jewish ritual and you're not welcome. Leave us with our grief."

No one spoke until the Germans were out of earshot. "Yaakov," one of the men said. "Was that so smart? They will not like it. Look—at the castle—they are watching. The officers. You have spit in their faces in front of the entire camp. They cannot allow it to pass—"

"We'll see. Meanwhile, we proceed as before. Do we have a carpenter?" A man stepped forward. "There's some old lumber in back of the second barracks. Take another man and get enough to make a Star of David for a headstone."

"I'll need nails, Yaakov. And I have no tools."

"Think, man!" Yaakov erupted, then more quietly, "Splice the wood together. Use shoelaces, your belt. Anything. Hurry up. I want to get this done."

They completed the burial without further incident. When the Germans paid no attention to them as the day went by, by afternoon, the men began to gloat, to revel in their triumph. Yaakov said nothing. He knew it was not over yet, would never be until they were free again.

The men were fed in the open, lining up by company with their mess gear. A truck drew up and the mess detail dished an unsavory stew out of huge kettles. Yaakov took up a position to one side, as if overseeing the process. It was than that the prim major appeared, a mocking smile on his aristocratic face. He gave a stiff bow and an exaggerated salute.

"Excuse me, sergeant," he drawled. "Will you come with me, please? The commandant would appreciate the pleasure of your company, if you are not otherwise engaged."

The commandant's office was a large cheerful room with antique furniture and a massive fireplace. A huge oil painting of Adolf Hitler graced one wall and a boar's head another. The commandant, in the uniform of a general, sat behind a table of highly polished dark woods inlaid with ivory. He was entirely bald with a pinched nose and lively eyes. He smiled pleasantly when the major led Yaakov into the office and invited him to sit down.

"I prefer to stand," Yaakov said in formal German, remaining at attention.

The general took a cigaret and offered Yaakov one.

"No thank you."

The general shrugged and lit his own. "Your name is Yeshivat," he said. He waited but Yaakov made no reply. "Is that correct?"

"My name is Yeshivat."

"A Palestinian Jew."

"Correct."

The general leaned back in his chair, smoking, appraising Yaakov reflectively. "Tell me, Yeshivat, what are you trying to prove?"

Yaakov allowed his pale eyes to come to rest on the general's face. The features were composed and at ease, the look of a man of broad experience, a man of varied tastes who was sure of himself. A man who recognized his own strengths and weaknesses. A realist.

"There's nothing to prove."

"Yet in the short time you've been here you've managed to call a great deal of attention to yourself and your people, and to antagonize my men and officers. To what purpose?"

"We are soldiers and expect to be treated as such."

"All the prisoners in this camp are soldiers," the general snapped, leaning forward, "and are treated accordingly."

"Then we have no complaint."

"But you are Jews," the general murmured, as if making a discovery. His smile was fleeting, disarming. "There is that difference."

"We are members of the English Army."

"Jews do not get much consideration in Germany, Yeshivat. I suppose you've heard."

"I heard."

"I could have you all shot."

"I don't think so. Things are not quite what they appear to be, general. Even prisoners of war hear the news. We know that the British have turned Rommel back in North Africa. We know the Russians are fighting back harder than ever, that Sicily has fallen to the Allies and the

Americans have landed in Italy. No, I don't think you will shoot two hundred British soldiers."

The smooth cultivated face stiffened and the mouth thinned out. "You overestimate the situation. It is only a question of time until we defeat the Allies. As for you Jews, no one cares whether you live or die."

"You're wrong, general. Kill us and you'd have an uprising on your hands from the rest of your prisoners."

"These Englishmen! Nonsense. They will do nothing to help a handful of Jews."

"Again wrong, general. You underestimate the British. Hitler didn't think they'd fight over Poland, but they did. You Germans were wrong to attack the Russians. To declare war on America. And you're wrong to think you can win this war." He measured the general. "But you don't believe that, general. You're too smart for that. You know Germany will be defeated and you must know that when it's over an accounting will be made. Someone will be charged with all the murders committed, with responsibility for the ovens."

"There is none of that in this camp!" the general said quickly. "Look here, Yeshivat," he went on, in a reasonable tone. "I run a smooth administration here. All this talk of killing—well, we will have no more of it."

"My men will be happy to hear that."

"But no trouble. No harassment of guards. And orders must be obeyed."

"All legitimate orders will be obeyed, when transmitted through me."

The general stared at him. "Very well. But I want your word that there will be no escape attempts made. I insist on your parole."

Yaakov smiled thinly. "A soldier-prisoner is obliged to escape. I will promise you this, I will not go until after all my men have left."

The general laughed uncertainly. At the door, the major joined in. "There is little chance of that," the general said. "I tell you, Yeshivat, I like you. You have the stuff good soldiers are made of. You are of German stock, naturally?"

"My father came from Poland."

The general exhaled. "Go back to the compound. And remember, no more trouble."

Yaakov stopped at the door. It was time to cement his triumph. "It's vital to the welfare of my men that they be provided with recreational facilities. I see none in the camp. We will want equipment for sports. Soccer balls and boxing gloves. Barbells. Also musical instruments. Guitars, accordions, and the like. I intend to form a soccer league among all the prisoners. If you wish to risk defeat, the guards may enter a team and compete."

The general's eyes were veiled. "Is there anything else?"

"One more thing. We would like to do our own cooking. Kosher, of course. To do so we will need stoves, pots, dishes—"

After Yaakov was gone, the general stared at the closed door with no change of expression. It was the prim major who broke the silence.

"Let me take care of him, sir. A bullet in the back—an attempted escape. With that kind of man, no one will question it."

"That kind of man," the general offered. "If the English have many like him the war must end very badly for us. Very badly."

NINE

*If you say in your heart, These nations
  are more than I and how can I dispossess
  them?
You shall not fear them but shall remember
  what the Lord thy God
did unto Pharaoh and unto all Egypt.*

—Deuteronomy

1967

I

Everything had changed in Israel.

More than 2,500,000 people lived in Galilee, in the wasp waist of the country so vulnerable to Jordan's Arab Legion, in the bleak Negev. In the Valley of the Martyrs, six million trees were planted to honor the victims of Germany and saplings were put down wherever possible to hold the soil in place and help irrigate the land.

New settlements had been created. There was Carmiel in Galilee and Arad in the Negev. There were villages along the frontiers and now Eilat could boast of a museum, a library, hotels, schools, an expanding population, and four piers.

Water was brought by pipeline and other carriers to the desert, to the new settlements. And though desalinization experiments continued at an increased tempo, water was still in short supply.

A nation that had grown from the seed of hard work and farming, had been transformed into a country of cities and city people. Only two percent of the population still lived on the kibbutzim, though they exerted a moral and philosophical influence far beyond their numbers.

There were other differences. Where work had become a national passion, 100,000 people were unable to find jobs. Where once Jews came in a flood, they arrived now in an uncertain trickle, fewer than 12,000 in the previous year. The crusading zeal was no longer apparent, replaced by a spreading disenchantment, a cynical sophistication, a growing hedonism that saw men in bermuda shorts and girls in miniskirts mingling with those in kaftans and long dresses. A nation built by pioneers took its ease at sidewalk cafes and danced the frug in discotheques.

And there were the Arabs. Rearming for another round in their continuing jihad, collecting allies, vowing to wipe out the Jewish State, indoctrinating an expanding population in hatred, training them for the deed. Technicians and officers came from the Soviet Union, from China, to teach the fellahin how to march, how to shoot rifles and ma-

347

chineguns, how to fly jet fighters, to operate the complex control systems of missiles.

On television, on radio, in the press, the Arabs vowed to destroy Israel, to wipe out its population, to complete the job begun by the Nazis. And they owned two billion dollars worth of Soviet arms with which to do the work.

The Arabs shrilled of battles yet to come, of nullifying the results of Sinai, of turning time back to the situation prior to 1948. And with only the United Nations Emergency Force along the frontier to restrain the Arabs, there were many Israelis who believed what they heard.

In the capitals of the world's great powers, and in the United Nations, diplomats stepped through a carefully arranged choreography. Encouraging words were murmured to Israel's representatives at the same time that they were warned to commit no act that might be termed aggressive. Arms were sold to the Arab nations by the United States and England. Anxious to further placate Abdel Nasser, the United States sent food and grain to Cairo. With the money saved, he bought more guns from Moscow.

Only France supplied arms to Israel, and those in limited amounts. The cost of self-defense was an intolerable burden on the already strained economy of the country. Reserve officers hoarded weapons and wondered how it would be possible to counter the firepower of Soviet tanks and planes if fighting should break out.

Life in the Promised Land was difficult and dangerous and people had little to look forward to. Some of them left the country but for most Israelis there was no place else to go. This was their last chance.

Nothing had changed in Israel.

II

It was early May, too soon for the rush of summer visitors seeking to escape the heat of the lowlands in the cool hills of Safad, and so Yaakov Yeshivat had no trouble finding a hotel to accommodate him. From his room, he could see a panorama of green terraces and white Arab villages, the roofs of the houses painted blue to discourage evil spirits.

He bathed, shaved, donned fresh khakis and a sweater; and went to a modestly-priced restaurant in Jerusalem Street that served an excellent *techina,* the ground sesame seeds that tasted so much like peanut butter.

He ate slowly, relishing the taste of the food, enjoying the attractive surroundings. More and more these days, he took pleasure in such things. He supposed that was a sign of the passing years, to care about sensual satisfactions that were not so strenuous.

A succession of blurred images illuminated his brain: the women he had known and loved. Not loved, he corrected silently. Enjoyed only, taken pleasure from, but not loved. He thought about Carol back in Haifa, his most recent friend. She was a little too plump, a little too blonde, a little too anxious to please. Still, a first-rate cook and she made no excessive demands. A grin lifted one corner of his wide mouth. Again food. He was getting old. Older, he corrected.

After dinner, he lit a cigar, a recently acquired habit, and strolled around the town. Safad appealed to Yaakov, it's history impressive.

A group of Jewish intellectuals had come there in order to escape the Spanish Inquisition. Inclined to a mystical interpretation of the Scriptures, the Cabala, they made the town a hub of religious and intellectual activity. In recent years, it had become an artist's colony.

It was during the War of Independence that Safad established itself firmly in the minds of all Israelis. Then it had been occupied by 12,000 Arabs, well-armed and strategically entrenched.

The Jewish inhabitants were mostly old people, helpless, given to prayer and little else, and afraid for their lives. To help them, 120 Palmach commandoes were sent to Safad. They carried with them a tiny mortar, a *davidka,* little more than a noisy toy. The commandoes arrived and promptly attacked, supported by their artillery—*davidka.* The tiny weapon arched its shells into the enemy lines with a hellishly loud roar. As if in response, the skies opened up and it began to rain.

That's all the Arabs needed. Convinced the Jews owned a secret weapon with which they were able to summon Divine assistance, they fled.

It was a nice story, Yaakov agreed, whenever he heard it repeated, rich with the suggestion of miracles. But it ignored the truth. The Arabs ran because they could not

349

face the fury of the Palmach attack; the victory had been made on the hills of Safad, not in Heaven.

It was colder now and he shivered, turned back toward the hotel. A good night's sleep and an early start would get him back to Jerusalem before sundown. He walked swiftly, looking neither right nor left, and was almost back to the hotel when he heard his name called. He turned and saw, striding toward him, a man rugged and dirty in muddied boots and a thick wool shirt. There was a stocking cap on his head and his mustache drooped past the corners of his mouth. Recognition came slowly.

"Levi?" he said. "Levi Landau?"

They embraced and Yaakov was surprised at the surge of emotion that gripped him. He pounded the younger man on the shoulder. "Ah, it is good to see you, Levi. Very good. Look at you! There is muscle on those bones of yours. And that mustache! Do I see gray hairs?"

There was genuine joy in Levi's open laughter. "Of course, gray. I'm getting to be almost as old as you are, Yaakov."

"Impossible. I am Methuselah reincarnate." He peered closely at the other man. "What are you, twenty-five, six?"

"I'm thirty-four."

Yaakov stared at him as if unable to comprehend the words. "I can remember—" He broke off, shaking his head, his white hair shimmering in the night air. "The last time I saw you was in Eilat. I brought young Simon and—"

"No," Levi said, grinning. "Think again. It was Masada, in nineteen-sixty-four."

Remembering, Yaakov smiled with recalled satisfaction. Yigael Yadin had called for diggers to help unearth the site of that ancient fortress. Advertisements had been placed in newspapers in Israel and in London and 5,000 volunteers had been used.

"Masada was something," Yaakov said. "That had meaning."

Levi grinned. "Ah, the soldier in you talks."

"Yes. Yes, the soldier. Imagine those Zealots, Jews like you and me, standing against the Roman Legions. How many were there?"

"Jews? Nine hundred and sixty. And Flavius Silva had the Roman Tenth Legion. Ten thousand soldiers."

"Think of that! And when the Jews couldn't fight any

350

more they killed themselves rather than surrender! Those were men, Levi. Fighting men."

His mind played back to *The War of the Jews*—the account written by Flavius Josephus, a renegade Jew—remembering the excitement generated by his description of the final assault on Masada. When the Legionaires finally reached the citadel they found the corpses of the defenders. An old woman and a younger one with five children were the only ones left alive to report on what had transpired there. Josephus had written of that too:

> They then chose ten men by lot out of them to slay all the rest, every one of whom lay himself down by his wife and children on the ground, and threw his arms about them, and they offered their necks to the stroke of those who by lot executed that melancholy office; and when these ten had, without fear, slain them all, they made the same rule of casting lots for themselves, that he whose lot it was should first kill the other nine, and after all should kill himself.

Yaakov's pale eyes, clear and shining, turned up to Levi. "Idiocy, to go on about something that happened nineteen centuries ago."

"It was a great moment in Jewish history."

"Yes, yes. That's why I insisted on working on the project. But Yadin would allow me only two weeks."

"That's all anyone was permitted."

"Your father was there," Yaakov said, frowning. "But at a different time."

"I know. Have you seen him recently, Yaakov?"

"To hell with him! I don't see him or think about him."

"Okay, *adoni*. He is not exactly my favorite person either."

They were walking side-by-side and now Yaakov stopped, looking at Levi from under bunched brows. "You still hold that against him? Mara Gabrielli?"

"Of course not!" Levi said too quickly. "I have not exactly been a celibate myself."

A reminiscent glitter lit Yaakov's eyes. "That Gabrielli was some fine-looking female. Amos must have been a special man to satisfy her." He made a sound of dismissal in the back of his throat. "Enough. I don't want to talk about your father. You, Levi? What are you doing in Safad?"

"To buy supplies. I'm in charge of a new kibbutz about

351

fifteen kilometers from here, near the frontier. I'm going back in the morning. Why don't you come along. An old kibbutznik like you, maybe you can give us a few good ideas."

"Yes, I can give you ideas. But I'm due in Jerusalem tomorrow."

"Give us one day. Maybe you're getting too soft for life on a kibbutz, even for a single day."

Yaakov pounded his stomach. "Feel that, if you think I'm soft."

"I'll drive you back to Safad myself. What do you say?"

"Is it true that you use machines to build the houses these days?"

"Yes. The houses are poured concrete. Prefabricated. Not very pretty, but practical. Mess halls, recreation room, the works."

"And defenses? On the Syrian border——"

"Come with me and see for yourself."

Yaakov glanced at the younger man. "Don't think that you have tricked me into going. I go because I am concerned about such things. What time do we leave?"

"Seven o'clock. In front of the hotel."

"Make it six."

When Levi pulled up in front of the hotel the next morning, Yaakov was waiting. He climbed in the jeep. "You're late," he growled.

Levi apologized and they drove in silence for a while. It was Yaakov who finally spoke.

"How is your family, Levi? Your mother?"

"She's in good health, though still a little vague about some things. She forgets sometimes—"

"The years—"

"No. When I visit, she sometimes calls me Joshua. She must miss him very much. We all do, I suppose."

"He was a dependable man," Yaakov said. "And your sister?"

Levi brightened. "As ever. Laughing and happy. A little heavier than before, which is right for the mother of three."

"And the American?"

"Hank is okay. More the Jew than you or me, Yaakov."

"And Simon? He should be in Nahal, doing some good."

"I don't know what he's doing. He insisted on going

352

abroad to school. Papa finally agreed and sent him off to America, to Princeton University."

"An excellent school. Einstein was there."

"Well, Simon isn't anymore. He quit school and moved to New York about six months ago. He's written mama once or twice, but no real information."

Yaakov said nothing. He wasn't sure he understood young people these days, with their independent ways and their rejection of the old values. He cleared his brain. "You like being a builder, Levi?"

"We could use more of it. Construction is way off. What do they say in the Knesset? Is there any sign of an upturn in the economy? Some rumors say—"

"Everything will be all right. In the next election, we'll kick Mapai out and Levi Eshkol too."

Levi looked at the older man. His weathered face, lined and seamed, still owned that determined thrust of jaw, the same aggressive glint of eye. They were a special breed, Levi reflected, the hard-bitten men like Yaakov, like Ben Gurion, fully committed and willing to fight for what they thought was right, no matter the odds. Here was Yaakov still thinking of political victory. Another man would have given up long ago.

The Landau Company strike had cost him a Knesset seat in 1961. Four years later, his hopes had been raised again when Ben Gurion had broken with Mapai as a direct outgrowth of the Lavon Affair and had formed a new party, Rafi. It was his hope to oust Levi Eshkol as Prime Minister and again take over that post himself. Dayan, Davidov, Yeshivat; among Ben Gurion's staunchest supporters, and they had anticipated a smashing victory. Instead, they won fewer than ten percent of the votes cast, a stunning defeat.

But one of the seats in the Knesset went to Yaakov Yeshivat.

"I should tell you," Levi said calmly. "I voted Mapai."

"Damn fool! And what did it get you? A leadership old and worn out, the party structure split. Mapai talks of moderation when they mean inaction and weakness. Next time it will be different. The young people will turn their backs on Eshkol. They need strong leaders, men of action whom they can depend on. Next time vote Rafi. For the Old Man. For me."

"What is Ben Gurion after?"

"Whatever's good for the country. Look at Eshkol. In the face of Arab threats, of raids and arms buildups, he

353

does nothing. He talks only. We need a man in charge who knows how to handle Nasser and those others."

"Ben Gurion's old, Yaakov. He must be eighty."

"He has more life in him than men half his age. Last time I was down to Sde Boker he said to me—oh, to hell with that. What about Moshe? *He* should be Premier."

"I'm not so sure he's the man for the job."

"Of course he is. Listen, I tell you—" He broke off abruptly. "I talk too much. Another sign of old age."

They drove the rest of the way in silence.

Kfar Glickman was little more than an idea. Some tents, rutted tracks that passed for roads, and a population of machines and workers. The machines—giant yellow earth-movers, bulldozers, graders, trucks, cement mixers—were all still.

"What is this?" Levi burst out, as the site came into view. "Why aren't they working?" He bore down on the accelerator and the jeep leaped ahead. Yaakov clutched for a handhold. They skidded to a stop in front of a half-finished building of rough concrete. A solemn group of men were gathered nearby. Levi hit the ground shouting. "Is this a holiday? I am gone for one night and everything stops. Avram! Where the goddamhell is Avram?"

A thick-necked man with a bullethead came lumbering out of the unfinished building. There was a grim expression on his round red face.

"Okay, let's have it, Avram. What's the holdup?"

"Trouble last night."

Levi's eyes slitted and he swore under his breath. "Tell me."

"Last night, this morning, actually, while it was still dark. They hit us."

"Arabs?" Yaakov said.

Avram looked at him, his small eyes quick and wary. He addressed himself to Levi. "They blew up two dozers and the ditchdigger."

"Can they be fixed?"

"One of the dozers, maybe. The others not. There's more to come."

"Say."

"Murray went after them. He was killed. We lost their trail. They crossed that rocky stretch beyond the depression, all that shale."

"Did they go back toward the frontier?"

"Could be. Or they might have doubled back. There's

354

an Arab village about twenty-five kilometers from here, on our side of the frontier." He jerked his head toward the unfinished house. "We picked up two characters about thirty minutes ago. But they deny they're the ones."

Avram led them inside. Two Arabs sat on the ground, backs against the wall, heads bowed. They wore unpressed business suits and kaffiyehs.

"They say they're from Jerusalem," Avram said. "Visiting relatives in the village. Could be."

"Papers," Levi said.

"In order."

"They're city Arabs, all right," Yaakov said. "See the shoes. People from around here would be in sandals or work shoes." He spat and kicked dirt. "It's too perfect. I don't like it. An attack, then these two show up, all innocent and proper."

"What do you think we should do," Levi said.

"Make them talk," Yaakov said.

"How?" Avram said. He was a construction foreman, accustomed to hard work, to machines, unused to this kind of thing.

"Kill one and the other will talk," Yaakov said, without expression.

One of the Arabs lifted his head. "Shalom," he said in accented Hebrew to Yaakov. "Would you truly shoot down an old acquaintance?"

Yaakov peered at him. The features were familiar yet different.

"You don't remember," the Arab said. "We met only twice and for short periods. I am Mejjid al-Hadad, friend to Amos Landau. Years ago he prevailed upon you to interview me and you did so. But there was no help you could give."

The features were thicker, the eyes hollowed, but familiar. "I remember. You ran away when the fighting began, then came back."

Mejjid heaved himself erect. He stood straight, his gaze level, steady. "Why are we being detained in this manner? We are Israeli citizens and have done nothing. You are a Jew, effendi, a member of the parliament, a hero of many wars. I am but a poor Arab without rights but my friend and I are innocent of any wrongdoing. We were visiting my cousin Asaf and were on our way home. Has that become a crime in Israel?"

"There was a raid here last night," Yaakov said. "A man was murdered."

"Jews are murdered and Arabs are killed," Mejjid said. "A fine distinction but meaningless to the dead."

Yaakov chose not to argue. Mejjid had a right to be bitter but there was no way of helping him. He was an Arab, and in a beleaguered Israel, an object of suspicion and distrust.

"What is your cousin's name?" Yaakov said.

"Asaf Simhoni."

"We will look into it, of course."

"Of course, effendi. I would do no less."

"Who is the young man with you?"

"He is named Farog. He serves me in my declining years in place of my oldest son who was killed in Sinai."

Yaakov grunted. He swung around to face Levi. "I am for letting them go."

"They could be the ones," Avram said.

"Yes," Yaakov said, suddenly weary. "They could be but there is no reason to think they are. I say let them go."

Levi wet his lips. "All right," he said.

"Allah the merciful and compassionate will bless you a thousand times, effendi," Mejjid said.

"Be careful, Mejjid," Yaakov said tightly. "Next time you might not be as lucky."

Yaakov watched them back out of the unfinished building.

"You might be wrong," Levi said.

"I was right," Yaakov replied. He made a mental note to tell Milovan Levin about this. The Security Service might be interested in Mejjid.

III

Amos gazed at his naked image in the long mirror on the back of the closet door and approved of what he saw. True, the body reflected lacked the taut hardness of his youth but he had brought it back into good trim. Exercise and diet. Those were the keys. Calisthenics for twenty minutes before breakfast each morning and each afternoon an hour in the gymnasium at the factory. More calisthenics, steam and a rubdown. And whenever possible, he walked. It was worth the effort. A man not only looked better; he felt better.

He turned away, put on his pajamas and got into bed. Ruth was waiting for him. She smiled sleepily and he kissed her cheek.

"Goodnight, dear," she murmured.

"Goodnight." He switched off the light and cradled his head in his hands. "Have you heard from Simon?" he said, after a moment. He asked that same question almost every night these days and with cause. It had been weeks since Simon's last letter.

"It isn't right for him to ignore us that way," Ruth complained. "He knows how we worry."

"I've been thinking," he said slowly. "Doing some quiet investigating. Suppose I were to sell the business, the factory, the shops, all of it. There would be enough money for us with plenty left over for the children after we're gone."

She raised up onto her elbow and gazed at him in the dark. He was an amazing man, this husband of hers; whenever she decided that she knew everything there was to know about him, he did something surprising.

"Without the business, what would you do?"

"We could travel," he said. "You'd like that, I think. France, England. We could go to America and visit Simon."

"Oh, Amos, that would be so nice—" She stopped abruptly. "But I couldn't."

"Why not?"

"Rena and the babies. She needs me. If I went away ____"

He began to laugh. "I think Rena can manage very well without you, without both of us."

She lowered herself back to her pillow. "Amos, could we go to California? I would like that, to see where they make films."

"Yes," he murmured. "It will take some time to arrange but there are some prospective buyers. At my age, who needs hard work?"

She made no answer and he rolled onto his side and a few minutes later was asleep. The next morning, refreshed and full of energy, he arrived at his office to find a letter waiting. It was from Mara Gabrielli.

IV

Yaakov strode through the entrance hall of the King David Hotel and went down to the Regency Grill on the level below. He spotted Uri Davidov alone at a table in the far corner of the room. Davidov rose. He looked handsome and younger than his years in a finely-tailored tan gabardine suit. They shook hands.

"Shalom, Yeshivat."

"Shalom, Davidov."

Davidov sat down and Yaakov did the same. He felt clumsy and out-of-place in a khaki shirt and his old tweed jacket. He had never learned to be at ease with Davidov, now one of the Defense Force's Alufs, leaders of the highest rank. There was about him still that physical and intellectual rigidity that had always antagonized Yaakov.

"Will you have a cocktail?" Davidov asked.

A *cocktail*. No one else Yaakov knew would have used that word. "A martini," Yaakov said. "On ice." He saw the glimmer of surprise in Davidov's eyes. The old pioneer drinking martinis. It was incongruous. Carol had taught him about martinis. Like the Americans, she had insisted, over ice with only a suggestion of vermouth and a lemon twist.

"Political life seems to suit you," Davidov said. "You're looking very well."

"Too much talk," Yaakov muttered. "And none of it straight. But it has to be done." His pale eyes fastened on the younger man. "You would be good at it."

Davidov laughed easily and studied his glass. "Consider this, Yeshivat. The reason you dislike me is not because of the differences between us, but because of the similarities."

Davidov with his long soft hair and that aristocratic face put Yaakov in mind of those effete English officers who used to decorate the King David in the Mandatory days. But with a difference. Davidov was shrewd and tough and said exactly what was on his mind.

"Okay, *adoni*," Yaakov said. "We don't like each other. It isn't written that we must."

"I don't dislike *you*. Matter of fact, I am quite fond of you."

The waiter brought Yaakov's martini and asked if they were ready to order.

"I'm having the mixed grill," Davidov said. "You should give the Strogonoff a try. They do it quite well here."

Strogonoff appealed to Yaakov. "A small steak," he rasped perversely. "Rare."

Davidov emitted a small knowing laugh and lifted his glass. *"L'chaim."*

Yaakov echoed the toast and sipped the martini. "Why did you ask me here? Not to be friendly."

Davidov's full mouth drew down and an opaque veil was lowered over his intelligent eyes. "You're right. Conditions with the Arabs worsen each day."

"I know that."

"Did you know that since 1948 there have been more than one hundred thousand incidents? It has gotten so bad that our responses must be made with overwhelming force, as at Es Samu back in November."

Yaakov made a fist and lifted it. "Sometimes I think there must be a better way to solve problems than a quick blow. It doesn't seem to work."

"True enough. Shukhairy's Palestine Liberation Army people keep coming over from Gaza and across the Jordan frontier. And the Syrians keep violating our territory. They shell settlements and snipe at farmers. In January, they placed some Russian T-34 tanks onto the heights above Kinneret and we had to destroy them. There have been artillery duels and you know about the air battle in February. We shot down six of their planes."

"Davidov," Yaakov said elaborately, "for the history lesson, thanks. Please, to the point. There's a soccer game this afternoon and I want to go. Since I became a politician I have to worry about the Orthodox vote so I can't go out in public on Saturdays."

Davidov gave no indication that he understood. "Events move swiftly these days, too swiftly. Those colonels running things in Syria are all hot bloods calling for action and they're going to be trapped by their own rhetoric. We have reasons to believe that Nasser, though he makes a lot of noise, would prefer to leave matters as they are. But he's in trouble politically. King Faisal, for example, presents him with a real threat for the leadership of the Arab world, such as it is."

"What about King Hussein?"

"He would like to act as a moderating force, but since Es Samu his hands are tied. That raid was a mistake. I said so then and I think so still."

"Eshkol," Yaakov snorted. "The raid was only a political move to relieve him of pressure."

"Perhaps not. In any case, Hussein could be overthrown or assassinated by some fanatic the way his grandfather was. He's the only Arab leader with a grain of common sense, the only one with an awareness of where the self-interest of his own people lies."

"We should give him all possible help."

"Our patrols along the Jordan border are told to be very cautious, to avoid contact wherever possible. But after all is said, Nasser remains the problem. He is hungry to lead the Arab nation, as he calls it, to greater glory, to become a third power on the world scene. But right now his colleagues jeer at him, claim he hides behind the UN Emergency Force."

"Behind a pane of glass, they say."

"Yes, and sooner or later he will have to act."

"And then?"

"Then we shall react, of course."

The waiter brought their food and left. Yaakov picked up his fork and began to eat. "This is a political problem. We need a government and a premier that acts firmly and without hesitation. It's time Moshe came forward. He should be our next Prime Minister."

"I am not here to discuss political matters. As far as Moshe is concerned, I know only this—like me, he is concerned about our defense preparations and has requested permission to inspect positions in the south."

"He's back on active duty?"

"A precautionary measure, to bring him up to date."

Yaakov sliced a neat square out of the center of his steak. It ran blood and he chewed it with relish. "What does Rabin have to say?"

"As Chief of Staff, Itzhak will utter no criticism of his superiors. Whatever defense plans are made, after all, are his. Remember, Eshkol is not only Prime Minister but Minister of Defense as well."

"What has this to do with me? I am not even in the reserves any more. Just an unimportant politician."

Davidov addressed his lunch for a long moment, assembling his thoughts, choosing his words. "General Rabin is instituting contingency plans," he said, with quiet formality. "Experienced officers, men tested in combat, men who can do the things that need doing, are being invited to come back."

"Mobilization?"

"It may not come to that. But we want to be ready. There is so much to do and so little time. Come back to active duty, Yeshivat. There are battle plans to be worked out, logistics, communications to be established, other men to be chosen. You would have to resign from the Knesset, of course. Dual service is forbidden."

He laid his utensils aside. "Matters are as serious as this?"

"We can't afford not to be prepared. Will you join us?"

A sense of exhilaration rode through Yaakov's middle. "When do I start?"

"You will have to create a good excuse for resigning from the Knesset. We must be careful to alarm no one."

"Ah," Yaakov said, mouth flexing. "I will claim illness, the decrepitude of age. Nothing but the warm dry desert will cure what ails me." His suppressed laughter was edged with joy. "It is true. I will become whole again." He sliced off another piece of steak. "I tell you, Davidov, this could almost make me like you. Almost."

Amos Landau was waiting when Yaakov got back to his office. The sight of his former friend sent a hot flood running into his bowels and sweat broke across his shoulders. He had to fight back the impulse to embrace Amos, to say how many times he had thought of him in friendship, of how he missed their visits, their talks. Even the arguments. Instead, he kept his craggy face expressionless.

Amos stood up and smiled uncertainly. "Shalom, Yaakov."

"What are you doing here, Landau?"

The smile evaporated and the soft brown eyes glazed over. "I have a problem and there was no one else to turn to."

"A political matter?" Yaakov said stonily.

"You could say that."

"Come inside."

In his private office, Yaakov motioned Amos to a chair. There was a strangeness to all this, as if he were obligated to perform in a particular manner, but unsure of what it was. He cleared his throat.

"A political matter, you said?"

"I am here for a favor."

Yaakov gazed past Amos. A favor. To come for a

favor indicated the importance of the mission. Business, Yaakov assumed. Amos was after some advantage to increase his profits. To that end, there was nothing a capitalist wouldn't do.

"You remember Mara Gabrielli?" Amos said.

Yaakov concealed his surprise, said nothing. He watched Amos draw a pink envelope out of his pocket, extracting a single sheet of paper. "From Mara," Amos said. "She is in trouble."

"And she wrote to you, after so many years, after—?"

Amos shrugged. "There was no one else, I suppose."

"An important cinema star, rich, famous. What trouble could she have?"

"I'm not sure I really understand. It seems she became involved with a man, a much younger man. He brought her to a villa in the south of France, posing as a very wealthy person. Now it turns out that he is merely a fortune-hunter who wants to become a motion picture producer."

"And needs Gabrielli to star for him?"

Amos nodded. "He's holding her, actually keeping her a prisoner, locked up, until she agrees and signs a contract."

"Insanity. Such things don't happen."

"Mara says the young man has a friend, a male friend, and there are two other men, hired thugs from the sound of it. She can't get away."

"And the letter?" Yaakov said skeptically.

"Mara became ill and a doctor was summoned. She pressed it on him, asked him to mail it, and say nothing. Apparently he did."

"Why should this concern you?"

"Mara and I were once very close. I remember her fondly."

"She ran away with another man."

"That was long ago, Yaakov. I remember mostly the nice things, how good she was to me, for me. She was young and frivolous, ambitious, I suppose. I don't blame her now."

"What am I supposed to do about this?"

"Mara is an Israeli and very well known. Because of what she has become, she belongs to all of us. I would not want to see her hurt or her reputation stained."

"From what I have heard, her reputation could not be worse."

"Please. Will you help?"

"Why me?"

362

"Because you know how such affairs should be handled. Because you have had experience in these things."

Yaakov stood up, went to the window and looked out. He saw nothing, his vision blurred and out of focus. "Whatever is going on, you're asking me to perform an illegal act, to violate the sovereignty of France. If it got out—" He swung around. "Oh, hell, give me the letter."

Amos did so. "The address is there."

"This interview never happened," Yaakov said thinly. "No matter what the outcome, I know nothing about this business and neither do you. It must never be spoken about. Understood? The risks are very great."

"I understand." Amos stood up and held out his hand. "Thank you, Yaakov."

"I will see what I can do. Now you must excuse me. I have a lot of work." Yaakov was unable to muster enough strength to take Amos' hand and he loathed that weakness in himself.

V

May may be the most pleasant month in New York City. The mild weather allows the pollutants to rise above the city but it is warm enough so that the girls can shed their winter coats. The sight of all those animated busts and bottoms shimmering under spring finery charges the streets with color and liveliness, infuses the males of the city with a fresh awareness of their manliness.

Simon Landau was otherwise occupied, far above it all. Wearing only pale blue swim shorts, he stretched out on the terrace of Marjorie Cloud's twenty-first-floor apartment overlooking Sutton Place, the East River, and the southern reaches of Manhattan. He lay on his stomach on an air mattress and read *The Times* enjoying the penetrating warmth of the westering sun on his back.

He read the story through to the end, then turned back to the front page and read it again. He did not hear Marjorie come into the apartment, nor was he aware of when she came out on the terrace.

She crossed over to where he lay and, kneeling, kissed the back of his neck.

"Did you miss me, darling?" she said lightly. She fingered the thick black hair curling behind his ears and felt the familiar craving seep through her middle. It was ridiculous, she told herself, to let herself go over this boy, to feel so strongly about him. But she did. Had since they first met.

She straightened up and sighed. In her early thirties, Marjorie Cloud owned the clear, unlined face of a woman ten years her junior. And a body to match. Tall, with round hips and good shoulders, she had a high neat bust and long legs. A former photographer's model, she had married a man twenty-seven years her senior when she was twenty-one. Seven years later, she divorced him. The settlement included this cooperative apartment, a house in Westport, another in Key West, a Bentley limousine, a half-a-million dollars in blue chip stocks and bonds, and fifteen hundred dollars a month alimony until she remarried—something she had no intention of doing.

"Simon, darling. You could say hello to me."

"Hello," he mumbled.

Her eyes worked down the length of his body. He was beautiful. Lean and muscular, in marvelous proportion, with just enough hair on his chest and legs.

She had first seen him at a party. He had been involved in an argument, some dispute about the relative merits of Camus and Sartre. She had had no interest in the details of the discussion; but from the beginning she had craved him, craved to surround all that passion, to feel that concentrated energy and rage inside her, to absorb some of it into her own flesh.

A week later she phoned him and invited him to a dinner party. She kept him there afterwards, took him to bed and it had been everything she anticipated and more. She invited him to move in the next morning. He laughed at her and went away. Three weeks passed before she was able to see him again and this time he stayed for four days. They began to see each other regularly after that and a month later he did move in. That was almost three months ago and he was as removed and unconcerned today as he had been then. Outside of bed, and too often there, he seemed cool and detached, stepping through the motions without interest. Perhaps it was that remoteness that continued to excite and provoke her, to rouse her to greater heights each time they made love. She was sure about one thing; she needed this boy as she had never needed anyone else.

"Darling," she said, tracing the line of his spine into the hollow of his back with her fingertips. "We have a few hours before we're due at Leona's. Guess what I would like to do to you."

He looked up at her. "There's going to be another war," he said evenly.

"What are you talking about?" Her eyes rode over the headlines and she laughed with relief. "Oh, sweetie, you *know* there's always a crisis of some sort in the Middle East. It doesn't *mean* anything."

"The Arabs are mobilizing."

"All for show purposes. Empty talk. They're not going to do anything foolish. Besides, you're here with me. Safe and happy. Here. Here is something to take your mind off guns and other nasty things."

She bent forward and her mouth came down on the tight flesh of his flanks, the lips working, the tongue damp and hot. Her hand moved on him and he shifted onto his back, watching with mild interest. She was very good at what she did.

That night, in the oversized bed listening to a news broadcast while she undressed, he learned that Gamal Abdel Nasser had requested Secretary General U Thant to remove the United Nations Emergency Force from the 117-mile Egyptian-Israeli border.

"They really are going to fight," Simon said, trying to understand what it was he felt. "They really are."

"No," she said, coming out of her dressing room. She wore a sheer lace nightgown that enhanced her full womanly figure. "It's only politics."

"They kept saying they intended to wipe Israel out and now they're going to do it."

She laughed nervously and switched off the radio. "Don't be silly. It couldn't happen. The world would never stand for anything like that, the United States wouldn't."

He stared up at her. "The world will stand for anything, Marjorie. Anything at all. As for this country, well, there's Vietnam. Washington isn't going to lift a finger for Israel."

"Don't think about it. It's going to be all right. You're not a part of that anymore. It has nothing to do with you, darling. You belong here with me."

His eyes were blank and he made no reply.

"Tomorrow," she murmured, hovering over him, stroking the inside of his thighs. "Tomorrow we'll buy you something terribly expensive and exciting. Some new clothes. I know! We'll go away, a trip. To Las Vegas. You've never been and you'll love it. The gambling. The shows. It'll be exciting for you."

She covered his mouth with her own, hands reaching, urging his body to respond, being as provocative as she knew how to be. This time it didn't work.

VI

Amos spent the morning in the factory and when he returned to his office it was to find a message from Yaakov asking him to call.

Yaakov wasted no time on amenities. "That matter we discussed, I have some news."

"Is she all right?"

Yaakov hesitated. "Yes. Listen, Landau, I think we should meet somewhere and talk. These calls are too vulnerable."

"I don't understand."

"Never mind. You know the Cafe Brussels?"

"Yes."

"Meet me in an hour."

Amos was already there when Yaakov arrived. "Why all this mystery? Is there something wrong?"

"Nothing wrong. I wanted to be sure of privacy. First, Gabrielli is out of that villa. A couple of my contacts did the job. Those boys who were holding her—not so much, all talk and very little trouble when the action started."

"And Mara?"

"My people suggested she might want to come home, to Israel. She laughed at them. She went to Italy. There are more good times to be found there, I guess."

Amos discovered he had been holding his breath. He exhaled. "I appreciate what you did, Yaakov. Thank you."

Yaakov made a sound of acceptance deep in his chest and looked at his big square hands. "There is something else." When Amos said nothing, he went on. "You keep up with the news. You know the UN has pulled its people off the Egyptian border."

"That surprised me."

"Not me. I never trusted U Thant. One word from Nasser and he jumped around like a puppet."

"What does it mean?"

"Nothing has changed. As always, there is no one to protect us but ourselves. In case anyone doubted that, U Thant made it clear." Yaakov glanced up at Amos. "You know I resigned from the Knesset."

"I heard that you weren't well. You don't look ill to me."

"I've never been better," broke out of Yaakov. Then, more softly, "I am back on active duty."

Amos shook his head. He was not surprised. That was where Yaakov belonged, in uniform.

"Things have been allowed to go slack," Yaakov was saying. "It is one thing for men to train once a month but that barely prepares them to fight. Steps are being taken to put matters right and to do that experienced people are needed. That's why they called me up again, why I wanted to see you. I'm authorized to invite you back into uniform. Would you be interested in taking command of an armored regiment?"

Amos felt his hands grow cold and damp and his mouth went dry. An armored regiment. All those men and machines. The responsibility . . .

"I'm out of touch," he said. "I've been retired."

"Stop wasting time with talk and you'll have more of it to get back in touch. You know tanks. You've commanded one and you commanded a battalion. That business of yours, I know how many people you employ. That takes brains, I suppose, to build a big business. To lead all those people, is not exactly easy. You're stubborn and wrong about a lot of things but we need men like you now. Most of our commanders are young, too young. A little seasoning is important. That's it, Landau. Say yes or say no."

Amos thought about Ruth, about leaving her alone. About Rena, and his grandchildren. About his sons. About Joshua. He made up his mind.

"I say yes."

"Naturally," Yaakov muttered, standing. "Get your affairs in order. You have three days."

On the same day that Amos went back on active duty, Egypt announced that it was shutting the Strait of Tiran to all Israeli shipping. With its troops again occupying Sharm el-Sheikh, the port of Eilat was closed down.

"We pity you Jews," cried the Voice of the Arabs over Radio Cairo. "By God, we pity you. This is our revenge for Suez and the 1956 aggression."

VII

In New York, the United Nations was summoned into special session to consider the Middle East and what could be done to calm that inflamed situation.

Arab leaders, many of them antagonistic to Gamal Abdel Nasser, hurried to Cairo to pledge him their allegiance in this moment of his need. Jordan's King Hussein, insulted and castigated by Nasser's propagandists for his pro-Western stance, placed his English-trained Legion under the command of an Egyptian general.

In the Mediterranean, the U.S. Sixth Fleet made ready for action and ten Soviet warships emerged from the Black Sea, sailed through the Dardanelles and into Middle Eastern waters.

In the UN Building alongside the East River, Arab delegates insisted that there was no cause for alarm, that there was no crisis, that the Jews were given to exaggeration. The claim was echoed by the Soviet representative.

England's diplomats spoke of the possibility of assembling an international fleet to challenge the Egyptian blockade of the Strait of Tiran, emphasizing the international nature of this body of water. The United States supported the plan.

England changed its mind, lost all enthusiasm for testing the blockade, proposed instead a conference with the Soviet Union, the United States, France and itself participating.

The Russians said no.

The Americans said an international fleet should be formed.

Abba Eban, Israel's Foreign Minister, went to Paris and spoke to President De Gaulle. The President said Israel should practice restraint. Eban went to London and spoke to Prime Minister Wilson. The Prime Minister said Israel should practice restraint. Eban went to Washington and spoke to President Johnson. The President said Israel should practice restraint.

In Cairo, army units paraded through the streets, past thousands of wildly chanting people, heading for Sinai. Armored divisions, including the latest Soviet improvements in tanks and halftracks and artillery, were on display. Overhead, Russian jets zoomed by in tight formations. Western observers were impressed. This time, as Colonel Nasser had insisted all along, it was going to be different.

It was announced that troops from Iraq were flying in to fight alongside their Egyptian brothers. From Algeria, the Sudan, Saudi Arabia, Lebanon, from Arab rulers great and small, from landholders and impoverished fellahin, came pledges of assistance and loyalty against the common foe. And the sound of Gamal Nasser's voice on Radio Cairo brought passionate cheers.

"We face you in battle," Nasser declared emotionally, "and are burning with desire to start in order to obtain revenge. This will make the world realize what the Arabs are and what the Jews are."

Amos Landau wiped the sweat from his forehead and waited for the men to assemble under the camouflage netting. Benches had been arranged in rows facing the blackboard. He watched them file into place, most of them so young, years younger than he was. Perhaps Yeshivat had been right and a bit of age and experience was in order, a necessary leavening factor.

But could he keep up with them? Could he cause them to believe in his judgment, to trust him and accept his decisions, to follow where he led?

Would he be able to lead?

Once he had, but that was eleven years before. Eleven years of good living, of soft living, of self-indulgence. Still, the time had not been entirely wasted. Building the Landau Company had demanded a certain narrow purpose and cerebral toughness, commitment and flexibility.

Conflict of one kind or another was a daily occurrence in business. There were competitors and suppliers and salesmen and shippers and buyers. And the union. He drew the thick hot desert air into his lungs. Whoever bested Yaakov Yeshivat in a fight could be proud. Yeshivat did not lose often and when he did it did not happen easily.

The men were seated and waiting. He turned to the blackboard and in great bold strokes chalked the number 1,200 on it.

"Chaverim," he said grimly. "That is how many tanks our Egyptian friends own. We possess far fewer. We also have fewer planes, guns, and if it ever comes to it, we will have far fewer men. Add to this the 600 tanks the Syrians have, 130 more in Jordan plus the men and equipment of the other Arab countries, and the situation becomes clear."

An oppressive silence gathered under the camouflage net. A young captain, wearing earlocks and a yarmulke, raised his hand tentatively. "Under such circumstances, another war seems like madness. How can we possibly win?"

The silence thickened. These were men geared to consider only victory and the specter of defeat rocked them, made them uncertain. Amos knew he had to bring them back.

"How can we win?" he repeated thoughtfully. "We have a secret weapon," he answered, tapping his temple. "Jewish heads," he said, grinning. "We'll think of some way—"

Somebody laughed, then another, until all of them were laughing. He waited for it to peak, then cut them short with a gesture.

"I hope that this trouble will be settled peacefully, but we cannot anticipate that. Instead, we must plan to fight. To begin, I want every vehicle fueled and ready to go in a matter of minutes. I want every tank and gun carrier loaded with shells, the infantry able to advance in fifteen minutes."

A major from Headquarters stood up. "It won't be possible to maintain a full alert. We don't have men enough for that. Our tanks require three or four men each, depending on the model. We simply lack the manpower."

"I know. What I want is one man assigned to each armored vehicle, a veteran, a regular. He will be in charge. If and when there is mobilization, reservists will be assigned to each regular. Vital to us now is that each tank is brought to operating readiness as soon as possible. To this end, work must begin immediately. *This is top priority*. Also, I want repair units fully mobilized with spare parts for any eventuality. If a tank throws a tread it has to be replaced at once, in minutes, in seconds if possible. We have the trained personnel to do this and that provides us with a great advantage. In order to compensate for Arab numerical superiority, we must keep every piece of equipment in action as long as possible."

He let his eyes work over the assembled men. "We hope for peace, but we are going to plan to fight and to win. Think in terms of victory. From the start, every unit commander, every section chief, every tank officer, will have to operate at top efficiency, maintain maximum pressure on the enemy. There will be no time for rest or sleep until the guns are silent again. There will be no stopping and only one way to go—forward.

"Should you find yourself without immediate orders, your orders are to advance. Strike quick and hard. Bring every fight to its conclusion as rapidly as possible by using all available power.

"Bypass enemy strongpoints, isolate them. Later, they will be neutralized. Do not wait for supplies to catch up to you. Such things often take time and that is what we have little of. Surprise is our primary weapon. Use it at all times. Do the unexpected. Think, act, improvise. War never goes the way it is supposed to. Above all, take chances. Risk everything to win. Israel is at stake and all of our people. So gamble, gamble, gamble. . . ."

It could have been the board room of a large international corporation. The walls were paneled in dark wood and the table was long, solid, highly polished. The men seated around it could have been company managers or directors. For the most part, they were in their thirties and forties and of no particular distinction except for the gravity of expression that each of them wore as if part of a uniform.

The room was in the headquarters of the Israel Defense Forces and the men were the ranking officers of the armed services. All of them were in khakis and combat boots and some of them wore pistols on their belts. In the air-conditioned room, a few of them had buttoned their shirtsleeves at the wrist.

A slender, bald man with a quizzical smile on his narrow face, at the head of the table, cleared his throat and began to speak. The insignia of the Air Force was pinned to his shirt. "Gentlemen, we begin," he said in a mild voice. "If it comes to crunch, our strategy is simple, our tactics are simple—to end the Arab's warmaking potential as swiftly as possible. To this end, my boys have a job to do."

Halfway down the table, Yaakov Yeshivat slumped in his seat, fingers intertwined under his broad chin. He listened carefully. Without effective air cover, the ground forces would be in serious trouble in the open desert, undermanned and underequipped. Yet to protect them, Israel owned fewer than 400 planes, many of them propeller-driven and obsolete in terms of modern warfare. Against this, the Arab nations were able to put more than 1,000 planes in the air, many of them the most recent developments of Soviet technology. He forced his attention back to the speaker.

"We have, naturally, made evaluations of the situation, certain decisions. Should war come, the Air Force will provide support for all columns in Sinai from the first moment. More important over the long haul, we will strike at a certain number of Arab airdromes quite early. Our hope would be to put as many of their planes out of action as possible."

"Won't they detect our formations with their radar, be prepared?"

"A risk we take. Our planes will fly low in order to minimize the radar effectiveness. Some will come from over the Mediterranean. Others straight on from the base at Beersheba. The plan is to strike each airdrome at precisely the same moment and to keep hitting them for eighty minutes. This will require rather complicated take-off procedures and swift landing and refueling techniques in order to get the same planes turned around and back on target in short order. We're working on these details now."

"It sounds to me," Yaakov said gruffly, "that you are putting your pilots to the test. How many flights can a man make without rest?"

"At an estimate, three or four flights per man per day. It should be enough. Of course, we anticipate a certain mechanical fall-off in the effectiveness of the planes as the fighting continues. That can't be helped." He nodded in Yaakov's direction. "You have something more to say?"

"Two questions. First, and I'm thinking in terms of my own people, naturally."

"Naturally."

"If a strike is called, when will it come?"

"Ah! The key question. You tell me the best time." His eyes went from man to man inquiringly.

A stocky brigadier spoke. "Just after dark. We would have the advantage of lessening enemy visibility and——"

"And he would be expecting us, I think. Any other thoughts?"

"Before dawn. His people will still be asleep, those on duty tired and inattentive."

"Again, no. His radar people will be more alert then than at any other time, the only eyes and ears of the Arab. When and if we fly, we fly in the morning."

"But all bases will be on the alert, the men breakfasted and at work."

"Not quite. What do we know about the Arab, especially the Egyptian officer corps? When does he take his first tea break? At about eight in the morning, chaverim. And tea time, as the English have taught us, is a time for relaxation and fraternal exchanges."

A murmur of agreement went up around the table.

Another officer spoke. "After the initial strike, all other bases and units will be alerted. We can expect prompt retaliation from Jordan and Syria, possibly Lebanon."

"To deal with that, Uri Davidov."

Davidov unfolded his long frame and stood up, placed his fingertips on the table, supporting his weight easily. He looked around as if about to deliver a lecture. "The evaluations supplied by Shin Beit seem quite thorough. The Shin Beit people insist that they are easily the best intelligence service in the region and I pray they are right. As they tell it, it is a matter of fundamental psychology.

"If I may address myself to the various parts of the question, the last first. Lebanon will not fight. Period. The politicians have been arousing their people with the usual anti-Israel harangues but the Army men are realists. They have a fighting force of about 16,000 men and they understand that we are capable of destroying them in a very short time. We are committed to the idea that Lebanon's generals will not undertake an exercise in defeat.

"As to Jordan. Hussein is the nearest we have to a friend among the Arabs. He is sane with a reasonably sound grasp of the realities. Should fighting break out, it is our intention to contact him, to emphasize our desire for peace with him. We will let him know that we intend no aggressive moves in his direction. We hope he will understand and act in his own best interests.

373

"Now Syria." The aristocratic mouth curled disdainfully and there was scorn in his voice. "Their political leaders are a noisy lot echoing the policies of their friends in Moscow. Their rhetoric is more colorful than their ability to fight. Individually the Syrian is no less brave or dedicated than anyone else. What he lacks is proper leadership. There is no real backing of brains or military talent or courage.

"The Syrians have been largely responsible for the terrorist activity. They've mined our roads and shelled our villages and we're convinced that their continuous prodding has pushed Nasser to act as he has, to risk war in order to maintain his high place in the Arab firmament. If the guns go off, gentlemen, the Syrians will do little. But we shall not overlook them. We will clear the border, secure Galilee in the only way they understand. By force."

Yaakov looked up and met Davidov's glance. If only the tall general were not such a stuffed shirt, Yaakov speculated, he might be likeable. His thinking was often right and clear.

"The first part of the question," Davidov said. "After the initial strike, won't the Egyptians sound the alarm? In a word—no." He allowed himself a small, smug smile. "Again, a matter of knowing the enemy. When they are hit, the Egyptians will respond predictably. First, they will assemble all available information as to what is going on and that will take about an hour. Then another hour to reach a high level decision on what to do."

"And at that point," a colonel put in, "they will tell their allies."

"Not at all," Davidov replied cheerfully. "Have you ever known an Arab to admit the truth when the truth involves defeat? No, Nasser will immediately proclaim a great victory. He will shout it over the radio and the newspapers will print black headlines to confirm it. And Arabs everywhere will want to believe and so they will. Nasser will pontificate about destroying Israel and this will work to our advantage for it will mislead his friends and his people in the field. It will be easier for them to retreat or surrender or not to fight at all when they believe that elsewhere Egyptian arms are rolling up impressive victories. A man who expects to win isn't likely to be terribly concerned about being made prisoner for a few days. The Arab will prove helpful to us."

Yaakov didn't like it. It was all too pat, too easy. Strike

first, yes. Quickly, yes. But this was not 1948, not 1956. The changes were ominous.

All these blackboard calculations, this talk of psychology. Very nice, very neat. But did it really add up? Simple arithmetic provided a different conclusion. He measured the overwhelming power of the Arab military against the jumble that was Israel's soldiery, along with a *potpourri* of hardware from the United States, from France, from England.

This time Russian technicians worked closely with Egyptian forward units and there were missiles in Sinai that could knock out defense positions and bombers that could reach Tel Aviv or Haifa in a matter of minutes.

Time too was on the side of the Arabs. Israel lacked the manpower, the arms, the resources for an extended conflict. Either victory came soon or there could be no victory. And defeat would be total, the end of the country and its people.

He calculated the time necessary to put his brigade in fighting condition. Some reservists had already been mustered to active duty, but his table of organization fell short of what was needed to fight and win.

The report came over the eleven o'clock newscast, just a couple of sentences crowded into a roundup of world news. Anyone not paying close attention would have missed it. Simon snapped off the television set and lit a cigaret. It was almost funny but he couldn't laugh.

The sound of Marjorie singing drifted out to him. Her bath was finished and now she would be powdering and perfuming herself, readying her body for him. She was beautiful and passionate, agreeable to any suggestion. A most desirable woman and he didn't want her.

She called his name and he went into the bedroom. She was in bed, the sheet drawn chastely to her shoulders. She held out her arms invitingly.

"Take off that silly bathrobe, darling, and come here."

"Israel is buying gas masks from Germany," he said.

"Darling," she said, a hard edge creeping into the throaty voice. "Let's leave politics out of the bedroom for a change."

"Don't you see the joke? German gas masks for Jews?"

She threw back the sheet. "Come here," she murmured.

"They're going to fight again."

A quick expression of displeasure compressed her lips. "Nonsense, there's no sense to it." She smiled and her tone

375

became logical and sensible. "There are so many Arabs and so few Jews. That Prime Minister of yours, Ben Gurion. He's too smart to get into another war."

"Ben Gurion isn't the Prime Minister," he said flatly. He stared at her, legs parted, breasts flattened and sagging, raw hunger glittering in her withdrawn eyes. He turned away. She understood nothing, he told himself. The question of peace or war was not for Israel to decide.

"Everything is going to be all right," she was saying. "You'll see. The Jews are too smart to fight."

He jerked around, choking the hot response that surged into his throat. How blind she was! Tuned in on herself only, feeding her brain with platitudes and myths and easy answers.

"Those people," she went on blithely, "are always having a crisis of one sort or another. All that bluster and shouting. I suppose they enjoy it. It makes them feel important. Nothing will come of it."

A blurred image of Joshua blossomed brightly in his mind, that delicate, handsome face, the lambent eyes, the soft voice, the interest in the world, in people. The *concern*. Joshua would not have been here, would not have given himself to this woman, would not have allowed himself to become what Simon had become.

"They've been squabbling for weeks, it seems," Marjorie continued, one hand stroking absently at the underside of her left breast. "All that talk. If they were going to fight they would have started by now." Her fingers reached for the nipple and it came erect. "Come, sweetie," she said, lips hardly moving. "Come, come on. Make me happy, sweetie. Here, sweetie. Right here. . . ."

It was difficult for him but she was persistent and in time he performed to her taste.

He was asleep immediately after, plunging into the deep blackness for warmth and safety. An almost feminine darkness, all encompassing and reassuring in its furry thickness.

Gradually, the night gathered itself together, swirling clouds, black on deeper black, forming into an impenetrable cone. From out of that stirring funnel the sound came, distant and faint, disturbing, persistent, refusing to go away. He fought against acknowledgment, striving to erect a wall against it. No use. It fought back, a lilting chime designed to summon without offense. With insidious grace, it picked its way through the quilted layers of sleep to a responsive sector of his brain. He moaned a protest,

376

shifting his position, starting at the touch of flesh against his flesh. He rolled away from Marjorie and sat up.

The telephone rang again. He switched on the bedlamp and stared at the silver Tiffany clock on the night table. It was four in the morning.

"There's a call," he muttered.

She made no reply. Marjorie Cloud did not wake easily.

He lit a cigaret and looked at the gold-and-white imitation of a French telephone. He hated that telephone. He closed his eyes and picked it up.

"Yes," he said.

"Tel Aviv calling Mr. Simon Landau."

He forced the sleep out of his brain. "Speaking. This is Simon Landau."

"Go ahead, Tel Aviv. I have your party for you."

"Simon! Can you hear me, Simon?"

It was his mother, speaking in Hebrew, the voice shrilling across the immense distance, apologetic and sure of itself at the same time.

"Mama! Are you all right, mama?"

"How are you, Simon? Is it late or early in New York? Time confuses me. Are you all right, Simon?"

"I'm fine, mama."

"We also. Your papa, me, Rena, Levi, the children, Hank."

"Mama, why are you calling me?"

"I'm your mother. Why shouldn't I call if I want to? Simon, what is this place? This Mrs. Cloud? Is it a boarding house?"

He laughed, relief mingling with pleasure at the sound of his mother's voice. He hadn't realized how much he missed her. "Yes, a kind of boarding house. Mama, what's happening there? I keep reading things in the papers."

"We watch Cairo on the television. Your father bought a very nice set for me but all we can get is Arab programs. That Nasser keeps threatening us. I don't understand it, a nice looking man like that, always wanting to fight."

"Mama, is there going to be a war? From the reports we get, things seem to be growing calmer. If Nasser was going to make war he would've done it already. And, with every chance of surprise gone, Israel isn't going to attack the Arabs."

He heard her sigh over the distance. "Oh, Simon, I don't know. There was a parade in Tel Aviv a few days ago, the celebration of Independence. The newspapers said that the foreign diplomats stayed away as a protest. They think we're going to attack Damascus. Would we do that, Simon?"

"No, mama. Of course not."

"Everything is so complicated with your papa away. He's back in the Army, you know. A colonel. He came home the other night, the first time he had a good meal in a week."

"What about Levi?"

"He's a captain. Isn't that nice, a captain?"

"He's been recalled?"

"And Hank also. Rena's coming to stay with me until it's over, with the children. It'll be nice to have them."

Only the crackling of the long-distance wire disturbed the silence that followed. A swift panic rose up in Simon.

"Mama! Are you still there?"

The urgency in his voice broke through the wall of sleep that encased Marjorie Cloud. She rolled onto her back and sat up.

"What is it?" she muttered thickly.

"I'm here," his mother said.

"I was afraid we were cut off."

"Simon," Marjorie husked, with sleepy irritation. "Who is it at this absurd hour?"

"Simon," his mother said tentatively.

"Yes, mama."

"Don't you think you should come home?"

"Oh, mama," he said, stripped of all defenses abruptly, and vulnerable.

"What does she want?" Marjorie said.

"Dear, I think you should come home."

"You're not a child."

All the vagueness had gone out of Ruth's voice and the gentleness firmed up. "We all need you now, Simon."

His head began to move up and down in vigorous comprehension. "Yes, mama," he said.

"What was that all about?" Marjorie said, after he hung up, the swollen eyes wary.

"I'm going home," he said.

She stared at him uncomprehendingly. "No," she said finally.

"As soon as I can."

"No. No, you can't! It's insane. You hate it there, you told me. You hate your father, the way you lived. Nothing's changed."

"They need me."

"Stay here. With me. I've got a surprise for you. I rented a house in Acapulco. You'll love it there. Everybody goes. Everybody."

"I'm going back to Israel."

"It makes no sense. If they want to fight, let them. It's not your war."

He gazed at her with faint amusement. If not his war, whose?

Mejjid al-Hadad found it difficult to keep pace with the two officers. General Heikel was a tall man with an easy athletic stride, whose dark brown skin contrasted with the white of his tennis costume. He smiled tolerantly.

"Listen to the man rave, Hassan," he said to his companion. He used his racket as a pointer. One of the new lightweight steel models, just arrived from an old Royal Army friend in London, he was very anxious to try it out. "Look, man, look at those tanks, those mobile guns. Look at our men. Understand that we have more than 80,000 troops in Sinai. The Jews are not mad. They know our strength as well as we do. Attack, indeed."

Colonel Hassan laughed happily. He was pleased to see the General in such a fine frame of mind. It made life easier for Hassan. His mind ranged ahead to the upcoming tennis match. He intended to give the General a very good game. In the end, of course, he would lose. Close this time, as if he was really on his game. But as always, the General would win. He, Hassan, would take the first set, 7-5, perhaps. The second to the General. 6-3 would be a proper score. Then the third set. Hard-fought over the portable court the Headquarters carpenters had built. To provide a fast playing surface, tenting canvas had been cut and stitched to fit, stretched tight over the boards. The third set, a beauty! With some long volleys, a deep game, which the General enjoyed so much. Final score: 6-4. The General would be in a fine mood afterwards.

"If only the Jews would attack," Hassen offered. "Let them come here and General Heikel will wipe them out. Oh, our brave soldiers will crush them, disembowel them, slice away their manhood for all time. Soon the General will lead us into Jerusalem and Gamal Nasser will come to laugh in Ben Gurion's face."

"Ben Gurion is an old man," Mejjid said wearily. "He lives in the Negev."

"Then that one-eyed devil," General Heikel said, twirling the racket. The balance pleased him. "That Dayan.

We shall put out his other eye. When word comes from Cairo—" He let it hang.

"The Jews will not wait for Cairo to speak," Mejjid said. "They will strike first. In the name of Allah the wise and compassionate, hear my words and understand what I tell you. The time to attack is now, before they are ready. They are preparing for war."

"We know that is not so," Hassan said reprovingly. "Our Intelligence tells us that in the Jewish cities life goes on as always."

"Business as usual," Heikel laughed.

Hassan laughed obediently. "Exactly. And it would not be good business for them to fight. Not this time. Not without the British and the French to help."

"They will fight," Mejjid insisted. "They have begun to mobilize. They are very efficient. Word has gone out quietly and nearly eighty percent of their men are already in uniform. Men and women both."

Hassan slapped his handsome brown thigh happily. "A people who put their women in the Army are not a concern to us."

"They are deployed and ready. Dayan leads them now and he will order an attack."

Heikel dribbled a tennis ball off the new racket and it bounced away. Hassan retrieved it.

"Listen, *habibi*," Hassan said kindly. "You concern yourself unnecessarily. Our friends will not allow the Jews to act."

"And some of our enemies also," the General added.

"Brilliant of you to say that, general," Hassan said. "The British are not going to permit the Israelis to fight. London is too hungry for Arab oil. And the Americans. They will offer the usual platitudes and promises, but they will do nothing."

"Besides," Heikel said. "The Americans are determined that we should love them. They're like that. So you see, they will do nothing to open Aqaba for the Israelis even as they did nothing to gain the Jews access to Suez. Gamal Nasser has said there will be no war, that we have already won what we want without a shot being fired. He is right, of course. There will be no war."

Mejjid shook his head stubbornly. "The Jews will fight."

They were at courtside and the tight green sea of canvas stretched out in front of them. Two sergeants stood by to act as ballboys and a high chair had been specially built for a linesman.

"You must understand me," Mejjid pleaded.

Hassan smiled indulgently. "We have had good reports about you, dear man. Your organization is a fine one, a vital cog in El Fatah. But this time you are mistaken."

"Your loyalty and sincerity are deeply appreciated," Heikel said, wishing Mejjid would go away. "Cairo shall hear of the seriousness of your purpose."

"You refuse to listen?" Mejjid said.

"Return to Jerusalem," Hassan said. "Your place is there, your work is there. Sabotage the defense efforts of the Jews. Blow trucks up and pipelines. Cause terror among them. Kill them. And should you acquire information of value, send it along to us."

"No point in your coming yourself, old man," the general said. "After all, you're not so young any more. Send it on with a messenger. I'll give it my personal attention. Thank you so much for coming."

Hassan smiled graciously. "It's time for the General's game. Excuse us, please. And many thanks for your trouble."

They stepped onto the court and began to volley. Mejjid swung away. It would take a long time to get back to Jerusalem. Hassan was right; that's where he belonged.

Shalom.

In Tel Aviv, public transportation was unreliable. Bus drivers, the ticket-takers, had disappeared from their posts. And no taxis were to be seen. At night, Kol-Bo Shalom, the department store looming high over the city, was blacked out. Should Arab planes attack, it was hoped they would fail to see the huge building and would crash into it.

In Jerusalem, service at the King David was no longer as swift and impeccably correct as before. The doorman no longer was on duty, nor the bellmen, only two of the barmen, and there were unfamiliar, elderly faces behind the front desk. Housewives blacked out their homes and shopkeepers stripped display windows with tape. Lines of women and old people waited at hastily established blood banks.

Shalom.

In Haifa, air raid shelter signs were put up. Armed guards patrolled the waterfront and girls in uniform hurried to their posts. Men, exempted from military duty because they were too old or for health reasons, appeared at registration centers and insisted on being conscripted.

In the border villages, sandbags were filled and air raid trenches were dug. Wire fences were erected and women were taught how to fire machineguns.

Shalom.

Eilat, the door through which ninety percent of Israel's oil came from Iranian ports on the Persian Gulf, key to her trade with India and the East, with East Africa, was slammed shut. It meant the death of the country's tire industry, for it was to Eilat that Singapore's rubber was shipped and there manufactured into truck and car tires and shipped out again.

Kol Israel broadcast code names every thirty minutes. *The Last of the Just. Deep Roots. Limelight. Close Shave. Field of Gold. Bitter Rice. The Wedding March. Lovers of Zion.* Men heard, understood and responded.

Shalom.

The leaders of the Arab world pledged themselves, their armies, their people to the jihad, the holy war, declared by Gamal Abdel Nasser.

"This will be total war," Nasser told the fellahin. "Our basic aim is the destruction of Israel."

Moscow issued a statement: "He who would venture to unleash aggression would encounter not only the united strength of the Arab countries, but also resolute resistance to aggression on the part of the Soviet Union and all peace-loving states."

Shalom.

The President of the United States called for a reduction of tensions in the area and expressed the hope that the Secretary General of the United Nations, then on his way to Cairo, would be received with good will and faith. He outlined the history of the region and said the United States desired to maintain friendship with all parties and insisted that he was opposed to aggression.

U Thant arrived in Cairo and met with Colonel Nasser. For three hours, Nasser defended his blockade of Eilat and denounced the Israelis for being aggressors. U Thant cut his visit short and went back to the UN Secretariat in New York where the situation was under debate.

Moshe Dayan, as Israel's new Minister of Defense, met with members of the press. Questioned, he replied: "I personally would not expect nor want anyone else to fight for us. I wouldn't like American or British boys getting killed here in order to secure our safety."

Shalom.

382

The McClintock children were asleep and Mrs. Hoffman's middle daughter, Elsa, was sitting with them. Though Hank was due back with his unit the next morning, he and Rena decided to go to the cinema. It was one of those long American westerns, this one with Henry Fonda. Rena had a special liking for him and for westerns.

"The horses," she insisted, "are so beautiful."

Hank was bored but he made no complaint. In certain ways, he had always indulged his wife. And this kind of film was one of the ways. She clutched tightly at his hand and lived out the Technicolor action unfolding on the screen.

Abruptly the picture faded to black and the sound groaned to silence. A disappointed sigh rose up from the audience and protesting cries were hurled at the projectionist.

"What is it?" Rena said.

Hank shrugged. "Some trouble with the carbon arc—"

The houselights came on and a short stocky man trundled down the aisle to the front of the auditorium and held his hands up for silence. He waited until he had their attention.

"If you will look around, you will see policemen. We would appreciate it if all of you would file out at once. There is no immediate danger. Simply a precaution, you understand. Order will be appreciated. For efficiency's sake, the last rows first and so on and so on. Now, if you will begin—"

A suffocating silence descended over the audience. There was a momentary lull as understanding penetrated. This sort of thing happened from time to time and there had been occasions when theaters had been rocked by explosions, people injured and some killed.

There was the shuffling of hundreds of feet and the sound of seats being pushed back. Conversation was muted as the people began to leave.

Policemen and soldiers stood at the exits. Hank spoke to one of them. "A bomb, *adoni?* Is that it?"

The man nodded, eyes searching Hank's face. "It's already been found. We are looking for the man who placed it."

A hoarse cry came from the direction of the outer lobby and a woman's frightened cry cut through the night. There was sudden movement, awkward, violent. A blue

383

arm rose and descended swiftly and then another. The melee was over as abruptly as it had begun.

The stocky man who had ordered them to leave materialized. He owned a face bland and equivocal. "It is over, ladies and gentlemen," he said. "Thank you for cooperating. It is safe to go back inside now. The remainder of the film will be shown."

Hank turned to Rena. Her lips were pale and trembling. "Come, we'll go to a café, get some coffee."

She shook her head once. "Take me home, please. I want to go home to my babies."

The stocky man was a major in Shin Beit, Israel's intelligence service. With his bland features and agreeable manner he impressed some people as a retired businessman or a music teacher or a small shopkeeper. At this moment, in a tieless shirt and brown slacks, he perched on the corner of an old oak table in a room provided as a courtesy by the Police Department. Two men hovered over the prisoner who sat in a hard metal chair, chin on his chest.

For the most part, Milovan Levin found satisfaction in his work, satisfaction in matching wits with other men under tension for high stakes. The highest. He would have enjoyed the work more had not the results been so deadly, the methods as direct and cruel. Another man might have been inhibited by the imperfections of the job. Not Milovan Levin. He did what was required.

This prisoner, for example. Levin knew his name, knew that he was a Syrian born in a small agricultural village north of Damascus, and trained in that country in the use of explosives. Levin was almost sure that he knew when the prisoner had entered Israel, and by what route. Much information of this kind came to him from sources in Syria itself. Over the years, agents had worked their way into sensitive positions in Syria, and the other Arab nations, in the political bureaucracy, in industry, in the military itself. These men and women, many of them Jews of Yemeni or Iraqi descent, married and raised families, but remained loyal to Israel. Interestingly, it had not been this complex and efficient network which had turned up this man, this Farog Dibini. For that he owed a vote of thanks to Yaakov Yeshivat.

The two police investigators were making no progress with Farog, which did not surprise Levin. They tended to work along orthodox lines and Farog had been instructed thoroughly in how to resist them. Levin slid off the table and motioned the policemen aside. He stood in front of Farog and assessed him gravely.

"Say your name for me," he said.

"I am Namir Avatichi," Farog said, trying to arrange a smile on his small mouth.

Levin shook his head sadly. He had never enjoyed this part of the job but it saved time and, over the long haul, lives. "You're lying," he said gently. Farog dropped his head and Levin lifted his chin. "You are Farog Dibini."

"No, *adoni*, I—"

"You were born and raised in the village of the Mukhtar Yahaya."

"I am from Yemen. I came to Israel on the wings of the eagle."

Levin shook his head impatiently. "You were trained at El Fatah camp number seven and you have been under the authority of Mejjid al-Hadad for at least six months. Tonight you placed a bomb under seat number three in the fourteenth row of the cinema. The bomb was poorly made, Farog, and it might not have gone off, even if we did not find it. But you have done some good work as a saboteur. It was you who destroyed the heavy machines at Kfar Glickman a month ago." Levin smiled a small, understanding smile. "I am right?"

There was a pinched expression around Farog's mouth but his dark eyes remained steady. "No, *adoni*. I am Namir Avatichi. Born in Yemen in——"

It was a short blow, no more than eight inches, but delivered with practiced force, the bony fist twisting against Farog's nose at the moment of impact. Farog went over backwards onto the floor. Levin waited for him to come up into a sitting position. His nose was smashed. Blood streamed out of it and his dark eyes were tearing.

"I am Namir Avatichi. A Yemeni. My papers——"

"The papers are forged," Levin said matter-of-factly. He reached down and helped Farog to his feet, righted the metal chair. "Sit," he said. "I know that through al-Hadad you have worked with other terrorists. I want names and addresses. I want to know where the arms caches are, where explosives are stored. Are others expected soon from Syria and at what point will they be crossing the frontier?"

"I am a good Jew, *adoni*. See, my earlocks, and I wear a yarmulke."

Levin hit him again on the nose. Even as he went

385

tumbling to the floor, Farog screamed out his agony. He thrashed about in pain. Levin nodded to the policemen and they hauled him erect.

"Sooner or later you will tell us, Farog. Make it easy for yourself. Do it now. Refuse, and I will pluck out your left eye. Then the right eye. And the fingers of your right hand."

Farog held his nose and whimpered. "I am a Jew. You have no right."

Levin extended his hand, palm up, and one of the policemen placed a hunting knife in it. He tapped the broad blade against the edge of the table and the ominous sound lingered in the still room. Farog was unable to drag his eyes away from the blade.

"His pants," Levin said.

Farog wanted to scream, to protest, to explain that it was all a mistake, a sort of a game in which no harm was intended. He felt his trousers droop around his knees, felt his undershorts being stripped away, felt the two men hauling him onto the big table. They spread his legs with powerful hands and held him immobile, the oak table not unpleasant against his naked bottom. The gleaming blade came reaching for him, icy and bitter sharp against his scrotum. The pressure increased, thin, insistent, cutting . . .

He screamed.

"No! I will tell you everything! I will tell!"

The men released him and he sat up, looked down at himself in horror. A narrow trickle of crimson streaked the sac. A hollowness seeped into his stomach and he wanted to vomit. He placed both hands protectively over himself.

"You must promise," he said pleadingly, to Levin. "You must promise that I will not be harmed."

"Talk and you will be treated with consideration and fairness. Try to deceive me and I shall complete the operation."

Farog began to talk.

Within the next three hours, Shin Beit agents, and the police, arrested seventeen saboteurs, three of them women. Two arms caches were discovered and a blueprint for terror throughout the Jerusalem area which included the destruction of power stations, radio transmitters and telephone lines.

Levin personally headed the detail that went after Mejjid al-Hadad. He placed his men around Mejjid's house, trying to close off all avenues of escape. He hoped to be able to gain additional information from Mejjid. As leader of the ring, he would know other names, other plans, might be able to furnish knowledge about similar terrorist groups around the country.

Levin never discovered whether Mejjid had been warned of their coming by one of his colleagues or if he simply spotted them as they took up their positions. An agent spied the tall figure moving silently through the shadows at the rear of the house, his flowing white kaffiyeh making an excellent target. The agent called out a warning, identified himself and shouted for the man to halt. He ran.

Levin was in front of the house when the shots crashed out. Ordering his men to hold their positions, he headed around back. It was over when he got there. The agent stood over the body.

"He ran," the agent said, "then shot at me. I hit him twice."

Levin kneeled and rolled the body over. It was Mejjid al-Hadad, the handsome brown features frozen in place. He closed the dark eyes and said a silent prayer for the dead. "All right. What's everybody standing around for? Let's search the house. We've got work to do."

It was late at night but the London airport was crowded. Simon Landau stood on the line at the Alitalia reservations desk. He had been on line for almost an hour. And before that El Al, Pan American, BOAC, others that flew nearer to Israel.

When he reached the desk, the clerk stared unhappily at him, made no effort to be even professionally genial. "Yes," he said, unable to conceal traces of his cockney accent. "What can I do for you?"

"I want to go to Tel Aviv," Simon said. "Israel," he added carefully. "The first available flight, direct or otherwise."

The agent's eyes closed in weariness and fluttered open again. Two days of this. Israelis struggling to get back to their country. Mad, the lot. Couldn't they see that their ridiculous little country was going to be overrun by the Arabs? All of them were going to be killed.

"I'm sorry," he said automatically. "No airline is flying into Tel Aviv, or any other airfield in Israel. The crisis, you know."

Simon anticipated him. "What about Rome? Get me on the next flight. You can do that."

"All booked," the agent said. "But if you like, I'll put you on standby."

"What are the chances of getting on a flight?"

The agent softened momentarily. "Not so good. All the others, Israelis, too."

Simon nodded. He told the agent his name and started away. "Sir," the agent called after him. "Have you tried one of the unscheduled lines, perhaps to Yugoslavia or Greece. That would get you nearer, at least."

Simon looked at the man and nodded. "Thank you," he said. "I'll try." He turned away and a sense of hopelessness gripped him. He knew that he wasn't going to make it back in time. He had failed, and the guilt for that failure could never be shifted to anyone else.

Out of the black desert night they came, a baritone roar of engines—trucks, tanks, halftracks—sending up a swirling dust cloud. They formed a tight semi-circle and as if on signal their headlights were turned on, bathing the back end of the 6x6 in glaring white light. Soldiers made their way into the space in front of the vehicles and settled down on the ground.

After a while, an officer climbed onto the 6x6 and held up his hands for silence. "Chaverim, it is a known fact that nothing is too good for the men of Israel's Defense Forces——"

Hoots and catcalls greeted his words.

He waited for quiet. "You have the finest quarters of any army in the world," he went on lightly, "under this romantic desert sky——"

The catcalls returned.

"The best food——"

Derisive shouts.

"And now we bring you the finest of entertainers, the most beautiful woman in the world, Israel's gift to Hollywood and to the world. Chaverim, I give you—Mara Gabrielli!"

A throaty roar went up.

Two soldiers helped Mara onto the truck bed and someone handed a guitar up to her. She stood there, smiling, letting the sound of their approval wash over her. Tall, shapely in a black-and-white vinyl mini-skirt and a tight black sleeveless sweater, a spectacular figure. Let them look, let them enjoy.

From where Amos Landau stood, outside the perimeter of light, Mara seemed as beautiful as she had fifteen years before. The same girlish slimness, the flaring hips without bulges, the heavy breasts still full of promise. Her black hair, longer than he remembered, had been pulled tightly back and tied at the nape of her neck. Her smile was a brilliant arc against glowing olive skin. She belonged in films, Amos told himself, a creature for the world, the stuff of fantasy for all men.

She looped the guitar cord around her neck and plucked at the strings, sending base tones into the night. The soldiers grew quiet as she began to sing in Ladino, reminding them of her Sephardic beginnings, saying in song that she was one of them, one of the formerly dispersed come home. The words of *Los Bibilicos* were slow and romantic, creating images of nightbirds and flowering trees and people who suffer from love.

Then, in Hebrew, *Hana'ava Babanot,* ending:

"Stretch out your arms and embrace me
Hug me again and again."

The soldiers filled the desert air with their approval.

She sang in Greek about a girl who fell into a well; about a shepherd, in Rumanian; a gypsy, in Russian; of a bald mountain in America; of peace in German; of mules and boys and of God, closing finally with *Avadim Hayinu,* which was from the Passover Haggadah:

"Slaves we were,
And now we are free men."

They cheered and shouted her name and cried for more and she obliged them. And finally when it was over, they crowded around the truck, reached to help her to the ground, to touch her, to speak directly to her. A captain, her official escort, eased her out of the press of flesh.

"There's a schedule to meet, Miss Gabrielli," he reminded her.

"Ah, the schedule. Yes, yes. I'm coming." Blinking rapidly, trying not to allow what she felt to show, smiling at the smiling young faces, she trailed after the captain.

The captain stopped. She looked up and saw Amos Landau. He was different, yet she recognized him at once, and somehow the changes were meaningless. The same neat masculine form, the same warm expression, eyes level and warmly sympathetic. There was less hair and his cheeks were stubbled and there were lines, but he was no less attractive. She took a step toward him and held out her hand.

"Amos," she said.

He took her hand. "Shalom, Mara."

She kissed his cheek and the watching men approved. Amos blushed and Mara laughed.

"Miss Gabrielli," the captain said. "The schedule."

"You're a colonel, Amos?" she said.

"This is my command," he said, assessing her.

At this range, the changes of time were visible. The parchment configuration of her neck, the pouched eyes, marked with crimson hairlines, the cynical downturn of the sensual mouth. She brushed instinctively at her hair.

"From time to time," she said, with forced lightness, "I heard good things. About the Landau Company. You are to be congratulated."

He took no comfort in this meeting, wanted to say something appropriate and amusing. Nothing came. Seeing her now, he recalled something once heard or read. *"Every person past forty must be responsible for the way his face looks."*

Over the years there had been stories about her in the press, accounts that revealed as much by what they hadn't reported as by what they had. Of a notorious existence. Of three marriages and three divorces. Of a bullfighter in Madrid and a gambler in Las Vegas and a prizefighter in Rome and a rock-'n'-roll singer in London. There were brawls in nightclubs and at airports. And two arrests for possession of drugs. There had been apologies and explanations, excuses in recent years. Attempts to bolster a once spectacular career that was sagging weakly.

"I look tired," she said wistfully. "This tour is very wearing."

"You're more beautiful than ever."

"You lie very nicely, Amos." She looped her arm in his and they walked a few steps to one side. "I am grateful for what you did, the help you gave. There was no one else I could ask."

"That's what old friends are for."

"I don't deserve your friendship," she said very quietly. "That time with Salisbury, leaving that way, not even saying goodbye, just a note. I didn't have the courage to face you and all for that pig Salisbury."

He searched for something suitable to say. "You've made an important career for yourself, Mara. The whole world knows you. Israel is proud of you."

390

The sea-green eyes were clouded. "It's such a mess, my dear, and so am I. The newspapers printed some of it but the worst is too sordid and bloody to be told. The marriages, the affairs, the people hurt, the abortions. And once there was a child."

"I didn't know."

"I made a slight error at the time. I neglected to be married. But God has a way of dealing with such things. My son died when he was three, of pneumonia, Amos. He died in a very modern and expensive hospital in Hollywood where, of course, no one ever dies of pneumonia. All my fame and all my money couldn't save the life of that innocent little boy, Amos. So he died while his mother was in Cannes sleeping with some Italian producer whose name I can't even remember. My son was a very sweet boy, very beautiful and full of love."

"I'm sorry."

The corners of her mouth lifted briefly. "Me too." She gave him her hand again. "I must go. The schedule." She hesitated. "After that business at the chateau in France, I wasn't going to come home. I went on to Florence. But I had to come back. I suppose it was stupid after so long to come at a time like this. A person could get killed."

"You're an Israeli," he said.

She nodded. "It's that simple, isn't it?"

"Yes, but not so simple."

She took back her hand. "Take care of yourself, Amos, and give my best to Joshua."

"He's dead. In Sinai."

"Oh," she said, after a beat, "I didn't know."

She swung away, moving with the fluid grace of an athlete, long legs reaching. She climbed into the waiting jeep and disappeared into the night without a backward glance.

VIII

To those concerned with such things, the omens were good. The year had produced a fine harvest. And that winter snow had fallen around Jerusalem, an unusual phenomenon. And on this particular night, in the midst of the dry season, fat globs of rain fell on Tel Aviv.

There was more. According to the Hebrew calendar, this was *Nisan,* the same month in which the ancient Israelites had made their exodus from Egypt to wander in the wilderness of Sinai.

The kibbutz was still. Dark and cold, the Negev in the early morning hours of June 5. A guard huddled against the railing of his watchtower, impatient for his tour to end, anxious to get to the dining hall for some hot coffee, breakfast. On the ground, other guards tried to keep warm in their slit trenches, hugging themselves or hitting their hands together.

Without warning, the blackness was shattered by the explosion of mortar shells, looping over the frontier from Gaza, seeking the buildings of the kibbutz. Someone set off the siren alarm. An unnecessary precaution. The people of the kibbutz were already awake and, half-dressed, rushing to their defense positions.

Eleven other kibbutzim reported that they had come under attack.

At 07:55 hours that same morning, air raid alarms were sounded in Tel Aviv. Five minutes later, a message went out to airstrips north of the city, to another near Beersheba—

Battle Order of the Officer Commanding, Israeli Air Force. Urgent. To all Units:
Soldiers of the Air Force, the blustering and swashbuckling Egyptian Army is moving against us to annihilate our people...
Fly on, attack the enemy, pursue him to ruination, draw his fangs, scatter him in the wilderness, so that the people of Israel may live in peace in our land, and the future generations be secured.

The young men went running to their Mystères, Mirages, the Super Mystères. Minutes later they were airborne, jet engines screaming as they swept over the Mediterranean sparkling in the morning sun, flying low in the sea mist.

In tight formations of three or four planes, they swung south, keeping radio silence, teen-age pilots and middle-aged veterans of other wars, and professional flyers who days before were guiding El Al's Boeing 707s. They sped along the coastline.

A formation of twin-jet Vatour bombers led the way, never more than 100 feet above the sea. At Port Said, northernmost terminal of the Suez Canal, they hooked inland over Egypt, past Beni Sueir toward the bomber base at Luxor on the Nile.

Over enemy territory now, and certain that they had been spotted and identified, the pilots kept a sharp watch out for enemy fighter planes. For anti-aircraft fire. They encountered neither.

The target came into sight. They climbed to bombing altitudes, depositing their payloads on the neatly arranged TU-16s studding the runways below. This done, they swung back and made a strafing run, using 30mm cannons with deadly results.

Elsewhere, it was the same. The Mystères and the Mirages hit military airdromes at El Arish, Bir Tamada, Jebel Libni, Bir Gifgafa, all in Sinai. And in the Canal Zone, Fayid, Kabrit, Abu Suer. And Cairo West, Beni Sueir, Imshas, all in the Valley of the Nile. Russian-built MIGs and bombers were destroyed in their revetments. Radar installations that had not done their work were shot apart. Fuel tanks were blown up and trucks and buildings were wrecked by cannon and machinegun fire.

By 09:00, the first wave of planes had returned to their bases and were refueled. Minutes later they were back aloft, striking deep into Egyptian territory again. Some of them turned their attention to air bases in Syria, destroying that nation's air force on the ground. And Jordan was similarly hit. And Iraq. Twenty-five Arab bases were ripped apart, their Air Forces smashed as effective fighting instruments.

By mid-morning, the skies belonged to Israel.

In Cairo, the official radio declared the start of hostilities. People danced in the streets and cheered.

"Helas Tel Aviv!" they cried. "Tel Aviv is finished!"

"Our glorious and courageous pilots have shot down 24 Jewish jets," Cairo Radio boasted, then: "46!"

"60!"

"Nasser!" the people shouted. "Nasser!"

In Israel, Kol Israel summoned the remaining reservists to active duty. *Men At Work. Alternating Current. Good Friends. Wedding March.*

And between announcements, *Hatikvah* was played.

And *Jerusalem the Golden*. And the theme song from *The Bridge on the River Kwai*.

In Washington, a State Department spokesman said that the United States was ". . . neutral in thought, word and deed." The Secretary of State felt impelled to explain subsequently that this meant the United States was merely ". . . nonbelligerent," though of course not indifferent.

In England's House of Commons, the Foreign Secretary made it clear that "British concern is not to take sides."

And in Moscow, ". . . resolute support" for the Arabs was expressed and it was demanded that Israel stop fighting and pull back at once.

Inland from the Mediterranean, positioned in the orange groves and pointed like a giant arrow to the southwest, toward Sinai and the Gaza Strip, the armored battalion sat, quiet and immobile. Waiting. A collection of camouflaged crustaceans painted green and armed with deadly stingers, lumpish, vulnerable, resting on steel treads.

Men sat in the shade of tanks or halftracks and read. Others dozed under orange trees. Some listened to transistor radios and others talked and a few strummed guitars. A squad of riflemen, all from an Orthodox kibbutz in the north, danced a hora.

The command halftrack was crowded. At the rear, Spiegal pored over his maps. Born and raised in the Negev, he was one of Amos Landau's Desert Rats. Opposite Spiegal, picking her way forward now, was Edie Kazin, slight and dark, with round eyes that conveyed a perpetual innocence. Radio operator and official organizer, Edie Kazin ran the command halftrack with a graceful competence. Every chart in its place, field glasses properly stowed, clipboards stacked, wax pencils close at hand, submachine guns loaded and ready. Up front, just behind the driver, Jed Serlin, a transplanted Bostonian, baby-faced and freckled, with a frown of constant curiosity.

"Standby alert," Edie Kazin told him, with no anxiety. "The colonel should be here."

Serlin blew a kiss in her direction. "The colonel is here, sweetheart." He stamped down three times on the metal floor. Amos crawled out from under the halftrack, wiping sleep out of his eyes.

"What?" he said.

"Standby alert."

Amos climbed into the halftrack. "Notify all section commanders—crank 'em up."

The heat grew more intense and a shimmering haze rose off the dun-colored hills to their front. To Amos, all this was familiar. Emotionally, at least, it might have been 1948 or 1956. But it wasn't. This time would be different. Egypt owned the latest military hardware and with the help of the Russians had had time enough to learn to use it.

Edie Kazin returned from her radio. Her triangular face was grave and her round eyes concerned. "Kol Israel just announced it—we are at war."

"Confirm with Brigade, please," Amos said. "But first order the men to mount up."

"I think it is going to be rough," Serlin said, the freckled face serious.

"If anything should happen to me, Jed, you know the orders. Speed is paramount. Encircle them. Cut them off. Leave the mopping up for later. Attain primary targets as quickly as possible. If necessary, you will operate without further orders. You understand?"

"Nothing is going to happen to you, Amos."

"There will be shooting. It's best to be prepared."

"Colonel!" Edie Kazin called. "Brigade on the radio. They want to talk to you."

Three strides brought Amos to the rear. "Landau speaking," he said into the mouthpiece.

"Yeshivat here. It's begun."

"We heard."

"We're hitting into Sinai at three points. Move out, and let's get it over."

Amos swung up to the front of the halftrack. "Kadima!" he cried. "Let's go!"

The columns rumbled into motion, picking up speed as they went.

First contact was made south of Rahfa, an artillery strongpoint in Gaza. A jeep patrol scouting ahead captured two Egyptian soldiers. Questioning revealed information that failed to jibe with Intelligence reports.

"They must be lying," Serlin said.

"I don't think so," Amos indicated the map of the area. "We knew there was activity along here, and here. They've simply put in new works in the last few weeks."

"We can't go in there not knowing what they'll throw at us!"

"We'll go in. But first we'll soften them up a little. Tell Brigade I want an air strike right now."

Twenty minutes later the planes appeared. Squinting up at them, Serlin began to swear angrily. "They're Fougas! What are they trying to do to us? Are we so hard up for planes—?"

"We use what we've got," Amos said, with more assurance than he felt. The Fouga was an Israeli-built plane, propeller-driven, slow, designed for training purposes, not combat. The High Command had ordered them armed with machineguns and rockets, to be used for direct troop support. Their pilots were all over age flyers plucked out of their civilian jobs for this moment.

The Fougas came in low, almost too low, firing their rockets point-blank at the entrenched artillery below, making pass after pass despite the heavy flak until their ammunition was exhausted. When they finally withdrew, Amos ordered his tanks to advance.

They ran on under heavy defensive fire from a zig-zagged line of dug-in Stalin-3 tanks. The column spread into a battle formation, came on again, cannon thumping. A warning cry came over the radio.

"Mines!"

Amos trained his binoculars on the terrain ahead. They had studied aerial photographs of the mine field, each company commander, each tank commander. Every one of them knew where the soft spots were located, the openings.

"Lead company," he said. "Ahead."

"Lead company, ahead," Edie Kazin said into her radio. The right flank rolled forward, the commanders ducking inside their tanks now, buttoning up. From where Amos watched, they looked like a swarm of giant insects, jerking and bouncing, kicking sand, but moving immutably forward.

"Another fifty yards," Serlin said anxiously, "and they make their turn." He lifted his eyes from the map. "No!" he broke out. "Too soon. The fool is turning too early."

It was true. The lead tank had miscalculated, was swinging toward the fortifications far from the safe-point.

"Radio!" Amos yelled. "Call him off!"

It was too late. The tank made its turn and swerved ahead. At once, the tank lifted up onto its left tread, as if held aloft by a giant hoist. It toppled back to the ground, spinning in a tight little circle. It struck another mine and came to a stop. Black smoke came from its underside.

"Get out," Amos urged. "Come on. Out, out."

No one came out. Seconds later, the flames.

Amos went back to the radio. "Notify all commanders—use the disabled tank as a marker. They will turn into the mine field at a point to its left. Emphasize that. I am going in first. And they will follow."

"Move out," Serlin told the driver.

"Full speed," Amos said.

Small caliber bullets beat a tattoo on the armored sides of the halftrack and they all ducked as the driver maneuvered through the mine field. A sudden skidding turn to the left sent them all lurching and Amos fought for balance, coming erect. They had made it, were clear of the mines and had slid behind a low ridge. He looked back. The tanks were coming on and behind them the halftracks with their cargos of infantrymen.

A tank was hit; it hesitated, then kept moving. Another, like a creature gone mad, ran a blind course into the minefield. There were muffled explosions and the tank toppled onto its side. The hatch opened and a man crawled out, ran desperately for the safety zone, shirttails flapping. In mid-stride he jerked upright, crumpled onto his face. Amos turned away and watched the rest of the column come through, fan out across the sand.

Some of the halftracks began climbing the dunes. About halfway up, their treads lost purchase on the shifting sands.

Serlin yelled back at Edie Kazin. "Get those tracks off the high ground. Tell them to go around!" It was too late. The halftracks ground to a halt, unable to advance or retreat.

"We're lucky," Amos said. "If the Egyptians had any guns on this side of the crest, those tracks would be finished."

"Shall I send some tanks up there, pull them back?"

"Forget them for now. Get the infantry out and moving up. Send them straight ahead, but withhold the third company." He checked the Intelligence estimates of the defensive positions. "Here," he said, to Serlin. "Third company circles out here, to the south. Put them into this wadi for cover."

"That'll take them two miles out of the way."

"Two miles, but without having to fight. At this point, they double back and come up behind those people. In exactly sixty minutes, I want them to attack."

Serlin glanced at his watch. "And what do we do until then?"

"We are going to fight."

Casualty reports began to come in. Forty infantrymen were dead, and four tanks were destroyed, seven halftracks, a jeep. Many officers were killed and many more wounded.

Amos looked at Edie Kazin. She was pale and a nerve in her right eyelid leaped erratically. "We are all a little frightened, Edie," he said quietly.

"Shall I send the casualty report to Brigade," she said, in a steady voice.

He shook his head. "They have enough to consider without thinking about losses. And so do we."

Starting back to the radio, she glanced back. Her voice was almost inaudible through the noise of battle. "Are we going to lose this fight?"

"Losing is too expensive for us. We must win."

"See!" Serlin exclaimed.

Amos looked through his binoculars toward the left flank. The intensity of defensive firing had diminished.

"Third company must have broken through. They're hitting from behind."

Amos spoke with controlled excitement. "Now! Order everything forward. Every tank, every man. Let's go," he said to the driver. "You think I want to spend all day around here? Let's find a fight."

Hank McClintock sat in the coffee shop sipping tea and watching the commentator on the television set. The program came from Damascus. According to the commentator, disaster had overtaken Israel. Tel Aviv, he said, was no more. Haifa had been captured. Jerusalem was destroyed, burned out by Arab planes.

Hank heard his name called. He turned to see a portly man waving at him from behind the wheel of an old English sedan at the curb. "Is this all you have to do, *adoni*," he said, laughing, "with the country at war?"

"But all of us are dead," Hank called back cheerfully. "The Arabs say so. And you, Sarig, why do you go joy-riding on such a day?"

Sarig, an assistant professor of antiquity at Hebrew University, sobered immediately. "I'm heading for the Medical Center. We have to get the Chagall windows to a safe place."

Hank stood up. "I'll go with you." Carrying his 16mm sound camera and supply case, he got into the car.

Sarig put the sedan into gear and they rolled through the streets. "Funny, isn't it?" Sarig said, conversationally.

"What?"

"Hardly a man to be seen in the streets. As if it's a female world." He grinned in Hank's direction. "Makes me kind of uneasy."

"The Jordanians make me uneasy," Hank said, after a moment. "Do you think they will fight?"

Sarig lifted his hands off the wheel expressively and waited till the car swerved before replacing them. "Who ever knows about an Arab? I hear our people have been in touch with Hussein since fighting began this morning, saying we had no intention of violating Jordan's sovereignty or in any way committing violence against her."

Hank had gleaned the same information earlier from a military friend. He remained unconvinced.

"Will Hussein remain out of it?" he muttered, expecting no answer. "He's a prudent man and inclined to do what's right for his people."

Sarig snorted in contradiction. "I keep hearing that but I see little evidence of it. I believe what political leaders do and say in public. All those private gems we hear they drop behind closed doors don't add up. With an Egyptian general in charge of Hussein's army, I expect only the worst."

They were climbing steadily upwards past terraces to where the Hadassah-Hebrew University Medical Center was located, the largest hospital in the Middle East. The windows, each a vivid mosaic of stained glass depicting one of the tribes of ancient Israel, created by the artist Marc Chagall, had been installed in the hospital synagogue.

"It seems to me Hussein is in an intolerable position," Hank offered. "If he doesn't do what Nasser wants him to do, some fanatic will probably murder him the way they murdered his grandfather, Abdullah."

"Violence and killing," Sarig sighed. "Once they begin they breed more of the same."

"I've had a belly full of war, Sarig. Three years as an infantryman during World War II, Sinai, and now this. This is the worst."

"Why?"

"Because we can't afford even a single defeat. One setback could mean total disaster. The odds being what

399

they are, if the Arabs win there'll be no one left to save, if the world decides to act."

"Don't worry, *adoni*. The world will watch and talk and waggle remonstrating fingers afterwards if we are wiped out. It will do nothing." His expression hardened. "But we are not going to be wiped out. We are not going to lose."

Hank felt no reassurance. He glanced over at Sarig. "Your family," he said. "Are they in a safe place?"

"They are at home, where else?"

Hank made no reply. He had insisted that Rena and the children go to Tel Aviv and stay with her mother. There, at least, they would be removed from the ground fighting that might erupt in Jerusalem itself. She had not wanted to go and they had argued about it. In the end, she did as he wished but when they parted she had been silent and resentful. He wondered if he had done the right thing.

The medical center complex sprawled out ahead of them and Sarig drove directly to the small synagogue. Men were already working to dismantle the windows. Wooden crates were lined up to accept the precious glass.

Sarig called to one of the men laboring on the first window. "How does it go, Giora?"

The man straightened up and recognizing Sarig shook his head. "Terrible."

"You shouldn't be having trouble. Those windows were designed so they could be dismantled in an hour or so and packed away."

"A beautiful theory," Giora replied heatedly. "But somebody forgot about this damned hot dry air. The putty which was to remain pliable and easy to remove has hardened into place. We've got to cut the glass out of the lead frames. That's going to take time."

"Well, then I suppose we'd better not waste any talking."

"Mind if I take some pictures?" Hank said.

"Do whatever you like!" Giora said. "Sarig, go to the workshop. You'll find a jeweler's carborundum saw. I'm going to need it for this operation."

Sarig hurried away and Giora turned back to the window. Hank readied his camera, began shooting wild, capturing the men at their delicate work. This footage would add an extra dimension to what might be otherwise just another documentary film about war.

When he saw that Sarig had returned with the carborundum saw, had mounted the scaffolding to assist Giora, he took up a position that would allow him to shoot closeups of their hands at work on the glass. He had exposed no more than twenty seconds of film when the first shells exploded in the courtyard between the synagogue and the maternity clinic. Shrapnel whirred overhead and men scrambled for safety.

Sarig looked down at Hank. "There, *adoni*," he said, a wistful smile on his round face. "There is the true voice of King Hussein."

A flood of oaths broke out of Giora. "Damn them! They've damaged some of the windows! Have they no respect for art!"

Shaking his head, Giora turned back to the window, pulling a roll of scotch tape from his pocket.

General Heikel and Colonel Hassan ate breakfast in the shade of a camouflage net, thus avoiding much of the unpleasant morning heat. The orderly had cleared away the dishes and now they lingered over a second cup of peppermint tea and smoked American cigarets and planned a bridge game for that evening. Heikel considered bridge a challenge, a first-rate exercise for the military mind. It forced one to maintain a condition of alertness, allowing as it did room for maneuver within a proscribed area. He expressed the thought to Hassan, not for the first time.

"Excellent, General," Hassan said. "You have a way with words, of synthesizing an idea—"

"Now, Hassan," Heikel said modestly.

"I mean it, sir. I imagine you'd be a very fine writer."

"Interesting thing for you to say, Hassan. You see, I have been considering doing my memoirs. I am getting to about that age, you know."

"Nonsense, sir, if you don't mind my saying. You can't be more than a year or two older than I am."

A flight of four jets screamed overhead. "Ours?" the general said, with mild interest.

Hassan uncrossed his legs and went to the edge of the netting. Shielding his eyes, he looked after the planes as they sped south.

"Our MIGs, Hassan?" Heikel said. He tapped his cup with a spoon and the orderly brought more tea.

Hassan returned to his seat. "General, I could be wrong, of course, the distance and speed, but the silhouettes —I thought they were Mystères."

"Israelis?"

"I think so, sir."

Heikel made a sound back in his throat. "They do a

401

nice job, camouflaging them, I mean. Difficult for our gunners, I would imagine."

"Not too difficult, I'm sure."

Heikel put another cigaret in his holder and Hassan extended his lighter. "I suppose," Heikel said, "they're doing some reconnaissance. You know, Hassan, there is an amusing side to all this. They send their planes over to look us over and we do the same to them. We blow up a railway line or mine a road in Israel and their people hit one of our installations. Keeps everyone on his toes, so to speak, but it is rather futile."

A dull explosion sounded in the distance. Then, a string of them. And in counterpoint, the sharp, quick report of anti-aircraft guns.

"What do you suppose that's all about, Hassan?"

"They might have attacked the supply dumps, general."

"Oh, dear."

"Shall I give them a call, general?"

"I imagine our fighters are able to handle the situation without our help." A lingering sigh passed across his finely turned lips. "Oh, very well. Find out what's happening back there. And you might inform command that if the Jews are going to bomb our supply areas I recommend in the strongest terms that we do likewise to theirs. Patrol action is one thing, expected, reasonable and controlled. But these jets are an entirely different affair. As a matter of fact, Hassan, if those planes come this way again, tell our anti-aircraft people to let go with a few rounds. Good practice, you know. Teach those people where to fly and where not to, eh!"

Hassan rose and gave a friendly, smiling salute. "Whatever you say, general."

Levi Landau was prepared in every respect. Emotionally he had readied himself for this day, it seemed to him, all of his life. Had waited for it to come. He had trained himself, considered all the possibilities, the probabilities, decided how he would act in a variety of situations. There was a cold lump behind his navel, a rock of determination, and his brain was focused on what lay ahead, what had to be done. On what he was going to do.

Physically everything was in order. His body was lean and strong, healthy, the reflexes sharp and practiced. His gear was spotless and in perfect condition, the Uzi lovingly cleaned and wiped so that only a thin coating of oil remained to prevent jamming. In his boot he carried a heavy hunting knife, the blade carefully honed, the grip specially corded to prevent slipping.

And on his head he wore a bright red peaked cap, a gift sent from New York by Simon the previous summer. To keep the sun out of his eyes, Simon had written, explaining that this was a baseball cap, the prettiest one he could find. Levi agreed that it was a pretty cap.

He glanced down the line of trucks. His men were aboard and ready to go. Destination: El Arish, headquarters for the Egyptian Army in Sinai. They were to be flown in, landed in time to fight their way into the town. Maps and photographs had been studied and battle plans made.

A sense of exhilaration filtered through Levi's middle, a visceral anticipation. He clutched the Uzi more tightly. This time no slipups. This time he would fight. This time he would get *his* chance. He pounded his hands together to relieve the rising tension and moved over to the lead truck. One of the men had a transistor radio.

"Hey, Levi," a corporal cried, "Kol Israel says we shot down four hundred Arab planes."

"You believe everything you hear?" Levi said.

The corporal laughed without humor. "I thought only the Arabs lie."

"Let's hope Nasser doesn't surrender before we get there."

A jeep came bouncing down the line, skidding to a dusty stop. The battalion commander.

"Are your people ready to move?" he called to Levi.

"All ready."

"We're going to be under way in ten minutes."

"El Arish, look out!" a soldier shouted.

The battalion commander scowled. "Forget about El Arish," he said. "They don't need us in Sinai."

Levi felt the cold lump in his middle dissolve. "Jerusalem then? The fighting has begun there. We will liberate the Old City. To win in the center of——"

"We go in the other direction," the battalion commander snapped. "North of Kinneret."

"But nothing is happening there," Levi protested. "The Syrians will never fight. Everybody knows that."

"Orders, Levi. Load up."

Levi watched the jeep speed out of sight. No, he told himself. No, no, no. It couldn't be happening to him again. Not again. He deserved his chance.

403

It was night and the desert cold penetrated the layers of clothing to the bone. Infantrymen huddled together for warmth in the halftracks and trucks that transported them further south.

Orders had been explicit. Isolate and bypass, avoid prolonged combat if possible, smash through to Suez, cut off all escape routes for Nasser's army in the desert, occupy the East Bank of the canal and Sharm el-Sheikh, before world diplomatic pressure became too great to withstand, before a cease-fire was forced upon Israel.

Speed was all important.

The armored column ran with blackout lights. Radio silence to be maintained, except in emergencies. Amos Landau stood at his position in the command halftrack squinting into the darkness. There was nothing to see. Behind him, the radio began to crackle. He was at Edie Kazin's side in three strides. She handed him the microphone.

"It's Dorfman."

Dorfman was in charge of the advance party, a dozen AMX light tanks, plus a platoon of infantry in armored cars.

"Landau here, Dorfman. What is it?"

"We're in trouble," Dorfman said, voice edged with urgency. "Caught in a crossfire. There must be fifty of them, T-55s, throwing everything they've got at us."

"Can you pull back?"

"Not a chance. We walked right into a trap. Unless you can spring it, we've had it."

Amos called for a situation map, turned a flashlight on it, checked coordinates. "I've got you located, *adoni*," Amos said into the radio. "We're on our way, but it's going to take thirty minutes at least to get there. Can you hold out?"

"I'm not sure."

"You've got to! Use your speed, your maneuverability. Drive on them, head on, understand! Don't give them sitting targets. Keep moving."

"I'll do what I can."

"Mazel."

The radio went silent.

The Mogen David ambulance rolled toward Hayarkon Street. Rena McClintock, face fuller and her figure lushly maternal, sat in the back on the stretcher. Occasionally her eyes met those of the other two women, housewives

404

like herself, and they smiled at each other. No one spoke. It was as if they were made self-conscious by the nature of this work, by the intimacy of blood and the strangeness of their being here. The doctor, in his seat alongside the driver, twisted around.

"Everything all right, girls?" he said.

Everything was fine, they told him, and he faced front and never turned around again. He was a somber man with a thick rectangular mustache and tiny sober eyes. He sucked on an unlit pipe.

Rena was worried. She had never actually *seen* blood before and hoped she wouldn't be ill or faint or do something stupid.

Two middle-aged policemen stood on the sidewalk in front of Harold's Place when they drew up. The doctor introduced himself and shook hands with the policemen and Rena felt reassured by this concession to normalcy.

"These are my assistants," the doctor said, indicating the three women. "They'll bring the equipment."

"You ever been in a discotheque before, doctor?" one of the officers asked.

"Never."

"Well, you're in for an experience. Let's go downstairs."

Harold's Place was a melange of light and sound. Multi-colored flashers sent bursts of illumination across the room at irregular intervals and darkness alternated with yellow and red and blue. Loudspeakers filled the long narrow room with a jarring beat and the discordant wail of a singing group to which a collection of girls in mini-skirts and young men in wildly patterned trousers and shirts thumped their middles in some athletic approximation of the sex act.

At the sight of the new arrivals, especially the two policemen, Harold came rushing over. He was a short man with bleached yellow bangs and damp eyes and small red lips set in a perpetual purse. He milked his fingers apprehensively and clucked in a high tight voice.

"Really! Officers. Is it necessary? To come here this way! This place is clean. You know it is. *It is.* Absolutely clean. None of those girls work here any more. I assured the precinct commander. I assured him and I keep my word. You are inhibiting my customers and that is decidedly *unfair.*"

"Harold," one of the policemen said, with elaborate tolerance, "be quiet." He took in the room with a single gesture. "I hope the Arabs have their share of such types, otherwise we must lose the war."

"Really, officer," Harold protested loyally. "You have no right to insult——"

"Shut up, Harold," the other policeman said wearily.

"This is Doctor Seaver," the first policeman said. "He is going to allow you and your clients to contribute to the war effort, Harold."

Relief showed in Harold's face. A smile spread the plump little mouth. "Well! Why didn't you *say* so? A collection. Of *course!* I'll cut the music and turn up the lights. My people will be *glad* to give."

"Blood, Harold," the first policeman said dryly.

"Real blood, Harold, including yours."

Harold blanched. "You can't!" he gasped. "It's too vulgar. This is a place of fun. Oh, my goodness, not *blood.* Money yes, blood no."

"Blood, Harold," the second policeman said.

"For the wounded," Doctor Seaver said.

Harold braced himself. "I have rights. I can refuse."

"Blood," the first policeman said. "Or we are going to discover a number of violations, violations that will force us to close Harold's Place. Perhaps forever."

"Why me?" Harold said weakly. "Why pick on me?"

"Oh, it isn't just you," Doctor Seaver said cheerfully. "Our people are doing this all over Tel Aviv. There isn't time to wait for volunteers."

"You are going to cooperate," the first policeman said. "Aren't you, Harold."

"I hate cops," Harold said waspishly.

"Mrs. McClintock," the doctor put in smoothly, "will set things up. There are forms and things, you see. We'll need some tables so that the people can lie down. Now if you'll see to the lights and the music, Mr. Harold—"

"The blood you get, doctor," the second policeman said. "It won't be any good. Too much whisky in it."

The doctor nodded thoughtfully. "Perhaps it'll take the boys' minds off their troubles."

Government House perched on a hill southeast of Jerusalem, a comfortable and dignified complex. Constructed by the English to shelter their High Commissioner during the days of the Mandate, it had been used as headquarters by the United Nations Truce Supervision force. Its gardens remained a living testimonial to Imperial concern for beauty and gracious living and they provided a dramatic view of the Holy City and its environs, a panorama of Jewish-Christian history tucked into the distant dusty hills.

Shortly after fighting broke out in Jerusalem, Jordanian troops stormed Government House, occupying it without resistance from the UN soldiers on duty.

From an Israeli point-of-view, the situation was intolerable and orders were issued to drive the Arabs out, to take and hold Government House. Hank McClintock attached himself to the unit assigned the task.

He took his place in the fourth vehicle in the convoy and began shooting film as soon as they began to roll. They climbed toward their target, past a low wall on which, in white paint in English, someone had written— *Israel Wants Peace;* past a grove of olive trees; past a tank, charred and smoking, a still body hanging face down out of the hatch; past mortar crews setting up their weapons.

A shot rang out and the convoy stopped. Men leaped out of the trucks, dashing for either side of the road, taking what cover they could, sprawling into firing positions, looking up toward Government House. Sporadic riflefire broke out from the heights and the soldiers began to shoot back.

Hank ducked behind the low wall and found himself alongside two infantrymen. Their faces were grim, their hands tight on their weapons as they searched for targets. Hank adjusted his lens and began to film them, hoping to capture the fierce power in the kick of their rifles as they snapped off shot after ominous shot.

"Follow me!" an officer yelled, standing, running up the hill. Hank swung around, re-focused, and shot the action. The two soldiers hurdled the wall and followed the officer, zigzagging. Bullets kicked dust behind them. Without warning, one of them was jerked to an abrupt halt, as if tied to the end of a long rope which had reached its limit. He hung on the air for a long beat, then fell forward, blood gushing out of his nose. Hank gave the dead man five seconds of film, before directing his attention further up the hill.

Here diminutive forms dashed from rock to rock, tree to tree, stumbling sometimes, falling other times, waving at each other, their cries distant and unreal. To Hank, the dull crump of mortars and the sharper crack of rifles all seemed out of synchronization with the action. He ordered himself to get closer to it all.

He moved ahead in a half-crouch, picking his way

across the steep, uneven ground. A mortar shell whirred overhead and he dived for cover, shielding the camera with his body. A nearby explosion, and the earth shifted under him. Dirt splashed the back of his neck. Moments later he was up, hurrying forward. He didn't want to get left behind.

The advance section of AMXs were caught in a great bowl formed by a low circle of hills. In the dark, they scurried around like frightened mice, aware that no escape was possible, desperate to prolong the inevitable for as long as possible.

The T-55s, heavy-weight Soviet tanks, had almost closed a circle around the Israeli tanks, were blasting steadily at them with their powerful cannon.

Amos had stopped the headlong dash of his command within sight of the battle, placed his halftrack on a low ridge that supplied him with a clear view of the entire proceedings. He began dispersing his tanks strategically. His plan was simple: To come up behind the T-55s and strike a hard blow before they realized what was happening. Fifteen minutes later word reached him that all the tanks were at their jump-off places. He ordered the attack to begin.

In the next ten minutes, twenty-one T-55s were put out of action. Confusion took over in the darkness and here and there an Egyptian tank turned and fled. When some of his own tankers gave chase, Amos ordered them back.

"Let them go!" he cried. "Hit those still in the fight. Destroy as many as possible."

As first light broke in the east, Amos counted four of the enemy still fighting. Backed against the slope of a low rise, they were able with their superior cannon to hold off the Israeli tanks.

"Send the halftracks up the slope," Amos ordered Serlin, on duty at the radio. "They should be able to come in behind and to the side."

"Their guns won't penetrate that heavy side armor."

"Maybe not. But it'll give them something to think about, divert them for a few seconds. As soon as the tracks make contact, the tanks are to move in fast, finish them off."

The strategy worked. The Egyptian commanders turned away from their front, turrets swinging, firing toward the quick-moving halftracks. It was a futile effort and no hits were made. Before they could bring their guns back to bear, the Israeli tanks were able to advance to effective range, knocking out all four tanks.

Suddenly, all was still. The shooting stopped and the tanks were halted. Here and there a hatch opened and a form appeared to look around, to appreciate the dawn of another day, to count the enemy losses and try not to see their own, to complain about the early heat.

"We killed thirty-eight of their tanks," Serlin reported, "and captured three more intact."

"Assign one of our men to each of them," Amos said. "Send them back to the repair trucks. I want those Egyptian insignia painted out and replaced with ours and back in action, for us this time. Have we got any new intelligence information?"

"Yes sir." Serlin spread out his map. "Here, stretched out to here. An Arab strongpoint. Covering the track south. Set positions. Excellent defensive strength."

"Tanks?"

"Dug in for use as artillery."

"How recent is this information?"

"The Air Force sent a plane over last night. They've got some kind of an ultra-violet film that takes pictures in the dark. Anyway, that's what they said."

"It's going to slow us up," Amos muttered irritably.

"And we're short on ammunition. Last night used up quite a bit."

"Tell supply we must have more at once," Amos said, studying the map. He frowned. There was something distantly familiar about this terrain, as if he'd been here before, faced this same situation at an earlier time.

"Of course!"

He pointed at a seemingly barren expanse of desert. "Here, Serlin, I've been down here before, years ago, on an archaeological expedition. We spent three weeks tracing the ancient Roman roads into Egypt. Here, this place, Rafi Afirifi. An old road begins there and heads straight south, cutting enough to the east to avoid those Egyptian positions. It extends for at least ten miles."

"Will it support our tanks?"

"I don't know. First we'll have to find it and dig it out. I imagine it's covered with sand now. Get engineers on it at once. See if we can get some bulldozers up here. If not, lets hang some blades on our tanks. And every man can use a shovel." A brief rising laugh broke out of him. "Maybe we can profit from Caesar's Egyptian adventure with Cleopatra."

That night while the fighting went on, and in the windowless meeting chamber of the Knesset building in Jerusalem, Moshe Dayan was sworn in as Minister of Defense. Uri Davidov, handsome and well-tailored, stood to one side as the room filled up. He saluted formally when David Ben Gurion appeared, striding into the room in that peculiarly energetic way of his, the white aureole of hair flowing at each step. He greeted Abba Eban formally and spoke briefly to Menachim Beigin. The former chief of the Irgun had been appointed Minister Without Portfolio in an effort to provide national unity. Golda Meir, American-born and Eban's predecessor as Foreign Minister, joined the group around Ben Gurion.

Abba Eban detached himself and came over to where Davidov stood. "Tell me some pleasant tidings, Davidov. I have been dealing with politicians all day. How goes the fighting?"

"Our people have taken Government House."

"An omen of better things to come. What else?"

"These figures are accurate and confirmed by film. Our pilots have destroyed more than three hundred and fifty Arab planes. In the air and on the ground. Mostly the latter." He allowed a slow smile to bend the handsome mouth. "It seems that our Air Force planners underestimated our pilots. Some of them have flown as many as ten missions today. The average is about seven for each man, a very high figure, I'm told."

"They are good boys."

"They are excellent fighters, which is more to the point. Here's some interesting information. It was expected that their shooting accuracy would diminish in combat from training standards. Oddly, the reverse has been true. They shoot better in a real fight."

"And the aircraft? Are they holding up?"

"Also better than expected. Serviceability began at ninety-nine percent and has remained at that level."

"What of the ground fighting?"

"Oh, Israel has a distinct advantage there, Mr. Minister," David said soberly.

"And what is that advantage, General?"

"Our army has all the Jews."

410

IX

General Heikel watched the scout car brake to a halt. He drew a cigaret from the gold case and Hassan offered a light. Heikel leaned back and blew three full round rings. Never more than three. A superstition acquired during his training at England's Sandhurst. Besides, after three he lost the knack.

A lieutenant hurried under the camouflage net, concerned and tired. A pair of goggles were pushed up on his forehead and the circles of dust around his eyes gave him the expression of a bemused raccoon. He managed a proper salute and Heikel touched his swagger stick to the peak of his soft cap.

"Well, lieutenant?"

"We located the Israelis, sir. Their tanks are swinging back from the east at top speed. They bypassed the defenses at Rafi Afirifi by going into the desert."

"That's absurd!" Hassan drawled. "It simply can't be done. Tanks can't cross those dunes—"

"Nevertheless," the lieutenant insisted, "they did it. By that maneuver, they managed to isolate and make useless two armored battalions. By doing what we were told couldn't be done they——"

"That will be enough of that, lieutenant," Heikel said mildly.

The lieutenant swung back to the general, the raccoon eyes bright. "General, there's still a chance. Order the 3rd Regiment to intercept, bring the full regiment behind them. They're going to have to slow down at Wadi el Rahi and we can hit them at that point. Split their forces and destroy them. An air strike——"

Heikel studied the young officer with good-natured interest. The young ones, so full of battle fervor but with little understanding of all the ramifications of war, of tactics, or politics. The lieutenant had a good point. The Israelis had done what the High Command had insisted could not be done. And Heikel had set up his defenses accordingly. The big tanks had been dug in, their guns directed northward and all the fortifications, the trenches

411

and bunkers, had been built to stand off an attack from that direction. Yet the Jews were coming from out of the east. It made no sense to him and he punished his memory in an effort to make it turn loose a workable strategy for this unorthodox situation.

"These Israelis," Heikel said to Hassan, with grudging admiration, "simply have no grasp of fundamental tactics."

Hassan agreed. "Headquarters is packed and ready, general."

A slight dizziness gripped the lieutenant. He had not eaten since fighting began the previous morning, nor had he slept. Perhaps if he had been in better physical condition he might have understood the thinking of his superior officers. As it was, he grew more confused each minute.

"General," he said desperately, "there isn't much time. Give the order and our tanks can take up positions at the wadi before the Israelis get there. Our guns are superior, we'll blast them out of the desert. And when the planes come——"

Hassan laughed, a taut, rising sound. "Have you seen any planes, lieutenant?"

"Some, colonel. Israelis mostly. Where are our planes?"

"A good question," Heikel said darkly. "Here is abundant evidence that a field leader can trust no one, not even his own people. I've asked for air support a number of times——"

"Eight times by actual count," Hassan put in.

"Eight times," Heikel echoed. "And not a single plane has come. And do you know why, lieutenant? I will tell you, expand your military training, something no one tells you when you're in training. I have received no air cover because someone else, someone with more influence in Cairo, someone more inclined to play a sharp political game than I, is getting all of them. Oh, well, I've managed up to now without the air force and I'll go on. Issue orders to break camp, Hassan."

"But, general," the lieutenant persisted. "There's still a chance——"

Heikel unwound his tall, well-formed figure from the field chair and adjusted a pair of sunglasses into place. He smiled indulgently at the young officer. "I commend your zeal, lieutenant, and I'll remember it when this is over and we can get back to normalcy. But you don't understand the nature of things. I've received nothing but contradictory orders since hostilities began. Hold your position, they told me, pull back to the canal, wait for further orders, prepare to attack, receive reinforcements. Since last night at ten o'clock there has been no further word from headquarters. Now, our position here has become untenable. Your excellent report makes that clear. The Jews are in a position to strike a deadly blow at us from the flank and the rear. To resist would be sheer folly so—" his smile was charming, open, resigned. "We're pulling back, lieutenant, in order to be able to fight again another day. After all, lieutenant, I want to win this war as much as you do." He glanced over at Hassan. "Colonel, take this lieutenant's name. I want him made a captain, at least."

An hour after camp was broken, all order disappeared. Men and vehicles scattered across the desert, fleeing to the rear, hoping to make it across the Suez Canal before the Israelis caught up with them. Heikel found himself with Hassan and the driver in his command car, alone in the scorching wastelands.

They had gone only a few miles when the motor began to sputter.

"What is it?" Hassan demanded anxiously.

"I do not know, colonel," the driver replied, pumping the choke. "There seems to be something wrong."

"I can hear that for myself."

The engine ceased running and the command car lurched to a stop. Hassan swore and ordered the driver to find out what was wrong, to fix it.

"According to the gauge, colonel, we are out of petrol."

"Nonsense!" Heikel said peevishly. "I left orders for the tank to be filled at all times."

"Yes sir. It was filled when we left. I saw to it myself."

"Check the engine," Hassan said.

"Yes," Heikel said, leaning back and lighting another cigaret. "It could be the engine. They are forever malfunctioning."

The driver got out and did as he had been told. "The engine is in excellent condition, general," he reported proudly. "I take very fine care of it myself."

"Then what can it be, man?"

"The petrol," the driver said unhappily.

"Impossible," Heikel said.

"You must be mistaken," Hassan added.

The driver went around to the rear of the car and knelt down. One corner of the fuel tank had been chipped away, a tiny aperture, but large enough for the fuel to drain out as they had moved across the desert. He returned to the waiting officers, saluted crisply, told them what he had found.

"What does it mean?" Heikel asked plaintively.

"When the Israeli planes strafed," Hassan recalled. "It must have happened then."

"Yes sir!" the driver said, with sudden relief. He had been afraid the officers would blame him for this calamity.

"Ah, yes," Heikel said calmly. "There had to be some logical explanation. This driver is a good man. He always obeys orders."

"Yes sir," the driver agreed.

"Well," Heikel said pleasantly. "We'll just have to wait for someone to come along and give us a lift. Shouldn't take long, I suppose. Some water, please, driver."

It was tepid, tasteless, and the general wished he had thought to bring along a thermos of iced tea. Actually, Hassan should have remembered.

The temperature in the car began to climb and it was no cooler outside. With the sun almost directly overhead, there was no shade, except under the car itself, and the driver had appropriated that space. Heikel considered ordering him to surrender it. After all, rank did have its privileges. He decided that for a general to crawl under a command car lacked dignity.

The driver came rolling from under the car. "General," he said. "Listen."

They heard the sound of approaching motors.

"You," Heikel said to the driver. "Get up on top of that high dune and signal. Make them see you, understand!"

The driver was halfway to the top when a jeep came careening over the ridge, a halftrack in its wake, heading at an angle that would carry them away from the command car.

"Signal them!" Heikel cried. "They don't see us."

"They're Jews, general," Hassan said nervously.

"So! Do you prefer to die in this accursed desert to their company? I do not." He took a silk handkerchief out of his pocket and waved it frantically, shouting hoarsely at the same time.

The jeep wheeled back in their direction.

"See!" Heikel said triumphantly. "If they'd have gone on by there's no telling when someone else would've come along." His eyes widened and his voice grew shrill. "Take off that pistol, you imbecile! Are you trying to get us all killed!"

414

The jeep stopped a few yards away and a lean, dirty soldier got out, a submachinegun cradled in the crook of his arm. He eyed the two officers with distaste.

"All right," he said in flawed Arabic. "Both of you, take off your boots and your pants."

"You don't understand," Hassan protested. "This is——"

"Shut up," Heikel said. "Do as you're told."

"That's a good idea," the Israeli said. He glanced toward the dune where the general's driver stood watching uncertainly. He waved at the man who hesitated only briefly before starting back.

The halftrack ground to a jolting halt and Heikel spied a woman among its occupants. The Jews, he noted with disapproval, had little sense of what was right. Two men got out of the halftrack and came forward.

"We are fortunate," Heikel whispered to Hassan. "They are officers. They will see that we are properly treated."

Amos Landau studied the two Egyptians. A general and a colonel. An impressive catch, possibly even a valuable one. He looked at them enviously. They wore freshly pressed bush jackets and their red-trimmed garrison caps were crisp. His eyes worked down. Their undershorts were clean and neatly ironed. The taller of the two, the general, directed a friendly smile at Amos and saluted with his swagger stick.

"Hello, there," he said, in impeccably correct English. "I'm General Heikel and this is my aide, Colonel Hassan. May I have your name, please?"

"Amos Landau. Please, put your trousers back on. Both of you."

When Heikel was again properly clothed, he turned his attention back to Amos. "Colonel Landau, isn't it?"

"That's right, general."

"You're a professional, of course? A career soldier, like myself?" Heikel was anxious to establish an area of rapport, of common interest. That was vital in these matters."

"Not exactly," Amos said. "I'm a businessman."

"Of course," Heikel said agreeably. "And what business are you in?"

Amos glanced at Jed Serlin who lifted his brows, but said nothing. Amos looked at Edie Kazin whose wide eyes displayed a contrived indifference. He grunted and turned back to Heikel.

"I'm a manufacturer, general. Textiles."

"Excellent. We Egyptians have long dabbled in textiles.

Cottons especially. My wife's brother is a trader. Perhaps you know the name, Ibn el-Houk?"

Heikel was beginning to feel better about things. The Jew would understand this bond between them, business, and that would better the situation considerably. He gave the smile that had charmed so many English matrons and maidens. "We seem to have run out of petrol, colonel."

"Well," Amos said, looking back at Serlin. "What do you think we should do about this?"

The freckle-faced captain grinned. "Hell, colonel, we can't leave these fellows out here in the hot sun. Besides, we're all going to the same place, it seems to me, the Suez Canal. Let's give them a lift."

"A good idea, Jed," Amos said, then crisply: "Okay, let's move."

"You heard the man, general," Serlin said brusquely. "Into the halftrack."

Once under way, Amos gave his attention to the Egyptians. "That was your encampment we passed some miles back?" he began.

Heikel nodded amiably.

"Why did you leave? Why didn't you stand and fight?"

"Oh, we should have given you a good battle, had you come at us in proper fashion."

"Proper fashion?" Serlin broke out. "What does that mean?"

"Well, really, captain. From the north, of course. You must have gotten lost somehow, turned around. It's easy to do in the desert, to lose one's landmarks and so on. Let's be honest, Colonel Landau, for you to lead your command into the desert that way—" he shook his head in mild disapproval, "—a fundamental breach of good tactics. You must have known where our defenses were and to deliberately avoid them, to avoid a battle——"

There was a strange, alien echo to the words and Amos wondered if this was the effect the desert heat had on men's minds. What kind of an officer was this, to run before a shot had been fired, to abandon his men and equipment, to make no effort to resist, to find some flaw in the strategy that had resulted in a swift and easy victory. Anger clenched in his chest and he wanted to strike out.

"Why didn't you fight?" he persisted tightly.

"With what, my dear fellow? We were unable to get air support and your planes might have returned at any time. And since we are winning elsewhere, and with so little difficulty, it makes no sense to sacrifice lives unnecessarily. A temporary setback like this——"

"What are you saying?"

Heikel tried to be kind. "After all, colonel, our bombers have leveled Tel Aviv and Haifa and Jerusalem has fallen to our comrades from Jordan. It is simply a matter of hours, a day or two at most, before Israel is forced to surrender or be destroyed. You Jews are a practical people. You will do the prudent thing."

Amos turned his back on Heikel and stared at the sun-drenched panorama ahead. No communication was possible. They were involved in two different wars, two different worlds, this general and himself. No reconciliation was possible. Not only did they view history differently but they saw the present and the future through opposite ends of the telescope.

Amos knew that the Israeli drive into Sinai was two-thirds of the way to Suez; would soon close off all chances of escape for the eighty thousand men of Nasser's desert army; that Egyptians by the thousands were fleeing, leaving vehicles and guns and boots behind, hoping to find safety in the arid sands, thinking to make it to Mitla Pass, or to the Bir Gifgafa Road between the southern mountains and the great dunes that blocked off the center, or to the northern road at El Quantara, and then across the canal. Few of them would make it.

Amos knew also that the battle in Gaza was almost over, that the Palestine Liberation Army had been cut off, was finished as an effective fighting force.

He thought about Heikel's words. *None of Israel's cities had been bombed.* His family at home in Tel Aviv was safe and well. An image of his sons blossomed in his mind. He wondered if Levi was safe and was glad that Simon was in America and out of all this.

Radio Cairo beamed martial music over the airwaves. It was thirty-seven minutes past seven in the morning when the music broke off and an announcer's voice intruded. He read a communiqué from the Supreme Command of the Egyptian armed forces:

". . . It has now become certain that, in a comprehensive manner, the United States and Britain are taking part in the Israeli military aggression as far as the air operations are concerned. It has been fully proved that some of the British and American aircraft carriers are carrying out wide-scale activity in helping Israel.

417

"As to the Egyptian front, the American and British planes have created an air umbrella over Israel. As regards the Jordanian front, these planes are playing an actual role in the operations against the Jordanian forces, as was shown by the Jordanian radar screens which clearly showed this air activity in support of Israel."

The report was promptly denied in the United States and in England. The Soviet Union, its destroyers closely trailing the aircraft carriers of the American Sixth Fleet, aware of their every move, conspicuously offered no comment on the Egyptian claim.

To counter the report, the Israeli Intelligence Service revealed that it had listened in on a telephone conversation between Gamal Nasser and King Hussein and recorded it. A transcript of the conversation, the Israelis insisted, proved the falsity of the Arab charge, proved that talk of American-British intervention was a fable created by the Egyptian President. The transcript was released to the press:

Nasser:	"Hello. Will we say the U.S. and England or just the U.S.?"
Hussein:	"The U.S. and England."
Nasser:	"Does Britain have aircraft carriers?"
Hussein:	(Answer unintelligible.)
Nasser:	"Good. King Hussein will make an announcement and I will make an announcement. Thank you. Do not give up. Yes. Hello, good morning brother. Never mind, be strong. Yes, I hear."
Hussein:	"Mr. President, if you have something or any idea at all . . . at any time."
Nasser:	"We are fighting with all our strength and we have battles going on on every front all night and if we had any trouble in the fighting it does not matter, we will overcome this. God is with us. Will His Majesty make an announcement on the participation of Americans and the British?"
Hussein:	(Answer unintelligible.)
Nasser:	"A thousand thanks. Do not give up. We are with you with all our hearts and we are flying our planes over Israel today. Our planes are striking at Israel's airfields since morning."
Hussein:	"A thousand thanks. Be well."

In New York the United Nations passed a resolution calling on all participants in the fighting to agree to a ceasefire.

A Turk's moon hung low behind the Judean Hills and the air over Jerusalem was acrid with the scent of cordite. A clear soprano chime, the bell on the YMCA tower, declared that it was one A.M. Artillery boomed and searchlights picked out new targets for the big guns. The whine of Israeli jet planes drew Hank McClintock's attention.

Unable to sleep, he had nibbled some C-ration. Now he put the can aside and picked up his camera, made the necessary lens and shutter adjustments, and pointed it at the night sky. Two jets went diving toward targets in Jordan, then two more, tracers streaking before them. A rumbling explosion sounded and a wall of scarlet and yellow flame erupted in the distance. Hank held his camera on it, lifting it once as another flight of jets appeared, the fire a lure for their rockets.

After a while the planes went away, though the artillery continued to lob shells through the darkness in a certain hypnotic rhythm. Hank returned the camera to its case and settled back alongside the wall of a blown-out house assuring himself that the war would still be going on in the morning. Minutes later he was asleep.

He woke at first light, made some tea and nibbled a biscuit. A tank came rumbling up the road and he waved it down, asked for a ride.

"We're heading for the Mandelbaum Gate," the man in charge said.

"Good deal." Hank clambered aboard, finding a place for himself just behind the turret between two infantrymen. They both showed the effects of the war, weary and coated with dust. Both were unshaven and their eyes were lidded and streaked with red.

"Shalom," Hank said.

One of the soldiers glanced at the camera case and turned away in disgust. Neither man spoke.

They rolled into the Muslim Quarter of the Old City, past Via Dolorosa where Jesus carried the Cross up to the Hill of the Skull. Looking over the rooftops of the flat Arab houses, Hank was able to see some of the bare stones of the Wailing Wall.

"Ir Hakodish," one of the soldiers muttered.

"And like Moses with the Promised Land," the second

419

soldier rasped sullenly, "we too are denied access to the Holy Place."

"Not for long," the other man replied.

They came in sight of a squad of paratroopers in their red berets, turning into a side street. Collecting his equipment, Hank leaped off the slow-moving tank and trailed after them.

Here the streets were little more than alleyways, shadowed, the buildings seeming to lean in on each other. The soldiers spread out, holding to either side of the narrow way, eyes alert and searching, weapons ready.

Hank ran ahead, filmed them coming on. A sniper's bullet, ricocheting off the wall above his head, sent him ducking into a doorway. He turned his camera on the troopers as they fired back.

"I got him!" somebody cried and the squad resumed its cautious advance.

It was strangely quiet and Hank felt it on his skin, thick and chilling, wrong somehow, all that silence in the midst of battle. They said you never hear the shot that kills you, he remembered uncomfortably, and his head came up and he strained to see behind each window and parapet. A machinegun broke the stillness and men shouted at each other and some began to run.

Hank sprinted for cover, heaved himself into a shallow drainage ditch. He landed in a foul-smelling trickle of moisture. Two soldiers were sprawled out a few feet away.

One of them lifted his head. He was dark-skinned with a thick Oriental mustache and soft, serious eyes. "You would do better with a gun, *adoni*," he said affably.

"I suppose you're right," Hank managed, keeping his head down.

A grenade exploded and shrapnel whizzed overhead. "I believe some place else would be much safer," the soldier said. He glanced around. "See. Ahead is an alley. I think in there the machinegun will not be able to depress enough to shoot at us. Perhaps from there I will be able to kill the gunners." He looked back at Hank. "Come along," he said gravely. "You may make some very nice pictures, if you do."

"What about your friend?" Hank said.

"Oh, he's dead, shot just before you got here."

The mustached soldier came erect effortlessly. He dashed forward, changing direction abruptly, crouching low and moving fast. The machinegunner spotted him, unloosed a trail of slugs. Hank held his breath until the soldier made it into the alley.

Now it was his turn. He knew the machinegun was waiting for him. He considered staying where he was but rejected it; sooner or later, some Arab would think to roll a grenade into the ditch.

"Hey!"

He looked up. The mustached soldier was waving to him from the alley.

"Come on, *adoni!* What are you waiting for?"

A Uzi lay under the dead soldier and Hank worked it free. Slinging it over his shoulder, camera in hand, he forced himself out of the ditch and ran as fast as he could. The machinegun began to bark.

In the alley, the soldier was waiting, smoking a cigaret. He watched Hank, fighting for breath, collapse against the wall. He took a long drag and extended the cigaret. Hank shook his head.

"I don't smoke."

The soldier nodded seriously. "It is not so good for you. Ah, you brought the Uzi. Excellent. It will be of more value than the camera. I am going after the machinegun. Would you like to help?"

Without waiting for an answer, he reached for the low overhang of the blue-painted house and swung himself gracefully onto the roof. He reached down and offered his hand. Hank took it.

They stepped carefully over the rooftops, taking cover behind chimneys and parapets. Ahead of them, the machinegun chattered occasionally. It stopped suddenly and a hoarse Arabic curse punctuated the stillness.

"Jammed," the soldier whispered to Hank. "Come on. We'll get them now."

Hank put the camera aside and unslung the Uzi.

They approached the right flank of the machinegun. It was the ammunition feeder who spotted them. He responded with good speed, snatching up his rifle, bringing it to bear. Hank's companion let go with a short burst and the man's face disappeared. The gunner and his other helper whirled, reaching for their sidearms.

Hank searched for the trigger of the Uzi. The joints of his hand felt fused, his finger frozen and useless. He made a massive effort and at once the Uzi danced in his hands. A scream was cut off in the gunner's chest and he died choking on his own blood. The mustached soldier killed the other Arab with a two-second burst.

421

"Very commendable," he commented mildly, "for a man who takes pictures. Look." He pointed deeper into the Muslim quarter. Hank followed the gesture. A squad of Arab Legionaires advanced along a twisting street, some two hundred yards away. "Come on. Let's give them back some of their own."

They shifted the machinegun to the other side of the roof and, while Hank sandbagged the legs, the mustached soldier cleared the chamber and zeroed in on the advancing Arabs. "Keep the ammunition belt clear," he ordered, then began to fire.

He worked the trigger in four and five second bursts, compensating quickly for misses. Two Arabs went down on the second burst and another on the third. Then the others broke for cover. A very good soldier, he traversed the width of the street, riding the trigger at the same time. Three more Legionaires fell.

"What now?" Hank said. "You think they'll come back?"

The soldier smoothed his mustache. "No. But we should try to find some more of them. It is expected of us, you see."

Yaakov Yeshivat hunched over the map studying the red and black lines that traced the Israeli advance. It was hard to believe. He checked the combat reports once more, studied the positions of the various units. The results were the same. To all practical purposes, the war in Sinai was over.

The skies were clear of enemy planes and the desert, except for the thousands of fleeing Arabs, belonged to the Israeli Army. The projected timetable had been exceeded on every front. A sense of gloomy frustration ballooned in his gut and he pounded a fist into his palm. To be virtually excluded from this fantastic victory, to be pinned down in the rear with the pencil-pushers and plotters instead of being where the action was. Damn all such orders—stay at your headquarters.

That was all right for Davidov. He was a perfect rear-echelon thinker, content with the maps and rosters. But not Yeshivat. Yeshivat was a fighter. It had been a mistake to accept a brigade. A regiment, all right. A battalion would have been even better. Then he could have gotten into the heart of it with the men.

A sigh passed out of him. He supposed Davidov was right. His experience, his knowledge, all made him more valuable as a maker of plans and decisions. Still, what harm would there be if he should join an advance patrol, before it all ended.

The field radio began to crackle and he looked up expectantly. "It's Colonel Landau," the operator said.

Yaakov went over to the radio. "Yeshivat here. What's going on?"

"Some of my men would like to go swimming. What do you say to that?"

Annoyance crept into Yaakov's voice. "You have time for jokes, Landau, I do not." Then, sudden understanding. A pleased grin pulled at his broad mouth and his pale eyes glittered with excitement. "You're there! You're at the canal!"

"Yes. For about thirty minutes. They had a few tanks and some infantry waiting, barging them across. I imagine they thought they could hold us here and open a gap for their people to get back."

"And?"

"And we knocked them all out. The East Bank is ours. Send me boats and pontoons, some engineers. There's nothing that can stop me and once I'm on the other side I can take my men into Cairo in a couple of hours!"

There was no missing the anticipatory excitement in Amos' voice and it was contagious. Why not, Yaakov asked himself. The Egyptians were thoroughly beaten, demoralized. A strike into the heartland of the country would finish them off for good, and all this nonsense about pushing the Jews into the sea. It was time someone taught the fellahin the facts of life. Hours, Amos had said. Yaakov let his mind play over the situation map on his desk. The other columns would be nearing the canal now. They too could cross, drive into Egypt proper, destroy Nasser's potential for mischief, insure peace for years to come.

The excitement oozed out of him, to be replaced by a sullen resentment. Every instinct crowded him into granting the permission Amos desired. He swore.

"Dig in," he bit off, "where you are. Hold your positions. You will not cross the canal. Repeat: you will *not* cross. Confirm."

"Yaakov, listen. Last time they stopped us ten miles away. Remember?"

"I remember. But it changes nothing."

"And so we've had to fight again. We can put Egypt out of business this time. There's nothing to stop us."

"You've got your orders," Yaakov said. "Do you understand them?"

"But why?"

"Because I too have my orders." The gravelly voice softened. "Orders from higher up, from Eshkol and Dayan, I suppose. There are, as always, political considerations."

"It's going to be 1956 over again."

"No," Yaakov shot back. "No, not this time. This time we'll keep what we take until there is a genuine peace. No one helped us this time and no one can make us give up what we've won." A quick flush of remembered warmth rose up in him. "You remember Ramat Yochanan, how it was?"

"I remember."

"Well, look at you, at the tough guy you've become."

"Nobody stays the same," Amos said.

"Yeshivat is the same."

"No, not even Yeshivat."

"Agh! Enough of this talk. There's still a war to fight." His voice took on an impersonal ring. "If your men want, they can have that swim."

Yaakov went back to his desk. It was reasonable, he assured himself, that a commander should study conditions in the field, let his men know that he cared. He turned to an aide.

"Get me a helicopter," he barked. "I want to find out for myself what's going on up there."

The Syrian Army had established a fortified position at Tel Fahar on a bluff looking down on the misty green hills of Galilee and the rich valley below. East of Kibbutz Dan, on the Israeli side of the frontier, Levi Landau's company waited in temporary defenses. As if to break the monotony of the bucolic scene, Syrian gunners lobbed an occasional shell into the hills behind them.

With daybreak, the Orthodox soldiers put on tefillin, began to say their morning prayers. Levi watched with no particular interest. A soldier stretched out nearby turned on a transistor radio and the theme from *The Bridge on the River Kwai* filled the air.

"Get something else," Levi snapped. "I'm sick of that."

"Sure, Levi," the soldier said good naturedly. He turned the dial and the voice of Radio Damascus came on.

"You are miserable Jewish people," the announcer cried in Hebrew. "We will pluck out the other eye of your

Moshe Dayan. He will be blind, and it will be the blind leading the blind."

One of the Orthodox soldiers stopped praying and listened solemnly, the black phylacteries still on his forehead and on his left arm.

"Your army is surrendering everywhere," the announcer shrilled.

The head of the Orthodox soldier bobbed up and down in solemn acceptance.

"Jerusalem is burning. Tel Aviv is wiped out."

The soldier tugged nervously at his earlocks.

"Kill the bastard Zionists."

The Orthodox soldier frowned regretfully. "That man speaks a very poor Hebrew."

Mist covered the Mediterranean and drifted inland. Simon saw the mist as an encouraging sign. It meant the patrol boats would have more difficulty trying to find them. He marked it down as the first good thing that had happened since he left New York.

He made his way down the beach to the rendezvous point, a jut of land on the far side of a rocky eminence. To make this arrangement had taken all of his remaining money. In return he was to be put ashore in Israel within twenty-four hours. The captain spoke English with a thick Greek accent that under other circumstances might have sounded funny to Simon.

"For the right price," he had told Simon, "I carry any cargo, human or not. And when nothing is to transport, I fish a little bit, but it doesn't pay as well."

He was waiting on the beach, when Simon got there, a big man with the look of power to him. Simon greeted him and looked around.

"Where's the boat?" he asked.

"Back in Salonika," the captain said. In the swirling mist, his flat face seemed paler than usual, more dangerous. "You see this fog, kiddo, is not so good for sailing around in."

"But we have a deal."

"Sure, kiddo. Big deal. Tomorrow we have same deal. But tonight all we got is a fog."

"We must leave tonight," Simon insisted, a mood of desperation settling over him. Even the elements were conspiring against him. "I've got to get home right away."

"You get home a day later, it won't hurt nobody,

425

kiddo. In this weather, I don't go nowhere. It's too dangerous."

"That's why I am paying you so much, to take chances."

The captain scowled and jabbed a blunt forefinger in Simon's direction. "The boat is mine, and I say no chances. Not in this fog."

"But they're killing each other. My family is there. I have to get back."

The captain shrugged. "If it is clear, we leave the same time tomorrow." He turned away.

Simon grabbed his shoulder and pulled him around. "Tonight! You've got to take me tonight. There's no more time to waste."

The captain shrugged the hand away. "Tomorrow, I say."

"No. Tonight. I paid you."

"And I will complete the bargain, kiddo." He grinned thinly. "I never give back money, it's an evil practice."

"Take me tonight. Come on, you dumb bastard, are you afraid?"

Again that scowl, the flat face gathering together. "Tomorrow, kiddo, I told you. Jews and Arabs—kill yourselves if you want, what I care? But me you don't kill." He turned and walked away.

Simon caught up with him, yanked him around, clutching the front of his jacket. "Give me the money back! I'll get somebody else——"

The captain hit him in the belly with his right fist. It was a short, swift blow that sent the breath whooshing out of Simon. He doubled over, gasping, holding his middle against the pain that knifed into his paralyzed diaphragm. His mouth opened but no sound came out.

"Soft," the captain said, not unkindly. "How you going to win war, you're so soft?" He took a few steps away. "Come again tomorrow, kiddo. I be back, the weather's good. Otherwise, the day after."

Simon fell to his knees and listened to the captain's crunching footsteps recede until they mingled with the soft lapping of the night waves. It was a long time before his breathing returned to normal, before the ache in his middle subsided, before he was strong enough to stand and make the walk back into town.

The Israeli plan was strategically simple and historically correct. Take over the heights commanding Jerusalem and so cut the communications of the Arab Legion, completely encircle the Old City. It was the same battle plan followed by the Romans centuries before.

No bombs were dropped on the Old City. No artillery shelled the holy places of Islam or Christianity or Judaism. No mortars destroyed the remnants of the past. Instead the Israeli soldiers advanced on the Wailing Wall, house by house, street by street, fighting every step of the way, paying a high price in lives to protect all the sacred places.

To Jews, the area where Solomon's Temple once stood was known as Temple Mount. Destroyed in 586 B.C., it had been rebuilt by Herod, only to be razed by the Romans in 70 A.D. Only the Western wall was left standing, protected, legend had it, by six angels whose tears had seeped into the crevices hardening the cement for all time.

Hank McClintock, camera in his lap, the Uzi slung over his shoulder, rode toward the Wailing Wall in the rear seat of a mud-splattered jeep. Up ahead, trucks and armored cars inched forward a few feet at a time.

A gray-bearded man in a black kaftan and a fur-brimmed hat stood at the edge of the road and passed out leaflets to the soldiers. He handed one to the driver of the jeep and as he did Hank turned his camera on the old man. A gnarled, almost translucent hand came up to shield the ancient face.

"No graven images," the driver said, laughing. He gave Hank the leaflet. "Here. Take some pictures of this. He's one of those who insist only the Messiah can liberate Jews. He wants us to stop the war. The Arabs know better, I think."

After a while, the convoy picked up speed and they made it down the hillside and through the Dung Gate. Hank saw an Arab appear out of a side street, running hard. Guns began to cough and the Arab went spinning to the ground; he lay still, legs awkwardly turned. There was more shooting and the convoy ground to a halt.

"Take cover!" somebody yelled.

Hank crouched in back of the jeep and trained his camera on a squad of advancing infantrymen. A rifle shot came and they began to shoot back. Some of the men moved toward the houses alongside the road, firing as they went. Two men wearing long robes and kaffiyehs came out of a doorway with upraised hands. They were searched and handed back as the soldiers continued the search for snipers. Hank went after them.

The sound of shooting intensified. Hank took cover in a

427

doorway. He was able to see the golden dome of the Mosque of Omar, third holiest place of Islam, not far from the Wailing Wall.

Some of the Israeli soldiers ducked into a house and shots sounded inside. Moments later, a handful of Arabs in civilian clothes, hands high above their heads, came out, protesting that they were not soldiers. All of them were young, with the look of men who spent much of their time out of doors. A sergeant ordered them taken to the rear under guard.

The Israelis returned to their vehicles and the convoy edged forward through St. Stephen's Gate. A corpse lay face down near a sign that claimed this was where the mother of Jesus had been born. A machinegun chattered and mortar shells exploded beyond the roadway. Hank swung his camera around, trying to capture it all on film.

An Arab halftrack came clattering around a corner, face to face with an Israeli tank. Each vehicle came to an abrupt stop. For a microsecond, as if paralyzed by the sudden confrontation, neither crew did anything. Then the cannon of the tank belched and the halftrack shuddered. Another round and another. Each time the halftrack accepted the blow with quivering fortitude. Smoke began to rise out of the smashed engine. Hank pointed his camera, waiting for the crew to emerge. No one got out.

The advance continued. Staying off the road, Hank filmed the men as they scurried from one shelter to another, firing at snipers and mortar crews, attacking machineguns. He focused on a soldier as he pulled the pin from a grenade, followed the arc of the explosive charge against the high blue sky, captured the burst on a low rooftop. Another machinegun went silent.

"Move out!" an officer bellowed.

Suddenly men were running toward the Wailing Wall. And some were crying, their faces streaked with emotion. The Arabs were forgotten, and the danger. Hank went after them, listened to their hoarse cries.

"Oh, God, oh, my God! At last we are home!"

"Blessed is the Lord God!"

"We are back in the City of God!"

Hank charged forward, caught up in the pervading exaltation, the profound mood of timelessness, of being one with those of the past and those yet to come. He sprinted toward the ancient assemblage, one hundred feet of old stone with bits of weed and scrub grass growing from between the cracks. In the gripping passion of the moment he was unaware of the camera in his hand or of the Uzi bouncing off his back.

He never heard the shot that killed him.

The bullet came from far back in one of the winding streets, striking him in the right temple. Already dead, he kept on for three or four strides, sprawling finally to the cobblestoned street like a rag doll.

Soldiers had gained the Wailing Wall in numbers now. Some of them went to their knees and others placed their faces against the rocks and smelled the old smell and wept and prayed.

"Blessed is the Lord. Blessed is the King of the Universe who kept us in life and sustained us and enabled us to reach this time."

Before long other Israelis came to the Wall, the pious and the not so pious, the Orthodox and atheists, traditionalists and contemporary cynics. Hasidim in long black coats danced the hora with kibbutzniks in combat boots. Soldiers donned tefillin and rabbis wore blue-and-white-and-gold prayer shawls and others draped belts of ammunition around their shoulders. Fathers scribbled the names of their sons on scraps of paper and pushed them between the stones, as was traditional. And the leaders of the nation appeared. The Prime Minister, the Chief of Staff, ordinary soldiers carrying bazookas and machineguns, David Ben Gurion and Moshe Dayan and Uri Davidov, and more.

The Chief Rabbi of the Israeli Defense Forces came, cradling the Torah in his arms, and a path was opened for him to approach the Wailing Wall. He prayed and then he spoke.

"On our blood we took an oath that we will never give it up, we will never leave this place. The Wailing Wall belongs to us. The holy place was our place first, our place and God's place. From here we do not move. Never. Never."

And none who heard disagreed.

Jerusalem fell. And with its capture it became only a matter of time until the bulge on the West Bank of the Jordan River succumbed also to Israel. Nablus was taken with hardly a struggle and, driving up from Ramallah in the south and from Jenin in the north, Israeli soldiers forced the Arab Legionaires back across the river. At ten o'clock on Wednesday night, King Hussein said that his country would accept the UN ceasefire. He said too that

15,000 of his troops had been killed since the fighting began on Monday morning.

In Sinai, all escape routes were closed off to the fleeing Egyptians and every attempt to rescue them was turned back. Israeli torpedo boats landed at Sharm el-Sheikh and found it deserted, its garrison having fled into the desert, the Egyptians unwilling to fight to keep the Gulf of Aqaba closed to Israeli ships.

On Thursday, five battles were fought in Sinai, involving a thousand tanks. Each battle resulted in an Egyptian defeat. Just before midnight, the jihad ended when Cairo announced it was accepting the ceasefire.

Only Syria was left.

X

It was clear that they were going to fight. For the first time, Levi wondered how well he would acquit himself. As well as Joshua? As well as his father? For the first time, too, he wasn't sure of himself and that troubled him. He expected to experience fear, to anticipate the danger; but this sudden lack of confidence, this failure to *know* how he would act, and react, drew his nerves up taut and brought an ill-making sensation to the pit of his belly.

He forced his mind to the present, looking across at the Syrian side of the Huleh valley, assessing the steep ridges. An attacking force would find little cover up there and as they moved higher they would come under point blank fire from the tiered strongpoints. At that morning's briefing, they had been told that at the westernmost corner of the heights, spreading out over an area of some three hundred yards, was a complex of bunkers and trenches and pillboxes, integrated to support and protect each other. All the approaches were commanded by unobstructed fields of fire down to a wide belt of mines and barbed wire. It was not going to be easy.

He glanced back at his men, waiting for orders to attack. They knew that Egypt and Jordan had both stopped fighting. That meant little to any of them on this Friday morning. Their war was about to begin. No one was laughing and there was no music coming over the transistor radios. All the faces were alike now, grim, intense, the faces of men who knew exactly what lay ahead.

A flight of jet attack-bombers came diving out of the sky above the heights, dropping their payloads with tremendous accuracy. They were followed by another flight. And another. And when they departed, the artillery opened up again, pounding the Syrian positions. It had been going on steadily for hours, tons of high explosives spent; but through his field glasses, Levi could see no marked damage.

"So," a voice broke in, "what do you see?"

Levi swung around. Jacob was a tightly constructed twenty-one-year-old who commanded the second platoon. In civilian life, he was studying to be a doctor.

"I see a lot of Syrians looking down at us."

Jacob grunted. "I guess we're going to have to go up there and ask them to leave."

Levi lit a cigaret and inhaled. "They may not want to go."

"We'll convince them."

"Some war. The scientists invent hydrogen bombs and jet planes and napalm and I don't know what else. And still it ultimately comes down to one man facing another in some kind of a showdown."

"Like one of those crazy cowboy movies."

"Exactly."

"What I want to know is, where's John Wayne when you really need him?"

At 11:30 it began. The sappers led off, covered by an infantry platoon, trying to open a path through the minefield. A withering defensive fire forced them back. They regrouped and made another try. This time they kept going, defusing mines or exploding them. At last the signal was given for the infantry to move up.

Levi adjusted the crimson baseball hat in place and waved his men forward. There was no cover, no safe areas, nothing to do but charge up the steep incline and hope the Syrian soldiers missed.

Levi kept going, firing the Uzi from his hip, aware that there was little chance of hitting anyone. He spotted a low thrust of rock and dived behind it, rolling onto his back so he could see down the hill. His company was cut to ribbons. Corpses dotted the slope and here and there a wounded man tried to move, cried for help.

The armor was moving forward now, already under

fire. A tank, hit, came to a stop. A halftrack did a ground loop and turned onto its side. In less than five confused minutes, the armor was beaten back, leaving three tanks and seven halftracks on the hillside.

Levi glanced up ahead and saw that some of the sappers had made it up to the rows of concertina wire, were trying to cut their way through.

"Cover them." he shouted. "Covering fire!"

He directed his Uzi at the lip of the first tier and unloosed a long burst, another. Other men lifted their heads and began to shoot.

Even as he directed the fire, Levi's mind worked rapidly. The planes, the artillery, the armor, all had failed to do the job. This was work for men with rifles in their hands and bayonets on the rifles. There was no other way.

He rolled over on his back and signaled for his platoon leaders to assemble. No one came.

"Joachim is dead," a bespectacled soldier shouted over the din. "And so is Willi."

"What about Jacob?"

"Wounded."

"How bad?"

The soldier nodded. "Both legs. Very bad."

Levi filled his lungs with air. "Pass the word. We're going ahead. When I go, everybody goes. And there's no stopping until we are on top and clean them out. Okay?"

He waited three minutes then, clearing all distractions from his brain, he heaved himself erect, charged straight up the slope, shooting from the hip. He spotted the flash of a machinegun and dived for a shallow depression, rolling as he hit the ground. Rocks dug into his chest and thighs and it was difficult to breathe. A pulse pounded crazily in his temple and all sound was muffled and thick now. He rose quickly and fired a short burst. The machinegun answered. He reached for a grenade and pulled the pin. Bracing himself, he came up to one knee and threw as hard as he could. Even before he hit the ground, the machinegun was firing at him. He counted. Ten— nine—eight—seven—six—five— The grenade exploded. He came halfway up. The machinegun remained silent. He charged toward the gap in the wire, never looking back.

At the base of the first terrace, he was momentarily protected from the guns above. He scuttled west, seeking a way up. Above him a light machinegun began to bark, flanking the men coming through the minefield and the wire. He listened carefully, trying to estimate how far back on the terrace the gunner lay, trying to fix the position. Satisfied, he pulled the pins from his last two grenades. He took one long stride away from the bluff and let one go. Then the other. He heard a scream after the second explosion and the gun stopped shooting at the men coming up the hill.

Levi yelled at them, motioned for them to follow him, then continued on his way. Fifty feet further along he found what he was looking for, a natural set of steps in the vertical wall. He slung the Uzi and began to climb.

Very cautiously, he looked over the edge of the terrace. It was clear.

Following the run of the terrain, the defenses had been put down in a series of sharp turns and bends, extending forward or backward with no particular pattern. Fire trenches ran through the entire defensive maze, many of them eight feet deep and three feet wide, complete with underground rooms and gun emplacements, carved out of the heights in the years since 1948. Here everything was black stone and cement, a hive of connected strongpoints, enabling the Syrians to transfer troops with security in order to hold off attack at one position or another.

Other men made it onto the terrace. Levi ordered them against the wall of the second level. Beyond the corner of the nearest trench, they were safe from enemy fire, out of sight. Levi counted; there were twenty of them. He looked at his watch. It had taken them almost an hour-and-a-half to come this far.

"We can't wait for the others," he said. "We're going into the trenches. Every gun we knock out will make it easier for the others behind us. Fix bayonets."

A young soldier gasped. "Levi, I think I cannot kill a man with a bayonet."

Levi glared at him. "You will have to, *adoni,* or he will kill you. Up here, the choices are limited. Now, listen, all of you. You all studied the aerial photos of these trenches and heard the intelligence reports. They run in every direction. When we come to a branch, I want three or four men to follow it. Use grenades in the bunkers. You ought to be able to pick up more from their people. Stop for nothing. Leave the wounded behind. We've got to break this first trench and move on up to the next one. All right? All right. We go."

He took a deep breath and charged around the corner toward the leading edge of the trench, jumping without

433

hesitation. He hit the bottom and kept moving, the Uzi ready. The trench bent to the right and Levi followed it.

They saw each other at almost the same second but the Syrian soldier allowed himself the luxury of being surprised. Levi put three bullets into his chest and stepped over the corpse without pause.

The trench widened abruptly, split into two. Some of his men followed the second branch.

Without warning, three Arab soldiers materialized in front of Levi. One of them shouted the alarm and swung his rifle into a firing position. Levi killed him, then turned the Uzi on the others.

Ahead, another branch. And some yards beyond, the throaty coughing of a heavy machinegun. Crouching, he waved four of his men into the new trench and padded ahead. The machinegun was situated on a firing ledge, four steps up. He placed his back against the wall and snapped a new clip into the Uzi, waving the rest of his men to move on.

When they were all past, he took the steps two at a time, spraying the exposed backs of the three men huddled over the gun. He went after his people.

From up ahead he heard shrill warnings in Arabic. Then the high pitched Uzi's, the heavy sound of Russian-built rifles. He moved faster. Turning a corner, he saw one of his men battling a pair of Syrians with bayonet and rifle butt.

"Fall down!" he shouted in Hebrew and, as the man obeyed, he fired. Both Syrians died at once.

"My weapon is jammed," he said, waving the soldier on. "Go ahead. I'll catch up."

He tried to work the firing chamber clear. The bolt was stuck, a round jammed in at an impossible angle. Using his hunting knife, he struggled to loosen it.

The Arab officer burst out of a bunker with a long dagger in his right hand, screaming an ancient warcry.

Levi heaved the useless Uzi at him. It missed and the Arab came on. Levi backed off, extending the hunting knife. He had never been in a knife fight, had never trained for one, never imagined that he might be called upon to live or die by his skill with the blade.

The Syrian was very quick, limitless energy apparent in every sudden move. He faked a high thrust and Levi's left arm rose in a reflexive defensive gesture. The Syrian came under the arm, the long dagger swinging in a low arc.

Levi spun deperately, bouncing hard off the trench wall,

434

letting the momentum carry him out of range. He braced himself and kept his eyes fastened on the other man's blade. A lengthy inscription was etched on the gleaming steel, a ceremonial blade, perhaps an award for exemplary garrison service. Levi cleared his mind and tried to recall everything he had ever heard about knife-fighting.

He kept his legs under him, balanced on the balls of his feet, muscles ready but not too tense. He wished there was room to circle. But the narrow trench was restrictive. Backward or forward, life or death.

The Syrian lunged and Levi stumbled away, slipped, went down to one knee. The Syrian came on. Levi fended off the initial thrust with his forearm. He reached but failed to get the wrist. The Syrian struck again, a back-hand slice. Levi twisted down and away, his shirt ripped. There was a sudden sting in his left shoulder.

Instinctively, he kicked out with both feet, weight on his extended left arm, like a Russian peasant dancer. He made contact and the Syrian grunted as he fell. Levi went after him, stabbing with all his strength. It took three thrusts before the man died.

Levi wiped the blade clean on the Arab's uniform, careful not to look at the man's face. He did not want to remember him. He stood up and checked his shoulder. The wound was superficial. He retrieved the Uzi, cleared it, and advanced deeper into the trench.

The fighting continued hand-to-hand for the rest of the day. More and more Israelis made it into the defensive channels and as they cleared one terrace, they moved on to the next. It was at dusk, on the highest tier, when Levi came across the major. He was a man of no particular distinction in an ill-fitting uniform and a soiled kaffiyeh. There was blood smeared over his shirt and his left arm dangled uselessly. He clutched a pistol in his other hand.

When Levi came upon the major, his back was turned. Levi hesitated, a millisecond of humanity, of morality, of tenderness, even. The circumstances made it a mistake. The major whirled and fired the pistol.

A burning, a deep burning, spread down into Levi's guts, reached up into his stomach. He fell to his knees, aware that control over his body was fast draining away. He squeezed the trigger and the Uzi careened wildly in his hands. The major fell over dead.

Levi dropped the Uzi and flattened out on the ground. A scarlet mist settled over him. How silly. Simon's red baseball cap had tipped down in front of his eyes. A dim awareness told him that he was being blinded by his own blood. The little major had killed him.

A stupid mistake, he told himself with regret. His first mistake. He should have fired at once, finished the major before he was able to defend himself. An easy kill and he had failed to take it. Stupid! Stupid!

A chill caused him to shiver. The pain was not so bad now but he could feel life draining away with his blood. He pressed a hand against the wound, trying to hold back the ooze. To die when all need for taking chances was over. How stupid! With the battle almost won, the war almost won. Well, he thought with faint amusement. He had done it. Just like Joshua. Blackness closed in fast.

With the fall of Tel Fahar, all resistance went out of the Syrian Army. For the most part, they turned and ran. Israel's soldiers ranged across the heights blowing up bunkers, Soviet-built cannon and tanks. Others attacked bases of the terrorist raiders of El Fatah, destroying them, capturing Quneitra. Columns advanced deeper into the country along macadam roads.

The battle, which had begun on the Muslim sabbath, ended at 08:30 hours on the Jewish sabbath, when Syria agreed to the ceasefire.

Six days and it was over. Throughout Israel, amidst the ecstasy of victory, the ancient Hebrew prayer for the dead was mournfully chanted:

"He who maketh peace in His heavens, He will make peace for us and for all Israel—and say ye amen."

Amen.

XI

As quickly and informally as they had mobilized for war, the men of the Israel Defense Force went home. Back to the ways of Mea She'arim, to the kibbutzim of Galilee, to the groves of the Negev, to the shops and factories and schools, to the girls of Dizengoff Circle.

For Simon Landau the journey was more labored, the miles marked by strain and a growing sense of private failure. When he arrived finally at the house in Tel Aviv, all guards fell away and, for the first time since his childhood, he cried. Later, when he thought back on it, he realized that his mother had shed no tears. Instead, she had comforted and accepted him, murmured soothing platitudes in that warm vague style of hers.

It was when she told him about Levi that the confusion and fear-twisted together in a guilty clinch. He wanted to shriek out his despair and torment, to flail his flesh, to plead for punishment and for mercy.

"I've got to see him," he managed to get out.

"Tomorrow—" Ruth began, then broke off, seeing the haunted expression on her youngest son's face. She nodded. "He's in Jerusalem, at the Hadassāh Hospital. He's been very sick."

Simon found Levi in a wheelchair, sunning himself on the ward terrace. He sat with his head back, eyes closed, his expression relaxed and peaceful. His pale face was drawn and thin and his thick mustache drooped around the corners of his mouth.

"Shalom, Levi."

His eyelids fluttered, opened. Recognition came slowly. He spoke Simon's name with warm pleasure. Simon kissed his brother on the cheek and took his hand, measuring the man in the wheelchair. Levi looked different. Thinner than he remembered, his dark eyes deeper, some inner quiet was reflected in them.

"You're getting gray," Simon said, trying to keep it easy and gay. "Your mustache—"

"A bullet in the guts ages a man," Levi said, without self-pity. "You look well."

"You're going to be all right," Simon said anxiously. "I spoke to the doctor and he said——"

"Easy, little brother. They took out a yard or two of my intestines but a man's got about twenty-five feet of the stuff so who needs another yard?"

Both of them went silent, then made sporadic efforts to speak. Questions were asked and went unanswered and there were impulsive clutchings and embarrassed smiles.

"You saw mama?" Levi said finally.

"Yes. She seems better than I remembered. Stronger, more in control."

"That's what I thought, when she visited. I know why, too. Because she has to be. Here I am, shot up, an invalid for a few months at least. And Rena, in bad shape over Hank."

"He was a nice guy."

"That Hank, he was a *mensch*, that one." He squeezed Simon's arm but there was no strength in his hand. "It's a good thing you came back. You'll be able to take your old weak brother for walks and read to him." A soft, pleased laugh came out of him. "It will be good for papa, too, to have you home."

Simon's expression transformed quickly. The concern washed away, replaced by a mask of reserve. "How is papa?" he said, without interest.

"It's never been easy for him to understand you, Simon, about you turning away from the things he believes in and has lived by."

"The company, the business, it's not for me."

"Nor for me."

"In New York, they say everybody should do his own thing."

Simon exhaled softly. "I like that. Maybe we should allow papa to do his own thing, not condemn him so much for not being whatever we are."

"You sound like mama."

"Oh."

"She defends him all the time." Ideas swirled in his brain, a storm of words, half-formed thoughts, the synopses crackling wildly. "She told me I was self-righteous."

"It's a sin all of us suffer from in our youth."

A quizzical look came into Simon's hollow eyes. "She really loves him, Levi."

"People always have. Mama, Yaakov, Mara— They may betray him, get angry with him, be hurt by him. But they keep loving him. He's a man to be loved."

"When I said something critical about papa, mama asked me what solutions I could offer to the mysteries of life. Imagine that! The mysteries of life. Have you ever heard her use language that way."

"She's a surprising woman sometimes. Capable beyond anything I ever credited her with. And so is papa. It took me a long time to understand that. He's quite a guy, our father."

"I don't understand."

"I always blamed him for whatever was wrong with my life, with me, with the world. What a presumptuous bore I was. To think that only I had the answers, that papa knew nothing. All that anger I felt, that resentment. I was jealous, I guess. Papa had everything. He was a genuine hero. Mama loved him. He was a successful businessman.

And years ago he even had Mara Gabrielli." He laughed and the exertion made him cough.

Simon showed his concern. "Should I call the nurse?"

"I'm all right." He smiled briefly. "Don't you see the joke, Simon? Papa succeeded at everything he tried, fulfilled his responsibilities as best he could to the country, his family, to himself."

"What about Gabrielli? Was that right?"

Levi patted the youth's cheek. "Brother dear, you have become a young fogie. That Gabrielli is a marvelous-looking woman. Who could resist her? Could you, Simon? And are you so perfect, so pure? That was papa's affair—and mama's."

"I'm not sure I can forgive him."

"Don't be an ass. There's nothing to forgive. He's a man and he's lived his life, is living it. You and I should do as well." He put his hand to his middle. "I learned something the day I got this. It was all so quick, so many men dying and the rest of us killing. A man lives twenty, thirty years, Simon, but he can die in half of a second, afraid and alone. Men don't die pleasantly, you know. They cry and scream and choke on their own blood and vomit. Men live much better than they die and a lot of living is what papa's done, better than most of us. A little of his humanity would be good for each of us."

"Mama said almost the same thing."

Levi managed a cheerful grin. "In her old age, it's amazing how smart Mama is getting." He took his brother's hand again. "It's too soon to talk about such things, Simon, but I hope you'll stay with us for a while. We need you here at home. It's not fair to deprive all our young women of such a handsome fellow."

Simon averted his gaze. "I don't know what I'm going to do." He looked back at Levi. "And you?"

"I've been thinking about teaching, maybe, or the diplomatic service. The man that shot me, I killed him. And he wanted to kill me. The two of us, alone, acting like maddened animals. I imagine to him I was some kind of a devil. But I'm not and neither was he. Maybe if we could've talked to each other—" His eyes, hopeful and steady, rose up to Simon's. "I'm going to study Arabic. I think we have to explain ourselves to the Arabs, and get to understand them. We must talk to them," he ended with sudden intensity.

"But what if no one will listen?"

Yaakov Yeshivat established his headquarters in a tent on the outskirts of Gaza City. The sides were rolled up to admit the least stirring of air. But there was none. The heat was constant and thickly oppressive. Yaakov, seated behind the small field desk, trying to dispose of the accumulated paperwork, felt beads of sweat roll down into the hollow of his back.

An orderly appeared. "Colonel Landau is here."

"Send him in."

He sat back and tried to sort out the jumble of feelings in him; satisfaction that Amos had not been hurt and remembered anger that he had suffered a defeat at Landau's hands. He tried to place it in time—1960. Had it been that long? He cleared his mind when Amos ducked into the tent.

"Shalom, Landau," he said, with forced heartiness. "Sit down. Doesn't this damned heat ever let up? You want an orange drink? They're warm like camel piss."

"No, thanks."

"You look good. A little less hair."

"War does that to me."

"Me, it turns grayer."

"How's the work going in the refugee camps?"

Yaakov snorted and tugged at the loose folds of skin under his chin. "I've got men checking papers and searching for hidden guns, trying to identify members of the Palestine Liberation Army. They hide among the populace. It's slow work. I'm afraid a lot of those terrorists will get away."

"Not many. Not with you looking for them."

Yaakov grunted. "We'll see." His pale eyes came up to Amos. "You're all finished now. You're going home."

"The battalion is dissolved, the men gone, the equipment turned in, the paperwork done. Yes, I'm going home. Unless you've got another job for me."

"Nothing." He hesitated. "I'm sorry about your son-in-law. He was a nice boy."

"The will of God."

A frown brought a deep vertical crease between Yaakov's eyes. "With Joshua dead and Hank, you still believe?"

"Levi is going to live. I'm grateful for that. And Simon has come home."

"Not exactly miracles."

"We won the war," Amos said lightly. "That has to be one of God's miracles. By all logic, comparison of armies

440

and numbers, we should have been annihilated. Still we won. A miracle, I say."

"Agh! That's all a lot of crap. We won because we hit them early and hard. Because our people can improvise and fight creatively. Because we minimize our shortcomings and exploit theirs. We won because our soldiers are better trained and motivated, because for us to lose is unthinkable." A mocking grin turned the battered mouth. "We won because we had all the Jews."

"It's easy to make jokes now. It was not as easy as all that. Men died."

"We did not want the war," Yaakov said testily.

"We had it anyway. I think we have to try harder for peace."

"And the Arabs! Already they act as if they'd won, making demands, threatening us, talking again of wiping us out. We stand alone against them and always have. Even the French blame us for the war, that arrogant sonofabitch De Gaulle. The Americans say we must give up Sinai, the Gaza Strip, the West Bank. They want us to allow Syria to reoccupy the heights so they can bombard our people again. To hell with that! And those overcivilized bastards, the English. They instruct us to give back Old Jerusalem. Even India, with all the sanctimoniousness of the righteously incompetent, condemn us. Who stands for Israel? Who helps Israel except Israel? Talk and promises is what we get. But no one ran the blockade at Tiran. And the Suez Canal is still closed to our ships."

"You think we should keep the occupied land?"

"I say it is time the Arabs dealt directly with us. No more third parties, including that debating society at the UN. I say the only alternative to peace is war. You think I wanted to stop you at Suez? I did it because I had to, orders, political considerations, they said. I argued for driving through to Cairo, to Amman, to Damascus. If our boys were there now the Arabs would all understand the price of continuing this war. Next time we will go all the way."

"There mustn't be a next time."

"Hah! Already the Russians are replacing the equipment we destroyed. The Arabs talk of the next round."

"It has to be stopped. I don't want to lose any more sons."

"Tell me how," Yaakov said softly.

"I don't know." He straightened up and smiled briefly.

"Perhaps I will go into politics, too, the Knesset. I will see what Eshkol thinks. And you?"

"I'm through with all that. Words don't fit me right, only action. Maybe men like you are needed."

Amos stood up and held out his hand. "I better get started. Shalom, Yaakov." They shook hands and he started out. He hesitated in the entrance and turned back. "What happened between us, it's long past. Finished. When you're in Tel Aviv, come and visit your old friends."

"Yes," Yaakov said. "Of course."

Both of them understood that he wouldn't, that something essential between them had been destroyed and would never be replaced.

He was still attacking the paperwork the next afternoon when Uri Davidov arrived. The tall general was cool and confident in neat khakis. He seated himself without being asked and crossed his legs carefully.

"We have a new job for you, Yeshivat," he began without preliminary.

"What job?"

"We captured a considerable amount of hard goods on all fronts, especially Sinai."

"I know," Yaakov said dryly. "I was there."

Davidov gave no sign that he had heard. "Statistics are being compiled but we do know that the tanks number in the hundreds and there are armored cars, trucks. Also, thousands of artillery pieces, machineguns, rifles, ammunition, and so on. We also got our hands on a number of surface-to-air and surface-to-surface missiles. Soviet manufacture, all of them. The Egyptians with their usual high thoroughness failed to launch them."

"What's this got to do with me?"

"Only a small amount of this ordnance will fit into our military establishment. The problem is maintenance, spare parts, and the like."

"So?"

"You've had occasion to purchase weapons for Israel. You have contacts, know price schedules. We would like you to make the necessary arrangements to sell the surplus captured materiel."

It began in some dark niche in Yaakov, a distant stirring, taking shape and force, rushing upward in short bursts of energy. A throaty rumble, a growl of disbelief, a raucous eruption, until great gushing howls of laughter broke out of him. Tears began to roll down the rutted cheeks.

"Sell guns!" he gasped. "It *is* a miracle. Anything is possible. Israel, gun dealer to the world! What a joke! What an incredible joke on all of us!"

Davidov frowned and the fine brow creased in neat furrows. "Will you take the job?"

"Of course! Yes. Absolutely yes. Positively yes. Yes, yes, yes."

Davidov stood up. "Very well. In a few days the catalogues will be completed and I'll get in touch with you. Finish up here as soon as you can. Shalom, Yeshivat."

There was a sardonic, skeptical edge to the gravelly voice when Yaakov finally replied, "Shalom."

Shalom.

The world will be freed by our liberty, enriched by our wealth, magnified by our greatness. And whatever we attempt there to accomplish for our own welfare, will react powerfully and beneficially for the good of humanity.

— Theodore Herzl, *The Jewish State*

GENERAL
STAR

Woody Allen
0352300698 **Getting Even** (NF) 50p*

Maurice & Maralyn Bailey
0352300728 **117 Days Adrift (illus)** (NF) 65p*

Jackie Collins
0352300701 **Lovehead** 50p
0352398663 **The World is Full of Divorced Women** 50p
0352398752 **The World is Full of Married Men** 50p

Max Caulfield
0352398361 **Bruce Lee Lives?** 45p

Ray Connolly
0352300515 **A Girl Who Came to Stay** 55p

Eric Corder
0352300671 **Hellbottom** 75p*
0352300086 **The Long Tattoo** 40p*
0352398515 **Running Dogs** 60p*

Knight Isaacson
035239840X **The Store** 60p

Ronald Kirkbride
0352300817 **Some Darling Sin** 50p

Harry Lorayne & Jerry Lucas
0352398566 **The Memory Book** (NF) 60p*

Robin Maugham
0352398299 **The Sign** 55p*

Molly Parkin
0352300809 **Love All** 50p

John Rechy
0352300329 **The Fourth Angel** 45p*

Alan Sillitoe
The Loneliness of
0352300965 **the Long Distance Runner** 50p

*Not for sale in Canada

Alan Sillitoe

0352300949	**Men, Women and Children**	50p
0352398809	**The Ragman's Daughter**	50p
0352300981	**Saturday Night and Sunday Morning**	50p

Henry Sutton

| 0352300345 | **The Liberated** | 65p* |

Alexander Thynne

| 0352300183 | **Blue Blood** | 45p |

William Woolfolk

| 0352300914 | **The Overlords** | 75p* |

TANDEM

Gerty Agoston

| 0426162560 | **My Bed is Not for Sleeping** | 50p |
| 0426162641 | **My Carnal Confession** | 50p |

Robert Alley

| 0426168542 | **Shampoo** | 50p |

Aubrey Burgoyne

| 0426152026 | **The Amazons** | 45p |

Catherine Cookson

0426163796	**The Garment**	45p
0426163524	**Hannah Massey**	45p
0426163605	**Slinky Jane**	45p

Jim Dennis

| 0426144376 | **Dragon's Fists** | 35p |

Jean Francis

| 0426162803 | **Coming Again** | 45p |

Jane Gaskell

| 0426159586 | **The Dragon** | 45p |
| 0426159314 | **The Serpent** | 60p |

Marceline Gobineau

| 0426156919 | **Stephanie – The Passions of Spring** | 45p |

Joe Green

| 0426151496 | **House of Pleasure** | 50p |

*Not for sale in Canada